Frances Sherwood teaches at Indiana University. Her stories have twice won O. Henry Awards. *Vindication* is her first novel and has been nominated for a National Book Critics Circle Award in the United States.

'A brilliant novel, the author's talent quite obvious from the first page, *Vindication* can't fail to make an impact . . . this novel weaves historical fact with vibrant invention' *Ms London*

'A gripping tale' *Observer*

'Frances Sherwood's *Vindication* is startling, depressing, enlightening and unforgettable, and that doesn't begin to do it justice' *Newsweek*

'An arresting and convincing portrayal' *Publishers Weekly*

'It teems with historical figures and events brought to exuberant life by taut prose, keen imagination and insightful scholarship. This is historical fiction of a very high order indeed' *Miami Herald*

Vindication

FRANCES SHERWOOD

PHŒNIX

A PHOENIX PAPERBACK

First published in Great Britain by Phoenix House in 1993
This paperback edition published in 1994 by Phoenix,
a division of Orion Books Ltd,
Orion House, 5 Upper St Martin's Lane, London WC2H 9EA

Published by arrangement with Farrar Straus & Giroux Inc.,
19 Union Square West, New York, NY 10003

A CIP catalogue record for this book is available from the
British Library

ISBN: 1 85799 019 6

Printed and bound in Great Britain by
The Guernsey Press Co. Ltd, Guernsey Channel Islands

To my children, with love and gratitude

CONTENTS

Author's Note

VINDICATION *is a work of fiction. It is based on the life of Mary Wollstonecraft (1759–1797) but there are many deviations in the novel from the actual history of Mary Wollstonecraft and her contemporaries. They were the inspiration thanks to which an imaginative world of its own came into being.*

I am indebted to the National Endowment for the Arts for writing time for two summers (1990, 1991) and to Indiana University at South Bend for two summers abroad (1988, 1989) tracing Mary Wollstonecraft's footsteps.

FANNY

IT SEEMED that Fanny was there from the beginning. Fanny, however, was raised in Wales, and Mary, born in London in 1759, lived
in Spitalfields first and did not move to Wales until 1766. Actually,
they met in dame school when Mary was seven years old and Fanny
nine. Fanny was quick with numbers, Mary with letters. Mary wanted
to be famous like an actress. Fanny thought that was silly. Both of
them had drunkards for fathers. If Mary lived to a hundred, she would
not forget her father's beery breath. It was sour-pickle brine mixed
with spoiled milk. Fanny's father was a gentle, pathetic drunk. When
Mr. Wollstonecraft came back from the tavern, he was mean, kicking
aside whatever was in his way:

Dogs.

Cats.

Babies.

He would stride into the house without so much as scraping his
boots, and let loose his waters in the hearth, sputtering the flames into
a leaping dance along the logs.

"Ah," he would say, happy to have relieved himself, and wag at
whoever was handy. Then he would sit down for some serious
quarreling.

"Oh, Edward, Edward." Mrs. Wollstonecraft, wringing her hands
and dithering about, not knowing what to say or do, would ask God
what she had done to deserve such a husband, and little Mary, shielding
her two sisters, would cover her ears, close her eyes tight shut, and
be sick to her stomach. Because there was shouting and crying, stamping and falling, screaming and hitting, kicking and pleading. After, it
would become very quiet. You would be able to hear the wind outside
and strange, scary sounds you could not remember hearing. When the

quarrel would take up again, Mary put Fanny in mind, her face and form, something between her father and herself. It was that horrible.

"Oh, Edward."

Mary wondered, if *she* had fallen right down there and then and died, would that have made them stop? It did stop when her mother died. It was as if her mother and earth swallowed up and nullified all the years of animosity. No more Oh, Edward. No more sad wringing of hands. No more pleas to God.

What Mary remembered of her mother:

The things in her mother's china cabinet in Laugharne, Wales. There was the teapot of black, lead-glazed earthenware with a molded relief of twisted green vines and leaves. The coffeepot, used infrequently, had a china lamb on the lid, and the soup tureen was in the shape of a hen and chickens.

Her mother's bed gown was linen and cotton, expensively dyed dark purple, with borders of red and blue lilac. Mary liked to sit in her mother's bedroom, on the chintz coverlet, under the canopy, and watch her mother's maid dress her hair. The maid would take the strands up from the forehead and build up two sides like wings with packing underneath, holding it all firm with pins and pomatum. Then the maid would paint her mother's face white, put rouge on each cheek. Her mother had lost teeth with the having of children and used plumpers to fill out her cheeks. Otherwise, she was a lovely woman with bluebell eyes and her own long hair, when not powdered, the color of corn silk. The ideal mouth was Mary's mother's mouth, a rosebud. Fanny's mother was lean and shriveled, with the arms of a grasshopper.

Mary's mother had been born in 1732.

Mary was born in 1759. In 1765, her grandfather could point to his properties in Spitalfields, London, using his cane with one hand, his other hand on her shoulder:

"I built, Mary, my love, these three blocks of houses. Many houses, Miss Muffit, what do you think of that? Four floors each, French weavers, merci very kindly, their looms and madames, top floors for chimney sweeps, black birds in the attic, darling dear, and the Irish always in the basement where they belong."

Mary's grandfather could wet his finger, tell which way the wind was blowing even on a still day, and he bought vegetables in the market with care and attention, examining each cabbage as if it were a face. Mary's grandfather had large hands, bowed legs, a raised right shoulder from hunkering over the loom, and only five teeth. When Mary was little, her father was slender, upright, refined. He had all his teeth. When Mary lost her baby teeth, she and Fanny buried them by the ducking pond, said magic prayers over them for what they wished to become. Fanny wanted to be married to a handsome knight. Mary wanted to be free forever.

"I may not know how to read," her grandfather would say, "but, lucky for you and yours, Mary, I know how to count."

Mary's father had no trouble reading, but he talked slowly and too loudly, as if he thought others too stupid to understand his conversation. He considered himself better than everybody else in the world, particularly his wife. And when they left the city, Mary's father called his father a blithering idiot.

"The money is in town, *you* are the fool," her grandfather replied, shaking his fist. "Why do you think I came off the land and *your* fingernails be clean."

In his lifetime Edward Wollstonecraft Sr. had learned how to turn thread into cloth and cloth into bricks and bricks into shillings and shillings into pounds, so that his son, Mary's father, with his inheritance, could buy his high black riding boots, a red coat with a row of brass buttons, a brace of pistols and a pack of hunting dogs, and move straight out of London, first to Laugharne, then to Richmond, in the North Riding. Before they moved out of London, Mary's family lived in her grandfather's house. There was her mother and father, her big brother, Ned, and two sisters, Everina and Eliza. Charles came later. Every night from the nursery window, Mary would watch the night soil being removed from the jerichos in the yards. A silent army of masked men moved in, who, her grandfather told her, hauled it in carts to outside the city to the gardens where the vegetables brought into the city were grown.

The night-soil men were night birds and they made a sound like low humming which frightened Mary. She thought she might be taken away with them to a dark, wretched land of coal heaps and abandoned carriages, a country where shadow people worked by night and slept in the day.

"It is the round of life, Mary, my dear. Night soil, day soil, all the same." Her grandfather was not frightened of anything and he kept all in order. Mary told Fanny that she loved her grandfather. He was the only one.

When they moved away, out of the city to their own house, Mary's father's voice got louder and her mother's more piteous. He told Mary's mother she was a stupid woman, and he boxed her ears, punched her stomach.

"Grief and lamentation. Oh, Edward, Edward, how can you," her mother would sob, throwing herself at his feet, holding on to his dirty boots so he could not move.

The children hid in the cupboard behind the stairs. Eliza would cry softly to herself and Everina bit her nails down to the blood. Ned clenched his fists and gnawed at his knuckles.

Mary would stay until she could not stand it and then would rush out.

"Hit me." Mary snatched up the hairbrush as shield, held it fast. "Go ahead and hit me, instead."

The blow seemed to come not from his hand but from something larger and outside, like the wind, for the force of it would knock her over to the floor, which tasted of grit and earth, blood.

"Oh, Mary, Mary, my dear little girl." Annie the maid was the one to pick her up. "So bold, so foolish. You cannot fight a big man. Did you think you could fight a man, lass?"

Annie licked her tender spots, going round and round the bruises until they were a slobbery mess. She would lick Mary's dirty face and tongue her eyes open like a mother dog's.

"See, not so bad. You still live."

Sometimes, after these things, Mary wet the bed, so that her dolls smelled and had to be thrown out the window to the boiling tub below in the yard. Then her mother would beat her.

"Bread and water for a week, you nasty girl."

Her grandfather always sent her a new dolly, Mary told Fanny.

Mary's first doll had a wooden head, silk upper arms sewn to its body and attached with wire to wooden forearms and hands. She had green glass eyes, a gown of green silk with a closely fitted bodice, quilted petticoat, and braid-trimmed shoes. Her name was Mary, and Mary would strap Mary to her back as she made her way through the fields around Laugharne Castle.

The ruins of the castle is where they would all play, Everina, Eliza, Ned, and Mary. King, queen, ladies-in-waiting.

Mary was the queen, and her sisters did as they were told. Ned was the king and told Mary what to do, and Charles not yet born.

The estuary near Laugharne was full of sea gulls and herons, sandpipers and cormorants. Low tide brought little sinking holes where the clams lived. Mary and her sisters liked to take off their shoes, have the wetness ooze between their toes, forgetting the penalty.

"You are filthy," their father shouted before beating them, making Mary feel that her evil deed was much more than just muddying her skirts. Mary told Fanny he made her believe her very being was dirty and at fault.

Laugharne Castle had big gaping holes where Cromwell had laid siege and there was a lane nearby called Deadman's Lane where the blood had run down like a river. That is what Ned said.

"Blood River, Deadman's Lane, River Blood, take your pick." He brandished his stick as if it were a real sword. Mary used the same stick when she was Queen Elizabeth making Ned a knight of the realm, sing la-ti-da.

Ned said he wished it was back in Cromwell's time and he a soldier true to the king. Eliza with her pretty blond hair and china-blue eyes wanted it to be the time of Henry VIII and she a great lady. Everina was too much of a killjoy to wish anything. Mary told them she wanted it to be the future, not backward, for she could imagine a time when she could study books like Ned and have her very own horse. Ned said be quiet, that would never be. You might as well wear breeches, he snickered. In the nursery he rode his wooden horse up and down, declaring for all and sundry: I am master here.

It was Annie, the maid, who took Mary to buy books on Saturday market to the traveling cart where the man sold little books for children at a penny apiece along with ribbons and cloths, pots and pans, and ballad sheets commemorating in song and story the latest highwayman hanged in London town.

Thus, Mary read *Dick Whittington and His Cat, Mother Hubbard and Her Dog, Jack the Giant-Killer, The History of Tom Thumb, Cinderella and Her Glass Slipper*.

She read aloud to her sisters, outside, in the tall grass of the fields and behind bushes, in the hollows or in the bottom of a rowboat on the black beach. She showed them letters, how to link the words, form the sentences. Just as Annie had taught her. By the time Mary met Fanny, she could read well.

Mary's mother taught her that carriage, motion, manners, and address began with a well-disciplined body, that the body at all times should express a light, floating quality, that it was important to position the head and limbs in an unaffected manner, the upper arms curving gently away from the torso, hands held palms up, one resting lightly on top of the other.

Nobody was allowed to touch Ned's books, but once during his lesson time with his tutor, Mary sneaked a book.

The book was titled:

BIOGRAPHY OF A BOY
or,
Characteristic Histories
Calculated
To Impress Young Minds
with an Admiration
of
Virtuous Principles
and
Detestation
of
Vicious Ones
by Mrs. Pilkington

Mary could understand why that was such a secret book.

Because
Her
Father
Did
Not
Detest
Vicious
Principles
and
her
mother
did not
know
a
Principle
from
a
Porcupine

Furthermore, if the author, Mrs. Pilkington, was indeed a lady, why did she not write books on virtue for young ladies? Surely that was more important than standing properly with your hands folded just so. Since Mary knew how to write, she thought she might write Mrs. Pilkington a letter suggesting such a book for girls. Girls must be . . . Mary thought . . . kind, compassionate, that is what such a book would say. Mary would put in other things, too. Girls must be smart, she would start with, and strong, a whole host of things, but not dutiful and obedient, for that assumed a mother and father who were intelligent and rational.

Fanny taught her the words "intelligent" and "rational" when Mary was ten. They had never popped up in any of the fairy tales Mary read. At dame school Fanny, a little older, was full of words as well as a host of jump-rope songs and string games like Cat's Cradle and Spiderweb and Dog Cage and Around the World. Fanny had legs long as a stork's. Once they climbed to the top of a very dangerous tree, daring each other back and forth:

"I dare you."

"I dare *you*."

"I dared you first."

Then, shaded by an umbrella of leaves, Mary began to explain her hard life.

"It started like a dream."

The voices in the dream were soft and beguiling, insinuating themselves into Mary's sleep, cutting into the woolly layers of sleep like soft scissors.

"Oh, Edward, please do not tell me that." Her mother's voice was shrill, pitiful, as if on the edge of the windowsill.

"Yes, you are, God be my witness, a whore and worse, worse than a whore. You are a terrible person."

Her father's voice was low and rumbling, as thunder starts at a distance, grows louder, and finally cracks right next to one's ear.

"How can I be such a terrible person, Edward, when I love you so, am your wife, the mother of your children, the mistress of your heart."

"And stupid and silly."

"Please, Edward, please forgive me."

Mary would wonder what wretched thing her mother had done to be such a terrible person. She tried to remember what she, Mary, had done in the course of the day, the week. Could it be her fault? Fanny said no, not your fault.

"And you are not comely, not comely at all, anymore, anymore."

When her father had been to the tavern he repeated words. But it was true that she, Mary, was not comely. Did that merit a beating?

"Oh, God have mercy on me, Edward."

"May He, may He indeed."

Each word of her mother's would contain more tears. Each word of her father's would get harder and harder. Hers overflowed, his became stone, and Mary would feel she was in a rushing river being pelted by branches or rocks like an adulteress or a witch. Then her mother would be dragged off the bed, hitting the floor, and unless Mary could manage to get inside their room, her mother would be killed.

"Open the door," Mary would scream, kicking the door. "Let me in."

At such times Mary found herself in a strange, unrecognizable fury, kicking and banging the door, raising a great racket. She felt brave enough to die. She wanted to die. She wanted to kill him, then die. She wanted her mother to die, too, and everybody, her sisters, Ned, the whole world, to die and keep dying right up to the end of the world.

"Open the door, open . . ."

"What do you want, you little hussy?" The door ajar a tiny crack, Mary would push her way in and throw herself across her mother's poor prone body.

"Mother, Mother."

"Get her off me, Edward, get this child off me. Go. Go. Leave be. Annie, Annie, come and get Mary."

Her father wrenched her off her mother's body.

"No, no," Mary would scream.

"Annie, take her, take her away."

Annie had to drag her, kicking and screaming, back to the nursery.

"Annie, keep the animal locked in a cage. She needs a cage, by God." Mrs. Wollstonecraft, trailing behind, her hair undone, her bodice open, flinging her hands heavenward, declared Mary hopeless and asked God to give her strength. "I refuse to have that child anywhere in my sight."

The trip down the hall to the nursery, her mother in great disarray, her brother sneering and clicking at her, and her sisters sniffling in fear, was the worst part of the whole thing.

"See," Ned would say.

"See," Everina would sneer.

Eliza would start crying. "I did not do anything."

"Who said you did, you ninny."

"I was not talking to you, Ned, Mr. Nosey."

"Come, Mary, my love," Annie would soothe. "It is only husband and wife. God is love. Do not distress yourself. Your Annie is here. Shh, shh, there, there."

"It was husband and wife," Mary told Fanny in the tree. "Is it intelligent and rational?"

Fanny pondered a row of ants making their way across up the trunk of the tree. "It does not sound so. I have brought my brush. Let me do your hair."

Mary's mother, after these commotions, stayed abed two or three days, cold compresses across her red eyes, the curtains pulled and her room filled with gloom and a musty smell. Annie had to trot up and down the stairs day and night fetching cups of tea and spirits.

"Mamma, are you sick?" Mary, standing at the door, the other children in a gaggle behind her, got a peek at gray pillows and dingy sheets. Mary thought of her mother's bed with its canopy and curtains as a tent on a battlefield where the wounded and impaired were brought. King Arthur would have a little pennant, purple for royalty, flying from the top. If she could be anybody in history, and it had to be in history and not the future, she would want to be Merlin. Merlin always knew what to say.

"Mamma, please?"

Muffled sobs.

"Mamma?"

"Go away, you bothersome child."

"Shall I bring you . . ."

"Annie, Annie, take that abominable Mary away from me."

Annie would scoop Mary up, scat the other children back to the nursery.

"Hey nonny nonny, but you are such a big girl, a heavy girl, it is a wonder I can still carry you. Are you twelve or eleven?"

Annie carried her at the side of her waist like vegetables. Annie smelled of ginger and anise, ancient sweat. Her hair was a nest of lice, as if her brain was abuzz with little white ideas. She let Mary stand above her every Saturday night and pick through for lice with a fine-tooth comb. Mary liked to squeeze the little bugs between her fingernails, drop them in the bucket of water by her side. After a while, Annie would begin to purr like a cat and unloose her bodice so that her breasts would hang out. She would ask Mary to smear lard over the large, brown nipples, and then carefully, so as not to lose a grain, Annie would sprinkle sugar round and round.

"Suck, Mistress Mary, suck them."

Annie had a third nipple, this one pink and very moist, like un-cooked chicken, under her skirts.

"Do I have to, Annie?"

But there was no use in the asking. Mary's head would be clapped between, her ears muffed in folds of flesh until with a kind of yelp and spasm Annie would let her go, asking to be kissed straightaway on the lips.

"Let me see what I taste like," Annie would say, like the parson in the chapel, who would always say: Bow your heads, let us give thanks straightaway.

During service, Mary liked to watch out of the window for the pale horse that came to munch in the graveyard. It had a freckled rump and sweet face, huge yellow teeth.

"Should you tell a living soul about this," Annie would incant each time, sprinkling more stolen sugar on Mary's salty tongue, "God will smite you dead, and I will have to cut your heart up into little pieces for the evening stew."

"Can I tell Fanny? Just Fanny?"

"Do you want to die?" Annie's eyes would squint and blaze like a pig's on the way to slaughter. Mary imagined her heart diced and slivered, strewn in a field, melting in the sun. God and Annie in league would be something to behold. Annie would hold the knife. God would hold Mary down.

"It behooves me to make this observation," the parson said on Sunday. "The youth of our land is in great danger of distraction and eventual perdition. The ranks are being assembled. Be wary, I caution you, of distraction. Beelzebub is afoot. Wingèd merchants are hovering. Lucifer himself is creeping ever so stealthily. Do not be misled down the sorry, wide, naked, nettle-filled, neck-reckless road of Satan."

Mary hardly dared make her way home. She kept her hands around her neck—neck-reckless, not she—and her lips, her sinful Annie-sucking lips, pressed in. Who knew what might lie in wait, a whole array, dozens of bad baby devils ready to jump out and sting at you like a squadron of bumblebees. She imagined the chief he-devil, Lucifer himself, to be a snake, but in clothes like the clothes she had seen worn by Sir Walter Raleigh in a book about Queen Elizabeth. Was it a doublet or a dublin they wore, a ruffled collar? He would wear a golden crown as befit the king of hell, but up close you would be able to see that the snake was a snake except for the legs. He would have that awful snake head with that wide, sneaky snake smile, man legs, hoofed, of course. Maybe he would keep his neck folded down so you could not tell right off, and then it would kind of rock up, get long like a turtle's, with wrinkles in it. Fanny said that the devil was like God, you could not see him. Why does everybody imagine him all the same, then, Mary wanted to know. Because we see pictures, Fanny answered. But how do we know how to make pictures? Somebody made a devil picture a long time ago. And everybody copied? Right. Fanny looked at Mary as if she were a dunce, so she did not ask how that long-time-ago person knew to draw the devil.

"Little girl, little girl," the on-the-road devil would say in a voice both scary and nice at the same time.

"Cannot be late for dinner, Mr. Devil."

"Do you think the devil is rational and intelligent?" Mary asked Fanny. "If he is not imaginary."

"Maybe intelligent, but hardly rational."

Mary thought the two went together.

"For how could a rational being disdain God's love, Mary?"

"I suppose."

When Mrs. Wollstonecraft finally got out of bed after one of her tiffs with Mr. Wollstonecraft, she would go about with an injured air for several days, stepping slowly and carefully, sighing heavily every so often, shaking her head sadly whenever she saw Mr. Wollstonecraft, sniffing into her lace handkerchief, heaving her big chest with great longing, and gazing sadly out the window at the meadow where the sheep grazed.

In a few days, Mary's father would begin to wait with great solicitude on his wife, doing her small favors, begging her to please eat a morsel, calling her dear and my darling. He gave her little gifts, sent her to the dressmaker. All the children got new clothes, too, and little cakes.

It started with a little smile, a sniff turning into a small giggle.

"Oh, Edward."

He would begin to pinch and pull at her, and sit across from her, his legs spread far apart.

"I do not understand," Mary told Fanny under their secret hideout bush (which, if anybody found out, would be death to the traitor), "how they can hate and then . . ."

"That is the way grownups are," Fanny said.

The Wollstonecraft children stayed huddled in the corners. Ned picked his nose and ate the snot from his fingers. Eliza's nose ran and she wiped it on her sleeve. Everina was working on a sampler in cross-stitch that said: Home Is Where the Heart Is. She had gotten the house with the chimney done, was on the alphabet. Mary was reading a book called *The Strange Adventures of Count de Vinevil*. Annie went about her tasks not meeting anybody's eyes and humming to herself. Mary put her head in her book. The dogs glanced up from their dozing by the hearth at the slightest sound. One of them whimpered in his sleep and wiggled his legs as if running.

Later, if Mary should put her ear to her parents' bedroom door, she would hear not the sounds of battle but the cooing sound of pigeons in their coop.

The peace might stretch into days and weeks, and playing midwife in the hollows with Fanny and putting sticks up her bottom for purges, and poultices on her chest for fever, and rags in the front for the monthlies, and plugs in her ears for runny ears, and cloth up her nose for the ague, and then being summoned to church by the Sunday bell, having a nice dinner of potted venison, plain pudding and oyster loaves, falling asleep without crying, Mary would wonder if it had ever really happened, the blows and tears, the crashing and kicking. Were they not a happy family, after all? Had it been a dream, in fact, the shouting? But just as she was beginning to be less wary and the tightness in her chest was loosening a little, there would be a subtle change in the air, in the house, on people's faces, signaling a turn. Her father's voice would alter at times, his "my dears" would have a slight edge to them, and her mother would hold her body closer to herself, as if all she contained existed within her own skin, and nothing else was certain. Little spats would start up, nothing serious or of great consequence, almost anything would do. There were little traps set everywhere in the house.

"Two loaves lost at the bakery?"

Hardly her mother's fault, not even Annie's, for all the loaves which were taken to the big ovens at the bakery were marked W for Wollstonecraft. Their own kitchen in Laugharne had no oven, only the open hearth kept aflame by the bellows puffa-puffed by a village boy and the spit turned by dogs in a tread-wheel. It was a middling house with sculleries and pantry, a washhouse, but no laundry, no buttery, no dairy, no brewery, no bakery, and the bread had to be taken on Thursdays down to King Street.

Her father was the one who measured out the flour and kept the key to the tea caddy, and he let Annie sell the old tea leaves to the beggars who came to the back, collecting from her each week, and not trusting anybody, anybody at all, parceling out the household money in grudge and suspicion. Each week he counted out the sheets and guarded the bread loaves as if they were made of gold.

"Two loaves, two whole loaves lost?"

"But, Edward, my husband . . ."

Edward Wollstonecraft was flush with liquor, pinpricks of spite purpled his nostrils. He had one long ugly hair sticking out of his nose like a saber, and his little piggy eyes spoke treachery and condemnation, and the spittle on his lips formed up so that he talked in spray. With one sweep of his hand he brushed all the dishes and food off the table. The dogs went mad, snuffling up all the food, and one even eating a broken plate with gravy on it and cutting his mouth.

"I am going to leave," Mary mumbled to her sisters in the stairway cupboard, where they were all jammed together.

"You are eleven years old," Eliza said. "How can you leave?"

"It is not fair," Mary hissed. "Can you not see that?"

"He is our father."

"Yes, but does that alone give him right?"

"Where will you go?"

"You will see. I am going to go. I am going to live with the gypsies and tell fortunes, or be with Fanny in her bed in her house."

"You are not going anywhere," Ned said, cuffing Mary. "How can you go anywhere until you get married?"

"I am not getting married."

"You will get married," Ned said. "It is God's law. And if you do not, you will be a spinster and starve all your life forever and ever in the poorhouse."

"I will starve, then."

"If you starve, you will die."

"I am going to die, then."

"You are not going to die," Ned said. "Unless I say so."

"I can live with Fanny."

"Her father is a drunk, too," Everina said.

"How do you know?" Eliza asked.

"At least here," Ned said, "you know the worst."

"Do I?"

"The worst is if the house fell down, and snakes crawled over you," Everina said.

"If there was no food for a hundred days, and then it rained, that would be it," Eliza said.

"We could all die in a big pile and then rot," Ned said. "That would be the worst."

The worst came on a day Mary was to call the Day of the Dogs, a gray, cold day, with fog rolling in from the sea like big bales of hay. Mary had her doll strapped to her back and she was hungry. Up the hill she went, and around a grove of oaks.

Ahead was the house. Smoke was coming up from the chimney. Tea will be soon, she said to herself, thinking of the warm liquid settling at the base of her belly, and hoping for hot buttered muffins.

As she got closer to the house, she noticed something hanging from the large oak near the front door. She was not sure what she was seeing. In *Jack the Giant-Killer*, a whole giant house bloomed at the end of the stalk. Fe Fi Fo Fum. On closer look, Mary thought that they were sacks dangling from ropes. Maybe it was venison wrapped in cloth to air and age. Her father had gone hunting that morning.

Then her eyes blurred. And her mouth went dry. She could not tell what she was seeing, for it was quite impossible that it should be what it was, and her mind could not take it in to make sense of it, and Dear God, she breathed, have mercy on such as I.

Her father's five hunting dogs were dangling, hanged by the neck, eyes bulging.

Mary vomited, stumbled into the house. The girls were sobbing,

Ned hushed, Mrs. Wollstonecraft and Annie did not look anybody in the eye but bit their lips, went about setting tea. Mary dared not say a word.

"Leave them hanging," her father commanded that night. "Do not presume upon yourself to cut them down. They have disappointed me, do you understand. Understand? Leave them hanging. They have disappointed me."

The children cringed together. Annie's olive complexion was ashy and the big pores on her cheeks had turned into black dots. Mrs. Wollstonecraft's eyes were glittery with tears. She was big with child then. Charles.

Annie served them tea silently. The fire kept going out. Eliza sniffled and pulled at her dress. Everina clenched her teeth. Even Ned looked stricken.

"We are going to move shortly," Mr. Wollstonecraft announced. "To Yorkshire."

Everina and Eliza struck up a wail. Ned looked wounded. Mary could hear the wind start up and thought of the poor dogs swinging, bumping into each other.

"They must be cold," she said to her father.

"Who must?"

"The dogs. Please cut them down, Papa. Please."

She thought of the wind ruffling their fur, and that their tongues would be leather and their eyes frozen like marbles.

"Please."

"Hush, child." Annie put her hand on Mary's shoulder and her great breasts, which Mary had come to hate, sugar or no, brushed against her back, giving Mary goose bumps and shivers all up and down her back.

"I want you to cut them down," Mary said.

"Mind your manners." Mary's mother stood up, pulled at her bodice, put her finger to her nose. Mr. Wollstonecraft snorted.

The fire made shadows on the wall like the forest in *The History of Tom Thumb*.

I hate him, Mary thought, I hate them all, I hate it here, I hate everything. I hate myself, I hate the dogs, I hate Annie.

"I will not cut them down for three days," her father said. "I most definitely will not cut those ungrateful dogs down for three days and three nights."

He stood up, approaching Mary, and she flinched, anticipating the blow, but instead he reached out and tweaked Mrs. Wollstonecraft's breast. Mary was amazed. Did her mother make her breasts into sugar teats, too?

"Do not ask me why," Mr. Wollstonecraft continued, his face red and puffed, his pants stained, and his stomach, now fat, tumbling out of his top. "Do not ask me why I hanged those silly dogs. I have my own good reasons."

Mary was eleven years old and knew that dogs and all dumb beasts were innocent of any crime requiring hanging.

"Why, you ask me why, Mary, did I hear a why, you ask me why?"

"No, no, I do not ask why." Mary began to shake. She knew her father was unintelligent and irrational.

"Do not be impertinent to your father." And her mother flicked Mary's cheek with her fingernail in such a way that a small cut formed which never healed properly and looked like a piece of moon caught under her eye.

"Ouch," Mary cried.

Her mother said: "Serves you right."

"You want to know why?" her father bellowed. "I will tell you why:

"To teach them a lesson."

"What?" Mary felt confused. What lesson? Her cheek burned. A little trail of blood was running down her cheek, dripping onto her neck. She wiped her face with the palm of her hand. If the blood fell on her collar, it would leave a stain and she would be beaten. She would be beaten in any event. All that was necessary was to leave her bed in the morning, or even stay in it, or to smile or to cry, to eat, not to eat, run outside, run to school, do well in school, do badly. It all equaled a beating.

"Everybody to bed," Mrs. Wollstonecraft said.

"No tea?" Ned asked.

"Naughty children do not get tea, Ned, you know that."

"I was good," Ned said.

"Me, too," Eliza said.

"I am always good," Everina affirmed.

"Dear little children," the parson at the church said that Sunday, "it is a glorious Sunday. Let us kneel down and praise God. You must remember that you will not be abandoned."

Mary, who had been looking out the window, waiting patiently for the freckled horse to appear in the graveyard, turned around. Not abandoned?

"I gather you unto me. Jesus will save you."

Mary walked quietly up to the pulpit, grabbed the parson's legs.

"Save me," she pleaded. "Save *me*."

Mrs. Wollstonecraft screeched. "Oh, my God. Annie get her. Get her out of there."

Everybody else laughed. Annie came forth to get her.

"Take her outside, Annie, immediately."

Mary was set in the church graveyard, where the pale old horse with the freckled rear was munching the grass between the graves. It turned to look at her, rolling its bulgy eyes and exposing its large yellow teeth. It was spring. Narcissus and daffa-down-lily were blooming. The air was balmy and kind, yet Mary had to clamp her hands over her ears, because she kept hearing it, because it had been imprinted on her heart:

"I hanged them to teach them a lesson, to teach you a lesson. Let that be a lesson to you all. A lesson, do you hear, a lesson."

CHAPTER 2

MRS. DAWSON had blisters on her arms and legs which she prodded and picked with her long fingernails. Sores on her lips she tongued open like little pot lids. Her spectacles did not help, for she must squeeze her eyes to see anything far or close, and she could not hear properly but must ask What say? What say? constantly. At Bath, where people went for holiday and mineral baths, she and Mary lived in two miserable rooms.

Mary at twenty-two, plump and pert, serious and full of ideas, was a lady's companion to Mrs. Dawson at Bath. This was Mary's employment after her needlework with Fanny and she could not abide Mrs. Dawson. What saved her mind and manner at Bath was a bakery. The tearoom was where Mary spent her free time, sipping countless cups of tea and writing letters. She felt elegant and literary.

July 3, 1781

Dear Fanny, What shall I tell you?
How shall I distinguish myself?
What is important?
The bakery kitchen has a massive trestle table, a baker's peel, a great oven, and a roasting pit. A young boy is used to feed the bundle of faggots to the oven which they let burn down to a fine ash, which is raked, and when the stones are the right temperature, in go the nicely shaped loaves and the buns which are served to guests with curd cheese, beaten egg and fruits, very nice indeed. It is quite novel to sit in a kitchen and not fear for your life. People passing in the street look in at me through the window as if I belonged here. Fanny, I must admit that I am not as comely as

*Eliza or as quick as Everina, but I have high hopes. I feel I have
survived my childhood for a reason. Is this silly?*

July 24, 1781

*Dear Fanny, You will think me presumptuous, and indeed I am,
for I cannot help but feel that all I do, my little employments, are
a form of apprenticeship. I am reading Mary Astell's* A Serious
Proposal to the Ladies. *Could I be destined for something beyond
the ordinary lot of our sex? So much to learn.*

Mrs. Dawson, Mary's employer, took it upon herself to teach Mary
a lesson or two. Moral instruction was her forte.

"At the tea shop again? If you think life is a basket full of posies,
all chickens come home to roost, and she who dandles, dawdles last.
What? What did you say? Smiling is the devil's work, Mary. Why are
you so late? Dreaming away? What is that in your hand?" Mrs. Dawson
fingered one of her scabs.

"Nothing, Mrs. Dawson."

"Nothing? Then why do you hold it back?" Mrs. Dawson hobbled
about angrily. "You dare to tell me nothing. You dare to bring into
my abode some object, scrap of paper, piece of food which you are
ashamed to show me?" The little squares of carpet, the dark obtrusive
furniture were Mrs. Dawson's realm, her life. "You are up to no good.
I can see it on your desperate face." Cook, in the kitchen, winked at
Mary. The kitchen was a small galley with room for only one. The
cook, rather rotund, squeezed in and out morning and night, wedged
herself between the stove and the cutting board. She sang sad Sicilian
songs in a feeble soprano warble as if caught in a cage. Mary felt sorrow
for her.

"Are you two up to something? I saw Cook wink."

"I was in the tearoom drinking tea," Mary admitted. She had to
stand up directly opposite Mrs. Dawson most of the time. Mary was
taller by a head. Sitting meant knee to knee.

"Mary, you are doomed to an ill fate if you do not learn to mind.
And you will not be permitted to see any of the festivities, as they are
called, for such sights do a young girl violence."

"Not the sedan-chair racing, ma'am?"

"Definitely not."

Every Tuesday at Bath there was sedan-chair racing. There was a portrait studio where one could have one's portrait painted. In the morning, people went on horse rides through the meadows and rolling hills surrounding Bath, and on Monday and Thursday, regaled by French horns and clarinets, people attended the public breakfast. There were other concerts and formal cotillions and country-dances in the Assembly rooms, and always the hubbub of the baths themselves. These were palatial and splendid and beautiful. Fully clothed people would bathe and throw each other from the balcony into the water. Dogs and cats were thrown, too, amid giggles and screams. In the Pump Room they served the same medicinal waters bathed in below, what matter. It was all such fun. The baths were full of echoes and chambers, odd spots behind pillars, and broken statuary. There had been baths there in Roman times. Mary could imagine togas, shields, laurel wreaths, declamations of philosophy, bronze bodies, black curls shiny as olives, brown thonged sandals.

Once she and Mrs. Dawson rode in a punt down the Avon River, passing the cattle market, where the farmers loaded cattle driven down from the hills to be taken to the Bristol docks. In the distance was Bramton Mill, where they made gunpowder, and site of the duel in which Viscount Du Barry died.

July 30, 1781

The story is, dear Fanny, that his seconds carried him down to the nearest tavern, stopped for a refreshment. Laying Du Barry out, they went inside for a good drink. However, Du Barry was not dead yet. But he did die waiting for them to finish their drinks, and so they buried him at the back of the tavern. Later he was dug up and given a proper burial in St. Michael's churchyard.

The river Avon in Bath was full of eels and brown trout and chub and carp and pike and perch and freshwater crayfish. Most notable was the bridge from where they had once thrown witches. If these women drowned, they were innocent and given a Christian burial. If they floated, they were hauled up and burned at the stake. Sally Wistock had been one such victim. A herbalist whom people from miles around visited for cures, she was denounced by an unhappy patient who did not recover from shingles. The poor lady floated.

Mrs. Dawson's rooms at Bath were so tight and spare that most of the time Mary felt folded in half. The furnishings were velvet, scratchy to the touch and unpleasant to the eye. The curtains, tasseled, dusty, a dismal blue, blocked each window. Mrs. Dawson liked to have a fire going no matter what the temperature, and the small, dirty kitchen with a huge oven helped to keep the place insufferably hot. Mrs. Dawson and Mary slept opposite each other, and whatever time Mary looked, Mrs. Dawson would have her eyes open, staring straight at her.

For serious talks about Mary's moral turpitude, Mrs. Dawson sat in the rocker. She rocked to emphasize certain key issues.

"That you cannot offer up a decent prayer to Him who made thee distresses me no end, and makes me wonder, Mary, if you are, indeed, a suitable companion for a God-fearing woman such as myself who has dedicated her life to good works and better thoughts, if I must say so myself."

"But I did pray, Mrs. Dawson, I do pray." At least Mary tried hard to pray.

"Jezebel, do not compound your evil with lies. I took you on as a favor to your dear father. No, I did not see your lips move in church today."

"I can read without moving my lips, and prayer is internal."

"And impudent. Lying on the one hand. Then the evilness of it all. Young lady, watch yourself with rapt vigilance. When Mr. Dawson was alive, may he live forever in heaven, he would not stand for surliness, no indeed, he would take a switch, and I, too, had I not gout and a poor, weak heart, and shortness of breath, and palsy in my limbs, and can barely see or hear and am not long for this world as it is, would punish you in a most corporeal manner. Kneel now and beg His forgiveness, do as you are told, child. Remember you are nothing and came from nothing and will go back to nothing. Remember you are nothing."

Mary did remember. She would be struck by the notion in the middle of tea or outside somewhere or in a boat or just walking along. I am nothing. Nothing. She wondered if this is what it was to be grown up, to feel so inconsequential.

August 12, 1781

Mrs. Dawson, dear Fanny, is a fit rival for my father. They are friends, which is how I came to be employed, and they must have trained in the same school, suckled at the same breast, been of one womb, for they see eye to eye, hear ear to ear and utter with one voice: Woe, Woe unto you or would have us like Dante's vision of Hell abandon hope. But I will not. Do you hear, I will not give in, Fanny.

"Did you say something?"

"Is that all, ma'am?"

"No."

"Yes?"

"Did you say something?"

"No, ma'am."

"Speak up."

"Nothing, ma'am."

"Good," Mrs. Dawson said. "I want you to get me a nice fish for dinner, Mary. A red one. Do you understand? Can you accomplish that task? Is that too much to ask? A nice red fish? To bring back to Cook. Cook wants a fish, does she not?"

Mary looked at Cook. Cook shrugged.

"Are you being rude?"

"Not at all."

"Are you being rude again?"

"No, no."

Mary went into her little room. She had to move sideways between her bed and Mrs. Dawson's bed. The wardrobe was at one end against the window. It seemed a waste, for she had only two dresses and a night shift and Mrs. Dawson had only three dresses. Mary would have much preferred to have some light come in the room. She sighed. She got out her straw bonnet, tied the silk ribbons. Fanny, she thought, I am being sent on a ridiculous errand by an autocratic, scabby, sanctimonious . . .

"Do I hear a complaint?"

"Oh no, Mrs. Dawson."

The fish market at Bath was on the waterfront. The sloping tables were lined with rows of fish with large, glassy eyes and sleek, neat bodies. Mary wanted to run her fingers along the scales, console them, saying it's all right, fishies. When she was a little girl she had taken a fish to bed with her in the hopes she and the fish would wake up together. After looking at all the fish carefully, Mary bought the prettiest fish of all. It was the color of a teakettle, coppery and bright, the overlapping scales covering all but the soft white belly.

The woman put the fish in Mary's bag, gave her the change. They were to have the fish for dinner, some nice boiled potatoes, a custard, tea. That is what Cook said when Mary had gone into the kitchen before leaving. Earlier in the day Mary had picked some watercress from the stream which ran down to the river. So they would have that, too. She walked back along the gardens before turning up into a dark alley, thinking of how the food would look on her plate. The fish would sit next to the potato and the watercress would be like a little garland all around. The custard would be in a small cup and slip down her throat smoothly.

That night, if Mrs. Dawson permitted her to have the candle, Mary also planned to read before falling asleep. She had a book from the bookstall, Rousseau's *Emile*. She could place it in the Bible, hide it that way, and she would make her lips move.

"What?"

There was a shadow, a form, something in front of her. Was it a wolf? The thing became tall, got taller, it was growing big as a bear, bigger than a bear, it covered the sky.

"Fanny," Mary wailed.

It grabbed her wrist. Then she felt a cool object at her throat.

"Oh, God, help me," she screamed. It was the devil. Mrs. Dawson had been right. She was evil. The devil had come for her. It was a lesser devil or Lucifer himself or another devil or something dead and awful risen from the grave. Oh, no.

"Help!" she screamed piteously, her words coming out a gurgle.

"Shush," it spat.

For a moment Mary felt relieved. It was not a devil. It was just a man, a big burly man. But then he pressed the knife tip into her neck, taking a little nick.

"Please, please," Mary pleaded. "Please. You can have the fish, the shilling. Take them. Please do not hurt me."

"Shut your mouth."

"Oh no. Oh, God. Oh, please do not hurt me."

They were all alone. Just faceless, closed-up buildings. The rows of houses seemed forever away. Suddenly Mary wanted Mrs. Dawson. Anybody would do. She could have been way up in the sky or on the sun for all the help she would get. She would die, die painfully, and nobody would ever know. People would be eating dinner, coming in from work, and she would be dead, punished.

"Dear God, help me," she muttered.

"I do not like your looks," the man said.

"What?"

"I do not like your looks, so I will have to kill you."

Mary did not understand.

He moved his hand against her breasts.

"Oh no, oh no." He was going to cut off her breasts. She knew it. "Dear God," she prayed. "I am sorry I have neglected you . . ."

Mary thought she heard rustling. Her ears, her heart strained to hear something, anything.

"So you will have to pleasure me."

"What?" she gasped.

"Just so. Kneel down."

Was she to pray again as she had for Mrs. Dawson. Why did not God hear her. She feared this man was also going to chop off her head.

"Kneel." He grabbed her hair, pushed her down.

"Have mercy on me. Please." She thought of her sisters, Fanny, even her mother. She began to recite what she always did when she was in trouble:

"A is an acorn that grows on an oak; B is a boy who delights in his book; C is a canister, holds Mamma's teas; D is a drum you may sound as you please . . ."

The man dropped his breeches, poked something toward her mouth, and started to breathe very fast.

"Open your mouth," he commanded. "Open your mouth. And if you bite me I will kill you."

But at that moment there was the sound of laughter.

"Oh, Mirabel, you are terrible." A man's voice came through the night. "To say such, and before your mother. My dear, it was positively . . ."

"Say anything," the man hissed, pulling Mary's head back by her hair, "and I will come back to kill you."

Quickly he pulled up his pants, ran back along the alley down toward the fish market.

"What are you doing sitting in the pathway, miss?" A man took her arm, pulled her up. "Are you ill?"

"No, no, I am fine." Mary could not say much. Her teeth were chattering. She was shaking all over.

"You have taken a chill," the lady said. "Shall we see you home?"

"No, no." Say anything, he had said, and I will come back to kill you. Just like Annie was going to kill her, too, if she said anything.

"This is the direction for the river, is it not?" they asked.

Mary felt skirts brush against her.

"Such a curious creature sitting in the path. Do you think she is all right? Servant girls these days swoon away at the slightest. Do you think she is quite right?" There were giggles, and then day folded over on them and it was quiet again.

I have to get home, Mary said to herself. He might come back. I have to get home. Gingerly she moved her legs, which scissored beneath her. She put one foot out, raised up on one knee, pulled the other foot out, braced herself, and had gone a step. I can walk, she said to herself, I can still walk. Carefully she extended one leg, then the other. Again. Another step. I can walk, I can still walk. She began to walk a little faster. She stumbled, righted herself, kept on. The air cut against her face. She heard slashing sounds coming from the street. Carriages, she said to herself, just carriages. Far better than humans. Her heart was racing, keeping pace with her legs. She was running. Something stung her, stuck to the tears drying on her face. Dear God,

I can run, she sobbed, I can still run. Ahead were the houses. They beckoned to her. I am still alive, she whispered. I am alive. But she remembered the words: I do not like your looks. You deserve to die. Tell anybody and you are dead. Tell anybody and your heart will be sliced up for stew. She was on the cobblestone street. She was in front of the house. She rang the bell, heard Mrs. Dawson hobbling to the door. The door swung open.

"Where have you been? Do you realize how late it is? Do you want to starve me to death. You are trying to kill me. I know it. I know you are trying to kill me." Mrs. Dawson clutched at her shoulder. "You do. You do want me to starve to death. Where is the fish? You lost the fish? Look at you, girl. Good money and where is it?" Cook looked alarmed. Her large chest heaved up and down. Then Mary saw that there was somebody in the other room. Had the man come back to get her? "Mr. Dawson, had he been alive, would have made sure that you paid for it. Do you realize that I pay you good wages to be my companion. What are you going to eat now? Air? Water? Fire? What do you think God would think if He could see you. Your clothes are dirty. Your face is dirty. Where is your other shoe? Is that blood on your neck? What is that on your ear? Have you no respect?"

"I am tired, Mrs. Dawson, have mercy."

"What? What did you say?"

"God saw. God did see me."

But, Mary conjectured, if He saw, why did He not help when I needed Him. Unless it was God who sent those people on the path. It was. It had to be.

"Your sister is here," Mrs. Dawson said finally.

"My sister?"

"She is packing your things."

"You are letting me go, Mrs. Dawson?"

"Yes, I am."

Everina appeared in the doorway to the bedroom. She looked worn and as stern as ever. Her hips had gotten heavier, though.

"Everina," Mary said. "What?"

"Your mother is sick," Mrs. Dawson said. "But do not for one second think I am going to hire you back. The world is not run on charity for girls like you. I am going to have to write your father about how much a disappointment you were to me."

"How sick is she?" Mary asked.

"Sick," Everina said.

"She is dying," Mary said. "Is she dying?"

"Somebody has to nurse her," Everina explained. "Eliza has her baby. I have my job."

"Some people think all they need to do is smile and curtsy, that they can spend the day drinking tea and eating tarts," Mrs. Dawson said. "Do not deny it. I have seen you at the bakery. Some people think they are better than other people. Well, they will find out exactly how good they are. Get on with you and do not ask for any back wages. I am not charging you for the fish, and another thing you must realize is that not everybody in this world is going to love you because you are young. Do you have anything to say for yourself? Thought so."

"Mrs. Dawson," Mary began, looking into Mrs. Dawson's squinting eyes. She was going to tell her how she had hated it all—the sermons, the sideways life, the heat and dark, but instead she looked at Cook. "Mrs. Dawson," Mary said. "Thank you for everything."

"We can take the return coach to London," Everina said, "and then the coach up to Yorkshire."

"I have taken the liberty of letting your sister get your things assembled. Goodbye. And do not come back for further employment. You are walking straight into perdition with an attitude like that. You will learn. You will be brought low. And yes, I have learned my lesson. Wayward girls like you deserve what they get. I hope that you have learned your lesson, too, that in the future you will fear God and mind your manners." Mrs. Dawson picked at a scab, rubbed her eyes. "You can never be too sorry, if you ask me. Remember that as you go through life. Never too sorry."

"Never too sorry," Everina parroted in the coach. "And do not forget it, you naughty girl. Tell me, what is wrong with the woman's skin? What did you do to her?"

"Nothing."

"Cast a spell?"

"Hush, Everina."

"I would, the ninny. She is going to meet her Maker crusty as a dried-out toad. And that cook. I am sure you three had a jolly time."

When Mary walked into her mother's sickroom, shuttered and smelling of brandy and diarrhea, old blood, copper tubing, she was reminded of her fear in the alley with the man ready to kill her.

"Who is there?" Her mother rose up on her elbows, fingered the air like bread dough. "Who is there? Answer me, who is there?"

"Mary."

"Mary who?"

"Mary, your daughter Mary, Mary Wollstonecraft."

"Oh, it is you."

Who else.

CHAPTER 3

IN THE FAMILY they were sunshine or rain. Eliza was rain, and she, Mary, sunshine, but it was not happiness, she knew, that made her sunshine. It was quickness. Mary had to keep moving or she would stop altogether, fall into rain. Everina was always the storm coming —the heavy stillness and then the rumble. Fanny, Mary's friend, was light and airy, a sunny day with an ominous cast, a little like a billowy cloud edged in black. As a grown woman, Fanny still looked like a child, but had developed a racking grown-up cough, and fainted easily. She would wake up on a pillowcase ribboned in blood.

Eliza *was* sanguine until she lost her baby. Truly. And she always gave the impression of expectation. For her wedding, she wore a wreath of lilies in her hair and a lovely cream satin with an embroidered and quilted petticoat. She looked like the Queen of the May. Mary and Fanny, who came up to Yorkshire, had worked until past midnight four nights in a row, sewing the dress. Mary's dress for the wedding, a sky-blue, with a fringed hem and lacing at the bodice, was given to Fanny when Fanny got married several years later. At both ceremonies, Fanny's and Eliza's, Mary had a feeling in her stomach as if a sharp stone had lodged itself and would not go up or down. And midway through Eliza's ceremony Mary thought she might spit up the tea and bread she had at breakfast. Everina had to take one arm and Fanny the other. It was a presentiment. This was before Mary was Mrs. Dawson's companion, before Mrs. Wollstonecraft became ill, and before Mary was summoned home to nurse her.

By the time the Bishops (Eliza and Mr. Bishop) came for Mrs. Wollstonecraft's funeral, Eliza had the baby, called Mary Frances after Mary and her friend Fanny. Mr. Bishop was, Mary observed, very like their father in temperament. He was brusque and blustery. Mary wondered if that was Eliza's only idea of a man—that is, a manly, manfully, manhood, mannish, man. She, Mary, vowed never to be associated with anybody who had the slightest resemblance to their middle-aged father. From a distance, she could recognize all the attributes, which were physical as well as temperamental—the large, beefy face, red nose, heavy hands, the gait and footstep of a bull. To compound the problem, if Bishop was their father in face and manner, then Eliza was their mother in her best days: cornsilk hair, sky-blue eyes, sweet expression. There had been a flurry of suitors for Eliza, all completely unsuitable as far as Mary was concerned, and Mr. Bishop the very worst.

"His manly grace," Eliza explained. "It would not do to give him no for an answer. And, of course, I have no dowry."

There was no dowry for any of the girls. Their father had seen to that. And Mr. Bishop's manly grace, Mary noted, consisted of enormous height, tight trousers stuck in short boots, short jacket, tight sleeves, and a wide-cut collar, and head of flaming red hair. Mary conjectured that perhaps Mr. Bishop had taken liberties before the marriage, because not only did the child fall fast upon the nuptials, but Mr. Bishop was both forceful in manner and formidable in body. It would not do to give him no for an answer.

Mr. Bishop was "in shipping," whatever that meant. After their mother's funeral, when Mary lived in a room below the Bishop apartment in London, she found out that it meant that he was a clerk in a shipping office. Mary had been under the impression that he lifted ships with his bare hands and set them in the sea like Gulliver. No, he sat on a tall stool, copied documents on a heavy wooden desk, and at the end of every day humbly took his pages into the office of one Mr. Jones, who was given to shouting orders and tearing improperly copied documents into a hundred small pieces and throwing them behind his back. Mr. Bishop regaled Eliza and Mary with such accounts. Sometimes, after laughing heartily, he would break into tears.

Following their mother's funeral, April 22, 1782, Mary went with Eliza and Mr. Bishop back to London—Spitalfields, to be exact, to one of their grandfather's old houses now belonging to their brother Ned, who himself lived in a fine white house, neoclassical in style, designed by Robert Adam and situated near Russell Square.

Ned never invited them there. Mary did not even know his address. Russell Square seemed another world, away from Spitalfields and her small room with its ugly awkward chair and table, its straw mattress. She was right below the Bishops and could hear them walking about, talking loudly. When the baby cried, Mr. Bishop cursed.

Mary spent her days reading romances, like *Love Intrigues; or History of the Amours of Bosvil and Galesia* by Jane Barker. When she read them she entered into a daze, forgetting that she had no money, that she must find employment, that nobody was going to marry her, that Ned her brother would not help her, that her mother was dead and her father a fool. But when Mary looked out of her one narrow window at the vegetable market, she remembered that her grandfather had left his money equally to the grandchildren but that Ned Wollstonecraft had contrived, in a court of law, to have it all come to him, the oldest son, as was traditional. Mary and Eliza and Everina had inherited some money from their mother, yet it would hardly do for very long. Everina had secured a position as a governess in Scotland.

September 12, 1782
Dear Fanny, Do you think I shall ever be famous? If so, it must fall from the sky like manna. It will not emanate from these walls nor find its way up the dirty stairs. And I must become very famous indeed to escape these confines. I am far away from all hope.

None of the heroines she read about in her novels was famous, but many were born rich and all inspired the love of at least one man. In a world of her own dreaming, Mary did not claim the rats which ran about like white foxes in the night, or the heavy grime on the hem of her dress, did not notice Eliza's bruises, and the thuds and slams, curses, and the late-night wailing of the baby.

"That," Mary said, pointing to a green bruise one day. "What is that?" Eliza looked as if she had been crying, too.

"Oh, that. I fell."

"And you fell yesterday and the day before that?"

"I cannot remember, perhaps I brushed up against the stonework of the fireplace."

When Eliza proceeded to nurse little Mary Frances, Mary could see that Eliza's breasts were marked by teeth as if an animal had attacked her there, too.

"Rats, Eliza?" Mary hissed.

"Little Mary suckled too hard. That is it."

Sometimes Eliza's lips were cracked and cut. "I am such a clumsy woman."

Eliza's nose, come to think of it, bled often. "I have had nosebleeds since I was a child."

Her cheeks were often black-and-blue. "My cheek is not black-and-blue."

"Your cheek *is* black-and-blue. I have eyes in my head, Eliza Wollstonecraft. What is it?"

"Eliza Bishop, if you please."

"If *you* please. You married him. The brute. Are we to repeat family history unto the seventh generation? Bishop, Wollstonecraft, does it matter?"

"And you are jealous that I have a man." Eliza, finished with nursing her child, buttoned her top, took on a haughty air, pushing her head forward like a chicken pecking crumbs. "Look at you, you have nothing."

"Of what, pray tell, am I jealous? Of getting knocked about, kicked and scratched, bitten and mauled? A man, what is that to have? I would rather have a bear. Anyway, I am not dead yet."

"I am married, Mary, and you are not. That is why you are jealous."

"God save me from marriage, my dear. I have seen quite enough."

"I cannot help it that you hate men."

"Hate men? I do not hate men. I hate violence. I hate the oppression of the weak by the strong. Women put up with too much for the sake of marriage."

"High-sounding words. If you could, you, too, would marry. Would you rather put up with the poorhouse?"

"Not at all, Eliza, you are not a fool. I taught you how to read. You should know . . ." Mary remembered the women in the novels. They were happy once married.

"What should I know?"

Mary put her head against the wall. In books, life was not life.

"What is there to know, Mary? Can I make a living on my own? Can you? Where would I be without the protection of a man."

"You call that protection?"

The world was a hateful place with no refuge. Her sister was beautiful and intelligent. The baby was lovely.

"You know how to think, Eliza. Think a little." Mary began to sob. "Oh, Eliza, my darling, think a little for yourself, of yourself."

"I am thinking. But it does me no good, Mary. You think. Are you much better off than I am? What happens when Mother's money runs out? Mrs. Dawson will not have you back. What are you going to do?"

Mary came over, knelt in front of her sister. Tears were draining off Eliza's face, falling from her chin onto her baby's face.

"I do not know what to do," Eliza whispered. "Help me."

"A is an acorn that grows on the oak; B is who a boy who delights in his book; C is a canister, holds Mamma's teas . . ."

"Oh, Mary, not that. Please. The alphabet is not going to help you."

"How do you know?"

Maybe Eliza was right. The alphabet was not going to help anybody. Maybe marriage at any cost was the only answer. Her heroines were married by the end of the book. A husband would feed one, that at least. There would be breakfasts and dinners, suppers and teas. Mary liked to lie abed, daydream about jelly and jam, soft bread, dumplings and stew, a nice piece of sausage with a roasted potato. At night, in her dreams, she set an enormous table. In the middle was green-pea soup, to be removed and replaced with fish baked in pastry. At the top was a roast sirloin of beef and the base was turkey boiled in prune sauce. On the left were veal cutlets and lemons, and on the right, oyster loaves. The table would gleam with silver and glassware.

Waking up, Mary had nothing to eat except her muddy tea. Then she would have to remind herself to go outside, get some air, see the world, the real world, the world of others. But watching coaches pass in the street, she despaired of ever riding in a coach again. Hearing the pie man, she knew she could never buy a pie. Or go in a tea shop. Or buy a piece of new cloth. When one of her teeth became loose, she pulled it out herself, stanched the blood with a dirty rag.

"What is that?" Eliza asked, looking at the tooth on Mary's table.

"My tooth."

"Why do you put it there."

"To remind me to do something."

"Do what?"

"I am not sure yet. What is that on your head?"

"Ran into the poker in the dead of night."

"Yes, I heard," Mary replied. "I heard the poker talk. The poker warned you, did it not, that you were a bad, sinful woman, a bad mother, and a worse wife. I had not been aware that pokers could speak, Eliza."

"I'm thinking of going back to live with Father," Eliza whispered, looking over her shoulder.

"What a wonderful idea, Eliza. Then you can cower in the cupboard as you used to as a child."

"I am grown now, Father is old, it would be different."

Except for the large wound on her face, Eliza looked very fetching in a rucked bodice and overskirt caught up at the sides and back. After a session, Mr. Bishop would buy her trinkets, make a fuss, just as their father had with their mother.

"I think that is silly talk, Eliza. Father struck Everina during the wake, and would have hit you, too, had you not been married and your husband right there."

Their mother's funeral, in a rain that promised to turn into a light sleet, was dismal, more dismal than other funerals Mary had been to. At her grandfather's, there had been so many people that she, in the front row, feared being pushed into the grave. The parson had been drunk, telling them several times that Old Wollstonecraft was a merry old soul, and then back at the house everybody else, it seemed, had swiftly gotten drunk, too, and told ribald stories and sung songs that sounded like sea chanteys, with much heaving and hawing and downing of spirits.

At her mother's funeral, it was just the family. Ned actually was there, finely turned out in a huge woolly coat. His wife looked exquisite, even in the rain. She was wearing black silk tucked high under her breasts, and a flat hat with artificial flowers, the latest style. Their baby brother, Charles, home for two days from the Navy, looked bloated and angry. The girls huddled together, Mary, Eliza, and Everina, and Mr. Wollstonecraft stood alone, openly sipping his whisky. Bereaved, the parson said by way of excuse. At one point in the service, Mr. Wollstonecraft had turned around and, without even walking to the giant oak on the hill behind them, relieved himself in a great rush and splatter. Mary was mortified.

"Why did not Father hit *you* at the funeral, Mary?"

"Because he knows I would kill him if he did, that is why." It amazed Mary that she was speaking the truth. Yet currently anybody could have trod right over her and she would have said, Beg your pardon. She had been stronger then. Maybe now she was reading too many novels with submissive women. Maybe she should write her own novel about a different kind of woman.

"So you think Father is a bad idea."

"Yes, I do."

"What do you propose, then, Mary?"

"I do not know, Eliza. I am unable to know what to do with *myself*. Next month my money will be gone. Am I to starve? Go in the poorhouse for indigent women? What is to become of *me*?"

"You will perish. We will all perish," Eliza wailed, and the baby took it up. "We will perish miserably."

"My God, Eliza, do you believe so?"

"Yes, and it is not that bad with Mr. Bishop, Mary, really." Eliza was hiccupping and sniffing madly. "We make amends. It passes. At his job . . . well, he is having a few problems with Mr. Jones, and shortly . . . actually, he is looking for another position. Mr. Jones tore to pieces, making confetti, three of Mr. Bishop's documents last week. Three, Mary. Three days' work. Mr. Bishop is under a great deal of strain. I have learned to avoid certain subjects, to be careful."

Eliza had a habit of taking down a strand of hair, twisting it about her finger. She smiled at Mary, patted her hand. "I will be fine. Do not worry on my account."

That night Mary heard nothing, not a cry, not a bump, nothing.

"Good," she thought, returning by candlelight to a book. The heroine in a dress of striped silk and a hat with feathers was expecting a proposal daily. Mary vowed someday to have a dress like that. The heroine flung open the doors of the library, went out on the terrace, took a deep breath, and paced the grounds of the estate like a cat. What should she do, what should she do? The pages were dotted with candle wax. Mary would have to stop reading at night, for not only were the books costly but the candles added up. It seemed, though, that she could write a romance. But in hers the heroine, who would have to look like Fanny, that same pale complexion and ebony hair, would find meaningful work. What would she do, what could she do? Proposals were fine, but few and far between in the world, Mary thought. But in the world, work for respectable ladies was actually more rare than proposals. So her heroine would be strong-minded and wooed through the intellect. Her husband would be fine and intelligent, with a pale complexion and ebony hair. The heroine's wardrobe would consist of twenty dresses, seven hats, a parasol, six pairs of shoes.

"The dinner was burnt," Eliza explained a few days later.

"Hardly a reason," Mary said. "Hardly a reason at all for those bruises and that cut. Here." She handed Eliza a cup of tea, took the baby.

"But it was my fault."

"Do not be dense, Eliza. You have to leave the man. Anything is better."

Mary looked down at the baby, then around the room. She thought, this awful room, how happily I would leave it—the wretched bed, the toppling table, the rickety chair, the falling shelf, chipped plaster, cold floor—this is like all such rooms everywhere and always. We, the inhabitants, form a brotherhood of poverty and despair. I am poor. I do not live on an estate.

"Mary?"

And we, we here, we are always housed like this. Two miserable women with our dirty, straggly hair and few dresses and teary faces, with an underfed, crying child. The stricken and the lonely, the desperate . . . this is our estate, our community, our life.

"Mary, I cannot leave my husband, Mary. It is against the law of God and man." Eliza hugged her child to her.

"If the laws of God and man say you must look like that, be treated like that, the laws be damned."

Mary was wearing the black dress from the funeral. Her blue dress was folded nicely in her trunk. She had a green dress as well. Her pleated muslin in tatters was becoming part, with other rags, of a quilt she was sewing. On the shelf was the Bible, which she never read but had inherited from her grandfather. She picked it up, opened it, read:

> If thou faint in the day of adversity,
>   thy strength is small.
> If thou forbear to deliver them
>   that are drawn unto death, and those
> that are ready to be slain . . .

"We will both go somewhere. We will go together. Somewhere else." Mary got up, paced the grounds of her estate.

"And the baby?"

"The baby, too. We will all hide where Mr. Bishop cannot find us, somewhere safe, with a friend or protector. We have to . . ." And then it came to her. It was possible.

"But, Mary, where? A cave, some other country, America? Where?"

"Fanny's, we'll go to Fanny's. Fanny is in Hoxton."

"Fanny? Hoxton?"

"Fanny Blood. They have moved to Hoxton. They are civilized people. Her family will take us in."

"But they have no money. The father drinks."

"He is not vicious, and what little they have they will share. Besides, what are the choices? Who else would take us in? Not Ned, our own brother. Tell me, tell me any better than Fanny."

Mary was pacing fast, back and forth, almost skipping. That was it, the plan.

Eliza looked out of the window. "They are selling cabbages in the market," she said.

"It will be our grand escape, Eliza."

"But from what to what? It may be worse."

"The very worst is if the house falls down and snakes go over us," Mary teased.

"The worst? Worst is if we have no food for a hundred days and it rains."

"We have seen the worst, Eliza. It is the Day of the Dogs."

"I hope that *is* the worst, Mary."

The day of the grand escape was overcast and cold. A dense fog surrounded the city, and bells on coaches and boats on the Thames were the only things that penetrated the gloom. Mary had hired a coach. The coach was late. Mr. Bishop had been at work a good hour. He would not be due home until dinner at twelve. The baby was with the maid at the maid's house for an hour. They were to take the baby from the maid's house, continue on. The coach was a good hour late.

Furthermore, when Mary went upstairs to see if Eliza was ready, she found the whole apartment in great confusion. Drawers were gaping open and clothes, dishes, pots and pans were mixed up together on the floor and on the bed and on the table. Eliza in the middle of all was crying and pawing through a pile of clothes.

"I cannot find my locket," she cried.

"You do not need a locket, Eliza."

"It is Mamma's."

Eliza, the favorite of the girls, had gotten the little bit of jewelry along with her small inheritance.

"The coach is going to be here."

"We have to get the baby. Do not forget that, Mary."

"Where is your night shift?"

"I do not know," Eliza wailed.

"Elizabeth Wollstonecraft, do be rational."

"Elizabeth Bishop, please."

"Oh, God, child, just hurry." Mary picked up a dress, stuffed it in Eliza's trunk. There were already two dresses in it. Beneath them was the night shift.

"I hear something, Mary."

Mary ran to the window. "It is the coach. Hurry, Eliza."

"I have to get my baby's things together, Mary. Oh no, I will never be ready." Eliza began to weep. "My jewelry, everything is lost. I will never, never . . ."

"The coach is here."

"We cannot go yet. We cannot. All my worldly possessions, Mary, are in this room. Mary, I think I will have to, Mary, I will have to remain behind. You go. Go, go ahead. I cannot leave my things."

"Are you mad, Eliza?"

"The baby. My locket. The baby's things." Eliza began frantically running about.

Mary opened the window.

"We will be right down," she shouted to the coachman.

"I am going to get my belongings, put them in the coach. You be ready when I come back up. Eliza, you be ready. Do you hear me?"

Mary ran downstairs the two flights to the street. The cold hit her like a fist in the chest.

"I have a trunk," she gasped. "Will you help me."

The coachman grumbled and grumped but slowly took off his long overcoat and tall hat, putting them up on the buckboard, and followed her back upstairs. Each of them took a ring at the end, maneuvered the chest down the narrow stairway to the street and up on top of the coach. It was not heavy, just a few pans, a cup and saucer, plate, her shift, one daily dress, a petticoat and corset, taken from her mother's belongings, the sewn-together rags for the quilt, the Bible, a small picture of the actress Sarah Siddons, a Wedgwood vase taken from her father's house. Her penny novels she threw away.

"I will be right back," she told the coachman.

"And I will be needing to get home to my dinner," replied the coachman.

Eliza was still sitting in the middle of the floor, crying like a baby.

"Eliza," Mary said, "I am going. It is now or never. I will not help you again, do you understand? You must go if you are to go at all."

As she was speaking, Mary was buttoning Eliza's bag. "Where is your cloak?"

Eliza pointed. "Over there."

"That is a good girl."

Eliza stood up. Mary was fitting her cloak on her sister. She had none of her own.

"We are going to walk downstairs."

"My locket."

"We will have to go without it."

"My baby."

"We will stop for the baby."

Mary dragged Eliza by the hand. They were at the top of the stairs. Mary had the bag in her other hand.

"My baby, little Mary . . ."

"Yes, I know."

They were down one floor.

"Our mother gave me the locket. It was her mother's."

"Yes, yes. We will get a new locket."

"How can we get a new locket. We are poor."

"We will get a new locket, Eliza. Now, just come on."

They were on the second landing.

"It was in the shape of a heart, Mary."

"I remember."

"Little Mary . . ."

"Yes, yes, the baby."

"I have a terrible feeling, Mary, that I will never see . . ."

"Do not be so melodramatic, Eliza."

They were on the ground floor now. The landing was full of human excrement. People would duck in there from the street.

"Come quickly," Mary said, opening the door. The rush of cold shocked her again. The horses were pawing and steaming.

"We are ready," Mary announced. "If you would be so good as to help me with my sister's trunk."

The coachman sighed, "I do not want to be late for my dinner." But he took off his coat again. He helped Mary bring the trunk down the stairs, fitted Eliza's trunk next to Mary's. The women got in. Mary closed the door.

"Hoxton," she said, leaning her head out the window to give the street.

"The baby," Eliza said in a tiny mouse voice.

"Of course," Mary said.

"The locket."

Mary sighed. Eliza was twisting her wedding ring.

"We need to make a stop," Mary shouted to the coach, for they had taken off.

The coachman did not hear.

"We need to fetch her child, who is at the maid's."

The horses' hooves clipclopped over her voice.

"Mary."

"Please, sir." Mary stuck her body out of the coach. They were going so fast.

Then Mary saw Mr. Bishop walking toward their rooms. What was he doing on the street?

"We cannot stop, Eliza. Not now, not here."

"We have to."

"Sit low. Mr. Bishop is outside."

"Oh no!"

"Shh."

They scooted down in the seat. "A is an acorn," Mary whispered. She knew that by law Mr. Bishop owned Eliza, owned the baby. Eliza was as good as a runaway slave.

"The baby . . ." Eliza said in a tiny scared voice.

"We will bring the baby when we get settled." Would they then be put in Newgate as criminals? What was the law?

"But who will feed her?"

"The maid, Mr. Bishop's sisters, his mother, plenty of people. The child eats solid food. She will be fine."

"Do you think so?"

"I am sure."

They sat back up. Eliza commenced with twisting her ring. "I cannot get it off, Mary."

"Hot water and soap."

When Mary looked out the window, all she could see was gray, a misty gray as if they were traveling very slowly through an enchanted forest, shrouded in a magic spell. All the houses were trees and the people were fairy animals in human clothes. Deer and squirrels, big woodchucks, bears. She thought of the coach as a chariot, swimming through the dense atmosphere, leaving the ground and ascending to the heavens. She was terribly calm, calm as ice, but inside, lumped in her heart, was a rock of pure terror.

"It was Mother's locket, Mary."

"You will get over it."

"The baby. The baby, Mary."

Mary was silent.

"Do you not care? You are becoming a beast."

"I am becoming what I have to become, Eliza."

Mary felt very angry. Things were left up to her, and when they did not succeed, she was to blame. She did not know what they were going to do. Once at Fanny's, then what? Soon they would have no money. Perhaps Ned would help. But she knew better. Ned would not help. Somebody would help. Something would happen. It was her escape as well as Eliza's. But she was the one who had to make it possible. Sitting in that wretched room day after day had addled her brain and made her into a fixture. Had she stayed, years ahead somebody would have come in the room to dust her off like a statue, like furniture. Now she was free. She was on her own. No father to contend with, no Mrs. Dawson, no Spitalfields.

"What are you doing, Eliza."

"Biting my wedding ring off."

Eliza was gnawing on her wedding ring like a little rat. She was in a frenzy. Her mouth was foaming.

"Eliza, stop it."

Mary grabbed her hand away. "Do not do that. You will hurt yourself."

"Look," Eliza said, holding up her bare finger.

"You bit off your ring?"

"Yes," Eliza said. "All gone."

CHAPTER 4

MARY SLEPT with Fanny, and Eliza with Everina, who was "no longer needed" as a governess to five "incorrigible rapscallions," and had decided to throw in her lot with them. Fanny wore Mary's night shift, and Mary Fanny's, and Eliza and Everina, who could not trade clothes, shared a novel and a candle. All four of them were packed in one room the size of a shoe box. It was like Mrs. Dawson's all over again. Furthermore, their nightdresses were too thin and flimsy for the temperature. The fire, as usual, went out. And there was not enough wood, and what there was was damp, there was not enough money, not enough food. How familiarly tiresome it all was. Eliza was miserable. Fanny coughed continuously. Everina was ill-tempered, impatient. Mary wanted another cup of soup, she wanted to die.

Several years earlier, before Mrs. Dawson and Bath, Fanny and Mary had done needlework for fine ladies, sitting in another cold house all day long and through the long nights sewing their hearts out and fingers off. The smell of that hearth with the fire gone out and the damp air which seeped under the door made Fanny cough, as did the air in the Hoxton house. Maybe that was the beginning of her cough. She and Mary embroidered fine handiwork for the garments of the leisured, making a specialty of gathered bodices and puffed sleeves and pleated edges, rucked details and ribbon-trimmed petticoats. They were very careful not to get the drops of blood on the cloth from pricked fingers, for who likes bloodstains on her morning gown? Like little foxes nipping, those pricks on the raw fingers, and the feeble dawns signaled more of the same.

When Mary and Fanny had been little girls together at dame school, really just a large table in the churchyard where Mistress Grundy showed them their letters, Mary told Fanny her dreams of being a famous actress. She would go on stage in London, wear pretty dresses and ride in carriages and sedan chairs and eat out of silver dishes. She would drink coffee. When Mary's family moved to Yorkshire, Mary wrote long, passionate letters to Fanny. They were full of errors and smudges, grandiose plots and rose petals. Fanny penned careful little notes on crisp white paper edged in blue. Mary had been the optimist, Fanny more reticent. Mary was undaunted and unembarrassed, Fanny demure and modest. Friends forever.

"We can take in sewing again, as we did," Fanny suggested. Her hands were folded. She looked very sweet, even in distress.

"We are too intelligent for sewing, Fanny."

"*You* may be, Mary," Everina put in with a huff.

Everina was the practical sister.

"All of us are too intelligent to make a living with our hands, Everina. I want to live by my wits." Without enough sleep, Mary did not quite know what she was saying. Her ideas were scattered and frayed.

When she and Eliza arrived at Fanny Blood's house they were out of breath, as if they had run, not ridden in a carriage the whole way. Eliza had been hysterical. She was still not calm. The moment Everina stepped in the door she was eager to blame Mary for the absence of Eliza's baby. Then they had not known where everybody was going to sleep. Mary ended up in a small, narrow bed with Fanny. In the dark of that tiny room, Mary could not help but be conscious of Fanny beside her, her breath coming unevenly through her open mouth, her small teeth gleaming like porcelain, and the narrow chest moving in trembles and flutters. Fanny had broad, heavy hips, strange in one so thin.

"Not earn her living with her hands? And does she think she is a Rousseau or a Voltaire or a David Hume or a John Locke?" Everina smirked. "Can we be professional philosophers? I think, therefore I eat?"

"Woman does not live by bread alone, Everina," Fanny said.

"What does woman live by?"

"Love," Eliza answered.

"For God's sake, Eliza, I hate to think that," Everina spat.

"Just because you were never married, Everina."

"Because I am too clever, Eliza darling."

"You are not a genius, my dear. You are a woman."

"God gave woman reason, too," Fanny interceded.

"Oh, is that so? Reason and no jobs equals the same thing—hunger. But you, Fanny, have a family."

Fanny started to cough. Mary frowned at Everina. If anything, Fanny's family was more impoverished than the Wollstonecrafts.

They were all perched uncomfortably in the parlor, which had just one chaise and one chair. Mary sat on the arm of the chair and Eliza knelt on the floor as if ready for prayer service. Fanny lay on the chaise, with Everina perched at her feet.

"We may all be geniuses," Mary said.

"For all we know," Everina scoffed.

"Yes, and who made man exclusive judge of genius, if woman partake with him in the gift of reason?" Mary added.

"Hear, hear." Everina pulled at her skirts, which rode up at the waist. The house barely accommodated the extra guests. Mrs. Blood had gone to the country to visit her mother, Mrs. Applewhite. Mr. Blood was upstairs, sleeping most probably.

"Everina, you do not know what it is to lose a child."

"Eliza, we are going to get your child." Mary chopped the air with her hand. "I just cannot think of everything at once." The child haunted Mary. She knew it was lost, surely lost. It hovered in its little gown over her pillow nightly. That was another reason she could not sleep.

"I fear not, Mary. I fear I am never going to see my baby again, that is what I think each night as I . . ."

"Hush, do not go on so, Eliza, stop making such a fuss."

"Very well for you to say, Everina, you who will never . . ."

"Eliza."

Fanny left the room coughing.

"Sorry, Mary." Eliza hung her head, bit her lip.

"Who cares anyway," Everina said sadly, "if we all are geniuses."

"*I* care," Mary said.

"You do not matter," Everina insisted.

"I do so, as much as anybody else. Why do honors have to be

conferred by somebody at court or in the Royal Society. I say we are a roomful of geniuses. My saying it is enough. We are a roomful of geniuses."

"Mary." Eliza shook her head. "You have always been so head-strong."

As Eliza was pretty, so Everina was plain. Mary considered herself in between, middling in all things. Sometimes she wished she had Eliza's face and Everina's brain. Fanny, of all of them, was truly the most lovely, with rich black hair and eyes like bluebells, a soft white complexion, a slender waist and boy's chest. She needed care, a warm climate, good food, medicines. Mary wished she could provide all that.

"Anyway, why do I have to be a genius to be able to live the way I want, reading and writing, talking about what I know. People do not ask genius of every man who earns his living by his wits."

"You can be a governess, Mary." Eliza had never worked at anything. Everina called her helpless and hopeless, and as a child chanted: Eliza tells lies-a.

"Governess is to be an upper servant, Eliza."

"One who eats, Mary," Everina said. For all her talk of not eating, Everina looked as if she ate a great deal. She was heavy-haunched and full-faced. Her complexion resembled lard, creamy and thick, pocketed with air. Everina licked her fingers all the time, picked her teeth, and ran her tongue over her lips, as if feeding off her own flesh.

"We have to sew," Fanny said, entering the room again, with a handkerchief in her hand. "That is a real skill, is it not. Everything else is rather hazy and hard to discern. People do not buy intelligence or talent. They are not objects which have value in the world."

In the middle of a conversation, Fanny would turn her head aside, fall asleep. It seemed rude if you did not know she was ill.

"We cannot go back to that, Fanny. We cannot do that," Mary insisted. "We are too intelligent to be sewing for a living and to be at the whim and will of forces we have no part in making. We can read and write. We can think. That has to be worth something."

Mary had read the American Declaration of Independence and had been struck by the opening lines: "We hold these truths to be self-evident . . ." Secretly she aspired to such presumption.

"Speak for yourself," Everina said, looking at Eliza.

It was the early morning. *Nobody* had slept. Mr. Blood had come home very late, banged into things, stumbled around. Fanny had to take him upstairs by the arm, settle him down. Yes, Poppy, Fanny had soothed, Yes, Poppy.

Pacing back and forth in her black dress in that parlor, Mary said to herself: Do not look down and you will not be dizzy. It was like Spitalfields all over again, being in a locked box. Yet she was convinced that there was a key to this box as there had been to the other, that it could be opened, solved. Perhaps one only had to say the right thing and the box would open of itself, perhaps the key was as simple as a word. It could be as simple as a guessing game, a child's riddle.

What is the first thing Mother does in the morning? How many buttons on a parson's jacket? What did the Methodist say to the Dissenter?

Their limbs were stiff and aching. The parlor was small, parsimonious, with a chipped tea set, carpet of too bright a yellow, too dull a brown border, thin curtains, the uncomfortable chaise and chair.

"We are not to leave this room until we decide," Mary insisted.

"Locked in forever," Everina intoned melodramatically.

"What else can we do, Mary," Fanny asked. "Except sew."

"Fanny, you know French and fine needlework. Everina can do sums, and essay writing, geography and history. Eliza is good at penmanship and basic sewing, and I, I . . ."

"A school," Everina concluded. "Really, it is quite logical. A school for young women."

"Yes," Eliza said, clapping her hands. "Yes, a school for young women."

"School. A School for Scoundrels. A School for Scandals. A School of Fish," Mary declared.

"If a girl is rowing upstream and the current is flowing at ten miles an hour, and twenty branches impede the way and a school of fish recently unleashed is traveling at six miles an hour downstream, a thread extending around a perimeter," Everina asked, "what have we there?"

"This is the way the garden grows." Eliza danced.

"Bushes border the schoolhouse," Fanny exclaimed. "Do not destroy bushes, little children, for they provide shade and you need them in your games."

"Rows of desks," Mary described, making her hands flat, steady. "Women in caps, carrying pointers, yes, S is for slates, schoolmarms, sums and signification, girls, girls, at attention, girls."

"A school," Fanny declared, pressing her hands together. "A school."

The house they found in Newington Green for their school was a little way out of London. It had four large sunny rooms on the first floor, a little parlor, and upstairs were many small bedrooms. Quite suitable for a small day school with a few live-in students. Mary and Fanny shared a room. Everina and Eliza shared. They borrowed from their brother Ned enough for the first month's rent, slates, ink and quill, sand pots, bedding, food and fuel.

When Mary was growing up she was not taught embroidery and paper-cutting, wax-work, japanning, painting, moss-work, feather-work, and the art of polite conversation. She did not have a dance master, music teacher, or teacher of French. She was not groomed for marriage with a gentleman and a life of cards and visiting, trimming petticoats. She was glad of it now.

In their school they offered the traditional areas of feminine deportment, namely music, dancing, drawing, and needlework, but also the girls were taught writing, grammar, arithmetic, geography, French, an investigation of several orders of animals, and gardening. Mary also had the girls keep diaries, chart their progress toward virtue.

The first Sunday, Mary made the acquaintance of the famous Dissenting minister Dr. Richard Price, who was a friend of Jefferson, Franklin, Condorcet, Samuel Johnson, and Priestley.

"You sound like a Methodist," she teased, shaking his hand in turn on the church steps after the sermon. "Your sermon was so, so full of feeling."

Methodist, of course, was something not to be. It was the religion, emotional in nature, of the common people. John Wesley had set tents up when denied churches, and preached his sermon to shopkeepers, servant girls, and slop carriers alike.

"No, my dear. We Dissenters believe in the beneficent force of reason, not in emotional excess. As for Original Sin and the eternal punishments of Hell, we consider them myths. We are optimists. By the exercise of reason and practical intelligence we believe that this can be made a better world."

Mary raised her eyebrows. "That's wonderful."

He laughed. "Are you settled over there in the school?"

"Yes, Dr. Price. We have twelve girls, a lodger. It is going well."

"Would you like to come for tea sometime?"

"It sounds wonderful."

"And leave your talk of sin at home," he said, laughing.

She was not exactly sure what he meant, but if he meant not to worry about Eliza's baby, and whether or not Fanny was going to get better, or if the school would manage to last through the year, well, then, she would try, she would try not to worry for the little time it took to drink tea, exchange some pleasantries.

"People often told me growing up that I was bad," Mary said. "But"—and she had to search for the word—"I want to be good."

"You are. We are."

"I want to be good and something more than good."

She knew this was not the discussion to be having on the church steps, the congregation filing and eddying around them, ladies' skirts swishing and men's canes tapping impatiently.

"What do you want more than good."

"I want to . . ." She looked up at the sky. "I want my life to mean something. I do not think good goes with it. It is rather selfish, is it not?"

"All our lives mean something."

"No, they do not, Dr. Price. Except in the sense of: this wretched woman worked hard all her life and died."

"I beg to disagree, but each person has her or his gift, a moment of grace, if you will. Everyone, even the most wretched. It could be simply in the way one dies, how one wages the struggle, the smile. And this wretched man will talk about it with you at length at tea. Saturday tea."

Mary leaned up against the railing bounding the little stone platform and stairs adjacent to the church. She was weary from not sleeping. Fanny's face on the pillow was so composed, so perfect a human face. The ears tight against her head were pink and whorled like flat flowers in a book. The mouth was a little open, so the top teeth showed. Baby rabbit, Mary thought, my baby rabbit is dying.

"The wind," Mary said, looking up at the swaying branches of the trees.

"Oh, that," Dr. Price said, looking down at the ground. "I think it may rain later today," he said.

CHAPTER 5

THE SCHOOL was on one side of the Green and the Reverend Dr. Price's chapel was at a diagonal from the school and was flanked by rosebushes. The tea set in the rectory was painted with pale pink roses and the cups had a rose at the bottom, so that drinking your tea was like catching baby crabs in a crab pan, except they were roses. Mrs. Price was a plain, sweet woman with a pointy witch's chin and thin, sloping nose. She smelled strongly of rosewater and dressed like a little girl in flounces and ruffles, ribbons and frills, puffed sleeves and lace. She and Dr. Price had married for love, she said, and not regretted a moment.

"A marriage of true minds," her husband said.

The Reverend Dr. Price was dignified in demeanor, bandy-legged, and small; he wore a curly white wig and a parson's waistcoat, buckle shoes.

"You have the soul of a poet, my dear, and the brow of a teacher. Surely you should be able to combine the two and come out with an important work," he told Mary at one of their many Saturday-afternoon teas.

"Work? I, a work?" Mary was in her black dress, as usual.

"Book, as it is called in the trade."

"Why? How can you think of me as an author? I am hardly a teacher and less a scholar."

"Oh, but of course." Mrs. Price reclined on silk pillows with a rose motif of vines and tangled blossoms. "Only the scholars are permitted to write books."

"But I have no subject," Mary confessed.

"When I write my sermons," Dr. Price said, holding a finger heavenward, and his cup in his other hand, "I am not always writing about what I am then at the moment, or what I know at that moment to be true, or what I know to be true and false in general. Oh, no. Rarely. I write a hope and a wish, a wish to be, to become, to understand. Each sentence, every paragraph is a kind of exploration. I am finding myself in the writing. It is, and let me think, yes, if you will, a metaphysical hide-and-seek."

Mary sighed. It would be strange to find herself in the midst of words and sentences.

"Drink your tea, dear."

"So it is not answers, but mapmaking. And all of it is about virtue, how to live, how not to live, and each reader, my dear, takes the words to a different heart."

Dr. Price smiled. He looked like a happy fish.

"And so you say you want to make a mark, a mark with a stick, an implement, in the sands of time? How better?"

"When I was a child I wanted to be an actress like Sarah Siddons."

"Bosh," Dr. Price said. "Write the words the actresses say. Be a playwright, not a painted puppet."

"A woman?"

"What does that have to do with it? Look at Fanny Burney, at the woman playwright Aphra Behn, at Elizabeth Griffith. I could go on." Dr. Price waved his hand, indicating countless examples.

"But I have not the constitution, the education, the ability to concentrate. I fear for my sanity sometimes. There are days when I am on the edge of tears." She had never told anybody this before. "Sometimes I am so restless I do not know what to do. Sometimes I can talk all night, like King George, you know." She kept poor Fanny awake sometimes with her schemes and plans. She would use a whole week's supply of candles in a night, and then in the early hours of the morning, as the sky was lightening and the birds chirping, she must go for a walk in the wet grass. "I am too, too happy, and in the same day I can be sad beyond hope. Sometimes teaching the girls is all I can do. Sometimes I cannot do it very well. Sometimes I am magnificent at it. Sometimes I do not know what to do with myself, my hands, my eyes. I want to fling myself down on the grass, embrace it, thank it, each little stem of it. I want a beautiful blue dress, shimmery, the color of the ocean. I want to be the ocean and the clouds. No, not the clouds, that is too far away."

"Yes, why not. I feel exactly the same way, my dear, and I cannot write a word. I tell my good husband, Oh please, dear, have patience, for some days I am a rose."

"Do we not all suffer chaos and doubt and longing and hope, and especially the poets. Look at Gray and Cowper. And Milton, for God's sake," Dr. Price comforted.

"But why do you think I could write something? I must have more than a particular temperament. It is not enough for me to suffer chaos and doubt and longing. Writing comes from reason, not from the excess of emotion."

"You are clever, you have ideas. You are reasonable."

"Not all the time."

"Often enough."

"I *have* thought of writing a romance." Mary remembered her sour room in Spitalfields and how reading had delivered her out of pathos into meadows and fine houses, drawing rooms and pretty dresses, the chatter of teatime and the excitement of balls.

"Except it would be a romance against romance, against the need for romance. I do not mean love." Here she blushed. "I mean the flights of fancy romance engenders. Would that our daily life were such that it did not require those flights."

"Would that you might become rich," Mrs. Price said.

"Do you think like Hobbes we are of a bestial nature or with Rousseau that we are basically good?" Mary asked suddenly. "Of course, Dr. Price, I know. I know what you think, because you are a Christian."

"And you are not, my dear?"

"I am a woman."

"What does that mean?"

"I am not sure, except that most of what is written, what is, what exists in the world does not include me. Speculations about the nature of man mean the male, I am afraid. I think"—and she smiled—"along with Voltaire that this is not the best of all possible worlds."

"So, are we to tend our gardens?" Dr. Price was looking at her very intently.

"No, because we are responsible to each other. We are responsible."

"My brother's keeper?"

"Sister's."

"Come, dear, let us go to church." Mrs. Price stood up, took Mary's hand.

"Before we go, there is something else, something I must ask."

"Ask away," Dr. Price said.

"It is this: do you remember many weeks ago on the church steps I said I wished to be good?"

"Yes."

"It is this." Mary looked at the carpet. Roses like a profusion of clouds billowed beneath her. To walk would be to fly. To fly would be to fall. "Simply, I am not good."

"Come, come," Mrs. Price tsked.

"No, I am not, Mrs. Price. I must take responsibility for the evil I have done."

"Evil?" Dr. Price smiled. "I hardly think so."

Mary was biting her lower lip, Fanny's habit.

"It is truly bad," Mary continued. "I cannot say or think it away."

"Let God be the judge," Dr. Price cautioned. "Things happen for a reason."

"Bad things?"

"Sometimes. We learn from them."

Mrs. Price nodded in agreement.

"Tell me," Mary insisted, "is there a reason for a child's death. What does a dead child learn?"

"A dead child does not have to learn. Is there a dead child?"

"Eliza's. Eliza's child who was left behind with the father, that child died last week." Mary hung her head. "We learned of it yesterday. In a way I am responsible." She did not look up. "I carried my sister away from her husband and did not go back for the child. The child died of dysentery in the care of others."

"Your sister could have gone back for her own child."

"She was afraid."

"Why did you carry her away from the husband in the first place?"

"He beat her."

"Well, then. And the child may have died in any event. There was probably nothing you could do or not do."

"I am not able to accept that idea. Why act if all is to happen anyway? Is that not a kind of laziness, a moral sleep?"

Mrs. Price frowned.

"Yes, but is there no room for accident in your picture of the world? Surely you did not mean for the child to die."

"And we left in a great commotion and hurry. We were frightened."

"Well, then . . ." Dr. Price looked at Mary. "Do not be so harsh on yourself."

"I could have gone back. There is the just action, the right choice. What would Rousseau have done? Rousseau, or Hume, or Voltaire?"

"My dear, who knows."

"Are you saying that philosophy does not matter?"

"No, I am saying: let it rest. Allow yourself consolation."

"But I killed the child. How can I allow myself consolation?"

Dr. Price stood up.

"Nobody killed the child. The child took sick, is that right?"

"Yes."

"Would that we could control everything with our will."

"Dr. Price, I should have gone back."

"You had the school, Mary."

"Yes, I know, but I could have gone for the child. I let one thing and then another interfere, and then I forgot. I forgot for whole days. And after a while, I did not think of the baby at all."

"And Eliza?" Mrs. Price asked.

"I told Eliza that after the school went well, in a short time, when everything got settled, then I would go back for the baby."

"Well, then."

"Let us go into the church," Dr. Price suggested. "Let us pray quietly. Surely you must not plague yourself with these thoughts."

They went into the empty church, the three of them, passing through the side door connecting the parsonage with the vestibule leading into the right aisle. It was dusk and cool. They did not light the candles in the brackets on the wall, and easing herself down in the front pew, Mary had the distinct impression that she was sitting in the shade of a deep forest. It was so still and quiet that it was as if the hands of the clock were held fast and firmly, the world at rest. This moment is mine, Mary said to herself. I own it. She recalled her brother Ned parading back and forth along the nursery floor, saying: I am master here. But the church was not the mere nursery of an insignificant house in one corner of the world ruled over by a petty despot, but God's house and everywhere for all time. Under God, Dr. Price said, all are equal, prentice and master, man and woman. Therefore, she was master of herself, with only God above, and He rather far away at that.

The high-backed wooden pews had just been polished and the smell of wax combined with the fading bouquets on the altar. Dr. Price sat down far in the back. Mrs. Price walked back and forth between the rows, her rosy-pink skirts swishing; she suggested they sing a hymn, and leading in her high, pretty voice, she began:

> Come, holy Spirit, heavenly Dove,
> > With all thy quickening powers,
> Kindle a flame of sacred love
> > In these cold hearts of ours.
>
> Dear Lord! and shall we ever live
> > At this poor dying rate?
> Our love so faint, so cold to Thee,
> > And Thine to us so great?
>
> Come, holy Spirit, heavenly Dove,
> > With all thy quickening powers.
> Come, shed abroad a Saviour's love
> > And that shall kindle ours.

After a while, Mary crossed back to school, where Fanny and her sisters were waiting. A fine mist hung over the Green, dotting the slender twigs of the bushes with drops like beauty marks. In the spring, the students brought in bushes of delicate blooms, but they made Fanny sneeze and her eyes water, so they carried them out in the schoolyard and they made fences in the mud, wove them into pallets for their dolls.

Book, Mary thought, a book. My book. How a book. Why a book. Where a book. Who a book.

The lamps were lit in the upstairs bedrooms; a girl's shadow crossed the window. They were washing and saying their prayers.

Mary lay down on the damp grass, looked up at the little hook of the moon.

"I must become very intelligent," she said to the night sky.

From inside the school she could hear a girl cough. She felt poised, as she looked up at Jupiter, on the edge of a new century.

"Everything will be different, we will all be new. Our lives will be full of light and love. I live too much in the realm of passion," she breathed. "That is my problem. Fancies and phantoms."

Oh, well. She got up, brushed off her slightly damp skirts, made her way to the school. She fitted the key into the lock, opened the door. She could see down the hallway to the fireplace in the parlor. The chairs were drawn near it for warmth. Her two sisters, Everina and Eliza, were sewing. Fanny had fallen asleep, her delicate head thrown back and her wild, black hair fanning the wings of the chair. None of them was wearing her lace cap or apron, for they were relaxed, comfortable with each other.

Eliza would talk to her soon, she hoped. She would have to say something, a word. She would have to say how terrible she felt. Mary, I cannot say how terrible I feel. She would have to blame her and blame herself and blame life and God, certainly the Bishops. She would have to wonder, as Mary herself did, how she could have considered a child safe with a man who hurt women. She would have to ask herself all sorts of questions, and come up, as Mary had, with unsatisfactory answers, but still she must go on living.

We must go on living, Mary concluded. It is our duty.

CHAPTER 6

"EVERY ACTION is fraught with peril," Dr. Price said, fingering the thin leaves of his Bible. "But we must not give up. We must keep acting. Not to act, not to try is not human, not godly."

The congregation bowed their heads. Mrs. Price signaled hello to Mary from under her hat. The day was to go well. Eliza was talking to her. Mary and her sisters were to have lamb for dinner, with mint and apple sauce. Then Mary would lie down for an hour, get up, and go into the school office, work on the notes she was assembling for the proposed novel. The accounts had to be done, too.

"Every action is fraught with peril," she hummed to herself in the school office that evening. Fanny came in, sat down across from Mary. Mary did not look up from the accounts. The school had been going a year and it was supply time. Pens and slates, chalk, morning gruel, tea, wheat flour, sand for scouring pots, salt pork, blue wool for uniforms. Insects batted themselves against the glass chimney surrounding the oil lamp. They sounded like rain against the window, the first few drops. The lamp gave off a rancid smell which upset Mary's stomach, so she had to keep the window open. Outside, the crickets had started up in a high, shrill chorus. Mary felt her thoughts in competition with insects.

"I wish the crickets would take a night off," she said, still not looking up. Fanny sometimes sat across from her, quietly sewing or merely resting, serving as silent company for hours.

"I am going to get married and move to Portugal," Fanny said very quickly and quietly, her hands folded in on each other.

"What?" Mary wiped her nib off with a rag. "Pardon me, what did you say?"

"I am going to marry Hugh Skeys."

"Hugh Skeys, oh God." Mary felt her heart stop.

"Yes. Hugh Skeys."

Mary put her head in her hands.

"He cannot make you well." Mary felt short of breath. Hugh Skeys was undistinguished in every way. He had been courting Fanny on and off for years.

"Maybe he can. Portugal is a warm place. The sun shines."

"It shines here."

"Sometimes."

Mary looked at Fanny. Her friend was wearing a mauve dress, silk, a lace collar, straight little bodice with scalloped edges at the waist and puffed sleeves narrowing at the elbow. Of course Fanny was beautiful, but Mary realized it now with sadness. She wondered for the first time how Fanny could afford to dress so well. Of course a man would find her pretty.

"You are going to give yourself up to some man, Fanny? You need good English doctors, care, fresh air."

"Some man you speak of is the man I love, and I cannot afford good English doctors, Mary."

"We will be able to, soon."

"Mary, Hugh promises to take care of me."

"Why Portugal, why so far away?"

"He is in the wine business."

"Ah, yes. Whither thou goest . . ." Mary smiled wryly.

"I love him, Mary."

"What?" Mary shook her head back and forth. Her plain brown hair, usually bundled at the base of her neck, had escaped its net. She looked a fright, she knew.

"I love him."

"You think you do. What do you know of love?" Mary asked. "You know nothing of love."

"I beg your pardon. More than you."

"That was cruel." Mary felt stung.

"I am sorry."

"Love is . . . love is sacrifice, Fanny."

"It is?"

Mary looked about, blinked her eyes. "You are right. I do not know what it is, actually. You are exactly right. I know nothing. But love is not Portugal. They have earthquakes there."

"They have fires in London. Anyway, I want a child. Every woman wants a child."

"She does?" Mary shook her head again, bit her lip. "You know I will never see you again if you go away."

"Why?"

"Because you will be married, that is why, and living in a foreign country, Fanny. They have diseases there."

"Do not say that, Mary."

"It is true."

"Mary."

"How can you do this to me?"

"I am not doing anything to you, Mary."

Mary stood up, sniffed. "You are killing me and you know it."

"I am not. You should be happy for me."

"We promised each other never to marry."

"That was schoolgirl talk."

"Well, look at us. We are still in school." Before the burning in her eyes could become tears, Mary rushed out of the room and out of the school to the lilac bushes. She hid her head in the leaves. Both she and Fanny had agreed as girls in Laugharne that they would be friends for life. If one of them had been a man, they vowed, they would have married when they grew up. But, of course, they were not a man and a woman; rather, two women. But a life as schoolteachers, tucked together in the same house, reading the same books, talking and walking together, taking little trips here and there, gifts at Christmas, birthdays observed—these habits constituted a marriage of sorts, and far better, Mary believed, than the real marriages she had observed between brutish men and unthinking women.

Fanny came outside, put her hand on Mary's shoulder. "I want a real home, Mary."

"The school is a *real* home. What is a real home, anyway? Are you marrying a man or a house? We have a drawing room and a kitchen and servants and furniture, and members of the family. Heaven forbid that we live with friends. Oh, rue that day."

"I want a husband like other women. I want my own child."

"Have you ever talked to any married women? They are not distinguished by their happiness, to begin with."

"I want a man, Mary, to know a man. You would not understand that, but most women feel the same way."

Mary blinked very fast, put her hand to her head, wondered if she might be ill on the spot. She could feel the heat emanating from Fanny's skin. Fanny was flushed. Her teeth were set, and her breasts rose high; even her nostrils had a tilt and determination. A man, Mary thought, she wants a man. God help her.

Mary remembered her parents in their bedroom after a bad fight, the giggling and carrying on. She thought of dogs and horses coupling. Once two dogs had gotten stuck and they had howled in pain until her father separated them. She thought of Annie pressing her head down in the kitchen with all the smells and the little lice floating in the pail. And the man in Bath who must have her touch him at knife point, wagging his member in front of her face like a musty snake. Why would anybody want that?

"I am not brave like you, Mary. I cannot live all alone in the world without the protection of a man."

Mary did not know what *that* meant, for most men she knew about did not protect. On the contrary, they attacked.

"The climate of Portugal, the care of a husband, and the lack of duties will be good for my health. I will get brown as a berry and strong. My coughing will cease. My tuberculosis will be cured. I will have a bunch of brown, bouncing babies tumbling behind me, calling: Mother, Mother. Is that not good? Tell me, Mary."

"That is what you want?"

Mary felt that it would not come true. She believed that Fanny would not survive without her, that it was her will alone, the fact that Fanny was in her sight, that in itself kept Fanny alive. Out of sight would be out entirely. Furthermore, Mary suspected that Fanny was not strong enough to carry a child. Her body had all it could do to stay upright.

"I love you, Fanny."

Mary had never said those words to anybody ever before.

"I love you, too."

"You do not have to say that." Mary kicked her boot into the bush.

"But I do, I do love you."

"Stop saying it, Fanny. Stop it." Mary put her hands over her ears, ran inside, upstairs to their room.

She was well in her bed, the sheet over her head, when she heard Fanny come in.

"I know you are awake," Fanny said softly. "And I do not want you to worry about me. I will be just fine. You will see. The first child, if a girl, is yours, Mary, your namesake."

Mary froze at that. "Call the child something lucky," Mary said, not coming out from under the covers.

The day of the wedding was sunny, brittle, and cool. The air seemed so pure, so refined, that human figures appeared to move across the landscape in vivid outline, cutting the sky. Fanny wore Mary's blue dress, taken in, a night of sewing. She wore a flat straw hat forward on her face, trimmed with ribbons and tiny flowers. Hugh Skeys was heavy-waisted and thick-jowled. Not a romantic visage at all, according to Mary, in his yellow silk stockings and leather pumps, and with a gold-knobbed cane. Eliza was red-eyed and quiet. Everina was excited and happy. The girls in the school cheered their teacher. Dr. Price officiated at the ceremony.

"Dearly beloved," he began, his voice full and joyful. "We are gathered here in the sight of the Lord."

It was only after the coach had become a tiny toy in the distance and the dust settled that Mary went upstairs to have a serious cry on their little bed, which smelled just like Fanny; that is, faintly of tart green apples.

CHAPTER 7

MARY EXPECTED to meet Fanny in the hall or at breakfast, at every turn. Sometimes she thought she saw her at market or down the street or at church. A neck, a nose, a laugh. And then it never was Fanny, but some dull, unattractive replica. Mary did not say much. The girls at the school were also subdued, and it seemed that it got dark early that year. Mary went about in the evening lighting lamps slowly. Eliza, morose and weepy, would stop in the middle of something, stare into the distance. Everina was ill-tempered, caustic. Saturday afternoons Mary still spent in the rectory. Her discussions with Dr. Price were always heated and thought-provoking.

"You *are* a Methodist," Mary complained. "If you advocate anything other than reason." Sometimes she could imagine him, despite his measured tone, preaching to the rabble in the street with enthusiasm and fervor, like John Wesley.

"Must it be either/or, my dear? Cannot it be and/and, the rationality of the *philosophes* and Hume's sense impressions?"

"But they contradict each other, Dr. Price, their approaches to reality are so different. You are not an empiricist. All of your ideas are based on the notion of absolutes and a priori. You are a religious man."

"We build, my dear, we build, and do not knock over the staircase once we are on a higher step. It is not a mutually exclusive world we live in, and the life of the mind is manifold."

"You are saying that the life of the mind does not matter."

"Not at all."

"That it is a kind of game we play at."

"Be kind," Mrs. Price admonished.

"Kind? This is not about kindness, Mrs. Price. If our mind does not truly matter, that is, if we cannot understand the world, I might as well be my mother, who died not knowing how to read, or my father, who lives to kick dogs."

"Come, come." Mrs. Price puttered, bringing with her rosehip tea and the scent and sight of roses. "And how is dear Fanny. Her child is to be born before long, is that correct?"

"She is doing well, I think. Her letters say so."

Mary did not want to talk about Fanny.

Walking back across the Green, Mary thought of what she and Dr. Price had been discussing. According to Hume, she recalled, what we know was to be perceived through the senses. But could it not be that the process of cognition continues from that point, she thought; that is, what is perceived becomes part of mind, which transforms all to rational thought.

Mary saw Locke and Hume seated there, in the late-afternoon clouds, amiably sharing a pipe. She drew her shawl closer to her body. She had gotten thin lately and was aware of her bones. They knocked against each other. Her hair felt like straw. I have become a bookish spinster, she realized, in looks and mind. She was not unhappy over the thought. I am what I am, she said to herself. I have become what I do.

She remembered herself as the woman in the room who read novels about maidens in distress rescued by marriage. Now, under Dr. Price's direction, she was reading difficult, thoughtful books. If her mind was a blank tablet, as Locke suggested, it was now being filled by the accumulated thought of her time.

"A letter," Everina said, when Mary was in the hallway taking off her gloves.

Mary recognized the thin blue envelope. But it was not Fanny's hand. She took it to her office and, standing in front of her desk, used the letter knife. It was from Hugh Skeys.

September 1, 1785
You must come, Mary. Dear Fanny calls for you each day, saying from her bed when she wakes up: Is Mary here yet? Mary, I fear she will not live through the birth, which is early October. I beg you, come in all haste.

"What is it, Mary?" Eliza stood in the doorway.

"Can anything else be wrong?" This was Everina.

"It is Fanny. She is, she is . . ."

"Dead?" Everina always went to the worst.

"No, thank God, no. She is sick. I must go to her."

"It is not the best time, with school starting up for the year," Everina cautioned. "And how can we afford it?"

"When is anything ever the best time? When do we ever have the money? Ned. I will get it from Ned."

"But how will *we* manage, Mary?" Eliza moaned.

"You will manage because you will have to manage."

The notes for her novel which she had scribbled down at night and before classes would have to be put away. All would have to be postponed. They would have to hire an extra teacher. A Frenchwoman in the neighborhood who could do sums and knew geography and, of course, French was happy to step in. Everina was placed in charge of accounts; Eliza, the students. Mary gathered together her few things.

"The main thing to remember," Mary told Eliza as she was packing, "is that this is a school, not an asylum. You must be rational and intelligent at all times. Never let a girl tell you what to do. Rule fairly, but firmly. Little Jane needs her glass of milk each night and Ann Marie has to be made to practice her piano one hour each day. Keep them all to their schedules."

"Do you think Fanny is going to live?" Everina asked.

"Of course, Everina," Mary said over her shoulder. "You know men. Her husband is merely overexcited. She is sick, but surely not that sick. She is having a baby."

Eliza flinched.

"I mean, her husband does not know what to do with a baby and therefore is . . ."

Eliza looked stricken.

"And Everina," Mary began, turning now to her other sister. "Do not let the butcher sell you expensive cuts. The cook does very well with stews and marinade. And do not let any girl sleep in her shift more than a week without washing. We do not want vermin propagating upstairs. Make sure they brush their hair every night. No tangles. Susan needs a steady supply of storybooks. The child is voracious. Do not let them pick on Katherine. She is too sensitive and may take it to heart. And if you have a problem, go immediately to Dr. Price. That is, if you cannot solve it yourself."

Mary shut her portmanteau, looked at her sisters. They both looked back at her as if she were deserting them.

"This trip is not a good idea," Everina warned. She had her fists clenched and there was real anger in her voice.

"Do not go," Eliza begged. She sounded frightened.

"I have to. The claims of friendship supersede . . ."

"What?"

"Everything. Do you not understand? A web of loyalties is what holds us up. Without that, without each other . . ."

"You will miss your coach," Everina said. "A web of loyalties, indeed. Do you know how weak webs are?"

"I will be back within the month, I am sure."

"We will see," Everina said.

Mary turned to go down the steps. They both looked bewildered. Eliza was crying, Everina biting her lip.

"It will be fine," Mary called back to them.

Dr. Price was taking her in his chaise into London. From there she would take a coach to the coast.

"Remember, ladies," Mary shouted. "Reason and intelligence."

"No passion?" Everina countered. "No stupidity?"

But Mary did not hear. Already in the chaise, she faced forward, her mind set on her trip. She intended to speed to Portugal, make Fanny better, and come back immediately.

"My dear," Dr. Price said, leaving her at the coach stop in London. "Be strong."

"I am," Mary said.

"Be careful of that, then."

The boat Mary boarded for Lisbon was overloaded. Mary could see that right off, a bad sign. It lay low in the water as even more cargo was brought on by spindly Negroes in bare feet and ragged red-and-white-striped clothes, as if they had once been part of a vanquished army. It was a new brig, the *Justine*, with stern windows, a short foretopsail and topgallant yards. The canvas was of flax. The masts, yards, and booms were all wood and the hull was wood. The ship had to be pumped regularly and the decks had to be washed down several times a day, for the planking would dry and shrink, and the caulking between the planks would become loose and the seams leak. Not only that, but all the ropes had to be tended. Blocks had to be oiled. Mary felt apprehensive getting on board, and the sailors, who held her life in their hands, leered at her, and whenever she appeared on deck, they would watch her body as if it were dinner to be trapped and snared. Indeed, Mary felt like part of the livestock on board.

There was no singing of sea chanteys, no accordion playing, none of the picturesque habits she associated with the sea. There was an acrid and surly atmosphere on deck, and the heat, once they embarked, was continuous. The ocean spread itself out flat and solid as a pancake and was stubbornly still. The captain, in full wool topcoat and trousers, crossed his arms and did not budge from his station on the bow.

The water was so smooth Mary felt she could walk on it and not go under. It would be more like skating on fire than like walking on water. Not only that, but the air was dense with heat and her throat was dry and her eyes smarted. Loosening the collar of her black wool dress, Mary longed for a breeze. If the ship remained rooted in the Channel, Mary imagined that they would run out of food. She could visualize bodies being thrown overboard, hitting that solid-looking surface with whacks and smacks. She fantasized a circle of figures radiating from the boat like the marks on a sundial. And then the boards of the boat would rot and splinter, crumble and become wreckage strewn with the bodies about the flat, hard surface. It was the heat, she told herself, that made her imagine such dire events.

But, in reality, the sailors and the passengers, facing off, glared at one another. There was a rumor that there was a witch on board, that she had caused the winds to stop.

"She is the witch," one very scruffy sailor announced, pointing to Mary.

The captain walked between them like a princeling, a sweating one, his scabbard glinting and hinting in the sun.

"Hush," he said.

Then dark clouds gathered from the north like gray horses at the plow. The children on board got very quiet. Mothers bundled them down to the hold. Quick, quick, little chickens, down you go. Quick, quick, quick.

"Aye," the sailors agreed, "aye, down they go."

The captain was brusque and officious. "Look sharp, look sharp. Prepare for a storm." He unsheathed his sword, kissed it as if he lived in the seventeenth century, pointed it at the clouds. "I will kill it, kill the bad clouds," he said like somebody's father.

The sailors grumbled and groaned. They walked with limps, had parched lips, lost eyes, dirty bandanas, tarnished gold earrings, mangy pet parrots.

"He will kill the clouds," they sneered. "All very well for him to say."

Mary imagined dragons of the deep lounging about on the ocean floor, curling and uncurling their serpentine bodies.

"Best you go down, madame, with the children."

But Mary stayed on deck to watch. When the storm started, it was with a great cracking sound as if the sky were going to split apart. The ocean rose up in two gigantic curls like pictures of the Red Sea parting to let the Israelites go. A great rumble followed and then the boat groaned, heaved, lurched and bounced, tossed and turned. Waves got higher, higher still. And then a torrent of rain suddenly crashed down on the deck. One of the masts snapped. The sailors ran side to side, bow to stern. No sooner were they in one place than they were thrown across to another. The captain, however, stood his ground, sword raised.

"Dear God, preserve us and help us," Mary prayed. She prayed for her sisters, Everina and Eliza, for Fanny in Portugal. She thought of her life, her parents, that she would die not leaving a child on this earth. There was nothing to show for herself or of herself. She would vanish. No books written, no great accomplishments. Nothing to indicate her mind or presence had been on earth.

"I have not finished yet," she told God, "because I have not started. Please spare me a bit more time. Please. I promise to use it well."

She held on to the wooden banister of the captain's stairs. White waves rolled down like avalanches of snow and covered the deck in fizzy, bubbly foam which sparkled like banks of diamonds. The only passenger abovedeck, Mary held on to the wooden rail for dear life. But then she began to lose her hold on the captain's bridge, slipping, sliding down; she was sliding off the deck.

The last thing she remembered was a hand holding one of her feet fast.

CHAPTER 8

EVERYTHING on deck had been knocked down, barrels and coils of rope, bolts of cloth, geese in wooden crates, china layered in paper and packed in special boxes marked CHINA, jars of jam, sacks of potatoes, rice, the bodies but not heads of dolls, and ladies' dressing-table mirrors, spring shuttles for looms, many farm implements—Jethro Tull's seed-drill, combined plows and seed drills, grinding mills. All were being batted, tumbled back and forth, as the boat rocked side to side. Below, children were crying and babies shrieking. Mothers were going out of their mind. Grown men messed their pants.

Mary found herself standing in water, the bottom of her skirts and stockings completely wet. But she had not slipped off the boat. Somebody had saved her. One of the distasteful sailors had grabbed her leg, pulled her back. And now the motion of the storm seemed, very subtly, not as severe. They put her in the hold.

Down there, underneath the sound of pouring rain and the smack of waves against the sides of the boat, and the continuous thunder, and the cargo banging against the walls, there was another sound. It came at first as a murmur, then a chorus. The words emanating from each separate voice, coming from all corners, sounded in bits and pieces. Our Father, Blessed, Amen, Heaven, Will, Bread, Forgive, Holy Ghost, Done, World, Trespass, Be, Next, Give.

The words crisscrossed each other and wove themselves into a tenuous web. This is who we are and what we are, Mary thought, these words. This is the web of loyalty. I can die now, she said to herself. I am ready. I have lived and that is enough, that is all. She felt so relieved, so free. She only wished Dr. Price were there to share this with her.

And then Mary noticed that the boat was not rocking violently anymore and that the howl of the wind had gone away. The group of passengers stopped praying, stood still. The rain pelted, pelt, pel, pe p the deck, stopped. The ship shuddered, shook like a dog drying his wet fur, shook, shoo, sho, sh, steadied itself. They heard the sailors calling to each other, the captain barking orders:

"Count off. Who is missing. Look smart."

They waited, and then, one by one, the passengers emerged from the hold, the first of them lifting the trapdoor slowly, peeking, and then throwing it back. The sun had come out. It was day, not night.

Mary was the last to climb out. She took a deep breath. It was a beautiful day at sea, the end of the day. The sun was setting, the water lapped gently, and the boat bobbed. The air was brisk, tart. And the captain stood in the same position, as if his stance alone had saved the day and the boat.

It is over, Mary thought, all over. And then she heard it. From the bow of the boat came wailings, wailings from below the ship, from the water. Oh, God—Mary clutched her chest—people overboard. Piteous cries.

"Save me, save me."

Mary and some of the passengers and the sailors rushed to the edge of the boat. There were men in the sea on boards and trunks and holding on to any bit of wood or piece of junk they could. Rubbish and all sorts of cargo were floating along, and not too far away, Mary could see the wreckage of a ship, another ship. It was sinking and she knew that when it finally disappeared, it would suck all down with it.

"We need to get them on board before the other boat goes down. It will make a big swell, pull them with it," Mary shouted. "Get some rope."

The sailors began to rush about.

"Where are you going?" the captain asked.

"Sir, it is a wreck."

"Who gives the orders here? I am the captain, not you, madam."

"Sir, they are drowning. They will all perish."

"We all perish, anyway."

"But not now, not today," Mary protested. "It is not necessary. Some rope, all it would take is some rope."

"Nobody is to throw a rope or give a hand without my orders, do you understand?"

The sailors stopped. The wailing heightened.

"Save them," one of the male passengers said, "for the love of God."

"Yes, save them," another cried.

The sailors of the ship hung their heads. Save them, they murmured.

"The boat is overloaded as it is," the captain said. "This is a new crew never before out. We might sink ourselves if we take on additional weight. We do not want to get pulled down. We have our cargo to consider. It would be madness."

The cargo meant again: the ducks and geese, a few sheep, cows, and the scarlet-combed roosters. Bolts of cloth which had been through a long, circuitous process—the cotton picked in America, made into thread in England, sent to India to be woven there, dyed indigo and red, and printed with the shapes of elephants and rajas and slithery snakes all along the border east and west, wound in bolts and wrapped in burlap and tied up in brown, hairy twine. There were crates of pewter pots got in Yorkshire, and Wedgwood china, the deep blue of pagodas, and turtle meat pickled in brine, packed in jars, and every time the boat moved, the liquid in the jars would lap like waves, reminding the turtle meat of the sea they once lived in. Jams, jellies, plows, and planters, axes and shovels, loom parts.

"The cargo is already all ruined," Mary said. "It will have to be tossed over."

"It can be dried," the captain countered.

"Not all of it."

"Much of it."

"A little."

"More than you think."

"But they are men, men who will die, sir. Would you have that on your conscience?"

"She has a point, sir," the first mate said.

They were on the deck, the horde of them, passengers, sailors, the two rather shabby officers. The sails of the boat were rent and shreds flapped like pennants from the splintered skeletons of the masts. Cracked crates, and barrel hoops, rope, all sorts of things were strewn about. A lone goose from somewhere sauntered forth, arching his long neck, honking and snapping.

Mary thought of *The School of Manners, or Rules for Children's Behavior*, chapters 1 through 12, which she had dutifully memorized as a child and used in her school. She believed she had brought everything she would need for any eventuality on this trip. She had her traveling writing set—her inkwell, pounce pot, an amethyst seal, quill pens bought from a walking stationer.

She had her sewing basket with needles and threads and pins. She had her few medical supplies, bowls and bleeding cups, opium and laudanum.

None of this applied. She was prepared, but not prepared for this. She believed she was ready for every eventuality, that she had the fortitude, the reason, and the intelligence . . .

She remembered the verse which had inspired her when Eliza was still living with the awful Mr. Bishop.

> *If thou faint in the day of adversity,*
> *thy strength is small.*
> *If thou forbear to deliver them*
> *that are drawn unto death . . .*

Holding on to a rope, and scrambling up, she hoisted herself up on the edge of the ship. She balanced there, tried not to look down.

"If you do not take them aboard immediately, I will jump," she said.

"I cannot believe this," the captain said. "Do you know how unbecoming you are, a lady, you a lady."

"She is a witch," one of the crew said.

"I will jump," Mary repeated.

"You have lost your wits," the captain said.

"She is insane," one of the sailors said.

"Grab her," the captain ordered.

"You grab for me, I jump."

"She will not jump," the captain said.

"I will. I swear to God I will. I am not afraid." She trembled while she said this. At any second she could lose her footing and fall. She did not want to jump. The idea terrified her. The ocean would swallow her alive. Looking down, she thought she saw green castle turrets, the green spires of a city, government buildings, the roofs of houses. She would be impaled, speared through. There *could* be serpents. And for very certain she would die, die painfully and awfully. She did not want to jump, she did not even want to be so high. It was amazing that she had managed to get herself up there in the first place. She was frightened of heights. Yet, all in all, she knew very well that she could not live seeing those faces. They would come to her at night and at all hours of the day, just like Eliza's baby did. She must rescue those who were being taken away to death, not because of God or Jesus Christ or the Reverend Dr. Price or even Rousseau, Voltaire, or Locke, or Hume or Clarissa or Gulliver or the American revolutionary thinkers like Thomas Jefferson. It was simply what she knew of herself.

"They are men," Mary said. "We must honor that."

"Oh, all right," the captain said. "Haul them in."

CHAPTER 9

MARY ARRIVED in Lisbon on a feast day. When she disembarked from the boat, she vomited on the rough wooden boards of the pier. She vomited what appeared to be years of food, and in her wretched state she imagined animals and vegetables in whole form coming from her mouth and spilling out. They walked away mooing or squealing or with a flip or a flop slipped back into the sea. A man came selling real vegetables from a cart, holding them up one by one. He looked like her grandfather. Aye, but you are a sick lassie, he said in English. A woman she did not know, a prostitute, came forward, wiped her brow.

"*Cuidado*," she whispered. "*Cuidado*. Careful." And she handed Mary a little piece of marchpane candy in the shape of a pear. This is what it is like to be in a foreign country, Mary said to herself. Strange.

It was early in the morning on a festival day. Garlands of flowers and strings of prettily colored paper chains were stretched across the tiny twisty streets. The men were sawing and hammering, putting up booths by the sides of the houses. While the women washed snails, the older men played backgammon, dominoes, cards, and checkers on small tables nearby. Threading themselves through the midst of preparations, little girls pasted together the paper chains and hats, strings of lanterns.

"*Desculpeme*." Pardon me.

Mary felt she was on the other side of the globe and not simply across the Bay of Biscay. A light wind blew from the north, but it was a warm and gentle wind, altogether different from a British wind. The sun, too, had not the limited, singular, and feeble warmth of a British sunny day, exceptional and a favor. The light in Portugal was diffuse and continuous, part of the air. Tall palm trees lined the port, and other tropical vegetation banked the walls of the city. The houses were washed white, with red tile roofs, and at the end of every block of houses were fountains and pools for washing clothes. The women pomaded their black hair and wore their red skirts tight around their bottoms, flaring out with ruffles below. The men were dramatic, handsome, built like sharp, delicate birds. The old women wore black shawls over their heads. Church bells rang Matins and Mass, and the hour, and twelve o'clock, and time for dinner, and every fifteen minutes. The men's breeches were tight, rust and brown, and their shoes, black, shiny, were like little slippers. Walls and buildings, fountains and walkways were set in mosaic tiles. There was the occasional mournful sound of a guitar—Moorish melodies. The squares featured fountains with blue-and-green-tiled tubs. Fringes of fern brushed against Mary as she made her way to Fanny's house.

A carriage had taken her until the cobbled road became too narrow, and she had to walk with her bags the rest of the way. The driver indicated up the hill. Mary stopped at one of the fountains set in blue-and-green tile, moistened the hem of her dress, wiped her face. She was tired and hot, still a little sick.

Fanny's house was up against a hill, with a wrought-iron spiked fence surrounding it, but the gate was open. Mary cautiously entered a stone courtyard full of trees and birds. She pushed open the large wooden door to the house.

"Hello, is that you, Mary, have you come yet?"

The voice came from up the winding stairway.

"Yes," Mary said, her heart loud in her chest. "I am here."

"Hurry, Mary, hurry, I have to see you."

Dropping her bags, Mary ran up the stairs.

"The back bedroom, Mary. I am here."

Fanny was stretched out on a large, high bed, her cheeks unnaturally red and her blue eyes glittering like broken glass. She looked like a painted doll, waxy and wooden.

"Oh, Mary," Fanny cried. She opened her arms. "Mary, I can die now."

"Hush that. Nobody is going to die. Nobody." But Fanny was like a bundle of sticks in her arms.

"The baby died, Mary. Little Mary died. I had the baby and she was born, oh, Mary, born dead."

Fanny started to cry piteously. Mary did not care at all or that much or at least not as much about the baby. It was Fanny. It was all Fanny. Fanny was alive. That was the important thing.

"You will not die, Fanny. *You* will not. I promise."

But the smell of death, sickly sweet—old blood tinged with treacle—just as it had been in her mother's room, had already permeated Fanny's surroundings. It had taken charge, spread itself across the sheets and furniture, was tangled in Fanny's hair and rubbed on her lips and rested between the pages of the books and between the lines in the books. It came from Fanny's mouth and eyes.

"We need to have this place cleaned," Mary announced. "That's the first thing. You need sweet leaves to chew."

The first thing Mary did was to command the servants to scrub out the room and wash all the sheets, stringing them up on a line from the second floor to a tree resinous and medicinal-smelling, with sharp, long leaves and a long, smooth red trunk. Every corner of the house was washed with a heavy brush. Mary sprinkled rosewater around the bed. And she washed Fanny's thin body, which she lifted and carried all about the room and downstairs and into the street to the bench in front of the house.

"Look, look. There is an organ-grinder and monkey."

The monkey was in the square, wearing a little red cap and coat with gold buttons. He was losing his hair and danced very slowly and held out his hat, slanting his weary little head to one side. "He is dying, my monkey is dying," the man said in English. "He tries to keep up, but he is dying."

"Please do not die, little monkey," Fanny said. "Please do not die."

"Let us get out of here," Mary said angrily. "Do not touch the dirty monkey, Fanny. Come away."

Mary decided sea air would be beneficial. She arranged an expedition with Hugh Skeys. They went by carriage to the shore. Fanny's long, gauze gown fluttered in the wind. Spots of blood on the bodice where she had coughed made a bib of red jewels. Fanny clung to

Mary's neck like a child. Her husband, Hugh Skeys, looked away, squinted into the sun. He held a parasol Mary had brought in an attempt to be gay. The sand sifted between Mary's toes in hot little piles. Fanny dragged on her. The sea looked innocent, but Mary knew better.

When Fanny got coughing fits, Dr. Santos would be summoned. He wore smart little black boots, a silk-lined cape. Pressing Fanny's chest, feeling her wrist, applying cups to her back, he would whisper: "Shh, shh."

When Fanny had to be bled, the blood dribbled into the porcelain bowl like offerings to some obscure god. Dr. Santos, holding the bowl and swirling the blood, would say: *"Olbrigado, olbrigado."*

Mary would bury the blood in the back. She washed Fanny's long black hair, no longer thick and strong but limp and fine, in lemons and soap brought from England scented with apples and cranberries.

She rubbed pomade on Fanny's lips and polished her teeth with a brush until they gleamed like sharp little pearls.

"You must treat your teeth with respect, Fanny, for they have a secret life. They hanker after elephants, they want to march in battle across vast deserts. After many days they come to the walls of the city . . . Who is it, the gatekeeper asks. It is we, the teeth sing in chorus . . . Are you tired, Fanny?"

"It is fine, Mary, go on."

Mary wiped Fanny's face and neck, helped her change her shift. Fanny's room, though balconied and high-ceilinged, was hot and close. Mary had to fan her continually. And when she did so, the leaves of the tall lemon tree in the corner rustled like the forest.

"Another expedition is called for," Mary announced desperately. Mary and Fanny and Hugh Skeys wound their way on donkeys into the dusty hills, so that the bay looked like a puddle behind them and the only real thing in the whole world was themselves. Fanny was tied onto her animal and her body rocked back and forth like a flimsy doll, and she spit blood, soiling the patient donkey's thick, gray neck. They had to turn back. And it was the last time they all went out; Fanny thereafter stayed in her house, then her room.

The house was in the Alfama Quarter, a part of Lisbon all but untouched by the earthquake of 1755. It stood on one of the small, winding streets with blue-mosaic-tiled walkways and pots of geraniums; cages of twittering canaries hung out of windows. Water from an unclosed standpipe dripped down muddy, vine-covered walls in back of the house all day long, but it was a welcome sound, and on the hill overlooking the blue bay were the ruins of a castle where peacocks pranced, fixing their beady black eyes on little children who brought them bread.

Portuguese was a soft, slushy language. The Portuguese seemed aristocratic and graceful in bearing, very gentle. But one day Mary saw a line of slaves shackled by the neck being boarded for Brazil. They had hardly any clothes, their skins were dusty and caked with dirt, and, except for one crying baby, they were completely silent.

Fanny's house was next to a hill of packed mud filled with swallow nest holes. At night the birds returned in a huge tweeting stream, circling round and round while all the church bells rang for vespers, and then they dove into their holes. Twilight streaked the sky with soft pinks and blues and night would begin almost apologetically. That was when Fanny coughed the most. Every day seemed as hot as baked bread. Fanny's husband liked to keep the shutters closed, just as Mary's mother's shutters had been. But each morning Mary frantically threw them open, and she had the servants wash out the sheets in a big tub at the corner of the street. They hung them out either on the line to the red-barked tree or on the veranda to dry. They got down on their knees with good brushes and plenty of hot, boiled water and scrubbed the floor. They washed the walls, all the tables and chests in the house. They shook out the little rag carpets and beat the two Persian ones until dust rose in the air in thick clouds. Mary aired the linen and straightened the closets. She bought pots of flowers, burned incense. If it were clean enough, if she were busy enough . . . That's what she thought.

"It does no good," Hugh Skeys said in the drawing room.

Mary had come upon him with his head in his hands. A big man, he was defeated and powerless.

"I do not know what else to do," Mary said.

"Yes, I know that feeling."

"I—"

"I," he broke in, "will not know what to do with myself."

"Do not say that. You will not have to do anything. She will get better. I am going to make her better. God will not let her . . . She will become well again."

Hugh looked at her sadly.

So he loves her, Mary thought, he really loves her. It had never occurred to her that he might.

Daily, the warmest time, about two, Mary bathed Fanny with a soft rag and warm water and English soap. Each night she would brush Fanny's long, black hair, not hard, but gently, fifty strokes each side, so that it would shine, grow.

"Oh," Fanny would exclaim, "that feels wonderful."

Mary mixed a liniment out of mint and camphor, lard and bread mold, heated it up, rubbed Fanny's chest and back with it morning, noon, and night. She made Fanny get up out of bed, sit on the veranda in the sun, drink warm milk and eat the fried pastry dipped in sugar the Portuguese made. It will give you bulk, Mary said. The first week Mary had the cook make a big pot of oxtail soup, putting in leeks and carrots, squeezing lemons over the top. She fed Fanny baked bread with drizzled honey, and a roasted leg of lamb was carved up, the drippings used for pudding.

"Why are you doing all this for me?" Fanny asked feebly.

"You are an angel," Mary said, taking Fanny's paper-thin fingers to her lips.

"Then I am dead."

"No, no."

Mary felt her mother's death was a shadow compared to this. She remembered herself stirring her mother's sick rags in a large kettle over the fire, the winter land barren and bleak as far as the eye could see, and her thinking, My mother is dying, but it is not the end of the world. This was the end of the world, Fanny dying.

One night in November 1785, Mary looked down on the court-yard before closing the shutters and she saw, in the moonlight, flattened against the flagstones, a little red jacket. It was the monkey, his arms outstretched as if he were running from something but had been caught nonetheless by the ankles.

"Call the doctor," Mary cried.

"Mary," Hugh Skeys said. "You are beside yourself."

"Oh, call the doctor. Please."

Day by day Fanny became smaller as death enfolded her a little tighter, drawing together the strings, tying the knots, wrapping the shroud.

During this time, Mary's nights were full of dreams.

She is walking by the road. A series of bushes border the road and they are all aflame. Each bush burns brightly. She walks up to one and asks: Who are you? I am who I am, it answers. She walks up to another and it, too, says: I am who I am. They all have that answer. They are who they are. But who are you, she has to keep asking.

In another dream Mary had shortly before Fanny died, she heard the cats who lived on the street calling her, calling her name: Mary, Mary, Mary. But it was Fanny, Fanny calling. Mary went to sit beside her, hold her hand.

"Tell them," Fanny whispered. "Tell them I love them."

"Who?"

"Tell them all, Mary. Mary?"

"Yes."

"Tell them."

Mary sat beside Fanny until she fell asleep and Mary could hear the rasping breath, in and out. Then she got up and pushed open the shutters, looked out the window. It was not much of a moon, but she could see the figure, which did look like Dr. Santos, tiptoeing around in cape and Elizabethan doublet, very daintily on his hind paws. Mary began to shake. When she reached out to quickly, quietly close the shutters, she saw that the street was dark, empty. It was a fantasy.

"Kiss me," Fanny said softly.

"What?" Mary turned around.

"Kiss me."

Mary went over to the bed, leaned down. Fanny reached up with her frail arms, drew Mary's face to her mouth.

When people speak of passion, Mary thought, this is what they mean. I have walked through fire and am seared to the bone.

When she left the room, Fanny was sleeping with a smile on her face, and her hair fanned out on the pillow like the high black combs the Portuguese women wore in their hair. Mary went back to her own bed, lay down. She did not think she could sleep, but she did.

CHAPTER 10

IN THE DREAM, she is in a white house, a huge all-white house. The walls are white, the floor white, the rug and all the furniture, everything white. There is a spiral staircase. She slowly climbs it, and as she gets higher, she can see that there is one thing which is not white. It is a huge crack in the ceiling. Somehow she is able to get up high enough that she can put her hands around the crack, hoist herself out. She does so, and when she looks down, she sees that the house she has been in is a gigantic egg.

"Mary, Mary, you are talking in your sleep."

"What?" Mary sat up. "Where am I?"

"In your own bed, Mary. It is I, Eliza."

"Fanny."

"Do you not remember? You are home now."

She remembered: Fanny was dead.

Her own bed, and it was still evening, with the familiar sounds and smells, stew and porridge, little-girl perfume, chalk dust, gossip. It was damp, cold, English. The moon shone over the Green, flicking silver the tips of sticks, all that was left of the bushes. It was such a nice moon, Mary observed. Modest, pale, a quietly witty moon. Earlier, right after supper, she had gone out for just a moment and lain down under the lilac bushes, just winter branches. It was so familiar, so reassuring. Her life could go on, she knew that, now that she was home.

The bright light of morning showed the school office in disarray. Mary had postponed going in until after breakfast. Papers, books, pictures made by students, a fan, pots of face powder, a wig, somebody's dress, and a stuffed robin were all in a tumble. In the account book, Mary noted money spent for coach rides. Extra food had been bought—pies from the pie man, candy, treats.

"Eliza."

"Did you call me," Eliza said. She looked very brisk in a blue-and-white-striped dress, braided hair.

"What is this?" Mary pointed to the entry in the account book. "Coach rides?"

"The children were irritable, Mary. I did not know what to do with them," Eliza explained. "I thought it was the reasonable, intelligent thing to do."

"So you all got in the coach, bought pies?"

"Yes, that is it, exactly."

"Reasonable and intelligent and expensive. Get Everina in here right now."

"You need not be so stern," Eliza pouted.

"Get her."

"Very well," Eliza huffed. "If I must."

Everina was sensible. Mary knew that. She ran her hand over her hair, thought of the girls crammed in a coach, each with her pie.

"Yes, did you want to see me, Mary dear?"

Everina seemed to be wearing something new, too. A lace shawl. Pretty shoes.

"Mrs. McCormick, our lodger," Mary asked. "Where is her rent money?"

"Mrs. McCormick left, Mary," Everina replied.

"Left? Left?"

"Yes, Mary, left."

"Pray tell, why?"

"The noise, Mary."

"The noise? What noise?"

"At night. The girls."

"So why did you not make them quiet? There are only three girls boarding."

"We could not smother them, Mary," Eliza said. "That would have been most unreasonable and unintelligent, not to mention cruel."

Mary looked at Everina, who certainly in visage alone could inspire fear in most ten-year-old hearts.

"They would not mind me, Mary. I had to whip one girl, but she wrote to her mother and her mother removed her from school."

"Everina, you whipped a girl?"

"They do it in all the best schools, Mary. You know that."

"You would not quiet them but you whipped one?" Mary had to hold on to the desk for support.

"It is not fatal, Mary, after all."

Mary wanted to go back to bed immediately. She had just returned after a sea voyage, a coach trip in which she had to fear footpads and highwaymen, and several miles of walking. Her dearest, sweetest friend had died, and now it seemed that her school was falling down around her. Eliza and Everina could not even keep a little school together. Mary wanted to go to bed forever.

"So the choice was whip or let the nonsense continue?"

"Yes, that is quite so." Everina seemed satisfied with the explanation.

"You whipped a child? You did not get enough whipping as a child that you have to whip others? Are you women not intelligent? Do you not know children? Promise them an extra fifteen minutes of play outside before lunch and they will be little angels at night. How could you whip a helpless child?"

"It was not hard. She stood very still."

Mary studied Everina carefully.

"Actually, I was very restrained."

"After our childhood, Everina?"

"Because of our childhood, Mary. Think of what we would be without whippings."

"We would have been happy children, happy adults, without whippings." Mary wished she still had her faith, the faith that she had slowly been losing over the past years and that she felt she had lost altogether when she lost Fanny.

"Not necessarily, Mary. Anyway, the child is quite fine. She is a spoiled and destructive little girl. We are better off without her."

"Yes, but two gone, Mrs. McCormick and this, now this, so we have a lodger and a boarding student gone. The loss of that income, sisters, is something we cannot afford."

Mary had the account book out. "Paints and brushes? Sugared ginger? Ginger beer. Ten new slates? Baskets and bonnets? Rose withdrawn? Anne treated for a cut? Money borrowed from Dr. Price? Money borrowed? You borrowed money?"

"Yes, we ran out, Mary," Eliza admitted.

"But I left more than enough."

"For ordinary circumstances." Eliza blushed a little. She could be infuriatingly demure when she was wrong. For a moment, Mary could sympathize with Mr. Bishop, who had beaten Eliza black-and-blue. She immediately checked *that* thought. But to think that the school was meant to solve Eliza's and Everina's employment problems and to help Fanny. It was to make them all independent. It was to give them all a chance at a life that would be endurable. Now Fanny was dead, and Eliza and Everina were admittedly incompetent. Mary wanted to lie down and die right then and there.

Only the night before, she had thought of preparing class notes in the upstairs bedroom. She planned to teach the girls drawing, so that they would really look at the world. With the geography lessons she was going to combine history, and talk maybe about how the former determined the latter. Traveling had given her several ideas. If she was to survive Fanny, she had to make good use of her life. Otherwise, how could she forgive herself. The night before, with the floors below full of little sounds—the dishes being carried from the dining room, the voices of her sisters, children calling out—had given her hope. She realized that she liked school life, she liked seeing to the girls one by one, their coming into her office for tea, a little talk. She would suggest books, go with them to the little library they kept, take down a book, open it. You will find this useful. Read chapter 3. Closing up at night, locking all the doors and drawing shut the latches, making it all secure, made her secure. The school. Her school. Her only home.

"A few other girls have left, too, Mary."

Mary looked at Everina. And she had counted on her for good sense. Eliza was sentiment. Together they were the complete person. Except that the two really did not get along with each other. And all three of them failed miserably at whatever they did. It was almost as if Eliza and Everina had planned the failure to show her, destroy her. Could that be possible?

"Everina, how could you let this happen?"

Everina shrugged, looked Mary straight in the eye. She was being defiant.

"It happened," she said.

Everina turned around, went into the kitchen.

"Do not walk away from me," Mary said. "Do not turn your back on me."

"I can if I choose."

"No, you cannot."

Mary followed her into the kitchen, Eliza behind her.

Mary wondered where the cook was. There was a pile of dirty dishes in the pan under the pump. Carrot tops and pieces of onion were on the table. Flour coated the cupboard and something was rotting somewhere. A mouse or a misplaced piece of meat.

"Where is the cook?"

"Gone."

"My goodness." Mary had to sit down. "The whole thing is crumbling."

"You always thought you were better than anybody else," Everina spit out.

"Ah, and so you cut off your own nose to spite my face."

"Everina," Eliza cautioned. "Do not be mean."

"It is true. Mary always thought she was better."

"Better than you, apparently, at running a school," Mary returned.

"You are not better than I am," Everina said, leveling her voice. "You like to think you are, but you are not. I am the most clever."

"That may be true," Mary admitted, "but it does not mean anything and could actually mean ill if that cleverness is not used in the interest of good."

"As if you did."

"I do, actually. I try to, at least."

"Mother *hated* you. Your own mother."

"Do not be so mean, Everina. Just because I was Mother's favorite," Eliza said, interrupting.

Everina continued. "And Father hated you, too."

"It was no secret," Mary said. She looked at the carving knife on the dirty kitchen table. "No, no secret, and quite frankly I am happy they hated me. Their hatred made me strong. Their hatred will push me through life. To tell you the truth, I would hate it otherwise. Two such pathetic people hating me? It is a compliment."

Everina, despite her thick, heavy face, had a sharp little chin and a nose which could slice ice. Already there were lines going from her top lip to her nose, a group of them drawing her mouth together like a little purse.

"This school was for all of us, to free us. Now it is gone." Mary felt immensely weary. She would simply have to write the parents and say the school was closed. She would have to sell everything in the hope that it would bring enough to pay back Dr. Price. She would have to find new employment.

"At least we will be free of your domination. Do this, do that, fetch this, teach them one, two, three, could you bring in my night shift, who has been spending my money, well, you know what this means?" Everina put her hands on her hips, mocking Mary. "Oh, my head is so heavy because of all the ideas I have, oh dear, oh me. And she lords it over you, Eliza, because you let her. But Mary has no power over me. You think you are a man, Mary, is that not correct? You wish you were born a boy."

"I wish I were born a human being, Everina, and if that means man, yes. Yes, I want what men have. All their opportunities, all their privileges which are due me, all their power."

"And Fanny, you wanted to be married to dear, dead Fanny. To have and to hold until death did you part. You wanted to do things to her, with her. Do not deny it, I saw the way you looked at her. With longing, Mary, with longing."

"Do not say that," Mary screamed, going at Everina. "Do you dare to make filthy . . . to desecrate the memory of Fanny? Do you know what it is to watch somebody you care about die before you, day by day?"

Everina grabbed the knife.

"Hah, you challenge me to a duel, Everina, do you, my own sister? Tell me, what have you ever done for anybody? You demean the sweetest, kindest friend I ever had. You do not understand love or friendship, because you have never had it."

"You cannot even get a husband." Everina's hand was shaking. The knife rattled against the sink rim.

"And you? Do you have a husband, Everina? With a face designed to scare horses?"

"I had a husband," Eliza wailed. "Once I had a husband."

"Do not be such a sniveling baby," Mary hissed.

"And a baby," Eliza whined. "I had a baby until you came along, Mary."

"That is right. Mary took your baby. God giveth and God taketh away." Everina's mouth was twisted to the side, her eyes were narrowed. The kitchen had an iron range with a water heater. Everina had moved so that she had her back to it, and as Mary approached her she backed up until her dress was touching the oven door. Coals from the night before kept that door very hot.

"Any closer, Mary, and . . ."

"You will stab me? I dare you. I double-dare you."

"Mary," Eliza warned. "This is not the schoolyard. Everina, put down the knife and be sensible."

Mary moved closer.

"Stop, you two," Eliza cried. "For the love of God, stop."

Mary rushed Everina. Everina hit the edge of the stove.

"Ouch," she screamed, jumping forward and nearly nicking Mary with the knife. "Ants, ants all up my arm. Oh, no, my dress is singed. Look what you did, Mary. I am burned. Oh, no. And ants. Get some water. Help me." Everina started to cry piteously.

Eliza ran for the pump, rushed back with a bucket of water, splashed some water in the washing bowl, and, taking a cloth, cleaned Everina's arms.

"Turn around, Everina."

Mary lifted Everina's dress. There were no marks, nothing, not an injury, merely Everina's buttocks, which were as slack and huge and as wrinkled as an elephant's ear. Mary felt sorry for her.

"Let me see your dress, Everina, if that is harmed." Mary turned her gently around. There was a little line of soot, but that was all.

"Your dress is fine, too."

Everina put down the knife, hung her head. "I am sorry, Mary."

"I am sorry, too." Mary moved Everina to her, rested Everina's head on her shoulder. "I am sorry for us all."

"What are we going to do?" Eliza asked, hugging both her sisters.

"It is going to be every woman for herself," Mary answered.

"I am frightened," Everina said, sucking in her breath through her teeth.

"I wish I was still married," Eliza squeaked.

"No you do not," Everina corrected. "Bishop was a vicious pig and you know it."

"I am lost, then," Eliza said. "I have never worked except here."

"I suggest that we look for jobs as governesses."

"But you hate that, Mary," Eliza said. "You said it was like being an upper servant."

"It is."

"Do you hate me, Mary?"

"Everina," Mary said, wearily shaking her head. "What are we to do with you? How can I hate you, how can I hate anybody? Is not life difficult enough without hating?"

"But now we will not have the school," Eliza moaned.

"That is right, Eliza. No school."

Mary looked out of the window at the Green and across to Dr. Price's chapel. Cool air came in through the window, hinting winter. It is the end of a time, Mary thought sadly, yet she was sure that its lessons were not wasted. The thought of Mrs. Price's roses would come back to her, she believed, for the rest of her life. Dr. Price had taught her how to think. We keep going, she thought, until we reach the end.

CHAPTER 11

DR. PRICE told Mary that all stories had a secret meaning. For instance, the medieval story of *Sir Gawain and the Green Knight* was about Ireland *and* about constant rebirth. The head chopped off can be put back, Price had insisted. Nature is always there, reborn again, Mary, and the human spirit lives forever.

For some reason Dr. Price made that story sound pagan. He had come across it through contact with a literary gentleman. It was really a tale about a challenge in King Arthur's court. During the Christmas season, the story went, a Green Knight appeared before the Knights of the Round Table, inviting anybody brave enough to cut off his head. Sir Gawain comes forward, does the deed. But the Green Knight does not topple over and die. No, he merely picks up his head and states that in a year's time his adversary must be prepared to reap the consequences of his act. In a year's time Sir Gawain learns much of life and is spared the loss of his head.

Mary hoped the human spirit lived forever, but she felt very tired when she got to Ireland. It was her fourth employment in ten years. She was twenty-seven years old and had to beg her brother for enough money to purchase cloth for a cloak, her last request to him, she promised. She did not feel renewed, but she felt oddly strong and determined. She had her notes for her book with her. Ireland *was* green. And very poor. Except, of course, on the Kingsborough estate, which rose up from the countryside like a king's castle with walls, turrets, twists and turns, dungeons, halls, ballrooms, dressing rooms, pennants flapping in the wind, all that you could ask. As the coach approached the gatekeeper's house, Mary was sick with apprehension and doubt. Then the gatekeeper rushed out in full livery. He looked like a playing card, she a pauper. She *was* a pauper. Mary had learned

of the position through a friend of Dr. Price in the spring. Knowledge
of French was required. Mary did not speak French well and could
only read it with difficulty, but she applied anyway, for at that point
she had been desperate. I am tired, she said to herself, of always being
desperate. But what could she do? The school had closed; she had
nowhere to go.

You have very pretty penmanship, Lady Kingsborough wrote to
her, and I hope you will be able to train my girls likewise.

Mary wondered if the girls were incorrigible or likewise impaired,
for why should one not be able to train them. How old were these
girls? Lady Kingsborough seemed, in that letter, faintly confused, a
tad prickly. Her penmanship was spidery and spiky, the *k* a spear and
the *h* a musket. But Mary could not complain. She was a desperate
pauper, her mother was dead, her father remarried, her friend Fanny
Blood dead, and her sisters helpless. The one brother who could help
was cold as a stone. If must be, she would learn Hungarian to secure
a post.

In point of fact, the only available respectable professions open to
her were schoolmistress, which she had been, companion to a rich lady,
which she had been, seamstress, which she had been, and governess,
which she was now to be. Even should she have ten years of dame
school, this was the best job she could secure.

The other possibility, vague and yet tempting, was writing. She
planned to write. Dr. Price had seemed to think she could do it. Mrs.
Price had been adamant about it. Yes, yes, yes, women write books,
plays, novels. And more and more women were writing books in the
privacy of their homes, in much the same way letters were written.
Dr. Price told her of Eliza Fowler Haywood, who had written a novella
a month from 1725 to 1726 to support her two children. Laetitia
Pilkington, though dying destitute, had for a time supported herself
and children through her writing. Wonderful, Mary had replied, planning not to die destitute. But Dr. Price was right; most of the novels
were written by women in the privacy of their homes. They were
written in everyday language and they read like gossip, like conversation or a letter to a friend. A knowledge of the classics and Greek
and Roman languages was not required. Elevated diction and com-

plicated syntax were not necessary. Furthermore, the subject of most novels—affairs of the heart—was one anybody could speak about. Most of the scenes in novels took place in drawing rooms, a setting any woman was familiar with. The problems and solutions of the novel were internal—within the house, the room, the heart. A few pages every night, Mary reasoned, and in a few months she would have a book. With a book, she would have . . . she was not sure. Something. A hope.

She asked her brother Ned, who had inherited their grandfather's properties and was a successful solicitor, if he would pay for some blue wool to make a cloak to wear to Ireland. He complied, letting her know in no uncertain terms that it was the very last thing she could ever expect of him. As if, she ruefully noted, there was a list.

In a dream she had about that time, the blue cloak was as long as a wedding dress, and the children she was to attend to, the babies, rode on its train. The mistress, Lady Kingsborough, resembled her mother, and the master was mysteriously absent, the way men fade in and out of life and dreams like shadows and ghosts.

In reality, the three little girls, Mary's charges, were five, six, and seven. Lady Kingsborough was not blond, but had strong, black hair and snapping black eyes which flickered on and off.

"Well, so you ran a school," Lady Kingsborough said. "A jolly hurrah for you, but it will not help you here, nor any airs you may choose to put on. We are in the country, no society. Tenants, that is what we have. Muddy boots, sheep and pigs, the hunt, cow dung."

Lady Kingsborough happened to be no stranger to the lower orders herself. She was an appreciator par excellence of the canine species, keeping dogs on her lap and some at her feet, while others danced attendance at a distance, playing and prancing, rolling and lolling, and still more frolicked outside—spaniels, setters and terriers, retrievers, and poodles, about twenty-five in all.

"Romular, come here this instant, you naughty boy. Pepper, I will not countenance impudence. Mitzi, behave, behave yourself. I am warning you, Mitzi. Spot, Spot . . . Goodness, Miss Wollstonecraft, the life of a . . . well, let it not be said I do not try . . . I try, I try . . . Do I not try, my darlings?" The fur-backed, waggly-tailed contingent looked up expectantly, pawed the ground. Romular, or was it Mitzi. Pepper, it was Pepper who piddled on the slate floor. And the puppies pooped behind the chaise and next to the Windsor chair and over by the fireplace and under the window. Spot had a flea-and-tick problem. There were others with curious complications. Dity would not eat. Rover had disgusting sores on his back. Bet tried to run away all the time.

"God knows I try," their mistress sighed. "Pepper must be punished. To the dungeon, Pepper. Tread warily, Miss Wollstonecraft, tread warily."

Lady Kingsborough wore a taffeta dress for this meeting and for nearly the whole of the year. The bodice was salmon-colored, and the skirts silvery-gray. She looked like a big shimmery fish with a human head. Mary supposed that made Lady Kingsborough a mermaid. It had an overdress of net and it was simply the most beautiful dress Mary had ever seen, except that it was slightly soiled and smelled strongly of dog. The petticoats drooped a trifle, too. And there was a little rip in the hem, stains here and there. Holes under the arms. A burn spot on the seat.

"The children?" Mary asked timidly. She was standing in what she gathered was the reception room for servants and tenants, a great hall with a long, long table. At the end of the table Lady Kingsborough was ensconced on what seemed to be a throne.

"Delightful." Lady Kingsborough fastened her eyes on Mary again, went out of focus, came back in. "Delightful children, each and every one. Let's see, there is . . . yes, and the two boys, but the girls, there is . . . yes, the girls are your charges."

"May I meet them?"

"You will, yes, let us . . . well, and . . . soon enough. They are little gadabouts . . . the girls. The boys you need not bother with. I whip them myself once a month. School in the autumn . . . delightful children, just delightful. Theodora, watch yourself, young lady. Never get Newfoundlands, Miss Wollstonecraft. I am considering retrievers, Miss Wollstonecraft, what do you think? Mariella, come here to Mother."

"Definitely."

"Exactly my thoughts. Wonderful animals, strictly wonderful. Well, that is all, unless you have any questions. I am sure you will hate it here. I do. They always do, too, the governesses and tutors, but well, I will try. Will we not, little darlings?" They all stuck out their tongues, panted in eager agreement.

Mary's room was high up in one of the turrets, far from dogdom. When she opened the door, she threw herself across the bed. I am a princess, she said to herself. When she looked out the window at the grounds, she felt grand, even though the furnishings in her room were plain, like those in servants' quarters. With several candlesticks, a whale-oil lamp, she would be able to read into the night and do her scribbling in peace. The book she was planning was something that would console her for Fanny's death. Fanny would be in it, immortalized. Fanny is dead, Mary said to herself, rolling over to stare at the ceiling, but I will write about her, for her.

Mary got up, took her quills and inkpot, sheets of paper out of her trunk, and placed them on the desk. There, she said to herself, now sit down and write.

The lady of the house welcomed the beautiful young governess with a genteel sweep of the hand. It is all yours, my dear, each and every room, the grounds. I am sending you to the village tomorrow to be fitted for some new frocks. I think blue silk would become you. We dine early and have musical evenings. Do you play? Well, you could learn alongside the children. Mr. Tra-la-la comes every Wednesday. A wonderful man, to be sure, and so accomplished and patient and so very handsome. It is so sad that his dear wife died last year. And feel free to use the library. Unfortunately, it only contains some ten thousand volumes with strengths in philosophy and natural science. Lessons in the morning, afternoons for your own contemplation. We like chocolate very much and always have chocolate at three, tea at six, and supper at eight. If there is any way, at all, that I can make your stay more comfortable . . .

But there were evil sounds at night.

Sighs and lamentations. The strands of leaves from the old willow whipped and wound themselves . . .

Miranda opened the shutters, looked out on the moonlit moor. In the distance, barely discernible, was a figure on a horse. Could it be Marcel?

Mary shuddered, packed her materials, went downstairs.

I cannot write, she said to herself. I cannot write at all. I am a failure and a fraud.

The library in the mansion was a gentleman's library—with a ceiling as tall as a cathedral's, and spiderwebs everywhere. Unused and desolate, out of the way, it was too damp for a library, and all the leather bindings had a greenish tinge. Mary went to the window for some air. She did not feel like edification and self-improvement. She wished she could simply write a letter to Fanny. That would be far better than writing about her. Mary also missed England. She thought of Dr. Price, all the roses. There were no streets on the Kingsborough estate. There was the driveway, and beyond, the road, the one road out and in, and small brown paths looping up and around the meadows and small hills.

She should be happy. She had employment, food, shelter. It was not so awful to be a governess. The sun was shining. She would be going to dinner soon. The children, whom she would meet, would be good children. It was not the end of the world to be a governess. A lot of people were governesses. Her sisters were governesses. A governess never goes hungry. A governess is not in the poorhouse. A governess is not on the street. She should count her blessings, one, two, three, four, she should be happy, happy, happy, and happy. She burst into tears.

"Miss Wollstonecraft?"

She turned, quickly wiping her face with her sleeve.

"Beautiful day, is it not?"

It was a young man, or a boy, perhaps, slim, with hair more white than yellow which lay flat against his forehead like a house shingle. His complexion was exceedingly pale and he was dressed in red velvet breeches and waistcoat, almost Elizabethan in style, and curious tall black boots. He had been spying on her, she knew.

"Mother says you are to be the governess to the girls."

"Yes."

He had a soft, high voice, like a singer's. "Father is to see about you when he returns."

"How long has he been gone?"

"Three months."

"And when is he to be back?"

"I do not know."

See about her? What did *that* mean? That she would lose her employment?

"So who are you?"

"The oldest one. Richard the Cripple."

"The Cripple?"

"Like Richard III. And you are, let me guess, Mary the Sad."

"I am not sad."

"You were thinking of dying, leaving, despairing, were you not?"

"Good heavens, no." But she had been.

"Just what I thought. In fact, I think of it often. Whenever I have a free moment."

Mary laughed. She was being much too familiar. And he was. But the child was a child. What harm could come of it?

"You are quite comely," he said, "for a governess."

"Comely? Someone once said I was handsome. And what do you mean 'for a governess.' "

"Comely, let us settle for that."

"You are quite impudent for a child."

"I am not a child."

"Oh, I see. You are all grown, then."

"Probably I am. But you are quite pretty in a very subtle way."

Mary at twenty-seven: eyes that shifted colors in the light, a whimsical smile, round face, heavy lids, small sparrow-hawk nose, full figure, creamy skin. She could not pay for the flour to powder her hair or for a wig, and so her hair was long and quite thick. She could not dress it well herself, and wore it in a tight bun at the base of her neck.

"If I am pretty," she said, "it hardly matters, for nobody ever sees me, and year by year I will become plainer and plainer."

"My goodness, you *do* feel sorry for yourself."

"Are your sisters good students?"

"They cannot read. Why do you change the subject? *I* am looking at you."

"Really. Not at all?"

"No. What do you read? Do you read the usual books on manners and nursery tales? My mother reads vast amounts, you know."

"My mother could not read," Mary said. She was not surprised that Lady Kingsborough could. A lady, the mistress of this vast estate on which she was told were situated tenant houses, a chapel, a blacksmith, an apothecary, a public house, and a school for young children.

"What do you read?" He had an insistent manner. She saw him as peevish and difficult.

"What do *you* read?" she countered.

"I read Rousseau and Voltaire, Hume. Tom Paine's pamphlets, the novels of Henry Fielding, Defoe, Richardson, Dr. Price, of course. I also read the *Monthly Review* and the *Gentleman's Magazine*. Is that good enough for you? I read Latin and Greek, French, a little German. I am taking the year off from Eton."

"No sentimental novels?"

"Richardson."

"I am writing one," she said.

"Why?"

"For money, of course. I am also going to write a serious book on education. Yes, that is correct. I plan to distinguish myself in letters." Which was a sudden inspiration. She had never thought of a book on education, and to distinguish herself, gracious, how remote that seemed. Still. And he was only a child. It did not harm to dream in front of him.

"Ah," he responded. "Ambitious, are we?"

"I had the good fortune to become friends with a Dissenting minister, Dr. Richard Price of Newington Green, and he was kind enough to direct my reading and help me learn to think a little."

The young man, as these little masters would do, was amusing

himself. Mary knew that. As governess, she was nothing but an upper
servant, anyway. She turned back to the window. She should not talk
so much.

The heavy brocaded curtains smelled of mildew, and the floor,
uncarpeted, squeaked and cracked. Outside, peasants were loading
things on carts. I am twenty-seven years old, Mary said to herself, and
still making grand plans.

"Miss Wollstonecraft?"

"Yes?" She turned again to him. He was her height, but so in-
substantial he seemed smaller.

"Miss Wollstonecraft?"

"Yes . . . Master Kingsborough."

"Richard."

"Yes, Mr. Richard."

"Richard."

"Richard the Lionhearted."

"Richard III."

"No Richard I ever knew."

"Richer by far . . ."

"Recharge the cannon, my boys."

"Recherché."

She sighed. "You are clever, Richard, I grant you that."

"Who cares. I am utterly miserable, Mary."

"Oh dear." She put her hand to her throat. "You are?"

"Yes. Of course."

"But you are so rich."

"It does not seem to matter."

She was, of course, of two minds. Naturally, she felt sorry for him,
but then again, she did not.

"What is it?"

"I am . . ."

"Are you sick? Is that it?" She asked that because he looked
unwell. He was very frail, and his skin had a waxy pallor.

"In a manner of speaking."

"Will you be well soon?"

"Not ever."

"Oh."

"And you?" he asked gently.

"Me?" She smiled, walked over toward him. "For me it is that I have the wrong life. I do not belong here or actually anywhere. My ambitions exceed my talents and circumstances."

"You belong in a literary salon, you should be a Blue Stocking lady."

"Of course. But I am not rich or accomplished."

"Maybe you will be."

"But I am already old."

Mary walked up very closely to where he was standing. What color were his eyes? They seemed yellow. She put her finger on one of his eyelids.

"You have the eyes of a cat."

He grabbed her wrists, held them fast.

"Richard, what are you doing?"

He pulled her forward straight to his face.

"My God," she exclaimed. His round little mouth looked like a circle cut in the ice and his tongue was a fast red fish. It tasted that way, too, raw and slippery wet.

"Do you like to kiss?" he asked.

She had never kissed anybody before except Annie—the strange things she wanted—and Fanny.

"Have you kissed anybody?"

"Oh, yes," he answered.

"You have? Who?"

"Assorted servants."

"I beg your pardon." She turned to leave.

"Wait."

"This is ridiculous. One day here and I am kissing the young master. Do you realize that I have been let go from every employment I have ever had? And this, this is a major offense. You, you should not take advantage of those in weaker positions than yours. It is your fault. How old are you?"

"Sixteen."

"Sixteen?" She stamped her foot. "Sixteen, and you exploit servants. Well, I am not your servant. I am the governess. Your sisters are my students. I owe you nothing."

"I am not exploiting you. I thought you wanted me to kiss you. Please do not say such cruel things to me." He put his hand over his heart.

"It is an offense for which I could be let go."

"No, it is not. Nobody cares."

"Read *Moll Flanders*."

"I have. It is a silly novel."

"Yes, silly to you. Moll Flanders was discovered by the mother, that part? Remember. And the young master . . ."

"Miss Wollstonecraft, you are so funny."

"How dare you laugh at me."

But he laughed all the more, and he lost his footing, fell.

"Oh, God."

Mary shuddered. She had not noticed. One of his legs was much shorter than the other and was kept in a strange tall laced boot different from the other. He lay sprawled and helpless on the floor.

"Help me up?" he asked good-naturedly from below her.

"Yes." She reached down and found that he was so light she could have carried him around.

"Thank you," he said, upright and smilingly offering his arm. "They are expecting us for dinner, Miss Mary."

Richard the Cripple, Mary thought. My goodness. He is undaunted.

Dinner was on a royal table, long, mahogany, very heavy, not at all like the lighter-weight Chippendale furniture of London. The wind from the opened window set the great cut-glass chandelier tinkling like so many tiny, tiny bells. Lady Kingsborough was at the foot of the table, Mary to her right, Richard at her left, the other children ranged on either side. The head was left empty, since the master was away. Mary had on her nice green dress, but it appeared unnecessary to dress for dinner. Lady Kingsborough was in the same dress as before. And her dogs were arrayed about her, on her lap and on the floor.

"I think we should have a toast," Lady Kingsborough said. "A toast to our new governess."

"A toast, a toast," the little girls said.

All three were giggly and plump, with brown braids which stuck out at the sides of their heads at stiff angles.

"And how do you like the estate?" Lady Kingsborough had helped herself to some more wine.

"It is beautiful." Mary had not seen much. But it was grander than any place she had ever been.

"Yes, of course it is." Lady Kingsborough spilled her wine. "Oh dear. Bridget, Bridget. The Irish are so slow, have you noticed? Doggies, come lick up the wine."

The little girls, red-cheeked butterballs, looked down with embarrassment. Mary felt like saying: Look up, look up. It is quite all right. I do not care a fig what your mother does.

"The important thing to remember is that tomorrow we must eat lunch on the moor," Lady Kingsborough said. "My best doggies need to run a bit. The family will gather in a grand picnic."

"Three cheers," Richard said, looking right at Mary.

"Tra-la-la-la," the little girls responded. The other boy, seven or so, scowled.

"I will not go," he said.

"William, you must go," Richard said.

"I will not."

"And afterward we shall ride into the village," Lady Kingsborough said. "And buy some tarts."

"We want tarts, we want tarts," the three girls chanted.

"And maybe some nutmeg drops."

"Nutmeg drops, nutmeg drops."

"And tarts filled with red, purple, green, yellow, orange jam."

"Yellow jam?" William gasped.

"Pity you do not wish to join us." Lady Kingsborough helped herself to more wine.

"A pity, a pity."

"Hush, girls."

"Mother," William said.

"Yes, dear." Lady Kingsborough turned slowly, but nonetheless nearly fell off her chair.

"I want to go."

"That is Mother's precious boy. And a jolly good time will be had by all. You must excuse me, little chicks. Your mother has had a hard day and must retire early. Until tomorrow, tallyho and Godspeed and God rest ye merry, gentlemen, and . . ."

Watching Lady Kingsborough stumble out, Mary was reminded of her father and her childhood.

But that night she started to write her novel in earnest. It began:

> *In delineating the Heroine of this Fiction, the Author attempts to develop a character different from those generally portrayed. This woman is neither a Clarissa, a Lady G——, nor a Sophie . . . In an artless tale, without episodes, the mind of a woman who has thinking powers is displayed.*

Thinking powers? That did not sound too romantic. Furthermore, her own mind was hardly an example of thinking powers. There were too many things in it for her to think clearly—the school, Fanny in Portugal, how cruel Everina had been, how helpless Eliza was, the idea of emotion over reason, experience over pure thought, and notions of political justice and liberty, and the time in Bath, when the man was ready to threaten her because she was not fit to be looked at, Annie, her mother, and then, always, her father. It seemed a wonder that she could think at all. Now this boy. But if she did not write her books, and soon, she knew she would be lost. There would be nothing about herself to hold on to and take up with. Words would fall from her hands, colorless, lifeless, useless. She must not let duties and past circumstances hinder or stop her. Her best course of action would be to enjoy what there was to enjoy about the estate, and ignore whatever was distressing.

Dinner had been fowl with prune sauce, whole fish in pastry, green-pea soup, jams and pickles, potato pudding, and rich seed cake.

For the lunch in the country, they had thick loaves of bread and apple butter, cabbage salad, Cheshire cheese. Lady Kingsborough had her usual tea. Not the same tea as the children and Mary, of course.

It was a blank, gray afternoon, and they had traveled, all of them, bunched in a phaeton a good hour to a meadow of mostly mud. It seemed to take forever to get there. Richard had to be helped down. The little girls went into the little thicket of trees to play teatime with acorn cups and saucers Richard had made. He had to sit on a stump with his leg straight out. William read an adventure story about Tom Thumb, with a blanket wrapped around him. Lady Kingsborough stretched out on a cloth to take a little nap; her favorite dogs settled themselves on her shimmery gray skirts. Richard set out a chess set.

"I am not very good," Mary said.

"No matter. Neither am I."

But she knew he would be good, and he was, checkmating her in about ten moves. Beat by a boy. And the little girls sang from the shade of the trees: "Checkmate, checkmate, checkmate."

Richard did not have much hair on his face, but he had a soft, downy mustache, as some women do. Mary wanted to smooth her finger over it. Beat by a boy.

"My goodness," she said, feeling uncomfortable, "it must be getting late."

Richard got up, limped into the woods. "Nature," he said.

With her traveling quill-and-ink set Mary wrote a few lines that might be useful in her book about the education of girls.

> *Above all, try to teach them to combine their ideas. It is of more use than can be conceived, for a child to learn to compare things that are similar in some respects, and different in others. I wish them to be taught to think . . .*

"Tarts, tarts," the little girls chanted when they started back.

When lessons began the next day, Mary got up early, washed herself well, combed her hair carefully, smoothed her black dress with her palm. The schoolroom, right off the nursery, was a large, sunny room with the floors scrubbed clean and with child-size tables full of the swirls and strokes wood gets from being cleaned over many years with wire brushes. There was a map of the world; the continents were in pea green, the oceans baby blue. In the South Pacific there were little canoes full of Samoan warriors as described by Captain Cook, and the American continent had Indians behind fir trees and trappers on the borders.

"These are the countries of the world," Mary said, using a pointer. "Can you tell me where we are?"

"We are English, we are English."

"One at a time, please. Martha, could you show me where England is. Here, use the pointer."

"Will not," she said, pouting out her lips and hanging her head.

"Elizabeth."

"Do not have to."

"Anne."

"They will tell you if you beat them." William, the younger son, was at the door. "They have to be beat."

"No, they do not," Mary said.

"Mrs. Marsh beat us," Anne said hopefully.

"Miss Wollstonecraft does not."

"Beat us, beat us," they chanted.

Their little faces were turned to her like buttercups, open daisies. They were expectant little animals intent on danger.

Mary sighed. "Beating another person or even beating an animal is a base and emotional action. Thinking people, good people, do not beat those weaker than themselves."

"Oh, but they must be beat, Miss Mary, and you must be the beater." Lady Kingsborough appeared at the door, walked in clapping her hands together. "Am I right, girls?" It looked as if Lady Kingsborough had stepped on the front of her skirt, for a great bunch of loose fabric hung down. Her hair, too, was down around her shoulders in great disarray.

"I am sorry, madam." Mary hung her head. She had the dizzy feeling of being a baited bear.

"Treats and sweets for the good girls. Bread for boys and dogs. They are good dogs, Miss Wollstonecraft, very good dogs. I have a little switch which I use on them. The girls get a riding crop."

"I cannot beat them, Lady Kingsborough."

"Oh, but you must."

"We like it," Elizabeth said. "We like to be beaten."

"I do not like to be beaten," Mary said to them. "I was beaten as a child and I despised it, and I shall not beat you."

"Oh yes, indeed, but everything in its own good time." Lady Kingsborough wandered off. "You will beat them," she sang back. "Finally you will beat them."

Finally I will beat them? How strange, Mary thought, looking out over the brown fields from her bedroom. Have I wandered into a house of perdition, that I kiss and beat children? Or is this an asylum or a dream of an asylum? And I came here partly to write about thinking people. She turned to her papers. They were always there, no matter how bizarre downstairs was, the nursery, the kennel, the dining-room table. This was her peace and quiet.

Thoughts on the Education of Daughters—that is what she would call it. She had done several sections already: "The Nursery," "Moral Discipline," and "Artificial Manners." But who would read such a book, she wondered, who would care. She tucked herself down lower in her bed, hunched over her manuscript. What kind of world was it, she wondered, when both mother and children call for beatings?

Then she heard his footsteps, the drag of his heavy leg behind him, the other one swinging light. Badum, badum, badum.

"Mary," he said.

She poked her head out of her room. "I am not presentable," she said. "And I suppose you want to be beaten, too."

"I would not mind your lashes, Miss Mary quite contrary."

She jumped back in bed, hid under the covers, squashing her newly written papers. A is an acorn, B is a boy, C is for crying, and W is the wolf who stands at the door, she recited to herself.

"Mary, come out, please. I want to tell you something." She put her fingers out from under the cover. Then her whole hand appeared, her arms, and finally the crown of her head, her hair, her forehead, her eyes, her nose, her mouth, her chin.

"What?"

"Mary."

"You are being very childish."

"You are."

"I have a right to be."

He sat on the side of the bed, and she reached up and with a single finger she traced along his eyebrows, moving to his ears and nose, around his mouth.

"You are a very pretty boy," she said. "You are almost a girl."

"Do you like that, Mary?"

"Grown men scare me," she said.

"Why?"

"Because they beat you. Even standing next to a large man frightens me. They can grab you, push you down. You can never tell."

"I see."

She stroked his chin, his neck and collarbones, his shoulders. Working back up with the flat of her palm, she pressed his face flat, pinching the nose, rubbing the skull.

"That felt so good," he said.

Then he touched her face, her lids, running his finger along her lips, ringing her ears, her cheekbones. She ran her fingers down his cheeks, cupped his jaw. He touched her neck, felt for her shoulders, reached under her armpits. She felt his ears, behind his ears. He brought his hands from under her arms to her chest and very lightly to her breasts. She put her hand on his stomach. He opened his legs. She pressed down on him. He flecked her nipples with his thumbs.

It was only the afternoon, but after dinner he came back upstairs and the moon coming in at the window bathed them in an unearthly glow. She could see the blue veins in his forehead and the thin red filaments in his ears, the lines in his lips, and his eyes changed color as he looked at her, lightening with tenderness and then going darker as his look became more intense.

CHAPTER 12

July 3, 1787

Dear Eliza. These last months with the Kingsboroughs have been most interesting. It is a rather complicated family. They mean well, certainly, or . . . Lady Kingsborough is a beautiful woman who drinks brandy in her tea from the early morning and is quite besotted by teatime. Her drunkenness is not like our father's. It expresses itself in sloppiness and confusion. She sleeps at odd hours and anywhere. I came upon her on the floor of the library and had to fetch a servant to help me pick her up and take her to the bed. Later, when I looked in on her, I could see that she had vomited all over herself. We had to bath her. She was exceedingly angry.

My novel, Mary, a Fiction, *is about a young woman forced to marry against her will for reasons of property. She is quite unhappy, and her only solace is her dear, dear friend who dies. Bereft, all she can do is serve humanity as best she might. The other book,* Thoughts on the Education of Daughters, *is more practical in nature. The title speaks for itself. I have sent parts of both books to a publisher friend of Dr. Richard Price, do you remember the Minister and Dissenting thinker at Newington Green? He is the one who gave me enough faith in myself to enable me to write in the first place. He felt that faith in God encompassed faith in people, and yes, I am a person. Joseph Johnson, the publisher in London, is also a Dissenter. Dr. Price recommended him highly.*

Richard and Mary were in the nursery. Below, on the deep-green summer lawn, the girls were throwing a ball about with their other brother. Lady Kingsborough was napping. Mary liked to take tea in the nursery because the windows gave a full view of the stretch of meadows and the woods and brook beyond. The tiny steeple of the chapel hung like a needle from the sky. There were sheep and cows. The pigs were kept on the other side in little round pens. And the vegetable garden was outside the kitchen door, and beyond was a small orchard with trees heavy with black-hearted cherries and with ripe nectarines, golden pippins, several kinds of pears.

"Richard, you will marry a nice girl your age soon."

"I do not want to marry a nice girl."

He lurched over to stand in front of her. "Why do you always start this, Mary? We are happy."

"I am not happy. This is my job here, Richard, this is how I earn a living. I cannot go hungry. You remember *Moll Flanders*. The circumstances are most unusual."

"Can we move on to *Pamela*, at least, or *Clarissa*? Our situation is quite harmless."

"Think of me, for once."

"I think of you all the time."

"I cannot violate the trust your mother has put in me. I feel so hypocritical . . ."

"Trust? Trust? My mother is half clouded half the time and the other half fully so. She wants you to beat the children, and if you do not, you are to be in a sense thrashed yourself. It is a trap. You are caught whatever you do. My mother should be put in the madhouse. Do not consider her a person worthy of consideration."

"You are only sixteen."

"Quite irrelevant. And I am tired of hearing my age. I know how old I am, how young."

"Nonetheless, I would be let go if she . . ."

"I would marry you."

Mary threw her head back, and laughed heartily. "Come now."

"You laugh because of my foot," Richard said petulantly.

"No, no." She took his head in her hands. "Not your foot, my dear. Your age."

"Soon to be seventeen. Anyway, sixteen feels old on me, very old. People marry at that age. My parents were sixteen. I may not live forever, anyway."

"You will live a good while longer, that I am sure. I am not young. I am a spinster. Twenty-eight now. Nobody would have me."

"I would. And nobody would have *me*. They will all be happy it is all settled so nicely. The spinster and the cripple."

"The author and the heir."

"Of course. It all depends on how you look at it."

Mary had sent off both her books to the publisher. She was relieved and apprehensive. Richard was certain they would be published. Dr. Price, who had read bits of each, was certain, too. Meanwhile, the little girls were learning to read with an alphabet box, storybooks, and the oldest one by stitching samplers with verses on them.

> *Not land but learning*
> *Makes a man complete.*
> *Not birth but breeding*
> *Makes him truly great.*
>
> *Not wealth but wisdom*
> *Does adorn his state.*
> *Virtue and honor*
> *Makes him fortunate.*
>
> *Learning, Breeding, Wisdom.*
> *Get those three,*
> *Then wealth and honor*
> *Will attend thee.*

The oldest girl could in fact read simple stories. The youngest could do sums. The middle girl was beginning to speak up for herself. Sometimes all three would troop up to Mary's room early in the morning before anybody else was awake and crawl into bed with her. The baby liked to snuggle against her stomach and the oldest hovered at Mary's back, singing rub-a-dub-dub, and the middle girl got her legs. Once everybody was settled just right, they would all fall back asleep, holding very still so as not to disturb each other.

"What is this hive? This hovel?" Lady Kingsborough stood above them like a giant. Mary woke up in a state of confusion.

"What?"

"My girls are in *your* bed."

Lady Kingsborough extracted each girl, threw her on the floor. The dogs raced about, yelping ferociously.

"You are not babies anymore. And Miss Wollstonecraft, do you intend to woo my children away from me?"

"Do we get sweets today, Mother?" the youngest asked.

"Sweets, sweets, we want sweets."

The dogs leaped and pranced on their hind legs. Sweets, sweets, we want sweets.

"Come on downstairs and sweets it will be. Honestly, these days."

At lessons, Mary, talking about the Spanish Armada wrecked on the shoals of accident, took a good look at the girls. The oldest was writing on her slate, her little tongue sticking between her lips, in great concentration. The sun was hitting the top of her head, giving her a golden halo. My little puppies, Mary thought. My babies. Lady Kingsborough was right to be jealous.

That night she read part of her novel aloud to Richard.

> *Her sensibility prompted her to search for an object to love; on earth it was not to be found: her mother had often disappointed her, and the apparent partiality she shewed to her brother gave her exquisite pain—produced a kind of habitual melancholy, led her into a fondness for reading tales of woes, and made her almost realize the fictious distress.*
>
> *She had not any notion of death till a little chicken expired at her feet; and her father had a dog hung in a passion.*

"*Mary, a Fiction?*" Richard chuckled softly. "It sounds like *Mary, the Truth.*"

"In the book the heroine is married off for the purposes of joining two estates. The husband leaves for a trip shortly after the marriage, and the heroine, Mary, devotes herself to the care of her dearest, darling friend. She and the friend travel to Portugal, but the friend dies. There Mary falls in love with Henry, who also dies. She must return to her husband. The book ends:

*Her delicate state of health did not promise long life. In moments
of solitary sadness, a gleam of joy would dart across her mind—
She thought she was hastening to that world where there is neither
marrying nor giving in marriage.*

"You are breaking my heart." Richard put his hand on his heart.

"So you think it is not good, is that what you think?" Mary was
at her little writing desk by the window. Richard was flung across the
bed.

"It is a wonderful book, Mary, that is what I think."

"No, be honest."

"I am honest."

"Well, but you think it is too autobiographical."

"No."

"Why then the Mary, hah-hah, a fiction?"

"Teasing, Mary."

"Miss Mary, to you."

"And Sir, to you. You know I will inherit my father's title, and
his land and this house and all his properties. Will you marry me, Miss
Mary?"

"Hush."

"Do not hush me, I am weaker than you."

"You are not weaker."

"Oh, Mary, but I am. You are an author, soon to be a published
author."

"I do not feel that I am, that anything is different, that I merit
particular consideration."

Richard grabbed the curtain ropes, made a noose, put his head
through.

"Do not play that way." Mary shivered.

He hobbled forward. "Sometimes I *feel* that way. It would settle
everything. To think I must drag this heavy shoe about with me for
the rest of my life. And hear behind my back snickers and snarls."

"Stop feeling sorry for yourself. Alexander Pope was a hunchback.
Look at what he did."

"Yes, of course," he said wearily. "Good old Alexander, the hunchback." Richard twisted the curtain cords again. They were silken, with braided fringes at the end. The curtains themselves were a deep maroon velvet, probably originally hanging in a main bedroom. The little girls liked to wrap themselves up in them. You cannot find us, you cannot find us. Yes I can, yes I can. For their little legs would stick down. White silks and black buckles.

"You are not unhappy, Richard? Please, do not be."

"Oh, Mary, I am," he groaned.

"I am, too, Richard. I will always be that way."

But when several months later the letter came from the publisher, Joseph Johnson, accepting her books, Mary was extremely happy. She ran all over, up and down stairs, looking for Richard. She found him in her room, on her bed, reading her notes.

"Richard, what are you doing?"

"Spying, as you see, pretending I am a publisher . . ."

"No need, Richard, I am to be published."

She showed him the letter.

"Gracious," he said. "You *are* an author."

That night Mary drank a great deal of wine at dinner. Lady Kingsborough said it was good for her. She was an author-to-be, an extraordinary girl.

Then when Lady Kingsborough retired with her cup and pups, Mary and Richard drank more wine. Really, Mary could not remember feeling so jolly, so at ease.

That night the little girls *and* Richard crawled into her bed when she was asleep. They were all in a big pile. Two dogs joined them. Mary felt confused, as if her head were whirling around on its own. She wasn't sure where she was.

"I am their mother," Lady Kingsborough's shrill voice broke through. "I *am* their mother. *I* am their mother." It was the morning. The light was harsh.

"What?" Mary turned over, crushed a girl and a dog. Richard lifted his head from the pillow. Lady Kingsborough wobbled and wove in front of them.

"Lady Kingsborough," Mary gasped.

"Yes, I am Lady Kingsborough."

Perhaps Lady Kingsborough had not slept at all. Her dress was almost in tatters, and the stains had discolored the bodice to an unrecognizable beige.

"We all had bad dreams, Mother," Richard said.

"Do we get some treats?" one of the little girls asked.

"No. Please go to the nursery. Miss Wollstonecraft, I must tell you it is not fitting that my daughters' affections should go elsewhere. You teach them in the morning, play with them in the afternoon, and sleep with them at night. Where will it end, Miss Wollstonecraft? Where will it end? It is not healthy for little girls to be so attached to their governess. And you absolutely refuse to beat them, unheard of in this day and age. Fido, stop it. Mitzi, Mother is going to spank. Surely you understand the principle involved, Miss Wollstonecraft. The sanctity of the family is at issue here. Nothing could be more important. I do not want my children, my little girls, distracted from their rightful place. Rover, heel, heel. And so for that reason, and that reason alone, Miss Wollstonecraft, I am going to have to let you go. Defection in the family, now there is a trouble spot. There are so many situations for governesses, and of course your mother, your family, they would all be so happy to have you in *their* bosoms again. Excuse me, I must sit down. A bit faint. The heat, you know. Pepper, would you stop nipping Mamma's skirts. And so one family to another. My little girls are important to me. Soon they will be big girls, and what then. Ah yes, motherhood. It is a divine calling fit for angels and saints. Please leave by the end of the week. No ugly words, bad feelings. Simply depart from the premises. I truly think that best. Today, this afternoon, as soon as possible, with the greatest possible urgency, today, did I say that?"

The little girls set up a wail.

"Mother, Mary and I wish to get married."

"Do not be ridiculous, Richard."

"Mother."

"Go to your room this instant."

"We love each other," Richard protested, hobbling forth.

"They love each other," the little girls prattled. "They love each other."

"I have never heard anything so empty-headed in my life."

"Mother, please."

"Richard," Mary said. Her night shift had ridden up around her hips. Richard had slept with his clothes on all night. The little girls were strewn about the bed like rag dolls. Mary felt absolutely miserable.

"What you need, Richard, is a good purge," his mother said. "And maybe some new shoes."

"No, Mother."

"Everybody to their room instantly. I will not tolerate this." Lady Kingsborough turned heel, left.

"I am waiting for you," she called from the hall.

Mary's little room seemed more silent than silent with everybody gone. It seemed to Mary that if Richard had loved her as much as he professed he would have found some way to get a message to her or come himself. She waited for his soft knock on the door. She stayed up all night, her ears attuned. Was he locked up? Was there no servant to be trusted? Was everybody so frightened? Was she just another servant he had dallied with? And now was he ignoring her forever? She did not know. Trays of food were left outside her door as if she were a prisoner. The week was miserable; the moisture and gloom seemed to insinuate themselves between the cracks in the ceiling and were in endless supply. Mary folded her shift listlessly (she felt so weary), put her vase and portrait of Sarah Siddons (all she had), her few books (which were for naught) into her trunk. She was going—adding, she knew, to her growing list of failures. Her mother had hated her, she had not pleased Mrs. Dawson, the school in Newington Green had to be closed, and now this.

The afternoon of the last day, with the dogs nipping at her heels, Mary boarded the cart to the coach stop in town. This is the end of my life, Mary thought. The little girls and Richard were crying at their windows. Lady Kingsborough stood at the door, quite the queen of the realm in a new dress. Mary had imagined Lady Kingsborough's old dress turning in time from rags to tatters.

It was spring, 1788. Mary had nowhere to go, nobody to see, but she did have the address of the man who had taken her two books, *Mary, a Fiction* and *Thoughts on the Education of Daughters*.

Her publisher, Joseph Johnson, was at 72, St. Paul's Churchyard, London.

JOSEPH

CHAPTER 13

THE DOOR KNOCKER was in the shape of a curled-up hand, black as obsidian.

It was evening and had been drizzling all day in London. The sky was a threadbare blanket. Mary had taken a coach from her inn on the Strand to St. Paul's Churchyard. She surveyed the curve of red brick houses facing Wren's cathedral. They looked like the walls around the castle ruins she had played in as a child in Laugharne. Completing the circle, she had scanned the door lintels for number 72, St. Paul's Churchyard, found it.

Twenty-eight, nearly twenty-nine, a spinster with hardly a shilling to her name, she could not remember when things had gone well, and so for all her desire to turn around, go back, there was nowhere to return to and she had best acknowledge it. It was as if the world fell away behind her and she walked one step ahead of disaster. There had been no position she had not lost and no friend she had not forfeited. Nothing to do, then, but scrape her boots on the boot scrape, take a deep breath, and lift and drop the knocker. But then the thought occurred to her:

What if Joseph Johnson does not like me.

What if he finds me silly and stupid.

What if, what if.

It does not pay to think too hard on it, she countered, all that might be, not be, so be it, your mind going a hundred thoughts between one moment and the next. And she would be long dead before she knew her fate.

She let the knocker drop.

The sound echoed down a hall. There were no footsteps in the house, though the light from the many windows cast squares of gold onto the dark street.

"Oh." Mary sighed. "He is not going to answer. And I will have nowhere to go and must die on the street like an animal."

She thought of the body cart that came around the streets to pick up the impoverished dead. In her black dress she would look like a big crow or an eel.

"Look," somebody would say, "look, the chest moves and the heart lives."

Then they would send her, not to the common pauper's grave, but—worse—to the poorhouse. There she would be in her pious bonnet, at a long table in dim light, hemming gray sheets and clothes for the lying-in hospital and the orphanage, day in, day out, sunshine a memory, laughter an echo.

Where is this man, she nearly cried, he who is to save my life. *Somebody* was at home. Candles were lit. He had to be there. She could not endure it otherwise.

The black dress she was wearing, unfashionable and out of season for April 1788, was the one she wore to her mother's funeral and for everyday teaching of the Kingsborough girls. She knew it would not do for London. Furthermore, her bonnet ribbons hung limply from the straw brim like tired worms, and the wooden red cherries along the brim had lost their glossy color and were pale replicas of their former selves. She appeared bedraggled and lost, a real supplicant, not a soon-to-be published author.

Joseph Johnson will find me ugly, Mary knew this; his heart will turn to stone at the sight of me. I had better go back to the inn where the coach arrived and gather my wits over a glass of port or two, that would be the best thing.

However, on her arrival in London, when she passed through the tavern within the inn, a man with a pig under his arm had said: "I am a Tory, but Mr. Furless here, he's a Whig. Say howdy-do, Furless, to the lady." Mr. Furless stuck out his right front hoof like a proper pig.

Another man had asked her what her name was pretty please, and would she dance the quadrille thank you kindly.

They were insane, she reasoned. The world was mad. Furthermore, she had very little money for a stay at the inn. The last guineas Lady Kingsborough had paid her were used to travel from Ireland to

London. From the coast inland, Mary had worried about highwaymen, for they were reputed in that area to be everywhere—behind trees, in gullies, at the bottom of hills. They could pop out of bushes, slit your throat.

Mary raised the knocker one more time, let it thump down.

"Please God," she whispered, though she no longer believed, after Fanny's death. It was merely force of habit and extreme situations which brought out whatever residual piety she might have. "Please let him be home. It is my only chance."

"Coming, coming, hold your horses."

It was a thin, male-servant voice, but too pert by far for a servant. London, of course, encouraged airs among all and sundry. That she knew and deplored.

Then the door swung open, releasing a rush of light. Candle flames and lantern wicks, burning reeds, a whoosh of orange and blue from the fireplace flooded out onto the street, swept her up. Mercy, she thought, feeling scrambled, this is either church or hell.

"Yes, can I help you, madam?"

The servant, she could see, was part of the blaze. Framed in the doorway, he was luminous, a little witchy. Mary imagined him saying, as did the golden Lucifer, "I will not serve." For he was cocky and forward, and without a wig, no powder in his hair, but strands of black hair pulled back and tied behind his ears with a dirty rag. The rest fell forward in a clumsy curtain.

And the nose peeking through this mess was hardly worth mention. Small, a child's, utterly devoid of character. Mary observed the fingernails. Indeed, they were black-rimmed, broken, and very unsavory. How could a prominent publisher have such a servant?

"Mr. Johnson, if you please?" She had to be polite because her dress was dripping on the floor and she wished to see his master.

"Have you an appointment with Mr. Joseph Johnson?" The man was obviously untrained. Have an appointment, a Sunday night?

"Does he expect you? Have you left a calling card?"

"No." The walls were a paneled wainscot. It seemed to her like a ladies' choice. She had heard that Joseph Johnson was not a married man. Perhaps his sister had furnished the house and hired the servant.

"Joseph Johnson is my publisher," she said curtly. "He is publishing two of my books."

The cold was creeping up her back. She did not know how long she could take this interrogation, for she was sensitive to damp, although she could remember once running outside with her sisters, all of them children twirling round and round, their hair spinning out spongy wet as they sang. Rain, rain; rain, rain. Her brother Ned shouted from the window. Come inside this very minute; Father wishes to beat you.

"Ah yes, publisher. Johnson is your publisher?"

"He will be publishing two of my books, and he will be happy to see me." Mary was not sure of this, of course. Really, all she wanted to do was warm herself by the fire, have a nice cup of tea, and get an advance on a new book, so she could stay at the inn until she found employment. She could see herself back at the inn getting used to the pig, Furless, at your service, and telling her name pretty please, thank you, and saying: Yes, Old King George is a merry old soul. I drink to that. Here's a shilling for your thoughts.

"And you, my dear, who may you be, pray tell."

"Mary, Mary Wollstonecraft."

"Ah yes, so you are Miss Mary quite contrary."

"Mr. Johnson is not at home?"

"He is very much at home." Richard in Ireland had called her Miss Mary quite contrary. Who did this man think he was?

"May I see him? Johnson?"

"You are seeing, my dear. Joseph Johnson, at your service."

And he bowed before her as if she were the queen and he Sir Walter Raleigh come for a beheading.

"You, you?" And she had been worried about her dress, her hat, her state of poverty. This man was the Joseph Johnson she had heard of? This upstart was one of the leading publishers in London? This was *her* publisher?

"Not likely," she said.

"Yes, I, I. I have been Joseph Johnson since the day they christened me. It is so very likely as to be entirely true."

"But you . . ."

"Do not look like a publisher?"

"Well, I mean . . ."

"And all the better. Pray tell, what does a publisher look like? Must I wear spectacles? Be a Ben Franklin or Sam Johnson? Should I be fat and old? Do you want me to growl? Grr. You want me to dress better. No, my dear. I prefer to look like Mozart, the *young* Mozart."

"Mozart *is* young."

"You have a point there, but he was younger when he was younger, so to speak. He is a very pretty boy, is he not?"

"You wish to look like a prodigy?"

"I am the prodigal son in the flesh, for I have sinned. Yes, my daughter. Behold."

"My goodness. I thought I left the madhouse at the inn. Is all of London so inclined?"

"All of London. Yes. All. But, good heavens, you look drenched through and through. Come by the fire, warm yourself, my dear."

"Drenched?"

"Yes, drenched, wet, soaking, water tip to toe, drowned rat, oh ugly. Come along, tip-top, do not be a shy one. I do not bite, bite, snap, snap, though I pinch, pinch. No, no, I am harmless, my dear, quite harmless. They call me innocuous Johnson."

"They do?"

He lifted his upper lip on the side, gave out a little snarl. She shuddered. Then he flipped his hair out of his eyes, smiled broadly at her. He had the largest blue eyes she had ever seen. And to her now he seemed beautiful. Oh God, she thought.

"The fire, stand there by the fire, right there, a little to the right, yes, forward, do not singe your skirts, back away a little. Do not be shy. Yes, yes, that is the way."

"Mr. Johnson."

"Joseph, and you must take off your clothes immediately before you catch your death of cold. We cannot have you ill, now, can we? Indeed, we cannot." He busied himself setting her by the hearth and then stoking up the coals, and moving the wing chair closer to the heat. He was a putterer and his hands had a slight tremor. Was it gin poisoning, she wondered. Or perhaps he was epileptic. Perhaps the idea of an unclothed woman.

"Your belongings, my dear, dry clothes?"

"My trunk is at the inn." Mary said that very softly. In truth, there were only a few things in her trunk to change into.

"What?"

"My trunk is at the inn near the coach stop," she repeated loudly. She wondered where the real servants were. Were they lurking behind the corners or at the base of the stairs, hanging upside down from the rafters, hiding under the rug, behind the chair, in the fireplace ready to step out aflame, each word a fireball: Hot bricks in your bed, madam? poking their heads to see who she might be? Somebody without clothes or object to her name? She looked around the drawing room. It was sparsely furnished. A long table spanned its width. There were a few uncomfortable chairs, a beautiful gold-leaf grandfather clock, but most of all, papers and books spread out everywhere. It looked like a school.

"And claret, must get you a glass of claret straightaway."

"Claret?"

"Claret, my dear, alcohol, as in wine, beer, small beer, and whisky if I may make mention, and all the rest which warms the blood and clouds the brain, and truly you must change your clothes. Strong tea, black tea. Yes, yes."

"Truly I have hardly any clothes to change into." She was still standing, for had she sat on the upholstered chair, all would be wet and ruined. "My trunk is at the inn, but even there I have few other clothes to change into. It is a nearly empty trunk. I have my blue cloak . . ." The cloth for that cloak purchased with money borrowed from her brother so that she could appear before Lady Kingsborough as a proper governess.

"That is all? You have nothing else to your name?" Joseph asked.

"Rousseau's *Solitary Walker*, Shakespeare's tragedies, Young's *Night Thoughts*, Locke's *Essay Concerning Human Understanding*, Milton's *Paradise Lost*, a portrait of Mrs. Siddons, a green dress."

"Young's *Night Thoughts*? That *is* choice. Prone to the melancholy mood, are we? And, sweet child, books and no dresses? And a portrait of an actress? Ah, we do feel a wee bit sorry for ourself, do we not? Mrs. Siddons, of all people?"

"I know it is childish, but she was my inspiration. I saw her in Gay's *Beggar's Opera*."

"Ah yes, Captain Macheath, poor Polly Peachum." Johnson put his hand under his chin, curtsied, did a pirouette, became the injured little lady.

"You do not understand, Mr. Johnson. She was the first woman I ever saw on stage, on anything, anywhere, or knew about, the first female, somebody unlike my mother."

"And what is wrong with Mother, pray tell?"

Mary was silent.

"Ah, so we do not want to be Mother? Father? Do we wish to be Father?" Johnson pressed his fingers together in mock seriousness.

"Hardly."

"So Mamma and Papa are not your cup of tea. Luckily, my dear, there are other flavors."

Mary wanted to sit down in the wing chair and quietly go to sleep. But her dress was wet, and her host was too busy to understand her fatigue.

"But why choose a silly actress as your heroine? There are women, Miss Wollstonecraft, who actually *write* plays, nobler by far and great sufferers."

He clasped his chest, reeled about, fell on the floor. Mary looked down at him as he kicked and rolled about.

"Bravo." She clapped. But she had to ask herself: Is this a grown man?

"You are like Dr. Price, but also like my friend Richard. You are very playful."

"Is that good or bad?"

"Good."

"To think I may displease you." He put his hand over his eyes. "Alas."

"I must go back to the inn shortly."

"None of that. You are my honored guest."

It was late at night, raining hard, and she had been traveling several days. "Stay here?"

"Elizabeth Anspach, Aphra Behn, Mary Manley, I could go on and shall one day. But these ladies who put the words into the mouths of the little actresses who flit about tra-la-la-la are far more worth emulating than tra-las."

"As Dr. Price told me."

"A great and noble man, a gentleman of the cloth, a true . . ."

"Are you laughing at Dr. Price?"

"Good heavens, no. Anyway, my dear, you must undress, quiet down, be sensible. A little claret, maybe a meat pie, and I will fetch you a towel. You are a lovely young thing, you know."

"I am almost twenty-nine."

"Yes, well."

"I am not young and I need to hurry."

"To what?"

"To my life."

"But, my dear, you have arrived. You are here, at your life. Put yourself down, settle in. It is yours. You have been living it all along."

"No, Mr. Johnson, I have been dying it. I have frittered away my time and talent, such as it is. My life is . . ."

"Let me guess." He put his arm across his head. "Let me think. Ah, the vision is coming clear. You think your life is a wreck, a ruin, beyond repair, awful, sad, troubled . . . You do not know where you fit in, where you belong, if there is a place for you on the island, on the continent, on the globe, say, why not join our eating club. It meets every Thursday. Let me see . . . gray, such an unusual color for eyes."

Mary had eyes that shifted color, but she did not wish to explain. Perhaps they had gotten watered down as she walked in the rain. She had no umbrella and had occasionally raised her head to the sky to let the rain do its worst, as it always did.

"I am neither young nor lovely."

"Oh, stop. Neither am I. Do I care a fig? I say fie to the world that would insist on such standards. Wounded, sensitive girl, let me tell you how I have suffered . . . Mary, listen. Listen to me closely. This is the city. You are in the city now."

"What does that mean?"

"That means, be strong, live long. Let me get you my dressing gown. I will be within your sight shortly. Do not run away. I will not hurt you. I mean well."

She heard his feet go up the stairs. He was singing, Here's to age and ugliness, in a loud, booming voice. He was wearing slippers, and the cloth made a soft, brushing sound. Shh, shh; shh, shh. Like sleep.

"Here we are." The robe he brought down for her was real French silk, maroon with blue threads running through it like slender snakes.

"I cannot wear that," she said.

"Why not?" He looked hurt.

"Because it is too beautiful."

"Oh, come now. All this false modesty and self-importance."

"It is not false. I am not important."

"Mary, I am to leave the room. You are to take off your dress, place it by the hallway so that Mrs. Mason can dry it out for you tomorrow, and you are to wrap that dressing gown about you. Otherwise, you may find yourself a very sick little girl in the morning. And then you will have something to cry about."

She stood there forlornly.

"What is the matter now?"

"You never let me say a word," she said.

"Oh no, that is not true."

"It is." Her voice rose higher. "I cannot even think. Your antics and . . . you tell me what to do. I cannot do anything."

"Anything? What has there been to do? I believe you arrived on *my* doorstep a bare minute ago. And already you critique my social manner. But not think? And you say I keep you from thinking? You must think at all times, when you go out, when you come in, in the dining room, going to Jericho, even when you are asleep. Do you realize that dreams are a great source of . . . And you, for my tastes, exaggerate, make every little thing into a high bombastic drama. I welcome you and suddenly I am a great hindrance and I do not let you think. This we cannot tolerate."

"Bombastic?"

"Well, maybe not bombastic, maybe not high, but certainly dramatic. Low drama, melodrama. You say an actress is your heroine. *You* are an actress. Does it possibly occur to you that you make your own world of illusions, that the world is your stage and the repository of your illusions about the world . . . You make your life into a tragedy."

"Tragedy is about losing illusions, Joseph. And melodrama is about the dangers of illusions. Yet, if I did not have my illusions, where would I be? Back home. Alone. I would never have written a word, never have come here, never, never, never, never." She stamped her foot. "Never."

"See what I mean about you," he said. "You are . . ."

"Impossible?"

"Impossible. That is it, exactly."

"And you, Joseph Johnson, are, are . . ."

"Yes, yes, do not be shy, tell me the worst. Come on. Do not be a coward. I am not shy. Speak up, woman."

"I, I, I . . . think I am fond of you."

"I beg your pardon."

"No, no, I did not mean that. Goodness, I am sorry. How could I say that? It slipped out."

"Yes, well, slip it back in. I will leave you in peace, fetch the claret, see what is in the pantry. I do believe Mrs. Mason . . . Yes, yes, exactly."

An hour ago she had been on a stagecoach, two days before on a boat coming from Dublin, and here she was in London at her publisher's. She had written two books of little consequence—one on manners, the other a mere novel—and here he was inviting her in and talking to her, not like a woman, but as an equal, an equal friend.

Taking off her dress was like peeling an orange, which she had tasted for the first time in Portugal and it was so tart it had pursed her lips. When she got her stays off, she felt she had removed a suit of armor. For a moment she stood in front of the fire naked. How delicious that felt, all the spots where the stays had poked were free, and her skin unclung seemed stretchy and abundant. Even her insides—her heart and lungs, the long twisted rope of her intestines —seemed to expand. Quickly she drew the dressing gown about her, settled into the chair at last.

Tragedy? he said. She lived her life like tragedy? She knew exactly what he meant. Pride goes before a fall. Excess, enthusiasms were not part of her time. It was 1788, so close the door. This is our box. Please stay away from the edges. He was right. She desperately wanted to live as others did—contained, measured, rationally, with dignity and decorum. What was wrong with her? She could not explain her actions. She had summoned a boy into her bed for stroking like one of Lady Kingsborough's pet dogs, as Annie had treated her. She had felt passion for a boy. On the other side of things, she could not keep her friend Fanny alive. Her school, which was to be an example of its kind, failed miserably. Eliza was right to be bitter, for she, Mary, had let Eliza's child go, out of a kind of lazy selfishness. She could be indifferent to others. Her life was not only without reason but without rhyme. She was too emotional. The emotional had no place in her modus operandi. If anything, tragedy showed the failure of the emotional life. She did not want to be tragic, but rather Roman, stoic, courageous, calm, an example to other women.

Joseph Johnson's dressing gown, which he had placed on the chair, was delicious, like a coat of small, twisting snakes. Mary was reminded of the poisoned robe jealous Medea gave Creusa to wear on her wedding night, which clung, burned, clawed. Chunks of flesh fell from the young bride as she collapsed writhing on the ground. How wonderful, Mary thought, how awful.

Johnson's fire hissed and sputtered in the fireplace as the magic robe curled and uncurled itself. Mary's legs were discreetly tucked under her hips, but they tingled, each hair rising on end like a little soldier at attention. She could smell Joseph on his robe. He smelled of ink and paper, heather. Gratefully she put her head back, and in her dream she was in Ireland again and she was in a meadow and the open book was closed and the young master, Richard the Cripple, took her hand and put it against his cheek.

"I want to be the child," she said.

"You *are* the child," Richard replied.

CHAPTER 14

Oh but a merry man is Danny O'Malley,
A very handsome man from a green, green valley.
One, two, and four coaches to his name
Brought him this day to his hanging fame.
Oh, highwaymen, come listen to me,
Do not twaddle the ladies who make so free
Or you, too, shall fair thee fell
When all souls do unkindly tell.

The sun was splashing in the window in bright splotches. Mary found herself waking in the chair. She could hear horses on the street.

"Good morning, good morning, coffee, I am sure. Mrs. Mason, if you want to know, and please do not be shy and speak up, tell me your wishes, tell me your desires." Mrs. Mason leaned forward conspiratorially. "Tell me your deep, dark needs, my dear; Monday is hanging day, and I shall not be about much longer. Follow me to the kitchen for your coffee. I need to show you about the roast."

Mrs. Mason had the brisk manner of her employer, Johnson, but was easily twice his size and had a big bunch of brown hair in a braided corona around her head, a big black mole on her nose, and a big blue dress shaped like a tent. The woman needed no bustle, no announcement. She wobbled and bobbled wherever she went, and farted gently without excuse.

"Coffee? You have coffee?" Mary said. "It is so dear."

"Oh yes, but he must have it, the master. He just must. And refined sugar and tea and chocolate, all the new luxuries from far-distant ports. I believe he would send Captain Cook himself on errand if he thought there was some delicacy to be newly discovered."

"Where is he now?"

"Morning walk, madam. Every morning."

"My dress?"

"It is dry, rather stiff, I am afraid, but . . ."

"I have no choice."

"Your trunk, Miss Mary?"

"It is at the inn, the one in the Strand."

"Well, we will send for it, straightaway."

"But I do not know where I am going to stay."

"You must stay here. Johnson says so."

"He says so? Why?"

"Because, madam, you have no money and no place to stay and you are a writer and God is good."

"Mr. Johnson is good."

"Indeed he is, madam. Now you sit you right down and tell me the story in your book, the one about *Mary*. I so love a good cry. She had a dear friend, did she not? I have several minutes until hanging."

"A young woman forced into a marriage of convenience travels with her sickly friend," Mary recited.

"Ah, and this friend, somebody you know?"

"Yes, as a matter of fact."

"I thought so, I thought so." Mrs. Mason thumped about the kitchen. "I so love it when somebody dies."

"The friend dies."

"Oh, woe is me, Miss Mary. Friends dying galore. Here is your coffee. It is hot, sip carefully. It is so terrible when a loved one dies. I buried three children. I asked God to take me each time, take me instead, and take me with them. Just take me. But here I am, still here, fat and saucy. Explain the ways of our Maker to me and I will give you a pound."

"I cannot explain."

"Yes, I know. I know." Mrs. Mason clutched her chest. "It is a sad and sorrowful place where we live, Miss Mary, I tell you that. This London town."

"My friend was very dear to me."

"Oh, sorry is the day, madam, sorry is the day."

"When Fanny died, I wanted to die, too, just like you with your children. I had turned from Fanny's deathbed in Portugal, looked across the courtyard, and saw clothes on a line. Clothes. Can you imagine? Bright colors, white sleeves and ruffled skirts, men's breeches flapping in the wind. And a cat was walking along a fence. A cat. From somewhere, a child was calling for his mother. A child. The world was going on. Cats were alive and children called, clothes were hung out. All this was still going on. I could not believe it, I could not endure it, I would not have it. Stop, I wanted to scream, Fanny is dead. Nothing is ever going to be the same again. Stop everything, stop everybody."

"Oh my, my poor Miss Mary."

"But I went on, went back, arriving at the little school I ran in Newington Green in England only to discover that in my absence it had failed. That was when I had to go to Ireland. And from Ireland to London, Joseph Johnson's, where I slept last night in his robe and am now drinking fine imported coffee."

"Oh, but more's the pity, madam, I tell you. It sounds like a book, it does. You could just sit down and write it right down, it is so sad."

"In my book, *Mary*, the woman falls in love with a sensitive consumptive."

"Oh, pity the sick, madam. And beware of the sensitive consumptives. My destiny was read to me when I was a little girl. I was born in Norfolk. And there be many who read hands and throw cards in Norfolk. My reading said I would live a long and unhappy life. Sure enough, the next day I met a crude and coarse harpsichord player, only he would have me believe he was a gentleman what-have-you. And I have had my fill of fiddlers. Every man who can hold a piece of wood under his chin fancies himself a fiddler these days. And do not mention singers."

It was midmorning and Mary and Mrs. Mason were downstairs in the kitchen drinking coffee. Mrs. Mason had a beef roast turning on the spit. When she went to the hanging, Mary was to watch the roast and baste it evenly. The pan catching the drippings had to be moved about a bit under the spit right and left, as the gravy dropped. Later they were to use those drippings to make Yorkshire pudding.

"Your dress," Mrs. Mason said. "You should dress before Mr. Joseph returns. It does not do to dally about when the sun is up."

"Are there many who . . ." And Mary thought of how to phrase it. "Are there young ladies about in the morning, many of them, that is . . ."

"Cannot say that there is. But you must ask him yourself. He publishes many famous and infamous people. Mr. Johnson's guests number Tom Paine, who is a man who will damn himself to save us all, and William Blake, who has visions fixed in the crotch of his pants, methinks. Mr. Johnson publishes books against slavery in America and hanging here, though you must forgive me, I enjoy a good hanging myself, and he rails also against the whipping of animals, and he publishes books that says all children must go to school, *all* mind you, poor as well as rich, girls as well as boys. Miss Mary, you are in the company of a saint and a most strange man. Mr. Johnson says that all religions are one, though he is a Dissenter. That idea he got from that scary Mr. Blake. Papist and Jew going to heaven together and Church of England side by side? But as to young ladies lolling in his dressing gown in the morning, surely that is his very own business. Mr. Johnson is a man of many interests. He does not inquire after my private matters and so I let sleeping dogs lie and snore."

"Yes, of course."

Mary looked up. They were seated in the kitchen at a long table before the hearth. It was the basement of the house, and from the small window she could see people, or rather boots and shoes, on the cobblestones. Occasionally, a horse clip-clopped by.

"I do not inquire into somebody's business."

"Of course."

With her hair down around her shoulders and no face powder, Mary knew she must look like a bereft schoolgirl. But she felt, at least for the moment, secure, almost happy.

"You see, I lost my employment as a governess, Mrs. Mason. I knew nobody, and Joseph had accepted two of my books. I had hoped he would help me."

"To do what?"

"To become, well . . . known."

"Gracious." Mrs. Mason laughed, wrapping up cheese to be put in the cooler, and scraping the extra butter off the churn-staff. "First she is cashiered, and then she wants to be a princess."

"No, I just want . . ."

"What? Say it."

"I want people to see me, listen to me. All that I have undergone I want to be of use, not in vain."

"Aye, are we not all that way, my dear; we wish to be both kept and free. But I must go. Here is Mr. Johnson back."

They heard the door open, footsteps in the hallway, then coming down the stairs.

"Just going," Mrs. Mason said, passing him. "And mind the roast, dearie, will you."

"Yes, hello," Joseph said. He smiled, inclined his head, bowed a little, righted himself, leaned against the wall, swallowed, said Ahem, hung his overcoat on the hook behind the door, and sat down. He looked tired.

"No longer the governess for the Kingsboroughs." He smiled at her conspiratorially. "Coffee. I must have coffee." He lunged for the pot on the stove. "I have heard of them. Tell me, did you hang a dog or merely flog a dog?"

"I would never hang a dog," Mary said angrily.

"Lady Kingsborough is a wonder to behold, is she not, in her manor, yet very Gin Lane. And the young master? Fetching, but really too bad about the old leggy. I have a friend who knows them." Joseph's cheeks were red and his hair flown about. He must have his coffee and small beer and a good hunk of coarse brown bread. "Ireland, but English, is that right? They live in a castle, is that it?" He stuffed some bread in his mouth, sat down. "Like royalty."

"Not exactly."

"Yes, and you wrote that there were three precious little girls. How precious were they?" Joseph smiled wickedly.

"How was your walk, Mr. Johnson?"

"Marvelous, if you must know, Miss Wollstonecraft."

She had not gotten into her dress, not left the kitchen. It was a warm, hospitable place. Across from her chair was a row of copper cups and stewpans and saucepans and frying pans and rolling pins and baking tins and cake hoops and patty pans and dripping pans and sugar cutters and toasting forks and preserving pots, and . . .

"The difficulty with the Kingsboroughs had to do with the children. They grew too fond of me, and their mother grew less so."

"Ah, fond, fond will never do, and I suspect the young master is included. Tsk, tsk, distance, my dear, distance is always the best way to broach things."

"What things?"

"Anything, anything at all, especially to schoolchildren and poetic young men. People who live in the country are desperate for drama and attention."

He put his cup on the table, lowered his lids.

"But you must replace that sorry blue dress drying out upstairs, I think, quite frankly—not to be interfering in matters of wardrobe."

"Black." Was it that Johnson could not tell colors?

"Yes, of course. Tomorrow maybe we must be up and about, buying cloth and going to the dressmaker. I envision you in a green or maybe red."

"How can I buy clothes? I have no employment, no dowry, no money."

"That is a consideration. But perhaps your fortune will change. Some unexpected news arrives from the north, let us say. The mad king is unlaced from his strait waistcoat, digs deep into the Royal Treasury. Provisions are made. A messenger appears. It seems that you, Miss Wollstonecraft, are heir to a rather large fortune. A distant cousin of the Kingsboroughs has admired you from afar. We will have to think about all this in the afternoon when the sun is warm. So much easier to think then. A walk on the Strand perhaps will set things to rights. Yes, indeed, a walk is called for, a think, surely."

Joseph pressed his lips together, settled his hands on his lap. He was slight and delicately made, as if his creator was of two minds at once, male and female. Mary liked that. Most men she found distasteful, with their big stomachs, heavy lips, bad smells, eyes which bulged and rolled the moment a lady came into a room. She remembered in Richardson's *Clarissa* how Clarissa was so offended when the flaccid and fatuous Mr. Solmes (the suitor), pressing himself forward, accidentally stepped on her hoop.

She had to acknowledge not only that Joseph was gracious and kind but that they were sitting in a fine kitchen indeed, with an ice-cream maker and coffee mill, and through the little window at the top they could see the lacy, ruffled edges of fine petticoats and the smart, shiny boots of important men. It was so different from the kitchens she had grown up in, which were sooty and full of menace.

She looked at Joseph sideways. He had not changed his clothes since the day before; indeed, he had slept in them. His face, too, was rumpled and creased. But he seemed oblivious of adornment, and rattled on in great spirit.

"You must stay here. I insist, I mean if you will, you are invited, and I would be most happy. Upstairs are the servants' quarters, but you see I have no servants, believing as I must that we must serve ourselves and that such distinctions as master/servant are pernicious to all. Mrs. Mason, a most excellent woman, helps me with my meals. But she is not a servant."

"I see."

"And all such distinctions between people are false and arbitrary."

"Yes."

"Let us go upstairs to the drawing room."

The rain had stopped early that morning and through the windows—for Joseph had not bricked them up, as many did, in order to avoid paying the window tax—came enough light that they did not have to set out lamps or candles. She had fallen asleep in the chair in Joseph's dressing gown. Early in the morning, still half asleep, she had heard carts carrying food coming from the country to market.

"My dear, let me be frank. I have an altogether selfish motive in asking you to stay here." Joseph folded his hands together, paced before her. "Let me get right to the point. A friend, Thomas Christie, and I are starting a journal. When I saw you on my doorstep, I felt God had sent you. We need help, my dear little waif."

"A journal? I am not a waif."

"Yes, a monthly publication. I publish books. Why should I not publish a magazine."

"Really?"

"The title page would look like this."

And he jumped up, ran into the other room across the hall, and brought out a sheet. It said:

The Analytical Review
or
History of Literature
Domestic and Foreign
Containing
Scientific Abstracts of Important
and Interesting Works
Published in English;
A General Account of such
as are of less consequence,
with Short Characters,
Notices, or Reviews
of Valuable
Foreign Books;
Also the
Literary Intelligence of Europe, etc.

"Book reviews," she said. "A journal of book reviews?"

"That is to be precisely it, my dear."

"And what is it you wish me to do?" She imagined sweeping the floor of paper and sharpening pen nibs, pouring ink, straining sand, running errands, straightening desks, fetching cups of tea, taking the manuscript over to Fleet Street to the printer.

"Write. Write—what do you think I would ask you to do?"

"I? You mean that I should write reviews?"

"Yes, you, you. Who else is in this room at this moment?"

"The cat."

"I do not mean the cat, dear girl."

"As far as I know, there are no women working at magazines, Joseph. Except for the women's magazines . . ."

"So, surely, that should excite you, this chance. The only woman."

"Oh yes, but . . ."

"What is this 'Oh yes, but'?"

"Nothing. But I think it a shame to be the *only* woman."

"We presently have space for one person, one more person to help. Are you presently engaged in another undertaking?"

"No, I am not. It is just . . ."

"My dear, I assure you that you will have time to write books. *Pamela*s will come out of your ears. *Tom Jones*es will drip from your fingertips . . ."

"Joseph, you do not take me seriously."

"Ah, but I do."

He put his finger under her chin and she felt like a cat purring for its dinner.

"The reviews I would write, Joseph, how would they go, what would they be about, how can I learn these subjects?"

"You know them already, my dear." And he reached out to pat her knee, for by now his chair was very close to hers.

"What do I know?"

"You know what it is to be a woman."

"And you know what it is to be a man."

"Yes, exactly, but I am going to do the scientific articles. You would review books to do with women and children, books on manners and the proper education of children. Women's topics, what else?"

"Oh." A moment before, she had expected to sweep the floor, and now, she did not know why it was, but she felt disappointed. She hung her head, stared down. The sun seemed to have gone out a little, for the ray coming through the window was feeble and tentative. Mary sighed. Women's topics. She knew what that meant: female hygiene, childbirth, the proper way to curtsy, the art of counterfeit.

"What is the matter?"

"If I do the women's articles, why do you not do the men's articles?"

"There are no men's articles, in the sense you mean. But why consider your contribution trivial? Are children and their education of no consequence?"

"Review books on the education of children?"

"Were you not a governess and the headmistress of your own school?"

"Yes, yes I was. But my school failed, and I was let go as a governess."

"So you must have some ideas. Have you not just written a book on the education of daughters?"

"Ideas? Yes, I do, I do have ideas. I believe the early education of girls should not differ from that of boys, that they should learn rationality no less than . . . I believe that girls should make their bodies strong and useful . . ."

"Well, then."

"And . . ."

"And you must stay here in this house with me. That is definite."

"Your neighbors, people will think . . ."

"Think what?"

"That I am a fallen woman, that what they are witnessing is my daily fall."

She thought of Lucifer, Milton's friend, hurtling through the sky very slowly, head over heels.

"They will think what they will, and let us leave them to their faulty logic, for what do we care finally when all is said and done."

His eyes glazed over. She could tell he was not thinking of her at all, but of something else. Why *did* he want her to stay?

"For the truth of the matter is not that you are my finely kept mistress, that you will pleasure me in those ignoble ways, that we live in chaos betwixt sin and death . . ."

"Ignoble? Are you quoting Milton?"

"But that we are working together in the great cause of . . ."

"Yes, yes. Literature, letters, the life of the mind."

"Are you making fun of me, Miss Mary?"

"Heavens, no. Why would I do a thing like that?"

He sighed. "I am tired. Let me show you your room."

Johnson had made her take off her wet skirts the night before and placed them, with the petticoat, near the hallway. They had been like seaweed. Her bodice was as stiff as a drying starfish, and as muggy. The whalebone stays lay on the floor, a beached sea turtle.

The silk robe Joseph had loaned her was made by the French weavers who lived in France, and not those who lived and worked in Spitalfields, where she grew up. The night before, Joseph had gone down to the kitchen in the basement, holding a candlestick before him, to bring up claret, and later unlocked his tea caddy, gotten out tea and put the kettle on the coals of the fire. Meat pies, fruit pies, crumbs and flakes brown and buttery about her lap.

Joseph fed the fire, fed her. Now it was nearly afternoon when he led her up the winding stairs to her room in the attic with its low ceiling of dark wood beams, and the walls whitewashed clean, smelling of resin and rosewater.

"Your day will be your night," Joseph said. Mary thought of the poem "Nocturnal Reverie," by Anne Finch, Countess of Winchilsea, which ended with:

> *Till morning breaks, and all's confused again;*
> *Our cares, our toils, our clamours are renewed,*
> *Or pleasures, seldom reached, again pursued.*

The room was perfect. Each piece of furniture seemed necessary and natural. The table mushroomed from the floor sturdy and dark, polished in a gloss which invited the placement of white paper. The chair sprouted from the floor, the smell of earth still spread on its legs, and its arms held her like branches, firm and true. The bed was rooted, a flat patch of mattress, a plain coverlet of dull green.

"Nobody has ever been this good to me," she said to Joseph.

"That is too bad."

"My life has been a series of disasters, Joseph."

Joseph yawned. "Come on, Mary. Talk to anybody, it is the same story. It begins with getting born."

"It does?"

"So think of now. How are you now?"

"Now I am grateful to you."

"I do not know what to say, Mary. It is all too, too"—and he grasped his hands in front of him—"touching." He teetered back, braced himself against the wall.

"Silly goose," she said.

"Silly goose? I intend to go on stage one of these days and you will have to pay money to see this."

Mary got into her bed. It was just right, and she fell into a most delicious sleep.

CHAPTER 15

Joseph Johnson
requests the pleasure of your company
at Thursday-night dinner
72, St. Paul's Churchyard
London
Thursday, June 6th, 1788
5:00—10:00 p.m.
RSVP by June 1, Mary Wollstonecraft
72, St. Paul's Churchyard

It was a salon of sorts. There was the strange Mr. Blake, for one. No matter that he was funny-looking, Mr. Blake, the engraver, painter, poet, visionary, claimed to have seen the face of God in a tree, as if God were some large kite caught in the branches or a blinking owl with a long white beard living among leaves and berries.

"Blake, happy as a lark, sees God's face in flowers, too," Mrs. Mason said, beating her cake. "The man should be in an asylum, the amount of things he sees."

Mary imagined how terrifying it would be to look at a daisy and imagine God with the petals as hairy flames and face as a collapsing center. If he was religious, how was William Blake able to believe that he saw that face and not died? Moses, himself, had to turn away from God.

"I do not believe any of it, Joseph."

"Leave Blake alone. He is a mystic and a poet."

"What does *Himmel* mean?" She was working on her translation in the kitchen. Joseph had popped down for a coffee.

"Heaven."

"*Danke.*" She dipped her quill, scratched "heaven," worked to the end of the line, sprinkled sand. Translating had a soothing feel. The other language was like a house you went into and gradually became accustomed to.

"*Wahrheit?*"

"Truth."

While Mary worked at the long table downstairs, Joseph worked at the long table upstairs. He was getting a manuscript ready for the printer.

"Mr. William Blake is almost too dreamy to talk to," Mrs. Mason continued.

"He abides in his own birdcage of a mind."

"Do not we all?" Mrs. Mason wiped her mouth on her sleeve.

Actually, the Thursday-night eating club had discussed Bedlam in reference to Blake when it was found out that Blake gave his wife reading lessons out in the yard naked. Just teaching her to read, Blake protested, as if it came through the pores of the skin, and the more skin exposed, the faster the absorption. Everybody at Joseph's table laughed at that. Naked, they all repeated. Mary looked at Joseph, wondered how he might look naked, though she had seen his chest and back, the calves of his legs. He had a small but strong body. She wondered what it would be like to walk about unclothed, leaves and bushes brushing against your thighs and the breeze puckering your nipples like lips against pomegranates.

"And Paine. Paine is a pain," Mrs. Mason said. "Another one."

"Only a man, Mrs. Mason," Joseph said, reappearing downstairs.

Tom Paine, cordially invited to Thursday night, was a pamphleteer who had written bold words designed to inspire the Americans to throw off English tyranny.

"I am the Revolution," he was fond of saying, as if he carried within an eternal light of rebellion.

Mary found him to be only an ugly stay-maker with a mouth full of higgly-piggly teeth, his skin ruddy with pockmarks. He ate like a pig at slops, slurping his soup and burping his beef and farting his fritters. Mary could not stand to sit beside him. Where shall we put Paine? was the question at every dinner party. At the end of the table, was always the answer. But Paine could move a stone by his rhetoric, would die for you if you asked him, could design iron bridges. Listening to Tom Paine, Mary could believe that people had the power to change their lives, as in fact had happened when a handful of buckskin rustics, hiding in bushes with muskets, farmers from Concord and Lexington, defeated His Majesty's Army.

"King George was in his counting house and starting to go mad, though they had removed the restraints of his strait waistcoat, when that happened," Joseph said.

"I hope this is not one of your scandalous stories, Joseph." Mary was hoping to concentrate on her translation.

"Not at all. This story is treasonous. Pray let me continue.

"The latticed windows let in the most filtered of light onto the stone-flagged floor. George, pacing, tried not to step on a crack (that would spell death to the royal family), while phalanxes of redcoats with rows of brass buttons, Ready, Aim, Fire, went bravely to their death, row upon row upon row. When the drumbeat stopped and the smoke cleared, and the field was running ribbons of red and gold, what good were their wigs to them then?"

"Not funny, Joseph; men dying."

"Funny enough. When Adam delved and Eve did span, who was the gentleman, then. I ask you."

Joseph had toy soldiers, which he would set up in mock battle on gray Sunday afternoons, redcoats and the French, Austrians and Prussians.

"Wissenschaft?"

"Knowledge."

"Writing is a revolutionary act," Tom Paine told them all at one of the dinners.

"Hear, hear, my good fellow."

"You are positing an alternative world, one that was not there before, perhaps an ideal world, whatever you say. By that fact alone, writing is a revolutionary act."

"Vive la Révolution."

Joseph said to Mary that he was fearful that Paine would end up in a sorry way. A sickness, nobody to call, a wretched room somewhere with mice skittering along the floor and brown, damp sheets, a long fever, coughs into the night. I am the man who wrote *Common Sense*, he would tell the mice, I am the man who helped with the American Declaration of Independence and knew Jefferson and Franklin. The mice would titter, nibble at the sheets, squeak: "Is that so?"

"No," Mary chided. *"Nein, nein, nein."* But she was afraid it would happen to all of them, that they would die miserably and alone in seedy circumstances without benefit of any human comfort. Famous or not, was that the fate of old age? She knew she would never grow old.

"We are the bookworms," Joseph sang out in the kitchen. "We are the proud and happy bookworms."

Mary had gotten a new dress after the first month especially for the Thursday-night occasions. There had not been time earlier. The dressmaker said it was the latest fashion from Paris, with a crisscross shawl like Martha Washington's, high-waisted like Marie Antoinette's current style—everybody was being a peasant these days (J. J. Rousseau's influence), and of a green-and-white stripe, Catherine the Great's favorite colors—cotton imported from India. There was a touch of the harem in that dress, too, like the awning of a tent, and Mary, who had been to Portugal to nurse her dying friend Fanny Blood, recalled the wonderful blue-and-green-tile fountains at the end of the streets, nobody there, in the old Alfama Quarter, the afternoon hot and still, only the sound of the water falling.

"I hope my dress is not ending an English life," Mary said to Joseph, "putting English weavers out of work."

"Never mind that, Mary, my love."

Some of the English weavers were destroying their looms in protest over the cheaper Indian cloth. In France, Mary heard, the women wore their dresses damp in order to have them cling suggestively to their bodies, though some of them died of it. She wondered if Joseph would peer at her more carefully if her dress was damp.

"Have you read *The Wealth of Nations*, by Adam Smith," Mr. Fuseli politely asked Mary one time. He was another Thursday-night dinner guest.

"No, I have not."

"Should. It has been out fifteen years and explains how the world works."

Henry Fuseli was small, with a huge head which made him look like a great brown frog, and his eyes, which took one in as if one's skirt and bodice, shawl and stays, cap and stockings had dropped off and lay at one's feet, bulged unbecomingly. He was a famous artist, and rumored, though married, to like men as well as women in that way. Mary thought of two mustaches brushing. And his art was of the most salacious sort. What way did he like men? She would have to ask Mrs. Mason—she who had nine, or was it ten, children. At least they would know how to take off each other's cravats and tie them, too. Joseph had asked her to help him tie his cravat once and she had failed miserably.

"You have wonderful green eyes, like a snake's." Fuseli told her.

"Hazel. My eyes are hazel," though she knew they changed color according to the light.

Could he, an artist, not know colors like Joseph? That would be impossible. At least he did not see God's face right and left like that William Blake or think he was the Revolution.

"Do we have to invite Fuseli again, Joseph? Give me another word for monumental."

"Big, tremendous, huge, impressive. Of course. He is very popular at court."

"He is?"

"The king is going to designate him painter of the court or something like that. Royal Academy."

"Quite a distinction to be appointed by King George."

"Listen, Mary, we are not the only country run by a man on the verge of madness. I have heard some horrendous tales about Catherine the Great."

Mary narrowed her eyes.

"Tales? *Sagen Sie mir alles.*"

"You are learning, you are learning."

"What is *Dummkopf?*"

In Fuseli's picture *The Nightmare*, an impish devil was poised on the knee of a sleeping woman, her diaphanous gown nearly off, and within the curtains stood a horse with glaring orbs for eyes. It made Mary think of a passage from a poem by Edward Young which went:

From dreams, where thought in fancy's maze runs,
To reason, that heaven-lighted lamp in man,
Once more I wake; and at the destin'd hour,
Punctual as lovers to the moment sworn,
I keep my assignation with my woe.

"Her eyes are blue as the morning," Blake said. "Not green at all." Blake held his knife in a pretty way, much like a lady. Fuseli held his knife clutched in his paw like a barbarian. Joseph, of course, had his own way. He would cut everything up into small pieces and then eat delicately with his fingers. Sometimes he popped a morsel into Mary's mouth.

"My eyes are brownish."

"A revolutionary red," Paine insisted. "From staying up all night on the people's behalf."

"Gray as the sky, as a rainy sky."

"I see green, green eyes," Fuseli replied, as if that settled it. "Emerald green, cat green, green, et cetera."

"See what you will," Thomas Christie concluded, "but it can be empirically verified by experimentation that her eyes are brown."

"This *is* an empirical experiment, Thomas," Fuseli sneered.

"I abstain, then," Thomas Christie said. It was dinnertime and yet Christie looked as if he had just risen. Actually, he was always coming from some bed, since he read late into the night, and late in the afternoon. His ring of blond curls was in a jumble over his head. His cravat was askew. If Blake had his visions and Fuseli his fantasies and Paine his fanaticism and Christie his wine and ladies, what had Joseph?

Dr. George Fordyce, the physician, said nothing about Mary's eyes. He had his profession, was a member of the Royal College of Surgeons, and was a dour, most silent man.

"I have no eyes," Mary finally said. "They are a figment of your imagination. So if they exist, they are at your beck and call."

"Like Bishop Berkeley," Joseph said.

"All sensible things therefore are in themselves insensible, and to be perceived only by our ideas," Fuseli quoted.

"No, my dear friends," Mary pointed out. "Not like Bishop Berkeley, but like men, like people of your sex. Yes, you will have my eyes what you will, not what they are or what I like. They are hazel, but change in different light. They are *my* eyes."

Later Fuseli will tell her: *That* is when I knew I must have you. Beck and call. What a coup.

Several years later Godwin will say: It was *then* that I understood what a fine mind and excellent woman you were and that we must be united.

Blake will say that at that moment she inspired him to invite a second woman into his marriage.

And Dr. George Fordyce, some ten years thence, looking straight into her eyes, saw them change all different colors, going red to a bright, brilliant black, and green as spring meadows to autumn brown, to blue to gray to gone.

"Gentlemen, excuse me."

"Mary," Joseph said.

"I am going to bed."

Mary got up, tears in her eyes, pushed back her chair, nearly tipping it.

"Mary," Joseph said, following her into the hall.

"Why do I have to be a subject of discussion?" she hissed.

"No harm intended."

"I am tired of all this."

"Of all what? Friends? Good talk?"

"You are impossible, Joseph."

"I am?"

"*Ruhe!* What does that mean?"

"Be silent."

She turned to the stairs. He turned back to his guests.

"She gets that way," she heard him explain. "She can be very . . . but brilliant, a brilliant woman."

And then somebody opened the door and the wind blew, setting the chandelier tinkling, a hundred little pieces of glass knocking one against the other.

CHAPTER 16

July 14, 1788

Dear Everina,

Dr. Samuel Johnson when he was alive had his dinner with his group in his narrow, modest house right off Fleet Street. He had the actor Garrick and that officious fool, Boswell, who has had gonorrhea several times, the man could not leave well enough alone. Edmund Burke, that vacillating hypocrite, and Sir Joshua Reynolds, the portrait painter whom Blake hates with a weary and enduring passion, filled out their table. Our artists are Blake, Fuseli, Opie. Over there they were the aristocrats, the Blue Stockings. We, we, labor in the vineyard.

The food for these literary dinners can be quite exotic if one can afford: sea turtles from India and pickled mangoes from India, ketchups from China and Malaya, not to mention Cheddar and Gloucester cheeses right from England. People eat a great deal here in London. A regular dinner could be roast beef, roast pork, chicken, veal and ham pies, fish, tarts, cheese, puddings and fruit.

Mrs. Mason comes in early Thursday morning for the company dinner, a little past daylight. Puddings are her forte. Boiled and baked, rice or oatmeal, vermicelli, sago, custard. Sweet baked puddings can be done with curds, fruits and almonds. She can do puff pastry crusts for her puddings and uses carrots, spinach.

Mrs. Mason also fancies strawberry fritters and gooseberries, damsons, and celery. Our dinner may also have beetroot pancakes, described by Elizabeth Raffald in her The Experienced English Housekeeper as *"a pretty corner dish for dinner or supper."*

The recipe is as follows, Everina:

6 oz peeled cooked beetroot
2 tbs brandy
3 tbs double cream
4 egg yolks
2 tbs plain flour
1 tsp caster sugar
1 tsp grated nutmeg
clarified butter

Mash the beetroot as finely as possible and mix with the other ingredients. Heat a shallow layer of clarified butter in a frying pan. Drop the beetroot mixture from the point of a tablespoon into the butter and shake the pan to flatten if necessary. Turn down the heat, as these burn very easily. Turn the pancakes over—they will cook quickly. Wipe out the pan if necessary between batches. These unusual delicate pancakes are good hot or cold. Garnish with green sweetmeats, preserved apricots, or green sprigs of myrtle.

I sometimes review cookbooks for the Analytical Review *and know whereof I speak and can recommend without equivocation Mrs. Glasse's* The Art of Cookery made Plain and Easy. *Trusler in* The Honours of the Table, *1788, cautions us that you must avoid "smelling to the meat whilst on the fork" for that would show that you suspect the meat is tainted. Further, "It is exceedingly rude to scratch any part of your body, to spit, or blow your nose . . . to lean your elbows on the table, to sit too far from it, to pick your teeth before the dishes are removed."*

I remove myself after dinner, for that is when the port and pot are passed and the gentlemen relieve themselves right there in the dining room so as not to miss one single pearl of conversation. The pot is a large, vase-like bowl, Wedgwood, a Chinese motif, fit repository of many repasts. Two men must carry out and dump the slops.

Yours ever, Mary

In the morning, Mary would take a long walk, tramping down Thames Street and across London Bridge, going as far as the George Inn in Southwark. She would observe horses and coaches, grooms and ostlers, and servants shaking out rugs and sleeping quilts from the galleries. It would be early yet for sedan chairs, great ladies with their piled hair, fur-trimmed shawls, tasseled sashes, and Brussels lace. Passing the fanciest drapers on Ludgate Hill, where only the richest ladies and most successful prostitutes bought their cloth, Mary would dream of the time she could indulge her passion for pretty cloth. On some days, when she was less inclined to walk far, Mary would simply cross Blackfriars Bridge, but had to be careful of pickpockets and beggars. It would be too early for any but the most hardy prostitutes.

Afterward, she would return to do a full three hours' work on the translation she was doing for Joseph, now Necker's *De l'Importance des opinions religieuses/On the Importance of Religious Opinions*.

She was pretending French as she had German.

Often she and Joseph sat down to a pleasant luncheon in Bird-in-Hand Court, Cheapside—a joint of mutton they would have, cabbage, bread, and beer—and in the afternoon Joseph would go to the Chapter coffeehouse in Paternoster Row, where booksellers and writers sat and chatted about their business. No women, of course, and Mary had to console herself at the Thomas Twining Tea Shop for Ladies, and on Sundays at the Vauxhall Gardens and sometimes the New Tunbridge Wells tea gardens. She wished to frequent the famous Beefsteak Club in Fleet Street, or to go to the Kit-Kat, to eat among royalty. Not possible.

The *Analytical Review* was going well enough. Mary worked hard over her contributions. She felt she was making progress.

Article XIII, the *Analytical Review*, July 1788, *Emmeline, the Orphan of the Castle*, by Charlotte Smith, in 4 vols, Pr. 12s.

> *Few of the numerous productions termed novels claim any attention; and while we distinguish this one, we cannot help lamenting that it has the same tendency as the generality, whose preposterous sentiments our young females imbibe with such avidity. Vanity thus fostered takes deep root in the forming mind, and affectation*

banishes natural graces, or at least obscures them . . . But we
must observe that the false expectations these wild scenes excite
tend to debauch the mind and throw an insipid kind of uniformity
over the moderate and rational prospects of life, consequently adventures *are sought for and created, when duties are neglected,*
and content despised . . . Despair is not repentance, nor is contri-
tion of any use when it does not serve to strengthen resolutions of
amendment.

M.

When Mary read in print what she had written, she was astounded. How strong I sound, she thought, how confident, how sure
I am about what women need. Was this the bedraggled sparrow who
had knocked on Johnson's door less than a year ago? Sometimes when
she lay in bed now, she could not sleep with the many ideas which
chased around her head. They were like white foxes—tabula rasa, the
consent of the governed, liberty, moral knowledge, complex impressions, simple perceptions, good night, good night, good night.

MARY KNEW that Joseph favored anchovies with Parmesan cheese as a side dish, that he read each night, had *Tristram Shandy* by his bed, that he liked backgammon and could dance the quadrille, loved best the play *She Stoops to Conquer*.

His bedroom was two floors directly below hers. She imagined his candle sputtering by his bed, and the sheet about his knees and the shirt scrunched up above his chest. She would stretch herself out on the floor of her bedroom, the rough boards cold and scratchy, putting her arms like Christ in supreme agony.

Is this enough? she would ask the room, the sky, the night, the moon. Is this what you want? With Richard of the Little Foot, there had not been this torture. It had been sweet and tender and certainly until the end without a pang of mistrust. The friendship had flowed like soft liquid. This was quite the opposite.

Outside the window, the sky was dense and silent, the stars faraway and indifferent, and truth opaque, unattainable. Why do I not just die, Mary asked herself. All this distress, and for what? Nothing added up or evened out or made sense. She was always at odds with herself, a jangle of nerves; it was not fair.

All that it had taken was a few looks, a touch here and there, lightly on the shoulder, once on the waist, and constant, daily contact. Mary? Yes, Joseph. She turned to him like a sunflower, her face pure and open. In the back of her mind she could hear wind. She noticed his upper lip curved up in the middle. She wanted to touch him there.

These thoughts were unworthy, she believed, of an *Analytical* reviewer and translator and author and grown woman. Furthermore, what right did she have to indulge in this kind of childish nonsense? Had serious men like Ben Franklin, looking over his glasses quizzically,

had thoughts of a lascivious nature? Well, truthfully, she had heard
that he had an illegitimate child. Yet Sam Johnson, had he created an
uproar every time he crawled into his wife's bed? He had, she had
heard, though the woman was a good deal older than he, and boys at
his school had laughed to see such passion. Jefferson himself had a
Negro mistress, it was rumored. Mary imagined the fair-skinned red-
headed Jefferson, drawn, like a moth, to the warmer hue. So all were
liable and none invulnerable.

She was afraid, though, that she was the lone female of such
predisposition. There would be, no doubt, a special place for the likes
of her, a kind of celestial poorhouse overseen by Father Time and
monitored by Mother May I. John Wesley himself would disdain her
excess. She dared not think of the Reverend Dr. Price. John Calvin.
Thomas More. Assorted Popes. She stood accused. She loved Joseph.

And like Blake she began to see things in the light of present
obsessions. One vision was a steady parade of self-flagellating Spanish
monks, with whips and tortures, and in deep pain. These thirteenth-
century bridegrooms were engaged in a love so impossible that they
could only hope for purgation, sharp cuts, at the very least affixing the
dull ache which pervaded the body and muddled the brain to a definable
spot, a welt, a sore, a scratch, a bruise.

How ashamed she would be of herself, having such strange as-
sociations, and in apology would pull out clumps of her hair, think of
snow, not eat, turn to the wall, cry.

Usually, the inevitable end to her tortures was beyond her control.
No better than Annie, finding herself on her own bed or standing up
against the wall, or crouching like an animal, skin to her own skin,
joining herself to herself, she would hiss out at the last second his name:
Joseph.

This subterranean side lay buried while she did translations at
the long table, French and German, on bits and pieces of paper strewn
about with English and Blake's engravings. Reviews were quick; she
did not spend time muddling, but went straight to it. She read in bed
on good nights, and, right before falling asleep, began to plan out
Original Stories, a guide for parents.

Furthermore, she now had enough money to send Eliza and Everina, governesses in Scotland, a set sum every month and to buy fabric for her own dressing gown.

"A dressing gown?" Joseph asked.

"Yes, so I do not have to wear yours."

"Ah, yes."

"I want to buy the fabric for my new dressing gown on Monday, Joseph. I have already seen the cloth, an expensive Indian print at Robert Gibbons's drapery shop in Ludgate Hill. Red and blue flowers, golden fringe along the border."

The fabric lay waiting for her among the cambric and chintz, the Persian, the black bombazine, crepe, muslin, cottons, linens, and wools.

"I will take six yards of that," she heard herself saying, Joseph at her side. "I can afford it."

Joseph had in mind something crisp and ruffled, whereas she planned on something silky smooth. He thought a nice bright color. She knew it had to be muted. She wanted something like that first night, when, wearing his dressing gown, she felt there was something alive and dangerous on her. It would be a chemise. She would have the dressmaker sew a round, low neckline and a high waist, so that her heavy hips would fan out under their curtain of cloth like mutton chops, tasty and succulent, each jiggle a ripple, each breath a slight straining. Under the bust would be small gathers attending to the rise of flesh like cupped hands. The cloth, slippery and shimmery, would be a promise of what lay underneath, and could fall easily off her shoulders. It would be the texture of her fidelity and the color of her desire and the pattern of her love. Talisman, enticement, symbol, the dressing gown would determine the directions and motions of his heart.

"Monday," Joseph said, "there is to be a guest for dinner, not the usual Thursday group, but somebody I am cultivating."

"Cultivating?" Mary looked up from her work.

"Well, I have cultivated you, have I not?"

"I am not a hothouse flower, you know."

"Ah, the lady speaks back."

"Nor a child."

"That is what I love about you, Miss Cucumber."

He was always saying that, "what I love about you." Never "I love you."

Mary went downstairs to the kitchen. Mrs. Mason had come in that Sunday afternoon and was presently rolling out pastry. Sheets of it lay across the marble top of the kitchen table. It was still cool down there and Mary longed to put her face down, press her cheeks against the smooth surface of flour.

"Is this to be a grand dinner, then, tomorrow?" Mary asked.

"Go along with you, Miss Mary. Drink your coffee and be merry."

"Who is this person who is coming?"

"You look tired, child."

Did it show, then, could Mrs. Mason tell, Mary wondered. There was a dull, burnished looking-glass which hung by a gold chain near the front door, and when Mary looked in it in passing, unable to resist, she saw a depraved woman, her eyes ringed with dark circles like a forest animal's, her hair a fluff of disorder, her mouth set at a sluttish slant.

"Oh dear, oh dear, I look a fright, do I not?" she would say to herself falsetto, but seriously worried that it did show, her desperate nights, her depraved practices.

"So who is this person, Mrs. Mason? Tell me."

"Oh, Miss Mary."

"By the authority vested in me by our good King George, I, Mary Wollstonecraft, command you."

"A young man."

"A young man?"

"He is a writer."

"A young man?" Mary's spirits soared. She was deliriously happy. "Just a man? You are sure it is a young man, Mrs. Mason. You promise? Not a young lady?"

"Good God, Mary. I promise on my mother's grave and my father's head and . . ."

"I am satisfied. That is wonderful. A man. I am happy. The royalty and all the children of the realm thank you." Mary performed a deep bow.

"Get on with you."

"No, really, I *am* for once happy."

"Are you really?"

"Without a doubt, Mrs. Mason, without a doubt. Tomorrow will be a wonderful day."

"You base your happiness on something so small?"

"Is it small?"

"A thread, my dear, which may break at any time."

"No, you do not understand."

"But I do, love, I do."

CHAPTER 18

THE WEATHER, to start out with, was not that wonderful. It was one of those rare hot days in London, with the air thick and fetid, and the streets full of hungry, mangy dogs. St. Paul's dull green dome shimmered in the heat like a moldy breast. Mary woke that day out of sorts. Despite her high hopes, she had gone to bed peevish, Mrs. Mason's comment had troubled her, and that night she had dreams that made her cry in her sleep. Eliza's baby had hovered in the dark rafters. Once Mary had even gotten out of the bed, walked to the door, not knowing she was doing it.

Despite the heat, Joseph was unusually dressed for their morning walk. He appeared in vest and morning coat, and breeches and white silk stockings. He had new buckles on his shoes, and a cravat knotted stylishly in a bow, and flowing tails. It looked like a big silk moth at his neck. And his coat was an unsavory green.

"Dressing gown," he twittered as they rounded the corner of the block the draper's was on.

"Dressing gown," she sang back, regaining her spirits.

When she had entered the shop a week before, Mr. Gibbon had saluted her with: "Garden silks, Italian silks, Geneva silks, fine thread satins, both striped and plain, wools, cotton, mohair silks, Norwich crepes, silks for hoods and scarves, and right tartans."

But the street was empty now and eerily so. When they got to the shop it was boarded up. On the street, there were no street criers, no merchants, no bookstalls out, no wagons or fine ladies in phaeton or chaise. The place was completely empty.

A ballad sheet in a hot gust of wind blew against Mary, caught in her skirts, a three-legged cat hobbled in front of her, a woman hurried toward them.

"Where is everybody?" Mary asked.

"Gone to the hanging, dearie, four to be hanged."

Mary had to lean against Joseph for support.

"Of course," he said. "Monday is a hanging day, and all off to attend."

"Heaven help us," Mary replied, tasting again from deep in her throat the breakfast roll and butter, coffee.

"Have you never been to a hanging, my dear?" Joseph asked, twirling his cane.

"No."

"Not ever?" He tapped her skirt lightly.

"I do not want to go."

"Ah, then, you must, you surely must. It is a major spectacle of our time."

"I do not want to go."

"A venerable English custom, part of your education."

"You are mocking me."

"Indeed not. It *is* part of your education. Are you not a lady who wishes to write of serious matters?"

"Yes, but . . . I do not have to be in Bedlam to write of Bedlam, and to be in Bedlam probably means I cannot write of Bedlam."

"Mary, Mary. So emotional."

"That is not good, is it?"

"No. Not good at all."

"A feminine trait?"

"Decidedly."

"Joseph . . ."

"And to be able to look unflinching on all that is reality?"

"But you are against hanging, Joseph, you yourself . . ."

"Not only on principle, my dear, but because I have seen it. I know it from my experience. Have not Locke and Hume and . . ."

"Are you saying that we can only talk and write of what we directly . . . You are saying that."

"No, of course not. But when we can, we should, for, after all, we are cowards if we do not look the enemy in the face. Do you not think so?"

Joseph printed books against the slavery of the Negroes in America, Mary repeated to herself. He was a good man and a Dissenter who believed that people had the right to worship as they pleased. He even extended this to Jews and Catholics, Methodists and Quakers. Like Blake, he did not believe that children should be put to work, but rather sent to school. He thought animals should be treated kindly and women learn trades. He had looked much in the face, thought for himself. She was being foolish and skittish.

The hanging procession started out at Newgate. Led by the condemned carts, a long snake of people, raucous and drunken, made its way past St. Sepulchre's Church. They followed slowly, the S of the snake bulging out in bunches and bundles, along Snow Hill and down Holborn Hill, and from there down Oxford Street to Tyburn Road toward the ultimate destination, Tyburn Tree. The drums beat out a dirge.

Bum, bum, bum, bum, bum.

The sun by then was high in the sky and the slight wind of the morning had come to a dead standstill. Beads of sweat now gathered along Mary's upper lip. She could feel wetness between her stays, which were digging out of her bodice and would make, she knew, a ridge of welts under her breasts as if she had been cupped there for blood. Her thighs rubbed together and would, no doubt, be red on the insides.

Three of the criminals to be hanged that day were grown men of twenty or so, but one was only a boy, lean and crying like a baby.

They were arranged, all four, one for each cart, on their coffins while the chaplain in the first cart led them all in Psalms.

Earlier, St. Sepulchre's bell had pealed the funeral knell while the clerk intoned: "You that are condemned to die, repent with lamentable tears, ask the mercy of the Lord for salvation of your souls."

"What did they do," Mary asked a woman. It was the same one they had met on Ludgate Hill. She seemed to have attached herself to them.

"Why, love, they be thieves." The woman had no teeth and had to work her mouth like a cow. And several times along the way, she had stopped to open her legs, relieve herself like a cow in the field. No going into the alley and squatting like the other women, stepping daintily away from it, holding up her skirts. Oh no, this one cared nothing for that. Her great breasts dangled and dingled like a cow's. Her face spouted hair like an onion. Yet she was quite content with herself, that was clear.

"The young boy is a thief, too?" Mary asked.

"Aye, the worst of the lot. He broke into his master's drawers, he did, took out a pound, the rascal, bought tea and sugar, can you fancy that, a mere apprentice going into the shop pretty as you please, and a cup of gin, white bread la-ti-da, and they found him asleep way into the morning, seven or so, outside a bagnio, a wicked smile on his face. His first and only woman, I dare say."

The woman herself smelled of gin. Gin and damp rot. She was sewn into her clothes, Mary knew, as was the custom, sewn in for the whole year until Christmas or Easter bath. The skirts alone went up for business and pleasure. Meanwhile, vermin nested in the folds and wrinkles of the once blue cloth. Tracks and holes along the seams marked the march of bugs. Flies followed the bunched fabric of the woman's bustle, and old blood showed through in brown patches. Mary imagined wormy things squashed between her breasts, crabs grabbed into her crotch, and lice crawling willy-nilly through the hair on her head.

"The others," the woman continued, "they took bread, potatoes, a slab of salt pork."

"Ah, the lad is a pretty one," Joseph said.

"Pretty do not save him from the gallows, no, sir."

"Just a boy," Mary said.

So there were to be no bold and beautiful highwaymen throwing locks of hair to the mob of adoring women, and no wreaths of primroses circling their fated heads, no tearful poems recited before the cart rolled away, or rousing songs, flamboyant speeches, no stops at the halfway house in Holborn for a farewell drink and toast.

It was to be tawdry and pathetic, nothing for the ballad makers to compose on.

Yet the crowd was noisy and anxious. It was a treat, time off from work, a festival of sausages and pigs' ears, radishes and onions, along with gin and beer. Hawkers mingled right beneath the hanging tree, and the whores did good business leaning against carts and coaches and opening their legs wide beneath bushes so all could see their hairy masses like beards grown wild above pink folds of greedy, gaping mouths.

Yes, Mary thought, that is it, how it looks, ashamed for herself, for it was large and loose, not as she thought, crinkled and tucked in like the little curled flaps, the rooster comb she liked to twiddle on those desperate nights, and what she had tasted as a child on the seated Annie, the flavor of salted herring and Christmas anise cookies.

"Three rows a penny pins," sang a crier.

"Short, whites, and mid-dl-ings."

"Buy my dish of great eels?"

"Songs, a penny a sheet."

"Dumpling-ho."

"Joseph, I feel sick," she said. "I want to go home."

"Shortly," he said. "In a bit."

The boy, twelve at most, with matted curls, a sweet child's mouth, did not die all at once, but danced and dangled, choked and gagged, until his uncle and father, out of mercy, stepped forth and pulled on his legs. Then, with a gasp, dirtying himself, the poor baby died.

Mary lost her breakfast to the ground at that moment, where it was lapped up by two very eager dogs in short order. Joseph had to help her over to the base of a tree.

"A child, Joseph, a mere child." She eased herself down. The trunk reeked of pee. Somebody else had vomited nearby. Mary took a deep breath and leaned her head back, closed her eyes. I have to come to grips, she said to herself.

"What is life, dear," said the woman, "but a vale of tears? Envy the lad."

"But what he did . . ."

Mary remembered how she as a child had sneaked into the pantry to wet her fingers, stick them into the sugar (she had developed a taste for sweets). For that she had been beaten until she wet her skirts, but not hanged.

"It is enough, Mr. Wollstonecraft," Annie had said at the time. "The child is sorry."

Later Annie brought bread and water to the nursery, cooed from behind the door: "Miss Mary, Miss Mary."

Mrs. Wollstonecraft had forbidden her dinner or tea or warm rags to wash herself with.

Mary's older brother had stood guard at the door, riding his hobbyhorse back and forth.

"I am master here."

"Are you able to stand, Mary?"

"A is for Acorn, B is for Boy . . ."

"What?"

"Somehow I thought the reprieve would come, Joseph, as in *The Beggar's Opera*, saving him from the hanging. The horseman drawing up, the document unfurled, the seal and signature: King George III, His Majesty the King. A pardon."

"Oh, Mary, this is not a play." Joseph said it sadly, but his face was flushed and his hands could not hold still, the way he got when in the heat of a good conversation and he wished to say something, get a word in edgewise between Blake and Paine.

"Or Sir Gawain and the Green Knight. A new head. A new life. A chance."

"No, Mary."

Mary lost her supper that night. A nice Yorkshire pudding, roast beef, potted pigeon pie, and rich seedcake. Two meals gone in a day.

She was mortified this time, for the guest was there. It was the special occasion, actually, the young writer. They began with talk of the hanging.

"He was a pretty one, that child," Joseph said.

That was when Mary had to rush out to the garden, and Joseph, following, had stood with her, rubbing the back of her neck.

"There, there, Mary, be a sensible girl."

All the white or blue Michaelmas daisies which grew up around the jericho had closed their trumpets for the night, though the moon was as big and nearly as bright as the sun. It rose over the green dome of Wren's cathedral like a great creamy saucer.

"How can we permit it?"

"Oh, Mary, how can we permit anything?"

"But a child, Joseph, a mere hungry child."

"I know," he said. "I know."

Yet he seemed not to know, or at least the Joseph she knew seemed not to be there that night. All day he had been dithering about, acting strangely agitated, and at the hanging was not morose, greatly saddened, as she was, not quieted and slowed down, but somehow seemed buoyed up by it. She hated to think it, but he was like the members of the crowd, flushed and excited. He kept licking his lips, smoothing down his pants, and walking not carefully and a little tiptoe as usual, but more in kind of a prancy fashion as at a party.

"Perhaps you should go early to bed," Joseph said gently.

"Yes," she agreed. "I hate everything."

"Mary."

"Well, I do."

"You are overexerted, and long-drawn."

"A child was hanged, Joseph."

"Yes, yes, precisely that."

Mrs. Mason, who had come early to prepare the meal, had gone home an hour before. There were only the three of them in the house—Mary, Joseph, and that Mr. Smith. There was a lonely feel to the evening. Mary wished it were Thursday and the dining room full of noise and clatter, each person wanting to say his own piece. This Mr. Smith was full of silence, and he and Joseph exchanged long looks as if each held a secret the other knew. He had brought dark red roses. They were in a vase in the middle of the table. They looked like velvet, faintly ominous.

Mary went down to the kitchen for some water. As she worked the pump, she observed all the flies fallen to the floor. The lime on the walls killed them. Of course the ceiling was not coated with lime, for otherwise flies would fall into the food made at the table.

She looked at the sorry little row of them along the walls, their frail feet crumpled, their wings flaccid, their bodies crisp and air-light.

There had been suggestions made by civic-minded citizens about having the horses all wear bags under their tails, but surely the flies would follow the bags and still find their way into kitchens.

Mary drank a good bit of water. Her throat was dry and her mouth felt like sawdust, with the nasty taste of eggs. It must be the Yorkshire pudding, she thought. Then she went to the dining room, made her apologies to the guest, Mr. Smith, and climbed the stairs to her room.

It was such a hot evening, so extraordinarily close that, even with the window open and the sheets and coverlet thrown off, Mary could not sleep.

At least, she said to herself, I know what is terrible, and I know that I am a wicked, silly girl. Maybe I should die. That thought often crept up, had to be pushed back. Sometimes it would come upon her unawares, straight out of a sunny day or even when they (she and Joseph) might be at Vauxhall Gardens, strolling among the trees, which were fastened with paper moons and stars. I have to die neatly followed I have to become famous, or the order was: I have to become famous and I have to die. And sometimes it came directly out of the gloom of her desires, a kind of spiraling descent into her own darkness. I have to be dead. That was what lay on the other side of all her bright, snippy cleverness. She knew she was no better than the woman at the hanging she had disdained. Worse, for the vermin in her case lived inside her. Her heart was worm-eaten and her brains crawling with licentiousness. Her duty was to live, but she cared little for duty and often less for life.

She had to use the chamber pot. But surely, on such a night, she could walk outside, use the jericho. She heard the bells chime twelve times from St. Paul's. Oh dear, she thought, oh dear, it is quite late.

Tiptoeing down the stairs, she could hear them still talking, Joseph and Mr. Smith, but the voices were not coming from the dining room. The door of Joseph's bedroom was slightly open. That's where they were. How curious, she thought, and then she paused, got a glimpse. Dear God. She clutched her heart, thought she would faint.

His room.

The bed.

The coverlet in disarray.

Light enough to see, for the moon was right in the window, hung there, as if it, too, could not help looking.

The bed, the sheets, the carpet beside the bed, the floor shiny waxed, a brown sea of wood. And how she wanted to be lost in the swirls and did not want to see the feet, the feet on the rug, the naked feet, and, her eyes going up the leg, men's legs.

The boy's face was as smooth-cheeked as a girl's, and his long, womanish hair curled down his neck in a golden tumble, the band unloosed.

Dear God in heaven, Mary thought, give me strength to bear this.

For the boy's, man's, author's, person's buttocks were as smooth as milk and round as a pig-bladder ball.

That.

And Joseph Johnson was leaning into him, the young man, who was leaning against the bed, and whose stomach was against the side of the bed, and Joseph's legs were thrusting. The two men were joined, skin on skin.

That, too.

The young man, his head turned to the side, caught her eye.

This is the dream of love, she thought, feeling such pain as she could not imagine.

The scene of the hanging came back, the bewildered face of the child. She remembered Joseph's face once when he was looking at her when he thought she did not know. His expression was full of pity and distress. What is it, Joseph? she had wanted to ask. What am I to do with you, he silently replied. Now she knew, and was able to go back, take all the little parts and pieces, make them into one coherent picture.

She remembered seeing such a one before, a sodomite. He had been in stocks. This was when she was a child in Yorkshire. This man did not look womanish or delicate or in any way different from any regular man, but it was said that he was one, and so he was put there, his legs and arms fitted into the holes in the wood. All day he sat thus, and in the beginning, the morning, it was just schoolchildren jeering, and later women going to market spitting, and on about dinnertime, a large crowd of men gathered with heavy stones, and they threw them at him.

When they finally came from the jail to unloosen him from the platform, he was limp and his head lolled to one side. He was dead.

HENRY

CHAPTER 19

IN THE EIGHTEENTH CENTURY, eels were skinned alive and geese bled to death, horses flogged, dogs starved, bears baited, and children wandered the streets maimed for begging, their teeth pulled and hair cut for selling. In London in 1787, there were 166 offenses for which human beings could be hanged. In 1757, in France, Robert François Damiens, who had attempted the life of Louis XV, was drawn and quartered, his flesh torn with red-hot pincers, his hands burnt with sulphur, and finally, supposedly still alive, he was burned at the stake. English sailors and soldiers were routinely whipped. One, in 1727, said he had received 26,000 lashes.

When Mary lived in Spitalfields with her grandfather, there had been a chimney sweep who got caught in the chimney because he was too large, too old to be a sweep, and had died stuck. In Richardson's novel *Clarissa*, Clarissa is raped. Boswell, Dr. Johnson's loyal biographer, was plagued with gonorrhea nineteen times. In London, one in five babies died within its first year. During the height of the Terror in France, 1793–94, at least 250,000 Royalists and others were executed. Vico, in *Principles of a New Science*, stated that every age is imbued with a character, a point of view. Voltaire, in *Candide*, made clear that this is not the best of all possible worlds. Rousseau believed in the perfectibility of man, but made light of women's capacities.

Mary Wollstonecraft, in her book *Thoughts on the Education of Daughters*, wrote: "Most women, and men too, have no character at all. Just opinions and virtuous passions appear by starts."

In her third book, *Original Stories from Real Life*, Wollstonecraft showed the brutal social climate of the time in her story of crazy Robin:

> *The children begged in the day, and at night slept with their wretched father. Poverty and dirt soon robbed their cheeks of the*

roses which the country air made bloom with a peculiar freshness;
so that they soon caught a jail fever,—and died. The poor father,
who was now bereft of all his children, hung over their bed in
speechless anguish; not a groan or a tear escaped from him, whilst
he stood, two or three hours, in the same attitude, looking at the
dead bodies of his little darlings. The dog licked his hands, and
strove to attract his attention; but for awhile he seemed not to ob-
serve his caresses; when he did, he said, mournfully, thou wilt not
leave me—and then he began to laugh. The bodies were removed;
and he remained in an unsettled state, often frantic; at length the
frenzy subsided, and he grew melancholy and harmless.

An engraving by William Blake, in the second edition, illustrates
the scene.

CHAPTER 20

BREATHING was a major problem for Mary the morning after seeing Joseph with his friend. She could barely put on her skirt and bodice. Washing her face and hands at the bowl, she had to tell herself to stop crying, that she had hands, a face, legs, a life. She dropped the cloth. Scooping it up, she lost her balance, nearly fell. And when she went out to the chandler's shop for some bread and cheese (she knew she must eat, and what if Joseph were down in the kitchen?), her feet on the cobblestones (they were on the cobblestones, walking) could not be felt.

Blinking at the exquisite brightness of the day, she found that the world had been transformed. Overnight, buildings had shifted and changed shape. Shadows of strange animals, the size of giants, loomed over London Bridge and St. Paul's. One had a bear face, red eyes. The only bear Mary had ever seen was part of a little carnival from Italy. It had broken its leash and lunged at the circle of spectators. Some men had taken out guns, shot it. Pop, pop. Then it fell, obligingly, for surely those tiny guns, toys, could do no damage. Then it had obligingly died, giving up the game with a tiny smile on its face. A ribbon of bright-red blood dribbled out of its nostrils onto the street. Poor bear. The thought now made Mary cry. Everything made her cry. Her mother's indifference to her made her cry. What Annie had her do made her cry. Eliza's lost baby made her cry. Fanny's death made her cry. What a sorry and stupid life I have lived, she said to herself, crying afresh over the whole untidy bundle.

Furthermore, she was not seeing things in their accustomed light. St. Paul's Church Mary imagined to be the lair of snarling griffins with forked tongues, claws set to rake. The clergy had that kind of skin, she thought, metallically hued, scaly and cold to the touch. The church steeples appeared to have mouths—like eels she had seen hanging up in a stall by the Thames. She visualized green severed heads on pikes before the Tower of London as in the olden days. Obviously, the streets were not safe.

Returning home flustered and confused, she saw with relief that Joseph was still abed; she quickly went upstairs, got back in her bed, trembling and hugging her bread and cheese to her, ate from her fist, spreading crumbs on her sheets. All her bones ached, and her gums ached, too. Her teeth felt as if they were ready to fall out of her mouth. How could she eat? How could she live?

September 30, 1789

Dear Eliza, Have you ever wanted to die, yet been forced to live? I am that miserable. There is no hope for me. I am stricken with the truth. My life is over. Dread washes over me and clouds my eyes so that I can barely see. I am beyond relief. Had I known what it was to feel so, I should have never ventured beyond my shell of self. It does not pay to extend your arms, smile your smile, nod your head, be agreeable. What shall I do? Tell me. Write me. Save me.

October 24, 1789

Dear Mary, I suppose it is all to do with love. Surely that is something you should put behind you. Twenty-nine is it now? Have you no dignity? Let this be a lesson. Being a governess in Scotland is difficult enough for me without receiving desperate letters from you. Would that I had some man to moon over. Get over your lovesickness, stop exaggerating, stay alive, and do not fancy yourself mad, for God's sake. Do you know how lucky you are to be living by your wits? Is that what you tell me, that you are living by your wits? Please send any money you can spare. I need a winter cloak and yarn for mittens, a hat. Sincerely, your sister Eliza.

Mary threw Eliza's letter in the Thames. Looking out at the brackish twist of water as it curled below Putney Bridge, Mary could understand the sorrows of young Werther, Goethe's doomed lover. She understood how Werther could come to his early death through unrequited love. Though only a character in a book, a novel at that, Werther and his fate seemed very real to her. He was a warning, a cautionary figure. The first sight of Lotte, his beloved, should have signaled disaster to poor Werther. In *Sorrows*, Lotte's handshake portended the gun in Werther's hand: did he not feel the cold tube of the barrel in her powdery palm? And in her smile, apparently so sweet, could he not apprehend death's leer? All was a kind of a lie.

November 15, 1789

Dear Everina, How is it in a world full of cruelty and despair, with Bedlam, and Newgate, and His Majesty's conscripted army, and with hangings and children begging, chimney sweeps and those that tend the mills, sitting at looms until faint with hunger, defecating at the machine which cannot go untended, how is it with all the terrors of the world, that I, we, one can be so very hurt by the inattention of another? I do not understand. Pray keep me from self-indulgence.

Mary, Mind your manners and see to your duties to your family. You are no help to them in this sorry state.

Mary thought of stepping out in front of a horse or tossing herself off a bridge, or simply not eating or drinking water ever again, or going down into the kitchen with the knives, lining them up on the table, taking them to her heart one by one. It would not be difficult. Her mind, though teeming with terrible visions, was quite clear. It was moving about which was hard. Even combing her hair was almost too heavy a task for her. Her arms felt like logs, her legs like stones. A thick cloth curtain seemed to impede all her movements, wrap up her limbs. Daylight hurt her eyes. She had to shield her eyes from the glare. All noises came together and nothing could be distinguished from anything else—a donkey's bray, a baby's cry, the squeak of wagon wheels, the slap of the whip. Noise was a deep whirlpool, something that would take you down. Sights and images assaulted her. They could knock her over.

The only alternative was to rest deep within the cool earth, all the tattered edges of herself smoothed out, brought to rest, weighed down and fixed. She did not disdain the idea of worms eating out her eyes and wiggling through the sockets or having her tongue slivered by the sharp scissor wings of feasting flies zzzz or even having small, crawly bugs file into her ears. She could picture little black beetles swarming over her heart, making inways and byways, wearing it down into little roadways of red nub.

Everina wrote:

Gracious, you get so disgusting. The man does not even know you care for him, you say, and yet you want to die over him. What is the point? Tell him or not, but live with the consequences. Why do you not count your blessings for a change. Some of us have to work for a living. By the way, I was wondering if you could send a pound or two, now that you are quite the little authoress. Count your blessings, my dear.

Mary sat down upstairs in her room with quill and paper, counted her blessings. She (1) was thirty; (2) wrote for a magazine; (3) had written three books; (4) was healthy; (5) had a roof over her head; (6) was healthy; (7) had a roof over her head; (8) wrote for a magazine; (9) had two legs, (10) two arms, (11) two arms, (12) two legs and a face; and sometimes lying in bed, (13) she liked to hear the rain on the roof and the noise below of Mrs. Mason cleaning up the kitchen and Joseph settling in for a night of reading; and a roof over her head and she was thirty, not that it was a matter of choice, and everywhere she looked people were happy and healthy and she was happy and healthy.

Of course, she had not provided Eliza or Everina with the details. Could they understand the details? Eliza wrote:

Mary, Has this person given any indication that he loves you? Why not love somebody who will marry you, for God's sake. Some

nice old gentleman who does not require a dowry and wishes a
young wife. A nice widower.

A widower? Thank you, Eliza. Is that how you see me? Matched
with a doddering old man. Just because I am thirty? I am not
lined and ugly, all my limbs work well. I am pretty and lively.
How dare you confine me to a widower, smelling of stale death.

At night, horses galloped out of the creases of her dingy pillows,
settled themselves on the rough wooden boards of her floor, and thun-
dered in formation around her desk and dressing table. She dreamed
of the Four Horses of the Apocalypse: the white horse with the conqueror astride; and the red horse, scavenger of blood; the black horse
with the scales of justice; and the pale horse carrying Death on its
scrawny back.

In one of her dreams, those horses were combined into one mixed,
mottled creature of indeterminate sex. In another, the horse was a roan
stallion; in still another, an Arabian. A whole herd raced across the
desert, kicking up clouds of dusty sand. Then they stopped, turned
their heads to one side as if listening to something—a drumbeat or a
birdcall. One horse came forth, a huge gray with freckled haunches
like the horse of her Laugharne childhood, and began speaking to her.
Mary strained to understand. The voice was both loud and muffled.
It filled the desert, scattered the vultures, and set the herd off. Mary
could not understand what it was saying, though she felt the vibrations
beneath her, and the heat of his breath on her neck, and could see the
working of the big yellow teeth. What? What are you saying? Could
you repeat that?

She woke up with a start. Her chest of drawers, the desk, her
window assumed sinister shapes. Her pillows squeaked. Then she saw
that there was a cloud of mice skittering about on the floor, looping
along, hop skipping over each other, scouting for crumbs from her in-
bed meals. Sitting up, Mary shouted at them. Shoo, shoo, scat, scat.
She got up for the broom, gingerly made her way across the cold floor,
hoping not to slip or slide or step on a mouse. Her mouth tasted like

gummed-together gruel. Looking out of her window, she could see that the sky was beginning to lighten, soften. Day.

"Good morning," Joseph says when Mary comes downstairs. He is none the wiser, she thinks. "Sleep well?"

"Yes. I will see you later, Joseph. I will be working on the review today. If you need to take it to the printer tomorrow."

"Very well. I am glad to hear that. I had an unusual dream last night, Mary, about a stampede of horses going through the house. It seemed so real. I could hear them, Mary. They charged up the stairs right into your room. There they circled around and around your bed, raising dust, and singing at the top of their horse lungs."

"Do you remember the words of the song, Joseph?"

"It is hard to tell. They were very loud. But I think, in their tortured way, they were calling for help. Their mouths twisted and they ground the air and the sound came from very deep within their long throats. Such an effort to get it out. It was like a cry."

Mary escaped down Ludgate Hill, crossed Fleet Bridge over Fleet Ditch, holding her nose and not pausing to see all the refuse and offal, passed Fleet Prison, not granting an ear to the shouts and lamentations of all those housed for debt, went under Temple Bar and into the Strand. She stopped at St. James's Park. In the summer, there would be trees, flowers, rows of phlox and violet carnations, nasturtiums, the lake with ducks and cranes. Now it was gray, cold. Joseph's new coffeehouse was St. James's, where Dr. Johnson and Oliver Goldsmith, the playwright, had gone. Joseph had taken Mary once, as a treat. She was the only woman there besides the young woman at the counter serving the coffee. Everybody, she noticed, was taking snuff and sneezing. A large urn of water heating over the fire boiled over. Several men were doing business at their table. At the time, Mary had been thrilled. This is London, she had said to herself. This is life.

"You are looking thin, my dear," Joseph said over tea that evening. She had forced herself to walk and walk. "Is anything the matter?"

"No, nothing, Joseph." She did not look him in the eye, but kept her head down.

The teacup and saucer were of a Chinese mode, blue rimmed with a green-and-golden nightingale perched on a yellow-and-orange blossom. Suddenly Mary thought she had never seen anything quite so beautiful. For some reason Joseph had brought out his best things for tea this day.

"And you are very curt with me these days."

"Do not mean to be." And it was a warm day for late fall, the air soft and the colors of the bare trees a burnished brown and dark gray.

"So maybe an excursion is in order."

"An excursion?"

"While it is still somewhat warm. Vauxhall Gardens?"

Mary smiled. The tea cakes smelled wonderful. Mrs. Mason's currant jam went very nicely with them. Her tea cakes, both tender and flaky, could easily be the best in London.

"So she smiles, she eats. That is more like it. This evening?" Joseph leaned forward, tapped her gently on the knee.

"I have no dress suitable for Vauxhall Gardens."

"My dear, whatever you wear will be beautiful."

"You are doing it again."

"What?"

"Being charming."

"Oh my, how awful." He fluttered his hand to his chest.

"I want you to be sensible around me." She knit her eyebrows.

"How can I be sensible? I am insensible. See"—he held out his hand. "No sensation. Alas, when I was a wee lad in Birmingham, my mother . . ." His hand trembled a little.

"Joseph."

"My lady."

"I do not want you to be foolish."

"Ah, but I *am* a fool."

"Twice a fool if you make me leave."

He sucked in his breath.

"Make you leave? Have I, am I the one to make you so sad these last days of Pompeii?"

"See what I mean. You cannot even be serious when it *is* serious."

"All right. I swear, I swear I will be a . . ."

"Good boy."

"Good boy. I swear on Boswell's codpiece."

"Not that."

"After the cure, after a little trip to the apothecary, and a promise to poor Dr. Johnson and the ladies of the Strand and the acrobats at Covent Garden and the actresses at the Globe and the sundry lads and lassies that he had been cavorting with."

"Lads, Joseph? They put people in the stocks for that. There is the case of the . . ."

"Yes," Joseph said very softly. "I know, Mary. I know very well."

"Vauxhall Gardens," she said cheerily, seeing his distress.

"That will be wonderful. It will be an occasion."

The Vauxhall pleasure gardens had many gravel walks. Along the way they gazed at pillars and statues, pavilions and grottoes. Hedges and trees artfully lined the walkways. Joseph and Mary stopped in a pavilion for refreshments. Joseph had wine and cold meat. Mary had tea and cake.

Mary took Joseph's arm. For they were friends, were they not?

"Shall we go to the music room?"

"Yes," she said. They were friends.

The music room was a gigantic round hall with carvings and decorations, a domed ceiling. They sat on a bench by the wall and listened to five transverse flutists, and one harpsichordist, play music by Joseph Bodin de Boismortier. The ladies and gentlemen going by were dressed in bright colors of scarlet and pink.

"Are you happy, Mary?" Joseph looked at her closely.

She looked around. "I think I might be." Somehow the weight at the bottom of her lungs had lifted and she could breathe freely. "I feel I should dislike you, Joseph, but I cannot."

"Are you accustomed to disliking people?"

"Oh, yes. But one learns when to be circumspect."

"Hiding is not your nature."

"But learning is *not* nature."

"And what an apt little student you are. Perhaps we can only learn what we are, and in that way nature and civilization conspire."

Nature and civilization. The terms made Mary think of forests and columns.

"I think," she said. "I have been acting like a silly goose."

"Oh, my dear, welcome to the flock."

CHAPTER 21

"DREAMS, MY FRIENDS. Our dreams! They are the unknown territory that we artists must now explore," Henry Fuseli said at one of Joseph's Thursday dinners. Mary was not paying much attention. The Thursday-night dinners no longer held the attractions they did when she first came to London. She attended because she lived in the house and because they offered some variety in her life. The days were long and dreary to her. All of London seemed so dull in the early winter.

Dreams, unexplored region, art. Nobody replied. Fuseli was the acknowledged genius of the group, and Joseph had said to let him have his way. Later Mary would tell herself that was what led her astray, letting him have his way. Genius is not a pardon for everything, she reasoned. Not a pardon, but a permission, is how she saw it. Anyway, she should have known better. She had been clear-headed enough when she wrote Everina the day after she went with Fuseli to that tavern.

December 5, 1789

Sister, I have told you about these Thursday dinners where every-
body is supposed to be brilliant and is, except for me, for not only
am I undereducated and out of place, but also I am the only
woman. In order to talk, I have to shout. But everybody is shout-
ing. We shout revolution or the poverty question or the number of
prostitutes on the street, or whether it is necessary to resist tyranny
at the cost of one's life. We shout at the top of our lungs. "Free-
dom, freedom," goes the chant, each one of us pounding on the
table with our fists around our forks and knives, making Joseph's
good plates bounce and clatter. Important things, you see. And do

*I sit there like a figure out of the wax museum? No indeed. When
Joseph was talking about cruelty to animals, I boomed out:*

*"I often have quite extraordinary dreams in which horses fig-
ure prominently."*

"Is that so? I paint horses," said Mr. Fuseli.

*Mr. Fuseli has an overbearing manner and a distasteful way
of slurping his soup and is distressingly uninhibited with breaking
of wind. Fart free wherever you be, is what he always says with a
sly little chuckle. So disgusting. He has a huge head, a small
body, bulging eyes, and a thick German accent. The damp, muggy
smell of a frog precedes him everywhere he goes. Far be it from me
to criticize. I have nothing against frogs. As long as they stay in
their swamp. Nonetheless, he seems to think very highly of himself,
as if underneath or somewhere around, he is a prince. Needless to
say, and I do not care what Joseph says, I do not concur with the
genius designation. The man is a frog through and through. And
if you let genius have its way, who knows what havoc may be
released.*

*One more thing, Everina, Bishop Berkeley out for a stroll,
this Fuseli! His Grace walks in the cool of the night bringing the
world into existence through his bulgy-eye perception. That is how
he acts.*

Mary certainly did not like the way Fuseli said: I paint horses.
She thought he said it in such a way that one would be led to believe
that *he* invented horses through the act of *his* perception.

She narrowed her eyes, concentrated on her raspberry tart. Fuseli,
like Blake, also did engravings. He had done a series of paintings
illustrating some of Shakespeare's plays. It was said that he had in his
collection pictures of a suggestive nature. Mary could imagine. Surely
The Nightmare was one such sample. And Fuseli's picture of Bottom
in *A Midsummer Night's Dream*, a donkey with a smile, and Titania,
Queen of the Fairies, surrounding him with kisses and fairy stuff. Too
emotional, too lyrical, too finally duplicitous.

The Thursday-night dinners: Paine and Blake, Fuseli, Johnson,
Godwin, Christie. The literati, the cognoscenti, the illustri. Down the

street at Lady Pomeroy's were assembled the decadent and the effete set. Who knows what they ate or said, except that it was French.

Joseph's people feasted upon a roast haunch of venison, wholesome mulligatawny soup, and stewed plums.

"Dreams," Fuseli continued, "reveal what we really think."

What did Mary *really* think as she looked about the dining room with the proper white cloth, Wedgwood china, the tile-inlaid fireplace, Dutch, the chamber pot to match the dishes, the silver candle holders, the clock, the chandelier, its many glass droplets. Mary thought: I wish Fanny were alive to see me here, and my mother, who could not forgive that I was a woman and not a boy, and Mrs. Dawson, who derided and demeaned me, and Lady Kingsborough, who thought more of her dogs than of her children's education, and my brother Ned, who always acted so superior, and my father, who hated me. I want them all to see me in this fine dining room, eating fine food and talking a fine line twixt life as we know it and life as we want it.

"Dreams tell us who we are. As people, as a person." Fuseli waved his fork about as if conducting the discussion and conjuring a dream.

"Am I a horse, then?" Mary said archly. "Perish the thought."

Fuseli tucked in his chin, fondled his chest. He handled his person, Mary observed, as if he were in love with himself, petting and pawing and preening, making his flesh into bread dough with his fingers.

"Perhaps being a horse in your dreams gives you free rein, Mary." He smiled in a lopsided way.

"A packhorse?"

"No, my dear, I see you at the races, quite definitely, for you have the beautiful brown eyes of a thoroughbred." He gave her a tender look, and she thought, for a moment, he slipped his foot over hers.

"Before, you said they were green."

"They are beautiful eyes, Mary, great eyes, sweet eyes, but do not fidget so and hold still, and that nervous laugh—you are much too intense. Be calm, my dear, be calm. Your thoughts betray you."

"My thoughts betray me. What am I saying, then?" She looked at him straight on.

"Save me, save me. That is what I hear you call from deep within."

"You are not far from the truth," Joseph said.

"Yes he is. He is an ocean away from the truth." She was thinking: I hate you, I hate you. "I shall save myself, thank you kindly."

Fuseli reached across the table, grasped her hand. Everybody looked, of course. William Blake and Tom Paine and William Godwin and Joseph Johnson. Christie, who was napping under the table, appeared at that moment from below the tablecloth, drawing it about his ears like a lady's scarf.

"Pity a poor widow woman," he said, falsetto.

"Christie, come out from there."

"I hate horses, hate the races." Mary drew her hand back sharply, examined it for marks, the unsweet exchange of vermin. Was she now to smell like a frog, too? How dare he touch her. Anyway, was he not the one who fancied men as well as women. She was quite tired of that kind of consideration.

"They remind me of my father, the hunt, horses, sport, that is why."

Impertinent fool who dares to grab my hand, she wanted to add. She and Joseph, except for a few times, had at best brushed each other's clothes, her skirts whisking against his shoe tops, saying: whoosh, whoosh; and the barest tips of fingers had fluted against each other, tootalou, tootalou. There, right across the table, sat Joseph, daintily composed and ready for some pretty prank. Meanwhile, grease glistened on Fuseli's fat chin in a trail of diluted gold.

"My dear, what ails you?" Joseph asked, leaning across the table. "Your bile is up, is that it. What is it?"

"Oh, nothing," she replied. "Nothing is the matter."

"I did not mean to hurt your feelings with my rude remarks," Henry Fuseli said. "You are so sensitive, so fragile."

She turned to him, smiled.

"Such a sad smile, *mein Kind*." Fuseli reached for her hand again, thought better, withdrew. "Why so melancholy?"

"Why so melancholy, little lamb?" Blake echoed.

"Melancholy is a luxury of the upper classes," Paine pointed out.

"Paine, stop being such an insufferable revolutionary," Joseph said.

"If my belly is empty, I am melancholy."

"So eat up, Paine. Solve all your problems."

Mary tried to smile nicely. "It is just that my childhood, well, was not happy." She might as well tell them. It was boring enough at the table. "That was the start of it."

"Well, let it be the finish, too. Whose *was* happy?" Fuseli asked, throwing his arms to encompass the world. "Childhood."

"Yours was not, either?"

"Of course not. I could not do as I pleased. People hit me, pinched me, poked and shook me. I had to do as they said, and it was quite clear to me that they did not know anything."

"She has moods," Joseph said. "Good and bad. One right after the other."

Mary knew that Fuseli was not only an artist but a classicist fluent in Greek and Latin. He had been a scholar, a prodigy. Surely one cannot distinguish oneself at so early an age if chaos reigns in the home, she thought. Her own blossoming, if it was to be, would come at an advanced age. For surely it takes a while to overcome an inadequate education and an emotionally wrenching family life. By the time you do, and turn around, able to devote yourself to some other endeavor, you are old.

"So what I suggest, Mary, my dear," Fuseli continued, "if you permit me to be bold once again, is that we go on a walk and discover each other. Two unhappy children, *nicht wahr?*"

They were at one end of the table and the others had been discussing something else. Yet they all turned and looked at Mary at this point.

"Discover each other?"

"See the sights. And all the while you will be telling me whence you came and where you are headed and what is to happen along the way. *Die Wahrheit.*"

But I do not even like you, she wanted to say. "I do not know you," she did say.

"Well, this is the opportunity. Horace says: Ah yes, seize the day. *Carpe diem.* And seize your cloak. It is quite chilly out."

Mary had her blue cloak from the Kingsboroughs. The green-stripe taffeta cloth she had picked out in the late summer for her new dress was now too thin. She had to stuff rags in her stays, double up on petticoats. There were a frantic few minutes up in her attic room. Do not be silly, she told herself, I do not even like this man.

"Are you cold," Henry asked, giving her his arm as they set out.

"No."

He pressed her arm closely. She shivered a little.

"We will stop for some spirits. We need to elevate our blood."

In the fall, the leaves which fell off the trees and were raked into big piles were burned throughout London. It reminded Mary of war, Carthage, smoldering ruins. The air was mysterious at that time of year, one day warm, almost sultry, and next cold, as if months had passed in the night. A tree fully leaved might suddenly appear naked in the morning. Now, as they walked down Cheapside, they saw a group of soldiers on parade.

"We will go into an inn," Henry said, guiding her gently toward a coach stand and a sign which bore a hog's head draped in a red banner. "There is a pleasant, quiet tavern. You will be able to tell me your life story in peace."

"Why should you want to hear that?"

"Because I like you, that is why."

"But you like men, no?"

"Yes, of course. I like men and women and children and little dogs."

She let it go for the time. She had never been in a tavern to drink, only to fetch her father, and in an inn only when taking the coach, and in a coffeehouse only with Joseph. This tavern in an inn was a large room with thick wooden beams and iron candle holders. By the rough wooden bar was a huge hearth with a roaring fire. She felt grown up and slightly sinful.

"Are you warm?"

"Yes." Her cheeks were burning, actually. She had to shed her wrap and wished she could extract the rags from her corset and sleeves, saying at the end: Look, I am thin.

A barmaid came over, leaned forward, almost spilling her breasts in Henry's face.

"Hello, dearie. What's your pleasure?"

"A stout, an ale."

She noticed Henry staring at the woman's front and, when she turned, at her backside, which rippled and shook. Mary supposed that, as an artist, he was obliged to look hard at the world, store impressions. Nonetheless, she felt uncomfortable. He must have detected something, for when the woman came back with their drinks and had to lift her arms up to poke some loose hairs into her cap, Henry did not look up, but gazed straight at Mary.

"Start with your father, horses," he commanded.

"Yorkshire, the North Riding, Richmond."

Mary is fifteen in this memory. She wonders if there is any possibility for her beyond the damp walls of her family house and if harsh words and angry tantrums, weeping and sniveling are the way the rest of the world conducts its business.

Her father has a farm in Yorkshire, the usual failing farm—the mangy sheep, scrappy grass, a fallen-down barn, and the house cold and acrid, full of misunderstandings and angry words all the time. The Wollstonecrafts have six new dogs, scrawny, snarly ones, of course, and now there are horses, swayback and prone to lameness, not racehorses.

"Richmond was a center of horse racing, Henry. My father gambled on the thoroughbreds."

"To you, Mary." He lifted his stout.

"Thank you, Henry." She raised her ale.

"There is nothing like a good bottle of stout," he said.

"Really? Nothing?"

"Almost nothing."

"Do you want to hear the rest of this dreary tale, my life?"

"Yes, yes, go on, very interesting."

"Each morning the racehorses were brought out and exercised on the Green. Each week there was a racing meet. Then the people would come from all over Yorkshire. My father always lost a good deal of money on the races, which raised havoc in the house. I heard hooves all night. There was no money. My mother cried."

"Well, matter of fact, we were poor, too. Switzerland, that is where I come from."

"Outside the town there were lime kilns, where they made mortar and plaster, and on the hill was a castle built by Alan the Red, a relative of William the Conqueror. I used to go up in the tower with my sisters Eliza and Everina and my brother Edward, if he was so disposed, to play kings and queens. Just like Wales, the castle at Laugharne, where the Royalists held out for six weeks against Cromwell."

"Do you want another glass?"

"No, thank you."

"You do know I am married."

"Yes, I do. But I also thought you . . ."

"Right now I like you very much, you in particular; you are very strong, but you have a childlike vulnerability. Attractive. Self-pitying. Accomplished. You are a mass of contradictions, my dear. I think we shall get on famously. Your lower lip, full and quivering, a sure sign of sensuality. You."

"*You* are married." His comments disconcerted her.

"It was an interesting decision, I think. At the time there were several possibilities. I had to think in terms of a wife. That is quite different from mistress or companion . . . you know how it is." He sipped his stout noisily.

"I do not think that I do."

"Well, I said to her, I need somebody who can take care of my needs." He cleared his throat.

"Yes." She patted her hair.

"That is very important. But do not let me interrupt you. Go on. Fascinating, this Birmingham account."

"Yorkshire."

"That is what I said."

"I was the queen and my sisters ladies-in-waiting. Edward, of course, was the king and would tell the girls what to do: Kneel, kiss my hand, that sort of thing."

"I was a solitary child, Mary, I will be straight with you, moody and gloomy. My mother always worried that my head was too big. Too many thoughts can weigh one down, is what she always said."

"And your wife, what does she say?" Mary looked at him.

"She says . . . When my head gets hot, she rubs it with a cold cloth."

"The burdens of genius."

"I do not sleep with my wife, you know."

"No, I did not know." She looked down quickly.

"Here I am interrupting again. Hit me if I do it again. Can I see your breasts?"

"No."

He looked at her, held her gaze.

"Oh, you are a wise woman, Mary, do continue."

By Yorkshire, Mary was beginning to feel she was getting too old for childish games and would prefer to go up to the tower alone anyway sometimes. Dreaming off, she was able to see for miles around—the hills and dales, the river Swale. She could see the fields of rye and barley. Bluebells abounded. She could even see the town, the stocks and gallows, the ducking pond for gossips.

"The other day, when I was talking to Blake, William, I said, who is to stop us from doing exactly what we want. The world is full of ignoramuses. Mary, you and I are special people. We are out of the ordinary and ordinary rules do not apply to us."

"What?"

"That is it, Mary, that is it. I may be newer than you to England, but the world . . . Now I am interrupting again, but I know the ways of the world. You are not laughing at me again?"

"You have interrupted and I am going to hit you." She pressed his shoulder.

"No more interruptions, my dear, no more. I would love to see them, just as an artist. Your body is so soft-looking."

"I found a dead baby up there in the castle ruins," Mary said quickly. "It was wrapped in a raggedy cloth and it looked like dogs or perhaps rats had eaten its feet off. The tiny eyes were closed tight as if not to see her fate and her little fists were drawn up for sad protection."

"Did you tell anybody?"

"Of course not. For surely . . ."

"They would have burned the mother."

"This is hypothetical, but should I ever be with child without a husband, I would keep and raise the child."

"Nobody would talk to you again."

"Nobody talks to me now, except Joseph. He would not stop."

She was sure of that. She did not think Joseph would ever stop talking to her, no matter what. Mrs. Mason would talk to her, she with her nine surviving children.

"Children are everybody's responsibility." As she said that, she forgot for a moment the fact of Eliza's baby left behind, that she, Mary, did not go back for the child, as she had promised Eliza, and then, abandoned to Eliza's husband, the child had died. Little Mary Frances was named after her and Fanny Blood, her dearest friend. You are godmother, Eliza kept saying. Do you feel nothing?

"Just a quick look, Mary. I will not touch."

"No."

She could tell he was getting annoyed.

"I take you out, buy you ale, and . . ."

"For that I must show myself naked?"

His lower lip hung down. His eyes seemed to contract. "I understand the French women use sea sponges," he said.

"I beg your pardon."

"They have them tied on ribbons around their waist, always with them, handily, and ready for insertion." He withdrew something from his waistcoat.

"To kill girl children?" she asked.

"Girl children?"

"Certainly that is why the baby was left at the castle. Nobody wants a girl."

"They do not? You are a girl."

"Yes, I know. I was one of three girls."

"No, my dear, the sponge is not to directly kill a boy or girl, but to not beget any. To insert and to keep the two apart, to block." He held it up. It was a sea sponge, but looked like a little piece of chewed mutton.

"So they insert them . . . up . . ."

"Exactly. Pre-coitus. Up the tunnel."

Mary began coughing, nearly choking.

"If the English women would adopt such practices . . ."

Her coughing fit started again.

"Are you all right?"

He rose and came over to her and patted her back. "There, there." His hand stopped patting, started rubbing, going up along her shoulders and down her sides.

"I am fine," she said, abruptly standing up. "Let us go back."

"I think we will have to take a chaise. It is dark and pickpockets are about. Are you in so great a hurry that I cannot pay the woman?"

"No." She sighed, caught her breath. She felt very strange indeed, nerves ajangle, tight-chested, dry-mouthed, and a prickly, tingly burning up and down her legs, so that she had to duck into an alley before they rode back in order to relieve herself. He stood watch for her at the end of the alley by the street. She was utterly disgusted with herself, but what could she do.

"English women would do well to heed the sponge," he said in the vehicle. "Would you like this one? It has never been used."

"No, thank you, Henry."

"You are sure, now."

"I am not concerned with matters like that."

"Why not, Mary."

"Because I am interested, not in the personal, but the political."

"But of course. Everybody must say that."

Looking up at the spare black sky, she wondered what Richard the Cripple was doing. Reading, perhaps weeping a little. It would be cold and windy there.

That winter and the following spring and fall, every time she visited with Henry, walking about, eating out, and coming back to Joseph's afterward, she would feel annoyed and uncomfortable. They often had little spats. Henry said she was bad-tempered. She said he was spoiled. Sometimes she never wanted to see him again. It was such a strange friendship, teetering between love and hate, that often she wanted to give it up altogether. But then, when he missed the Thursday-night dinners once, twice in a row, she wanted to die.

CHAPTER 22

THE REVOLUTION in France was of great interest to Joseph's circle. Mary followed intently the reforms proposed for the education of women and the laws of marriage.

On November 4, 1789, Mary's friend and former mentor, the Reverend Dr. Richard Price, delivered a speech before the annual gathering in London of the Society Commemorating the Glorious Revolution of 1688, in which he expressed support for the Revolution in France. Edmund Burke, of the House of Commons, who had been sympathetic to the American Revolution, came out with his *Reflections on the Revolution in France* the following year, on the anniversary of Price's speech. Burke expressed dismay at the revolutionary attack on the aristocracy, defended the queen, Marie Antoinette. Burke championed the liberties that propertied Englishmen enjoyed under the rule of law. He stood in direct opposition to Price and the English Jacobins.

"Dr. Price," Mary told Joseph over their tea, "is the one who introduced the work of Rousseau and Locke and Hume to me. He also pointed out Aphra Behn, Susanna Centlivre, Mary Manley, Miss Astell, and Lady Montagu, in his discussion of British intellectual life. He suggested that I myself become a writer. He gave me your name. You know that. Surely the least I can do is defend him and his ideas in a short piece."

"Nobody talked to you like that before?"

"Nobody. He was wonderful. And he took me right in hand. This was when I had my little school at Newington Green with my sisters and Fanny Blood. Every Saturday afternoon, I would cross the Green to have tea with Dr. and Mrs. Price, and we would discuss the topic of the sermon to be given that Sunday. Price corresponded with Jefferson and Franklin across the ocean and Condorcet in France. He knew Dr. Johnson well, and Joseph Priestley is a friend. He is the one who told me that if I ever wrote a book I should send it to one Joseph Johnson, who, like himself, was a Dissenter in the full use of that word. So you see that is why I must write this defense."

"What is this short piece to be called?" Joseph appeared downcast.

"*A Vindication of the Rights of Man.*"

"Are you feeling well, Mary?"

"Yes, why?"

"You seem so . . ."

"Winter is drawing near again. You do not seem that well yourself."

"It sounds large to me, ambitious, this defense of Price."

"No, just a little pamphlet along the lines of what Paine would write. I shall attack Burke, defend the Revolution in France, give a short history of the struggle."

"Oh, is that all?"

"I am going to start tomorrow."

The next day Mary was working on this document when Joseph came upstairs, handed her an envelope with a red wax seal. She got her paper knife with the ivory handle, a gift from Joseph actually, and sliced open the top of the envelope, took out the heavy piece of cream paper, opened it. There was a drawing of a horse in the upper right-hand corner and in the middle of the page, in an ornate script, it said: I must see you. I have been having dreams.

"Can I see?" Joseph asked politely.

"No."

"Let me see."

She wrote down something, pushed the paper over to him.

It said: Joseph, mind your own business.

"What is it? What is the matter?"

"You ask me to help with the magazine. I help with the magazine. I write many, many articles. You want me to do translations. I do translations. I write a book for parents. You tell me you want me to do some serious work. Now, when I am doing serious work, you want to hinder me."

"No, no, on the contrary. I thought you received a personal letter."

"Yes, yes, and not just you, but Henry, too. I do not want love letters now, inquiries about my health. Leave me alone."

"Let me read a little of what you've written against Burke, and I will be quiet as a mouse."

She shoved him some pages.

Security of property! Behold, in a few words, the definition of English liberty . . . But softly—it is only the property of the rich that is secure; the man who lives by the sweat of his brow has no asylum from oppression; the strong man may enter—when was the castle of the poor sacred? . . . I cannot avoid expressing my surprise that when you recommended our form of government as a model, you did not caution the French against the arbitrary custom of pressing men for the sea service. You should have hinted to them, that property in England is much more secure than liberty, and not have concealed that the liberty of an honest mechanic—his all—is often sacrificed to secure the property of the rich. For it is a farce to pretend that a man fights for his country, his hearth, or his altars, when he has neither liberty nor property.

"My God, Mary, you are more revolutionary than Paine."

"It is the truth and everybody knows it. And I do not need Fuseli's attentions or your interference."

"Yes, I agree."

"I have my routine. I have my life. Everything is under control."

"You have your routine."

"Yes, I have my routine. And I am independent."

Indeed, though she lived with Joseph, for breakfast she would have bread and cheese; for dinner, sheep's trotters or pig's ear soused, cabbage or potatoes or parsnips. She and Johnson would sup together on cold neat's tongue, cold apple patsy, cold roast beef. They did daily tea with tea cakes and tarts.

She only had to buy coal for her grate and soap to wash her clothes. Her expenses were under one pound a week, for Johnson did not charge her rent and paid her a small sum for her work. Had she not been sending money to her sisters she could have bought food from the chandler's shop, the pie man, the stall, or the baker. She bought her clothes secondhand from the dealers in old clothes at the rag fair on Monmouth Street. Two new dresses, the green-and-white-striped, bought at the draper Robert Gibbon's in Ludgate Hill and sewn by a dressmaker at Cheapside, and a beautiful white dress in the French style, and later a shawl, pretty shoes. She bought new muslin and a strip of Belgian lace to make a new bed shift. And she had her dressing gown.

"You have your routine, but *is* everything under control?"

All was in order. What need had she, she said to herself, of a person's particular attentions, his dreams, his sponges, his wives, his predilections, what-have-you? If he wished to see her, he must wait until Thursday. And Johnson, Johnson would have to learn to be less jealous of her work.

Mrs. Mason, for that particular Thursday dinner, had made a salmagundi according to Hannah Glasse's *The Art of Cookery Made Plain and Easy*; that is, each part of the salad was kept separate and arranged in its own saucer. Had it been midsummer, the spaces between the saucers would have been filled with watercress and nasturtium.

"Mary is working on something quite important," Joseph announced to all and sundry at the dinner.

"Is this to be her big book, her famous book?" Fuseli asked.

"Go ahead, laugh at me," she said, tossing her head back. She was wearing the gauzy white dress in the French style, with a scarf turbaned on her head.

"I do not think this is going to be her big book, but it is getting close to it. That is what I think."

"Hear, hear," Christie said.

"There is talent at this table, mark my words," Paine said. "Some of us are to be known."

"Who is it going to be, Mr. Loud-Mouth, you?" Christie asked.

"Maybe. Maybe me. Maybe Blake. Maybe Fuseli. Maybe Mary," Paine said.

"Certainly not Blake," Christie countered. "He is too much the lunatic."

"Maybe all of us," Mary said.

"We shall stand," Joseph said, in fact standing and holding his port glass aloft, "we shall stand among the stellar lights of this place and time."

"All places," Paine growled. "All time."

"Mrs. Mason, bring more port. This calls for a toast."

"Everything calls for a toast," Christie remarked. "For you."

"Yes, and are you not glad, Christie, my lad?"

"I wish we were paid for our brilliance."

"I see you consider yourself a part of this glowing constellation, Christie."

"I must tell you my latest vision," Blake said, his eyes rolling. "And I must tell you that I care little for my reputation in this world."

"Pass the potatoes, Mary, my love."

Fuseli put his foot over hers. She moved it.

"A tree was filled with angels, bright angelic wings bespangling every bough like stars," Blake said.

"Have we not heard this vision before, Blake, old man?"

"No, Joseph, that other one was God, God in the tree. This is angels."

Mary gave Joseph a beady stare, as if to say, Not another holy tree.

"Gravy, please."

Joseph kicked Mary.

"Ouch."

"What is that, my dear." Fuseli was all concern. "Have we hurt ourself somewhere? Shall I kiss it?"

Joseph gloated.

Mary kicked Joseph.

"Somebody kicked me." That was Godwin, perfectly expendable in Mary's books, being both dull and ugly.

"Sorry, old chap."

Joseph looked down at his plate.

Mary was saying: "Price defended the storming of the Bastille, Burke attacked him."

"The lousy monarchist," Paine said. "We will show him a thing or two. Locke believes in the right of revolution."

"Well, I am telling you it must have been a sight to behold," Joseph was telling Paine, "the women shouting for bread at Versailles."

"Marie Antoinette did *not* say, 'Let them eat cake.' I know that story is abroad," Blake added, "but it is not correct."

"Do not tell me you defend her like Burke. I abhor queens and kings. They will all fall."

"No, Paine," Blake said. "I do not defend her. But occasionally some truth is in order from whatever quarter it comes."

"The Revolution in France is the most exciting thing to happen since the Americans," Mary said.

"I should like to capture those angels in a tree, Blake, in a drawing," Fuseli said.

"Once I imagined (and this was a moonlight night in Newington Green when I had my school), I imagined a tree caught with silver, as if the boughs were hair flowing out with lovely ornaments, or a net in the sea dotted with fish, the scales iridescent."

"Long live the people of Atlantis," Fuseli declared.

"Long live Locke," Paine countered.

"What has Atlantis to do with what we are discussing," Joseph asked, wiping his mouth daintily on his napkin.

"Just everything," Fuseli answered.

"Locke is quite dead," Mary said.

"They have been growing gills along their necks for decades," Blake said.

"That they forced the king and queen back to Paris, the crowd, the people, the pure power of it all. Let them eat cake, my foot, my arse, my little finger. Antoinette *did* say that, the virago."

"Locke's ideas will live forever," Paine amended. "That we have a right to life, liberty."

"I had a dream that the people of Atlantis were crying," Mary said. "Oh, great blubberers they were, standing there, row upon row, as their country went down." Fuseli actually looked sad.

"How like the Americans to put in happiness instead of prosperity in their declaration. Life. Liberty. Happiness," Paine mused. "Fuseli, the whole thing is going to spill over all of Europe. The world will never be the same. The Age of Innocence is over."

"Hear, hear, Paine," Christie said.

Wonderful, Mary thought, narrowing her eyes. Fuseli has dreams. He says the people of Atlantis have grown gills. Blake will have angels singing from trees. Monarchy is to fall across the world, according to Paine. If King Louis is to go, what of our own inadequate, foolish king?

"Excuse me." Somebody had put his foot on hers.

"Will everybody keep their feet to themselves," Mary announced.

"Atlantis will rise again," Henry Fuseli said, finger raised to the sky.

"Let us hope," Tom Paine said, "that their form of government is democratic. No green kings."

No doubt the *Analytical Review* would cover this great event, Mary surmised.

"The staff of the *Analytical Review* should be in France," she said. "You know how biased the English press is, and particularly against the French."

Mary imaged green prisoners held in check by nets and seaweed shackles. Merrie Olde England would never tolerate such difference, she knew, for if brown people were enslaved on plantations in America despite the rhetoric of freedom, green people in England would surely be put in Newgate. Was there a fair society anywhere?

"Opium dreams," Joseph teased. "That is all Atlantis is."

Opium. Everybody smiled, everybody's favorite. Or laudanum, everybody's second favorite, which was opium mixed with alcohol. Or plain old alcohol. Sherry or port, gin because it was so cheap. Or smoking tobacco from America. Now, there was a pleasure. Or snuff. Or chocolate. Coffee. Tea. Pleasures abounded.

"Do you have any?" Fuseli looked at Joseph.

"No. Mary used it."

"I did no such thing."

Sometimes they smoked it in the evening, she and Joseph. When it was cold and the wind was whipping and she was feeling particularly desolate, they would sit before the fire with the pipe, passing it back and forth. Not much needed to be said. And after a while the shadows in the room receded and the fire spread its warmth like yellow liquid, like melted gold, along the walls and in a river across the floor. At such times, Mary forgave her father almost and understood her mother somewhat, and wished well for her sisters sort of, and many harsh words that she could remember down the halls of her personal history book took back their sting. During such nights, all was possible, as long as one felt well enough in the morning.

"No wonder the French were up in arms. The wheat crop failed," Godwin said at the table in measured tones.

"Yes, Godwin, speak, speak."

"That exacerbated centuries of unfair taxation and neglect. The courts are so extravagant. The kings are incompetent. The country is falling down around their ears."

"Whereas everything is wonderful in England," Joseph said.

"Opium will be our downfall," Paine offered. "It is the scourge of mankind."

"Indeed," Christie said. "But a welcome one."

In England, children were fed opium to make them sleep and young ladies ate it sticky black and unmixed after tea. It was eaten in parlors and bedrooms, in coffeehouses and tea gardens, at the baths and coach stands, in clubs and at balls, in shops and Gin Lane. Mary had heard that Henry Fuseli was a devotee and derived his visions in a milky blur of laudanum. Whereas Blake came upon his visions naturally. Mary did not have visions except in her sleep, but she liked opium on occasion, and laudanum when she was distressed, and brandy to celebrate, and gin because it was cheap.

"We need something," Christie said, "or we shall go mad."

"I know what you are thinking of, old boy, but let me merely point to Hogarth's picture 'Bedlam,' the last in the series of *The Rake's Progress*. Crazed by syphilis," Henry Fuseli said. "Brings to mind a certain Mr. Boswell."

"Why is poor Boswell always in the thick of things here. Does anybody know the fellow?" Joseph asked.

"Does anybody want to know him," Fuseli countered. "The damn Tory."

Mary found Henry Fuseli intolerably rude.

"Henry, you are decadent." Joseph looked at him in such a way that she had a passing doubt about the two of them. But Fuseli was married, after all. "So, so decadent."

"We are not decadent," Fuseli insisted. "We are English."

"I am the Revolution," Paine shouted out.

"Paine, you are particularly revolting when you are besotted."

"What about the *Memoirs of a Woman of Pleasure*? Isn't that an English book?"

"You know about Fanny Hill, Mary?" Fuseli's frog eyes bulged.

Mary wanted to say: Keep your frogs to yourself.

"Everybody knows about Fanny Hill."

"They do?" Blake asked.

"I doubt it."

"Some people *are* born blind, Joseph," Christie admitted.

"Not the French," Paine added. "The men wear high-heeled shoes over there just as a matter of course," Paine said.

"It is what else they do with them," Christie put in.

"What else *do* they do with them?" Godwin wanted to know.

"Gluttony is our vice," Joseph said. "Would you pass the rack of lamb, please. And gout our national disease. The pudding, please. That is definite. More roast beef," he called down to Mrs. Mason.

"No, gluttony is not it at all. Other vices abound. Look at our friend Boswell," Blake pointed out.

"Yes, poor Dr. Johnson had to remain mute days on end, nobody to take down his memoirs, because Boswell was busy running to the apothecary." Mary had been to the Apothecaries Garden in Chelsea. It was full of rare and exotic plants from around the world, medicinal and otherwise. She wondered which one Boswell had to take.

"You mean hobbling. You cannot *run* to the apothecary with something like that, my good man, my good woman."

"Yes, I mean hobbling."

"Well, that must be when Johnson worked on the *Dictionary*," Paine said.

"You have it wrong. Boswell did not meet Johnson until after the *Dictionary*," Mary corrected.

"Exactly," Paine replied. "Thanks to Boswell, spelling is uniform."

"They say Johnson's wife was old," Joseph said, "poor fellow. And that she was a veritable virago."

"No older than you," Mary put in. "Veritable virago, is that your term, Joseph?" Mary was sensitive to references to women's ages. She had read some writer who asked what business women of forty had to do in the world. She hoped to live that long to show him.

"Mrs. Mason," Joseph shouted. "Port. Port. Bring on more decadence. More. That dreadful rack of lamb was cooking for a good three hours. I told Mrs. Mason not to rush it. Mrs. Mason, where are you?"

"What this country needs is a good strawberry tart," Fuseli said.

Mrs. Mason appeared with a silver tray.

"Just in time," Joseph said. The port was in a tall decanter and she set out Joseph's chunky cut-glass. There was mincemeat pie on the table; a line of ants clustered around the strawberry tarts and pie crumbs on the white cloth. Some mice were running along the baseboards.

"This is port, not sherry," Joseph said.

"That is correct, Mr. Johnson."

While the drawing room was sparse and unornamented, the dining room was lavish. The cloth, the chandelier, the sideboard with Wedgwood china, rosewood chairs with needlepoint seats of a man and a woman getting out of a carriage. Pink and blue, little dot eyes.

"Let us hear three cheers for good old John Locke," Henry said.

They lifted their port glasses. Cheers, cheers, cheers.

"Mary, do not dream off," Henry said.

"I am not dreaming off, I was merely thinking."

(Mary was to write her sisters later: It was during this rambling, funny talk about Atlantis, the rights of the Atlantian fishpeople, that I began thinking of a book I might write applying the rhetoric of Locke, all the revolutionary thought to the problem, or rather the issue, of women, our development, the necessity of *our* rights.)

"Do not think so much," Fuseli said then. "It is not becoming in a woman. Your eyebrows are twisting together like tree roots at war."

"Mary is very becoming when she thinks, very indeed, Henry."

"I am going to take Mary out for some air," Fuseli decided. "The air will do her good, Joseph, a world of good."

"She has all the air she can use right here in this house," Joseph said. "She does not need more air."

"I think Mary can speak for herself," Mary said. "And for her intake of air and everything else."

ALL DURING the dinner Mary wanted to go upstairs to her desk to gather her wits. She had an idea. She wanted to scribble out something, for she now remembered where she had seen the comment about women over forty. It was in the novel *Evelina*, by Fanny Burney. A rude and rapacious man says: "I don't know what the devil a woman lives for after forty: she is only in other folks' way."

Mary was thirty-one. Mrs. Johnson was forty-seven, Samuel twenty-six when they married. Yet she had heard that they loved each other. Had she lived, what would Mrs. Johnson have thought of Dr. Johnson's antics, his constant association with the lecherous Mr. Boswell, and Mr. Johnson's saving David Garrick from eviction, and Mr. Johnson swilling his drink at all hours of the night and day?

Mary had to write little notes to herself. Otherwise, she forgot things. Her desk was covered with slips of paper, random jottings. A quick sentence about Locke, Atlantis, women, age, that's what she wanted to put down, keep for later. Then she turned to her project defending Dr. Price and the Revolution in France. She attacked what she considered to be Burke's vanity, envy, ambition, infantile sensibility. An ad hominem argument, she knew, but was it not enough that he attacked Price?

Staying with her candle and feather, ink pot and page deep into the night, she felt like an island in a black ocean. She worked with her stays off. Outside, all was closed down save the few streets which had whale-oil lamps or the few windows bearing candles, sick people maybe, other writers, solitaires like herself. Once in a while she would hear a laughing voice downstairs, a coach, horses on cobbles, what-ho, whoa, who goes there. Then all sound would be swallowed up by the night except the scritch-scratch of her quill going across the page, the shifting of her silk robe, a sigh, Joseph on the stairway blowing his nose.

"Mary, how is it going?"

"Not well, Joseph, not well at all."

"Really?" He lowered his head on his arm.

"Really. In fact, I am seriously considering abandoning this project." She got up from her chair. Her back ached, her eyes itched, her fingers were red where she had pressed the quill.

"You do look tired," he said, wheezing a little.

She looked at Joseph. Another issue of the magazine was due out in a week. She had written two articles for it. They were already at the printer, four pages. Joseph looked thin. He was always ill with his lungs right before an issue came out. He and Christie would end up frantic before they got the issue to the printer. When the downstairs fire went out and they had not the time to build it again, Joseph wrapped his hands in rags to keep them warm. Christie would not sit or sleep at all, but worked straight from the floor under the table. Then Joseph would be sick and they would have to start the fire in the kitchen range so that Joseph might inhale the steam, drape the cloth, set the pots to boil so that he could breathe freely again.

"It sounded so impressive, and a rather impressive title."

"It is not good, Joseph. You would be embarrassed to publish such drivel."

"Would I, now?"

Joseph was wearing buckled breeches, striped stockings, a tight-fitting waistcoat, and no cravat; his high-stand collar was undone. He wore no wig, as always, and no powder in his hair, as always, to declare his republican allegiance, and as always his blue eyes gave him the look of innocence and irresponsibility, and sadness. William Blake had taken to wearing a red hat in identification with the French. Women on the street were in aprons and caps like the French peasants, or perhaps they wished to dress like Marie Antoinette, who played at looking poor not out of loyalty to her subjects but in fashion with Rousseau's praise of simple things, the country life. Mary still wore either her black dress, plain green, or her green-striped, sometimes her white. She had her new dressing gown. Without her stays and with her hair down, she knew she looked like a marketwoman, but it was just Joseph.

"I do not want you to strain yourself, my dear," Joseph said.

A while back, before she understood Joseph, Mary used to scribble little schoolgirl notes about expeditions she and Joseph would take.

OUR TRIP

I looking out the window of the coach seeing cows and sheep, his soft hand on mine. And as the sun goes down and twilight falls, he takes out our hamper, trying to hold our provisions steady as the coach lurches from side to side. He has a chicken leg, I a slice of roast. We sleep leaning against each other, my hand across his chest. What a darling couple, the other passengers say, nodding their heads in approval.

When we get there (a rustic cabin on a lake), we look all about, saying, Oh, see the buttercups and the minnows and pretty rocks. Look over here. And how softly the water ripples. There are crickets in the grass and ducks, of course, larger animals maybe, and I, carefully wending my way through the tall grass, come across a wolf. But I am not frightened. I look at him with a sense of recognition.

In the morning Joseph and I have to go to town and buy a few supplies. I absolutely have to have the ingredients for whipped syllabub—sherry, wine, cider, lemon or orange whey, all sweet, and the grated rind of one lemon. Joseph merely requires small beer. The men on the porch of the store, country folk in straw hats, tell us that the weather is going to change, but we say that we are leaving before then.

But they never took long, romantic trips. Such fantasies were given up long ago. Instead, they would have dangerous conversations about slim men with thin wrists and long fingers. And as they became closer friends, they moved to hair color, size, temperament, and cast of mind, she saying this, he saying that, she feeling that she was conspiring against herself, and he becoming more and more at ease.

And it did not stop there. On their morning walks, Joseph would use his cane to point out: Oh, there is a nice one, do you fancy him?

The world was ripe for the picking and they both looked at the same orchard. Her heart would trickle blood during these expeditions. She would be sick with longing and shame, and at the same time feel titillated by such talk. She would have a sour taste in her mouth. She would want to yell, Stop. But she could not. She hated herself, felt traitor to herself. Yet could not help herself.

"Well, Mary, do what you think best. Do not finish this *Vindication* thing. Paine is coming out with something, he tells me."

"What is that supposed to mean?" Sometimes Joseph could be so annoying. "What is he coming out with? What are you telling me?"

"Simply this: if you cannot finish it, do not finish it. I appreciate that it is very hard work, writing a pamphlet on a political issue, for a woman especially."

"For a woman especially?" Mary turned, facing him squarely, and put her hands on her hips.

"Arduous work, tedious, taxing, requiring tenacity, Mary."

He could be so prim and prissy, so fussy, so wrong.

"For a woman especially? You are terrible, tyrannical and two-faced. In point of fact, I am going to finish it. You will see. They will all see. Everybody will see."

The everybody she had in mind who would see included her father, who did not care what she did. Nobody cared. In her heart of hearts she knew.

"Men will see," she said lamely. What men, she wondered. All men? Mankind? "My future husband will see."

"Pray tell, who is that?"

"I do not know yet," Mary answered petulantly.

"Well, let me know when you know."

"You do not believe that I can finish, do you?"

"I will believe it when I see it, Mary."

"Women who read will see." Maybe women would, it occurred to her. Maybe women would read her because she was a woman, a woman of sense. "*You* will see."

"Very well, suit yourself," Joseph said, smiling, and turning to go. "Oh, by the way, Fuseli wants you to go with him somewhere. He is downstairs."

"Tell him I am busy."

"Mary, tell him yourself."

"Tell him I can see him the first part of next week."

"Will you be done by then?"

"Yes, I will be done, all done, done up, done ditty, done. And I am never, never going to take on a project like this again, I promise you. You can toast to it. Not for you, not for anybody. And can you have Mrs. Mason bring up my supper for a while?"

"Is that all you have to say?"

"Joseph," she said wistfully. "Joseph."

"What."

"Oh, it is nothing."

"Are you certain?"

"Yes."

CHAPTER 24

THEY WANT to make his skin into a coat and his tail into a switch, and his hooves glue and the eyes marbles, the teeth choppers. Mary follows him out into the street, tracing him by scent alone, for she cannot really see him. It is a warm, balmy night. The horse is waiting, and they get on it, ride to the coast. They talk softly to each other. But they cannot hear each other, for the rush of wind cancels sound. Now she is alone riding on the horse. She is trying to talk to the horse. She has to hear him through her fingers on his mouth, and her words sink into his neck. At one point she falls asleep, her head bumpity-bumps on his back and she dreams within her dream that she is on a rocking horse in the nursery and her brother is saying, as always: I am master here. When she wakes up from her dream within a dream, her mouth is full of sleep, sour gums, but her nose tells her that they are riding through the forest, and then comes the warm salt smell of the sea. She looks down, sees sand, and on the glistening particles, all held still for a single second, is a small dead mouse with his red insides showing. Red. But when she looks closer it is strawberries sprouting a beard of gray fuzzy mold.

"You were crying in your sleep," Joseph said, shaking her shoulder.

She opened her eyes. His hair was sticking up at the sides and down about his shoulders and he was in his snake-satin dressing gown, barefoot. He looked like a wolf or a red fox seated at the edge of her bed, a strange character in a puppet show, half human, half feral.

"I had a bad dream," she whispered.

"Shh," he said, stroking her face. "Shh, go back to sleep. Are you finished with the piece?"

"Yes, it is there on the desk."

Joseph went over, took up the stack of pages.

"Fleet Street first thing in the morning," he said. "This is the beginning."

Of what, Mary thought, falling back to sleep.

The next morning she could barely drag herself about. Fuseli appeared in the afternoon, very done up and rather nervous.

"You seem tired, my dear."

"No, Henry, not at all."

"But that is a fine dress."

"Thank you." She felt groggy and out of sorts.

They secured a phaeton as if bound for the sun or in this case the moon, for it was getting late and the air chilly and they rode over to Lincoln's Inn Fields to a grand fine house to visit a Mr. Andrews, a good friend of Henry Fuseli's, and a more distasteful man Mary could not imagine. Furthermore, when Mr. Andrews went out of the room, Fuseli grabbed her and kissed her hard right on the lips.

"Are you insane?" she said.

"Yes, yes I am. Shh, Mr. Andrews is coming back."

Mr. Andrews's house had a laundry and a stillroom, a buttery, a bakehouse, a dairy, and a brewery. Each floor had a privy with a system of pipes and traps. It was advanced, very formidable. Mr. Andrews was a scientist. He had a collection. Bits and pieces of ancient pottery, Greek statues, an Egyptian tomb. He had a skylight in his house, and a picture gallery filled with paintings by Hogarth, and in his library the glass cases contained leather volumes banded in gold—Swift and Defoe, Richardson—and bound issues of the *Gentleman's Magazine*, the *Tatler*, and the *Spectator*. But the *pièce de résistance* was kept in a locked closet.

"There is a skeleton in the closet," Mary gasped, opening the door.

"Oh, it is quite the thing," Fuseli said.

"Everyone must have one," Mr. Andrews confirmed.

"But who is this, where did you get him, her, it?" The last thing she wanted to do was end up in some gentleman's closet.

"Quite expensive," Fuseli said.

"Grave robbers," Mr. Andrews admitted. "We have to compete,

we private collectors, with the Royal College of Surgeons. It is neck and neck."

"I can imagine," Mary said icily. She did not like Mr. Andrews's booty. She preferred the collection at the British Museum. The baby alligator, with its dry, dusty skin and the patch of yellow on its belly and its row of tiny baby teeth, was like a member of the family. The big bearskin rug and dead sea turtle of that public collection seemed as if they were a part of somebody's private collection in a house. Mr. Andrews's, which was a house, seemed like a museum. The dark, dusty artifacts in the half light of the early evening had a strange aura, as if the world existed to be dead and then displayed.

"I do not want to end up part of a collection, Henry."

They had been drinking port in the library when the necessity of leaving grabbed her. She had to get out of there.

"Henry," she said softly.

Mr. Andrews had to be excused for a moment again; he would be right back.

"Is he going in his thing?" she whispered. Mary imagined him locked in one of his privy closets among all the pipes and tubes, seated on top of the porcelain bowl. "Tell him I have to go home."

"You do not have to go home."

"I want to go home."

Before she could blink, Henry was kneeling in front of her. "I dreamed of this," he said, drawing his hands down Mary's bodice. "We were at the seaside," he continued, "and you were lying on the boardwalk, naked, with a white silk sheet over you. I drew my hands down the sheet, and said: Let us go in and make love. You said: Yes."

"I want to go back, back home," she said to Henry, disengaging his hands, which had affixed themselves to her breasts like scalloped seashells. "I hate the seaside." She rose to her feet. "A is an ass," she hissed at him. "B is a beast, C is a callow idiot, D is a dastard and a devil."

"Why do you want to leave? It is so nice here."

"This place is out of a Gothic horror tale, Henry, a Castle of Otranto. It is not for live people. Everything is dead here. Mr. Andrews wants to stuff us, display us, and you want to ruin me. I have just finished writing a solid work of general interest and you treat me like a strumpet. I am tired."

"No, I am treating you like a woman, for a change."

"What do you mean?"

"I mean, everybody treats you as if you were a man, a block of wood. I see the woman underneath all the erudition."

"You do?"

"She is quivering: Take me, take me."

"She is?"

"She wants to be ravished."

"She does?"

"Yes, Mary, she does."

"Mr. Andrews," Mary, still standing, said as he reentered the room. "We must be going. It has been lovely. Thank you very much."

"Oh, but Mrs. Wollstonecraft."

"Miss Wollstonecraft."

"You have only just arrived."

"Yes, yes, but my mother is very ill, and my sister is distraught beyond description, and my brother, my brother is masterfully lame, a riding accident, and my father, he is dead."

"My gracious. Henry did not tell me of this." Mr. Andrews put his hand to his well-dressed heart. He was wearing a short red jacket and a cravat of green silk, tight yellow trousers tucked in soft-leather boots, and his hair was short, combed forward. He had a haughty and exhausted manner, as if the world were just too, too tedious.

"Yes, well, Henry wanted to spare you the details. Goodbye and God rest, Mr. Andrews. Charming house, I am sure."

"I cannot take you anyplace," Henry said as soon as they were outside, "without you making a scene. You are not on stage, you know. And this 'A is for acorn' business is not polite. You are not in baby school anymore. You think because you are a little intelligent . . . that you are an intelligent woman. Listen, men do not care for that, especially when it means criticism for them. Men do not like strange women. They like comfort. There are enough difficulties in the world without finding more in your home or bed. Intelligent women believe

they have a lot to offer the world? Do not shake your head. I know
you do. Well, my little friend from Birmingham . . ."

"Yorkshire and Wales, and before that, Spitalfields."

"Wherever they grow your kind, let me tell you," he muttered in
her ear, hurrying her along the street, "you think you have a lot to
offer the world, well, my child, people may not want what it is you
have to offer. That is right. Have you ever considered that? People,
men, like cooperative women, gentle women, happy women, gracious women, thankful women, sweet women, pretty women, kind
women . . ." At each appellation he stabbed the cobblestones with his
walking stick. "Above all, we like loyal women. Now, that is the world.
That is the way the world works. Accept it or . . ."

"Die?"

"No, do not overdramatize, accept it or accept the consequences.
That is just what I mean. Where did Joseph find you, pray tell, under
a thorn bush?"

"In a great house in Ireland, Henry. Well, here we are," Mary
said. She got out of the phaeton. "No, no, do not bother. All this man/
woman talk has certainly tired this little lady out. Thank you for a
lovely afternoon, Henry. It has been a pleasure. Was polite on that list,
polite women? Cooperative women, gracious women, women with
large breasts and big haunches, women with sponges up their canals.
Is that what men like? Thank you very much for telling me. Now I
can plan my life accordingly."

"Mary. Congratulations on the book. Joseph tells me it is brilliant."

"Oh, stuff and nonsense, Henry." She slipped into the house, ran
upstairs, undid her skirts and her stays, her garters and socks, her
shoes, her bodice, her collar, her shawl. She took down her hair,
being careful to remove the artificial violets she had on either side of
a tight roll. She washed her face of powder, her cheeks of rouge, her
eyes of kohl. Naked, she put on her dressing gown. There, that felt
better.

"What is for supper?" she shouted down to Mrs. Mason.

"Roast duck and plum pudding," Mrs. Mason shouted back.
"Fruit and cheese."

"I can hardly wait."

Her good mood held up through supper and then began to flag. She burst into tears at dessert.

"What?" Joseph asked. "What is it?"

"I am S," she said.

"Sweet dear, do not be sad."

"And T."

"Perhaps you should go to bed."

"I finish the book and is there one person in the world who is happy for me?"

"Yes. Two."

"You and Mrs. Mason. Wonderful. You know what I mean, Joseph."

Joseph was in his dressing gown and slippers. They were eating in the drawing room in front of the fire.

"I must learn," she said, "how to tread the middle ground between loneliness and freedom."

"Loneliness and freedom." Joseph shook his head. "That is hard."

"Maybe too hard." What did I do, she asked herself, to merit such an attack from Fuseli? For, despite herself, she had started to love him.

"What happened to fame? Is that any consolation, my dear? As I recall, you were interested in it."

"Oh, fame," she said wearily. "What difference if there is nobody close to share it with. Do you think that is the middle ground? Maybe I *am* famous or will be, but I do not feel anything. Is that the middle ground, neutral and nothing?"

"No, fame is the highroad, and it is lonely and free."

"I do not want to be part of anybody's collection, either."

"No."

"And I want to be appreciated for what I am, the full person— an adult woman, whatever that is."

"Yes."

"And I do not want somebody less intelligent than I telling me what to do."

"Yes, or no. I mean . . ."

"And I want somebody to bring me coffee in the morning."

"Yes."

"Not a servant, either. And I want someone to say: There, there, there, there."

"There, there, there, there."

"Oh, Joseph, not you."

CHAPTER 25

FUSELI WAS a collector of sorts, too. He had a collection of stuffed mammals. Small mammals in his study, and in summer, in the tree branches outside his window. He trapped them. The Fuselis lived on a close, shady street, Foley Street. Henry Fuseli and his wife occupied three floors, and they took in a lodger upstairs in the attic, a poor poet. Mary walked about the block, going up and down, trying to get a glimpse of Henry during the times he ignored her. All she saw was activity in the kitchen, the cook crystallizing some violets and cowslips, the boiling of jams, the making of pickles.

Mary never saw *him* there, his actual face or body passing in front of a window, but she knew when he was home by the boots left out by the boot scrape. The servant was negligent; they could easily have been stolen. Mary often wanted to knock on the door. Here, here are your boots. She did not, though, and really, she did not want him to see her spying this way. For her it was quite good enough to be in front of his house, on the same street, in his city. She marveled that they existed at the same time and had somehow met each other. She wished, though, her thoughts could enter the keyhole and see and hear everything—for instance, Henry in his nightshirt and nightcap. He no doubt kissed his wife on the forehead before each went to his or her respective bedroom. And they both would kiss the baby. And she, Mary, would be there, on his breath.

"I love my wife," Henry would say from time to time when he was in the mood to see Mary, take her for a stroll.

"Of course you love your wife." They could be in Kew Gardens, with the aviary and menagerie with the Chinese and Tartarian pheasants. The basin was stocked with waterfowl when he came out with his pronouncement.

"I do love her."

But the first time Mary saw Fuseli's wife, she was surprised. She found the woman to be plump and pretty, a fat little sparrow, brown and perky, but without a trace of intelligence in her face. The woman was rushing out of the house, her hand holding down her hat, her skirts billowing out in back of her. How can he love her, Mary wondered. How can an artist find inspiration in *that*. The woman was so ordinary. When once Mrs. Fuseli came to dinner at one of Joseph's Thursday nights, Mary saw that the woman was gap-toothed, like the Wife of Bath in Chaucer's *Canterbury Tales*, a sure sign of lasciviousness. Yet Henry had described her as cold, cold as ice. And such a common kind of charm. Henry kept his head down, did not look up during that dinner. His wife had nothing to say, either, and stared at Mary, the only other woman at the table, as if she were an exotic animal, something with fur and green claws.

A day or so after that dinner, Mary said to Joseph: "I do not understand anything anymore. I feel I am going a bit mad. I am frightened. Tell me, tell me something."

"Tell you what?" Joseph was poking around in his pipe.

"The world. Tell me of the world."

"Stick to your writing, Mary," Joseph said, putting his pipe down, sniffing a little as he took some snuff out of his box. The evening gloom swallowed his face, made his legs sticks. Compared to Henry, he was way too thin, hardly substantial.

"I do not want to hear that."

"I know. I know what you want to hear. But why do you care for one who will bring you pain? Is that what you want? What you think you deserve? Mary, have some patience. When did this obsession start? Surely your work holds more opportunity for success and happiness?"

Her pamphlet attacking Edmund Burke had been roundly attacked in its turn. Joseph was convinced that it was because she was a woman writing about the rights of man. Anyway, people were buying it, that was the important thing.

"My feelings for him crept up behind me," she answered. Compared to Richard, Henry was a grown man. Compared to Blake, he was funny. Compared to Paine, he was tolerant. Compared to Joseph, he was masculine. Compared to Christie, he was serious. He was not slim and delicate, fine-boned and dreamy, but he was a man of note and accomplishment, a famous artist. He wanted to draw her. His eyes when he looked at her were like fire. She felt consumed.

"Nobody else cares for me, Joseph," she said.

"Is that true, Mary?" Joseph sighed.

"Yes, it is."

"I care for you."

"As a friend."

"And so what is wrong with a friend. You will find that a friend will stand the test of time far better than these come-and-go lovers you see on the street. These things tend to be a great deal of trouble and grief."

"I will soon be thirty-two, Joseph."

"I am one hundred and two, Mary."

"I am lonely, Joseph."

"*I* am lonely," Joseph replied peevishly. "Everybody is always lonely. What happened to the middle ground between loneliness and freedom?"

"Henry knows so much about everything."

"About middle grounds? I doubt it. Oh, Mary." Joseph shook his head, sticking a good bit of snuff up his left nostril and sneezing. "He knows the classics, his craft. He is a brilliant man, but he does not know that much about anything practical, least of all you."

"He is your friend, you invited him here, how can you malign him, how can you not like him?"

"I like him. It is just . . ."

"Do you think he loves me, Joseph?"

"I feel old," Joseph said. "Ancient."

"Do you promise he loves me. Promise. Promise."

"The man is married, for one," Joseph said, pinching his nostrils.

"What is for two."

"You know."

Joseph had acquired a rocking chair in the Ben Franklin style. He rocked for hours. This is my thinking chair, he would say. The

thoughts are coming fast and furiously. Or: Mr. Joseph is in his thinking chair, come back later. Or: Let me get in my thinking chair and
I will have the answer shortly. Mary thought he was in fact getting
old.

"What does it matter that he is married?"

"Of course it matters. It matters, Mary. You cannot marry him."

"You know what I think of marriage, Joseph?"

"I know what you say about it, my dear."

"He has to love me, Joseph, or I am done for."

"No, you are not done for. But why this great importance? Is it
necessary to you to be loved, and by him?"

"Yes."

"But you were not loved until . . . or for a while, for many years
you were not loved romantically."

"Not now, either, is that what you think? Now I may die any
day."

"*I* will die, and soon, I know it, for I think I have the ague, or
some other nasty malady. I do not look forward to having my blood
let. Maybe you should fetch the quinine. Perish the thought of leeches,
such a nasty business."

"Do you promise that he will come this Thursday for dinner."
She had left her chair, was kneeling before Joseph.

"Promise, please promise me."

Joseph shook his head. "I may not be alive by Thursday dinner,
not that you care." Joseph pursed his lips. "And this is the woman
who has written many articles, three books, and is working on her
fourth, this kneeling, begging, pathetic creature? Where is your pride?"

"I have none."

"You must."

"You will not promise, is that it?"

She was nearly in tears.

"Mary, this is going too far. Can you see yourself? And the man
is not even handsome. He is fat and bulbous."

"He is clever and fascinating, and handsome is as handsome does."

"Yes, but is he kind?"

"Not especially. Not at all."

"Exactly what I thought. Have you not been hurt enough?"

"What are you talking about?"

"Your childhood, your employments, all your experience."

"That is over, Joseph."

"It is never over, Mary, unless you face it. And if you do not face it . . . Do you see how you are repeating yourself, my dear?"

"Stop this dame-school philosophizing, Joseph."

"Or is it that hurt is all you know, so that you seek it again and again."

"Now *you* are being silly."

"Am I?"

"You must promise. You must. I will die if you do not promise he loves me."

Joseph shook his head sadly, took her chin in both his hands. "Dear girl, you are so desperate. Nobody is going to die."

"You must promise. You must."

"I promise," he said. "I promise, I promise."

CHAPTER 26

"I LOVE MAN as my fellow," Mary wrote as a note which she placed in a hatbox labeled *Rights of Woman*, "but his sceptre, real, or usurped, extends not to me, unless the reason of an individual demands my homage; and even then the submission is to reason, and not to man."

November 23, 1791

A world of ideas exists outside my window and also within my own head, dear Eliza. I promised Fanny that I would make something of my life. Sometimes, often, always, I fear I will fail. I am, well, as you can gather through my hesitation, confused. Sometimes I do not know how I get my work done on the review or the translations or my own. My head is dizzy. And my vision blurred. Sometimes I feel my legs give way beneath me. Dear sister, I cannot divulge the details at this time.

Eliza wrote back:

A world of ideas outside your window and in your head? Indeed you must feel very dizzy. Why not take up backgammon. Not nearly so distressing as this preoccupation with men. Is that not it? There are some who can indulge; others do not have the temperament. Surely you take it all too seriously. The aristocracy has nothing else to do but flirt all day long. You cannot afford that pastime. Why do you insist on being one of those sentimental heroines you see in the penny novels read by shopgirls and idle women? Is that what you are doing with your education? As for me, I am the dreary governess of two spoiled girls. I know nobody and my days are not filled with the joys of jabber or the fawning

*attention of effete men such as yours. The colors here are black
and brown. Am I to make anything of my life? Hardly. For as
you well know, I am undone. My only chance of happiness is
dead and gone. You prattle to me of writing books and dalliance.
How dare you, you who separated me from the only source of joy
in my life.*

Thank you, Mary. Very much.

Mary hated Eliza for scolding her, making her feel guilty and miserable,
ugly and selfish. That morning—it was a fresh morning—she wrote
back hurriedly:

*Eliza, you talk of my education. What education? And, darling
girl, we did the right thing. You know we did the only thing we
could. I am so sorry about the baby, truly I am, as I have said so
many times.*

Mary hesitated to use the word "baby." She crossed that out and wrote
instead "I am so sorry for everything." For how were they to know
that Mr. Bishop's sister could not keep the child alive? It was not her
fault either. It was bound to happen even if Eliza kept the baby herself.
That is what Mary told herself. The child was not strong, not well.
She wrote on.

*How could you have left Mr. Bishop other than the way you did?
You forget the circumstances. But do forget the circumstances, forget it all. Please, I am struggling now to be strong of heart. Eliza,
darling, do not be cross. I, too, am miserable over the whole thing.
I suffer.*

Mary wrote another note for her book, put it in her hatbox, which
she kept on top of her wardrobe.

*Men have superior strength of body, but were it not for mistaken
notions of beauty, women would acquire sufficient strength to enable them to earn their own subsistence, the true definition of inde-*

*pendence; and to bear those bodily inconveniences and exertions
that are requisite to strengthen the mind.*

*Let us then, by being allowed to take the same exercise as
boys, not only during infancy, but youth, arrive at perfection of
body, that we may know how far the natural superiority of man
extends.*

Mary looked up from the paper she was writing on.

"My God, Henry, I haven't seen you in weeks."

Henry's face was red from climbing the stairs up to her room. "I
dreamed that I came over to your house, up to your attic bedroom,
and fed you breakfast with a baby spoon. You were naked. I was
naked."

"You had that dream before, Henry."

"I never want to stop dreaming it, Mary."

It was early morning and the smell of porridge permeated the
house. She wondered if he was making the dream up to go with the
porridge and the new red ribbons which she wore at her wrist.

"Get the porridge, a small spoon."

"Henry, I do not think this is a good idea."

"It is a wonderful idea. Anyway, it is not an idea. It is a dream.
It will be real, neither an idea nor a dream, once we act it. The word
made flesh. Does that not excite you? It has been so long in coming."

"Henry, I am writing. Anyway, it is too bizarre."

"It is wonderfully bizarre. Why not bizarre? I love bizarre. Bizarre
is the joy of my life. You know that."

"But I do not know how."

"How what? Bizarre?"

"You know."

He started to laugh. "Oh, Mary, you funny girl."

"I am not a girl, Henry. I have been a seamstress, a lady's companion, a schoolmistress, a governess, a writer. I have written one
novel, a book on manners, a book on the education of girls, a political
tract, and numerous book reviews. I am working on still another political piece, a book championing women's rights. No matter that at

the present time it consists of notes in a hatbox. Henry, I am a fully grown woman."

"Not quite a grown woman, apparently. Your education has been deficient in several respects, dear girl. Is that true? How can you call yourself a woman? Are you not eager after all this time?"

"*That* does not make you a woman." She felt affronted. "Anyway, I have come close. There *are* other forms of affection. Richard and I used to . . ."

"What? Who is Richard?"

"A boy."

"What did you do? You never told me. What did you . . . ?"

"Rub."

"Rub?"

"Rub."

"That is all you did, Mary?"

"It was nice rubbing. It was wonderful. There are other forms of affection besides, well, *it*, as I keep pointing out to you."

"There are?" He looked baffled.

"Henry, I must tell you that . . ."

"I love you when you are being stupid."

"I do believe you do." She pushed her chair back, gave him a good hard look. "The fact of the matter, Mr. Fuseli, is I do not know what to do."

"My dear, sweet, darling girl, I will show you what to do. It is not difficult. You will just know what to do. It will happen. Trust me. Now, what I want you to do first is go downstairs, get a bowl of porridge, the smallest spoon. That is all. Bring it back up."

"Henry."

"Go," he said. "And hurry."

She went downstairs, rummaged for a small spoon, dished out some porridge.

"Does Henry need a bowl?" Joseph asked archly.

"Yes." Her voice was a little faint, her hands shook.

"Are you feeling well, Mary?"

"Yes, fine. I feel fine."

I will never feel the same again, she said to herself. I will never *be* the same again. Slowly, not trusting her feet, she climbed up the stairs. Her hands quivering, nearly spilling everything, she set the two bowls on the table, handed Henry the spoon.

"Sit down," he said.

She sat in the chair.

"No, the bed, the edge of the bed."

She sat on the edge of the bed.

"Good."

Looking straight into her eyes, he undid her bodice, untied her skirts, loosened her hair. She felt laid open, as if her very skin had been unbuttoned, drawn apart.

"You do the stays," he whispered.

"I cannot." Her hands were trembling.

"I will help you."

He fumbled at the laces of her stays. She had to assist him. He kissed her neck. She stood up, unfastened herself, and there she was naked before a man. She did not hide herself, but was painfully aware of her stomach, which was soft and full, and her thighs, which were heavy and long. Her breasts hung down, but the nipples were hard, erect, and her mound felt like a hive of buzzing bees. She felt shame, but when she looked up, his eyes were soft.

"You are a beautiful woman," he said, "and I am going to paint you."

"When?"

"Soon." He nuzzled her ear, took a little nip.

"I am afraid," Mary said.

"You must trust me."

"I do, but . . ."

"This whole thing is about trust."

"I will be thirty-three years old soon, Henry."

"Oh, my. In that case, we had better stop right this instant."

"Yes, I think so." She wanted to cry.

"I am joking with you. Mary. Mary."

He started to kiss her face, her eyes, her mouth.

"You are beautiful," he said. "And I love you."

"You do?"

"Yes. But first you must sit down and have your porridge, like a good girl."

He brought it over. Then he stepped neatly out of his breeches, first slipping off his shoes. There he stood in stockings, shirt, and waistcoat; his member, coming out of its sheath like a tulip, looked at her, eye to eye.

"I want you to eat all this up," he said.

It is happening, she said to herself. It is happening to me. She wanted it to be over and also to slow itself down. She wanted it to be the whole world, so there was nothing else.

"Open wide," he said, putting the porridge bowl on the floor.

The thing, which he called George, after the king, was slick and salty. He rocked back and forth, rubbing it along the roof of her mouth, pushing it down so she thought she might choke. She could have bitten it off, she realized. She would rather have had the porridge, for this was too much like Annie and the man in Bath.

"Cover your teeth with your lips, for God's sake. Let your mouth go slack."

She thought she might vomit.

"Are you feeling fine, still?" he asked. "Kneel, stick your hips out."

She wanted her mouth back.

"Your tongue is wonderful. Rough. Like a cat's tongue."

Mary was still thinking of things. She thought of her mother and father, her sister and Mr. Bishop. She thought of Dr. Price and Lady Kingsborough and Richard and the little girls. She thought why, if the whole world was at it, why she should think this occasion so momentous, so significant. When he began running his fingers along the inside of her thighs, she stopped thinking, but then he turned her roughly over like a slab of bacon, threw her over on her back, bit her nipples very hard, which hurt, and then, charging like a bull, he entered her.

She wanted to scream because it burned like fire. She thought she was going to die. She thought she was going to split apart. She wanted him out, out of her, out of her room, to be able to gather herself back to herself. He straddled her across her legs so she could not move them. And when she heaved her body up, he met her with greater force, sighing his own name: "Henry, Henry, Henry."

He kept at it, not stopping, for what seemed years, making grunting noises like a pig at slops, moaning and groaning, until he finally started to throb like a robin redbreast and his eyes rolled back like one crazed, asleep, or dead, and he was:

"Finished."

"Henry," she mumbled.

"What say?"

"Henry," she wailed, gulping in air.

"You liked it. I knew you would."

"Oh, Henry," she cried pitifully.

"I knew you would be grateful to me." He leaned down, gave her a big, wet kiss, a little slap on her behind, whip-whap. "I knew you would be grateful. It is one of the wonderful things about life. Maybe the most wonderful." He gave her another little slap. "I know. An emotional moment. Done crying? You should clean up a bit. It is a bloody mess, is it not? I have to be going. Don't step in the porridge. Ta-ta."

CHAPTER 27

HAVE TO BE GOING. Clean up. Mary wrote another little note, put it in her hatbox. It said:

> *Women might certainly study the art of healing and be physicians as well as nurses . . . They might also study politics, and settle their benevolence on the broadest basis . . . Business of various kinds, they might likewise pursue, if they were educated in a more orderly manner, which might save many from common and legal prostitution.*

By legal prostitution she meant marriage.

Spinsters entered the life of prostitution for economic reasons, it was said.

She did not like his biting, either.

Common prostitution was the kind you saw on the streets.

Still, she wished he was not married.

There were thirty thousand of them in London.

She wished she did not love him. One loved one's lovers, did one not? He clearly was not worthy of her love. Who was?

She wished her book was going better.

Perhaps she was not a real writer. Perhaps she just fancied herself one in order to give her paltry life some meaning, a title.

She wished she knew why she was alive.

She wished they had not left the baby behind.

She wished Fanny had not died.

She wished she knew what her life meant. It was a confusion.

Eliza and Mary arrived at Fanny's home in Hoxton that fateful day; the coach horses were in a lather. It was not as they expected, for

Mary had envisioned a modest but cozy cottage, lace curtains in the window, thick pieces of bread and honey for breakfast, warm, balmy days. It was a tiny, drafty and damp, barely furnished hovel. The Bloods were nearly indigent. Fanny was desperately ill. What did that mean? Why was it always like that?

Once in Joseph's kitchen, she standing in the doorway, Fuseli in a chair, sunlight coming through the window facing on the street, the sound of children on the street, she said: "Henry, this is a golden moment, this is it, everything." She felt satisfied, contained, fulfilled.

"You are beautiful."

As nice as it was to hear that, she wished he had something else to say about her. True enough, she had never thought herself beautiful, and had such a statement been made when she was eighteen, it might have been of some use. She would have been an entirely different person. Now it came years after that person in Bath who wanted to kill her because she was so ugly, or so he said, settling for the very thing she did with Fuseli, who said she was beautiful and wanted to do it because she was beautiful, or so he said, and she strongly suspected Henry said it to her because, despite his notorious brilliance, he really had nothing else to say. Was this how men were?

Thereafter, Henry came on Friday afternoons, the day his wife visited her mother, and when Mrs. Mason had the afternoon off and Joseph had his meeting with Christie at the inn.

"As beautiful as you may find me, Henry," Mary answered that day, "I would rather be rich."

"Are you not rich?"

"Hardly."

The poorhouse was never far out of her mind. Whatever money she earned at the *Analytical Review* and through the sale of her books seemed to be frittered away on her sisters, and her clothing and simple needs.

"I will probably live with Joseph forever, always be poor."

She had added to her attic room curtains and linens and a chest for her clothes. Also, she had a weakness for pretty shoes and had a blue silk pair, a pair with roses needlepointed on the toes, green cotton embroidered with vines, with a small, stacked heel, and an elegant

black pair with buckles. That was all she had to her name. A few
books.

"And I am old."

"So you are a beautiful old woman."

"So you think I am old, do you?"

"Mary, you are mine, I am yours."

"Almost, Henry, almost."

Why was she so uncomfortable over the idea of his marriage, for
had she not written that the institution was legal prostitution? How
could one be jealous of a wife, for God's sake?

When they went to the British Museum, she and Henry stood in
front of the curiosities Captain Cook had gathered on his voyages
around the world. They had just paged through Mr. Garrick's collection of plays and they had seen the original Magna Carta. Of course,
it is all for men, all these rights. Was that not always the case?

"I love my wife," he said.

"Of course you do." Another verse in the litany.

"She is a wonderful woman."

"Of course she is." Was he trying to make her angry and mad?

Mary was not really thinking of Henry's wife. Or even Henry.
What she was thinking about, really, was her book. She had taken all
the notes out of her hatbox, spread them on the floor like playing cards,
and started to arrange them in a logical sequence.

The upper-right note:

*My own sex, I hope, will excuse me, if I treat them like rational
creatures, instead of flattering their fascinating graces, and view-
ing them as if they were in a state of perpetual childhood, unable
to stand alone. I earnestly wish to point out in what true dignity
and human happiness consists.*

Second row from the bottom, middle note:

*From every quarter have I heard exclamations against masculine
women; but where are they to be found? If by this appellation men
mean to inveigh against their ardor in hunting, shooting, gaming,*

*I shall most cordially join the cry; but if it be against the imitation
of manly virtues, or, more properly speaking, the attainment of
those talents and virtues, the exercise of which ennobles the human
character, and which raises females in the scale of animal being,
when they are comprehensively termed mankind; all those who
view them with a philosophic eye must, I should think, wish with
me, that they may every day grow more and more masculine.*

Bottom right, last row:

*The first object of laudable ambition is to obtain a character as a
human being, regardless of the distinction of sex.*

Observations on the State of Degradation:

*I wish to persuade women to endeavour to acquire strength, both
of mind and body, and to convince them that the soft phrases, sus-
ceptibility of heart, delicacy of sentiment, and refinement of taste,
are almost synonymous with epithets of weakness . . .*

Mary was amazed at the cumulative effect of what she had written.
Did these notes, perhaps by simple addition, equal a radical transfor-
mation of society in which reason prevailed and there was a total
leveling of distinctions between men and women? Hardly. Yet there
was something there. Was it that the notes worked a magic on each
other by simple proximity, each note influencing the other to speak in
one voice, alchemically transforming into a grand chorus of I AM THE
REVOLUTION?

Shades of Paine, how had she gotten there?

Could she take responsibility for her own impressions and observations?

Perhaps, in writing her reply to Burke in *A Vindication of the
Rights of Man*, in which she denied the validity of tradition and the
wisdom of antiquity, she had become used to thinking in a new and
unfettered way. Was she, then, free? Once she was free, did that mean
her mind could go anywhere?

I am born too soon, she said to herself.

But perhaps we are all born too soon, she argued.

To be born is too soon.

Or to be born is just right.

"Why," she asked Joseph, as they sat together in the evening over tea, "why am I two separate people? With Henry I am bound and restrained, gagged, submissive. I become this pretty girl, his girl, a plaything. Silly and foolish. Yet I truly love him. If I do not see him on Friday, my week is destroyed. If I do not see him at dinner on Thursday, I want to die. If he is not good to me, I want to be buried ten feet deep. Yet in my work I am free, and more than that, I advocate a life I do not live. You see, Joseph, I am writing about the necessity of rationality for our sex. My sex. I turn around and betray myself. I am betraying all who read me. I am not that person I wish to become. I am not rational. I am not independent. I am a fraud."

"Oh, so give up, go home, put your head under the covers."

"I cannot."

"You are just advising women to think for themselves. Think for yourself."

"I cannot. I am hopelessly weak."

"Mary, you judge yourself too harshly. Are we not all, male and female, of many sides, facets, my dear?" He crossed his legs demurely, dipped his finger in the tea, wet his lips with it.

"We are many facets in direct contradiction to each other, Joseph?"

"To be sure."

"What about reason? How, if we consider ourselves rational beings, can we reconcile irrational behavior?"

"We are not only angels, my dear, but animals. In the great chain of being, we are midway. We struggle, I will attest to that, to be higher on the chain. But we are where we are."

Mary blushed. "Then you think we are basically savages."

"I think we are basically everything. We are basically even plants, as Blake would have us. Worms, less than worms. But also, dear girl, stars. It is that finally which makes us unique, not our distance from animals, but our proximity *and* distance."

"Oh, no."

"Why 'oh, no'? Glory in our position. It is unique and wonderful. It means that we can understand so much."

"What if my book, the one I am writing now, what if it turns out to be important, Joseph, what then?"

"You become famous, is that not what you desire? So that Mrs. Dawson, Lady Kingsborough, your father, your sisters, each man on the street will turn and say: That is Mary Wollstonecraft. People who have mistreated you will feel guilty. People who have been kind to you will feel justified. Harmony and balance will reign supreme. You shall be queen of the universe."

Mary stared at the fire.

"Whoever will inherit this world, Mary, this new world, they will read and appreciate you. Think of them as company, the ones to come."

Mary got up, went over to Joseph, planted a kiss on his forehead.

"I wish you could be my father, my husband, something."

He smoothed her hair, patted her back.

"Sometimes I wish it could be different, too, Mary, between us. But it is not. And if it were different, *we* would be different, and perhaps we would not like each other so much. Let us be friends. Let us prove that friendship is the best of all possible worlds. Listen: 'But if the while I think on thee, dear friend,/All losses are restored and sorrows end.' William Shakespeare, Mary, William Shakespeare."

"That theater owner."

"And knockabout actor."

"That fanatic about ingratitude."

"And jealousy."

"And death."

"And death."

MARY'S BOOK *A Vindication of the Rights of Woman* came out in 1792. It was written in three months. The first few weeks, she brought together all her notes. Working night and day, she did not change her clothes often or bathe hardly at all. Eating at her desk, she drank Joseph's precious coffee and even smoked his pipe in order to stay up longer. Her mind should have been a fuzz and a blur on the second week of this, as she arranged entries under topics, but her mind worked precisely and meticulously. Then, as it came to writing and rewriting, the words did not flow, not that, but rather each sentence hovered, asked to be drawn down from the air and placed on the paper. Mary obliged. She marshaled the words, made them attend to duty, had them come out even. She began: "In the present state of society it appears necessary to go back to first principles in search of the most simple truths, and to dispute with some prevailing prejudice every inch of ground."

In *A Vindication*, Mary's message announced that women should assume responsibility for taking an active role in their own destiny; it stated that oppression, in whatever guise, degrades all concerned, asserted that discrimination by denying valuable human resources is costly, requested that sexual identity be built on strength, not weakness, and affirmed that family duties are *human* tasks, worthy of any rational individual.

Her work was a logical extension of the Enlightenment belief in the rights of man to the rights of woman. She suggested that women must be educated to be reasonable, and become reasonable to be virtuous, and virtuous so that all of society might be happier. If men were not reasonable, they would be sensualists and women slaves.

The salons and philanthropic circles immediately arrayed themselves against her. Horace Walpole called her a "hyena in petticoats." Hannah More, one of the Blue Stocking ladies, declared the idea of women's rights to citizenship, to vote, to perhaps hold public office, was so inherently ridiculous that she would not bother to read *A Vindication.*

"Here they call me an 'unsexed female,'" Mary pointed out to Joseph, who was rocking furiously in his rocking chair.

"Do not pay any attention to all of that," Joseph said. "People are buying your book. We'll want to print a second edition with your corrections before long."

"And they are not accustomed, these critics, to dealing with something of importance from a woman," Christie said from his perch on the floor.

"You are getting to be very well known indeed, Mary. I might even say you are getting notorious," Joseph continued.

But nobody recognized her on the street. Nothing was changed. She would walk along the bookstalls, run her fingers down the spines of her book. Mine, she would purr, mine. Do not touch the books, the seller would caution. And on Thursday nights she still had to shout to be heard. Everything was the same.

The streets around Russell Square were slushy with mud and refuse. Slops were everywhere. It was Friday afternoon.

"Russell Square, for God's sake," Henry said, "is getting worse every day."

"I am tired of the British Museum, Henry, with all the antiquities, the Egyptian, Etruscan, and Roman antiquities, and I am tired of Kew Gardens with its Temple of Bellona, Temple of Pan, Temple of Solitude, and I am tired of the shops on Whitechapel Street and Cheapside, and tired of Vauxhall Gardens, and . . ."

"Are you tired of me?"

"No, I am not saying that." He took her to these places, she knew, because if anybody saw them it would seem like a harmless enough excursion.

"Well, come along, then."

The sun was shining brightly, but it was a chilly, shrill day. She wore her new blue silk dress. Milk-blue silk ribbons fastened her shoes. She had an overcoat now. Also blue, dark blue, with a three-tier cape collar. Mary was partial to blue, even though indigo was the cheapest dye and the color of uniforms for charity schools. Those in the Blue Stocking circle, ironically, were fine, rich ladies who wore white silk stockings, but the one man in their midst had dared to wear blue wool stockings, hence their name.

"What are you thinking, Mary?"

She was thinking about one of Catharine Macaulay's arguments in her *Letters on Education*.

"Oh, about you. I am thinking just of you, Henry. You are so handsome."

"Please do not mock me, Mary. Stay kind."

"J. J. Rousseau feels that women should be coquettes. Do you agree? Catharine Macaulay says that Rousseau is a 'licentious pedant.' Are you in accord?"

"Far better both than either in isolation. But what are you talking about? I thought you adored Rousseau."

"Except for *Emile*, wherein he has the character Sophia nothing more than Emile's concubine."

"You do not wish to be somebody's concubine?"

"Certainly not."

"Mistress?"

"You love your wife as every good husband should," Mary said sternly, placing her finger along his nose. "It would be nice if I could move in with the two of you. I could sit in the cupboard under the stairs. Come out at night, as I recall you do not sleep with her."

"Do not be that way, Mary."

"What way? Seeing the facts?"

"She is a wonderful woman, my wife."

"She is so wonderful that you are not taking her to the British Museum today. I am tired of hearing how wonderful she is and how beautiful I am. I suspect both are falsehoods."

"Why this? Why now? What did I do?"

"What did you do? I can only see you when it is most convenient for you. I cannot visit you, write you, greet you if I pass you in the street."

"Yes. Am I not good to you? Did I hide that I was married?"

"Is that what men say? Being good to somebody, what does that mean exactly. I am not a horse that you do not flog. Kind owner, merciful master."

"Do not be an impossible girl, Mary, not now, not here."

"Not in Russell Square, you mean? Sometimes I think I am losing my mind, Henry. I do not know what I want, what I am doing. For all that I have done, I am no closer to what I want. Here I am in this nasty street."

"And I thought you would enjoy an outing."

"Ah, but I do. I enjoy an outing." She swung her arms and legs. "I so enjoy an outing, it is just that I am a little teary these days. I do not know what is wrong with me. I must think of something, a change. It cannot be as it is."

"Obviously, you are in a quandary."

How is it that at the height of pleasure I seek to destroy it, she asked herself. I gradually chip away at the edifice of my own happiness, eventually achieving the misery I always hope to avoid. What is wrong with me? When everything is so wonderful, why am I not in heavenly bliss?

He took her shoulders, turned her to him. "You are too clever for this kind of . . ."

"For what, Henry?" Mary had clenched her fists and was now stamping her foot hard. "I know what you are saying. I am too intelligent for moods, feelings. I do not require the basic human amenities. An intellectual woman has no heart, and therefore anything may be done to her. She will understand. She will not cry."

"The things you write about equality for women have gone to your head, my dear. I am the kindest of men. I wish you no harm. You are a very troubled person. You do not know *what* you want. You describe an ideal world, but you live in a real one. What is the harm of love? You knew I was married. Do you want me to stop, all this to stop? I can go away. We can stop for a while."

"Do not go away," she practically screamed. "Stay. Please, I am sorry, I am sorry, Henry." She grabbed his sleeve like a child. "It would destroy me for you to go away."

When he kissed her, she was glad. It was like a sealed promise. But she did not like him to do so in public.

"Not here, Henry, not now." She pushed him away.

"Here and now." He pulled her closer.

"Henry, stop. Henry, you know better."

In fact, Henry Fuseli knew eight languages, he knew how to produce a steady stream of risqué pictures, and he knew how to get elected to the Royal Academy.

"Is this not what you wanted? Love and kisses, Mary." He pushed her against an iron fence. The bars dug into her back. "Love and kisses, Mary, all yours."

"Will you give them to me forever, Henry? When I get old, older? When I am old?"

"Until you die, Mary, until you die," he said, slamming her harder.

CHAPTER 29

SHE HAD NOT BEEN ABLE to sleep the whole night before, thinking of it. And so it was Monday, and the three of them were seated in the Fuselis' parlor. Mrs. Fuseli, in a dotted-swiss dress, pink-sashed, was sweating profusely and strands of her hair kept sticking to her fat face. The maid fanned her mistress, while the Fuseli baby cried in some other room. Mary was fashionable in a high-waisted, low-necked dress with a muslin overskirt. Her stays were poking her. She had on a straw bonnet with lace trim and new shoes. She wore her hair plainly bundled up at the nape of her neck. Had she and Henry been alone, he would have lifted her hair, kissed her neck. But he was standing across the room in back of his wife, looking stern and distant and rather silly in a green waistcoat and lavender cravat. They were all dressed as if for a party, but Mary was finding it more like an inquisition.

"What I suggest," Mary said very rapidly, looking straight at Henry, whose eyes were shot through with annoyance. "What I suggest is a simple little arrangement. It is this: that we all three live together, as friends of course, purely platonic, and that we travel to France as sort of a family to observe the Revolution. I have been asked by Condorcet to look at plans for female education. Because of my book. He has read my book on women. I am quite famous in some quarters now. I have heard that John Adams has read my book aloud to his wife, Abigail, and they both love it. And Joseph wants me to write something for him on the Revolution while I am over there. You see, people want to read what I write."

She preened a little at that, but neither Mr. nor Mrs. Fuseli seemed impressed.

"Who is this woman," Mrs. Fuseli asked, "that she can push her way in here."

"A poor unfortunate being, my dear. Do not let her trouble you."

Mary's book *A Vindication of the Rights of Woman* had gone through two printings in two months. It was being read not only in England but on the Continent and now in America. She was, after Russia's Empress Catherine, the best-known woman in the world.

"Miss Wollstonecraft, I am going to have to ask you to leave." Henry was acting as if he did not know her. Miss Wollstonecraft.

"I could help with the child, be a second mother. You see, I have never been with a real family," Mary offered. "I am very fond of your husband"—Mary glanced at Fuseli, who was avoiding her eyes—"and I think we women could become friends. It would be a jolly trio." It had been a sudden inspiration, this solution.

"My God." Mrs. Fuseli put her hand to her heart. "What is this? Who let her in here?"

"As friends," Mary said quickly. "Merely as friends. All as friends."

She sneaked another glimpse at Henry. He rolled his eyes heavenward, as if she were mad, this the final stroke. When she had appeared unannounced, he looked as if he wanted to kill her on the spot with the wood ax or fire poker. But she had not been able to contain herself.

"Tea, anybody?" The downstairs maid trotted in with a tray of tea things which she set on the table. The silver pot and creamer looked tarnished, ready for a good polishing. Henry opened the cabinet, took out a bottle of whisky.

"Well, let me be honest, Mrs. Fuseli. I have admired your husband long and hard, Mrs. Fuseli. I make no denial of that. But platonically. His mind, my mind. This arrangement would be purely chaste, Mrs. Fuseli. Minds. You know, minds." Mary pointed to her head, his head. "A marriage of true minds." Mary was not sure of the extent of the woman's understanding. "Minds," she said again. Actually, she frankly doubted that Fuseli respected her mind.

"Marriage?" Mrs. Fuseli screeched.

"Like angels," Mary said. "We could all go to France like angels. Stardust."

Mrs. Fuseli said: "You are insane. You want to live with my husband?"

"Yes, how did you know?" Finally it was getting through to the woman.

"But he has never touched you, nor you he, and never will?"

"Absolutely, Mrs. Fuseli. No touching." Mary raised her hands in the air.

"Hogwash."

Henry took a big swig of whisky straight from the bottle, long and hard. Then he belched.

"William Blake proposed such a thing to his wife," Mary defended. "It is quite the thing nowadays."

"That fool Blake should have been put in Bedlam long ago," Mrs. Fuseli spat.

"He is merely idealistic, an idealist," Mary insisted. "What is wrong with that?"

"We do not live in a platonic realm, an ideal world with the Good, the True, and the Beautiful ruling our lives, Mary," Fuseli said. "Are you blind? This is the real world. Have we not had this discussion before? Are you not an empiricist, as you profess?"

"You talk to each other?" Mrs. Fuseli was aghast.

"We determine what is real," Mary said.

"Hogwash," Fuseli said.

"Sometimes I am an idealist."

"Double hogwash."

Mary was startled that husband and wife used the same expression. He said he just kissed the woman good night. But they had a child, a fact she had forgotten. And all those animals on his tree. Stuffed dead animals. They looked as if they had risen from the grave, a furry black beady-eyed brigade.

"*We* make the world," Mary continued. "It is all a matter of conditioning. Hume and Locke . . . Henry, this is a wonderful idea, can you not see that? Just because other people do not have the imagination. It would solve all our problems about seeing each other and the time to do it in."

"You see each other?" Mrs. Fuseli shrieked.

"Only our minds see each other," Mary assured. "Nothing visceral, mind you. Pure perception. Metaphysics."

"Leave my house immediately," Mrs. Fuseli said, balling her hands into fists. "Such filthy language."

"What?"

"Leave."

"Now, now, Sophia, we need not be rude to Miss Wollstone-craft."

"Who is being rude? This woman, this woman . . . is desecrating our home. Who is she? Who gives her the right to come in here and insult our marriage. Is this why you are so weak on Friday night and cannot do your husbandly duty? Is this the dirty smell I can detect on your flesh and your hair? Who gives her the right to come barging into my house . . ."

"Not divine right, Mrs. Fuseli, but the secular freedom of every citizen to determine his or her destiny, and I assure you . . ."

"Where did she come from, who is she?"

"A fiend. I am a fiend, Mrs. Fuseli."

Mrs. Fuseli dove back among the cushions. Happy now? Mary thought. Happy now? Yes, your husband sticks me every Friday morning, hard, deep. He calls out his own name, though, saying over and again: Henry. Surely we should compare notes. What lines does he read in your play?

"A lie," Fuseli said to his wife. "A complete falsehood, Sophia darling."

Mary had expected Henry to laugh at the fiend thing. He did not. Mrs. Fuseli, who had gotten up and was pacing, moved up against her husband. "Are you going to get her out of here, Henry? Or are we to send for the sheriff?"

"But we can all go to Paris together," Mary continued, helping herself to some tea. "Mrs. Fuseli? Some tea?"

"That fool Blake has put some mad, mad ideas in her head. She has gone too far. Sitting around that dinner table at Johnson's has addled her brain. What *do* you talk about there?"

"Atlantis," Mary answered.

"Atlantis? What is that?"

"An imaginary country, island, a place under the Atlantic Ocean."

Mrs. Fuseli rolled her eyes. "God help me."

"God helps those who help themselves, right, Henry? Not that I am religious. It exists as an idea, along with Atlantis," Mary said.

"Make her stop talking. She blasphemes. I am going to faint."

Henry stood stock-still, as if frozen. Mrs. Fuseli seemed at a loss.

"Do you hear me, Henry, I am going to faint."

"Yes, dear."

The woman pressed her face so far forward to Mary that Mary could see the pores in her cheeks.

"Henry is my husband, whore. We are married. This is our home. Get out. I never want to see you again, nor does he."

"Now, dear, do not be too harsh on the girl."

"Girl, girl? This is not a child we are dealing with, but a demented spinster."

"Just because I am not married does not make you better."

"Henry, either she leaves or I leave. Henry."

"Henry?" Mary asked in a small, faint voice. "Henry?"

He was going to betray her. She could feel it. He looked like a traitor to her. He had a traitor's little piggy eyes. And the tight snub nose of a traitor. And the thin curly lips of a traitor. And the woman was obviously a dolt whose notion of marriage and everything else was archaic and stultifying. Mary had heard that she was a butcher's daughter. For a moment, Mary pitied Henry. Did he not remember that they had all talked about it at the table, Johnson's Thursday night, and that everybody, including himself, believed that marriage should not be a restricting and oppressive institution? The mind *had* to be free. That is what *he* said.

After that, Mary had envisioned the three of them sailing for France, living in the midst of the Revolution. She would keep a journal. Henry would make drawings. Mrs. Fuseli would have to tend to housekeeping arrangements, see to tea, that sort of thing. After dinner, she and Henry would talk and talk and talk. Mrs. Fuseli, sitting some way off, doing needlepoint, would ask to be excused and would go up to her room early. See you in the morning, she would say to them both. They would hear the door close. Henry would look at her and she would look at him. He would take his finger, draw it along her jaw and chin. Then he would tongue her eyebrows.

"Close your eyes," he would say, leading her to the kitchen.

In the kitchen, he would press her flat on the floor.

"Pretend you are asleep," he would say. Obediently, she would go limp. Gently, he would pull her in front of the stove. He would then proceed to undress her, very slowly, very carefully. All her limbs were totally limp, for she was asleep. He would have difficulty pulling off her sleeves, undoing her stays, but she could not help him. She was asleep. Outside the window, they would hear the Revolution going on. Laughter and singing of the French national anthem would wrap around the house, her head, the night. She would smell wine, French bread, chocolate éclairs. Liberty, fraternity.

Instead, there she was in their ugly English parlor. How could an artist stand such a lack of any unifying aesthetic? A muted Oriental carpet and red-and-white-striped chairs of a shiny satin clashed in style and color, and the needlepoint fire screen, used to protect makeup from melting off the face, which was in the pattern of a lion surrounded by gold, was tattered, as if a cat had got to it. There was, in addition, a cut-glass chandelier suspended from the middle of the ceiling which hung too low and threatened to fall, and a spinning wheel with a leg broken, under a mahogany-framed picture of a castle frozen in ice (nothing of Henry's). There was a clavichord. Beige curtains fixed on top with clusters of chipped rosettes hung at the windows, and little Greek figures sat on the mantel as if intent on an errand. Mercury, Venus, somebody with a discus. Henry had given the woman a free hand.

"I am going to leave the room," Mrs. Fuseli said, getting up stiffly. "When I come back, I want her gone."

"This is utterly ridiculous," Henry whispered as soon as his wife left the room. "How dare you come to my house, disturb my family in the first place, and then with this. My God, have you no tact, no mercy, no sense of decency? And saying I stick you."

"I thought it. I did not say it."

"You said it."

"I am a little confused, to tell you the truth. I have not slept. I seem to spend all my time pacing and worrying about things."

"What are you worried about? You are famous."

"Do you still love me?" Mary whispered.

"Of course I do not love you. How can I love you after this?"

"You used to love me."

"Shh."

"But I love *you*, and things were getting bad, Henry. You know they were. I was bored. And when we saw each other it was such a strain. We have been together for a few years. It was time for the next stage. But, Henry, I think the main thing is that I am not suited to deception. This would be the perfect solution. The main thing is that we are together. That is the main thing."

"The main thing is your brain is addled or you are completely mad."

"And who started it, pray tell?"

"I did not mean for it to come to this."

"And what did you mean it to come to?"

"I must be left alone. I am an artist."

"I am a writer."

Fuseli laughed.

"I *am* a writer. I can say that now. I am also a person. You cannot do this to me."

"People perform torture on each other, Miss Wollstonecraft. They do everything and anything to each other."

"Because they forget they are human, that each of them, torturer and tortured, is human."

"Blake put you up to this, did he not?"

"Blake is a genius."

"Blake is a hack. He copies my work."

"Blake is a genius."

"I hope you do not think of yourself as a genius. If you were, you could not do what you are doing. And what does Blake have to do with this, anyway."

"Blake wants to create a new world of peace and harmony, Henry.

And Paine wants equality for all. It is a new world in the making at our Thursday-night table."

"Right."

"I am not doing anything unkind to you, unfair."

"Destroying my marriage, causing me immeasurable grief."

"Immeasurable? How can you measure what you have done to me. I was, I was . . ."

"A virgin," he said.

"Yes. And now nobody will marry me."

"Nobody would marry you, anyway."

"That is not true."

"It is true. It is. You are too old, too fat, too tall, too ugly, and too clever and too poor. You talk too much. Men want sweet, quiet, cooperative wives."

"Oh, Henry, how can you say such things again." She put her head in her hands, began to weep. "I am not poor anymore, you know."

"Well, buy yourself a husband. I have a wife."

"She does not have a single idea in her head, Henry, not one."

"She is my wife," he said harshly.

"Oh, blessed be."

"Have you no respect for anything?"

"Yes, for that which merits it, Henry."

"Get up immediately and leave this house. Stop being such a spoiled baby. You are always weeping and wailing."

"You, you are pompous, proprietorial, predatory, and you smell like a frog. What are those stuffed animals doing in your tree? Is it the museum of small-mammal slaughter? Foxes and poor little squirrels and baby pigs . . . with their marble eyes, perched up on the branches *au naturel*. And that weasel! It is disgusting."

"Wild boar, not pigs. That would not be sport. Baby boars."

"I thought you were an artist, that you loved freedom."

"This is completely nonsensical. Just go. You are having an attack of some kind. Everything was fine and you have destroyed it."

"What about Paris?"

"If you want to go to Paris, go. You do not need us to go to Paris. But leave this house. Go, go now, go forever."

He took hold of her collar, pulled her from her chair, and with considerable strength pushed her to the door. Grasping her waist, he opened the door and shoved her out. The door slammed behind her.

"Oh, God." The worst had happened. She was standing alone on his steps. She was so weak she could hardly stand. She was standing so defeated she could hardly breathe. She was breathing with such difficulty that she thought she might collapse.

"What am I going to do?" she asked the sky.

The sky was inscrutable.

"A is for acorn," she began. "B is for bad, bad boy."

Actually, the idea of joining Fuseli's household *had* come from Blake and Thursday night; it had seemed quite the comfortable and rational thing. Lately, all the time without Henry had been spent in thinking about him, and the time with him had been spent in thinking about other things. She did not seem to be able to concentrate. In Paris, the city of equality, liberty, and brotherhood, surely such an arrangement would be quite ordinary.

"Come out, come out, you coward. Face me whom you loved, face yourself," she shouted from his porch.

Henry did not come out. The house enfolded itself like a book shutting at the end of the story. The curtains were swiftly drawn. A maid came out and closed the shutters. The doors were latched. And the residence became an impregnable and opaque prison.

Had Mary found a brick or a rock, she would have heaved it through their domestic bliss, a falsehood to begin with, she was sure, and an accommodation to propriety to end with. She imagined the brick turning round and round, crashing through the shutter, hitting the glass and cascading through the air and entering their house, like hitting a pond. The big splash would throw out concentric ripples. That would give the lie to their masquerade. A brick on their floor.

She wanted them to know, Mrs. Fuseli so smug and self-satisfied, that what she called her marriage was all very fragile and prone to disaster. Mrs. Fuseli, she wanted to announce, your husband has kissed and tickled me in the British Museum, and exclaimed love and desire in Mr. Andrews's house, at Bedford Square, and promised love until I died in Russell Square, and promised eternal love in Kensington

Gardens. She would be grateful to be informed. Yours sincerely, very truly, Mary Wollstonecraft, the late author and dearly beloved of . . . He loves his wife.

But Mrs. Fuseli never appeared. Mary, who had been standing in the little patch of garden beside their house, sat down on the ground, and finally, exhausted and wretched, she lay down, stretching herself on the flat ground under a tree. After a while, the sky darkened. The stars were close and warm. Dear stars, she whispered, weeping, I love you.

In her dream, she and Henry were swimming in the black sky, connected by a kiss. Stars spattered their hair and groin. They showed the way to navigators in the middle of the sea.

In the morning, Mary, still flat on the ground, saw the Fuselis with the baby and maid all dressed for a trip. A carriage came and the carriage man went inside to fetch a trunk. Then they disappeared down the road. They had not seen her and she had not the energy to get up. It was, again, a warm day, and about noon a parade of ants trooped around her, gingerly avoiding the puddle of urine seeping below her dress. The stuffed animals in the tree branches looked down piteously with their beady-black glass eyes. The weasel seemed to hiss.

That night the stars, more bold, drawing close to get a good look, peered down on her face. Mary, Mary, they brushed her face softly with light, Mary, get up, Mary. Showers of brilliance exploded in bright bits and pops above her. She was not asleep or awake. She felt wonderful. She remembered sweet Richard.

The next day the sun started to move toward her, lodged itself in a tree just as Blake had foretold, the angel tree, so that the stuffed fox was ablaze and the ferret was aflame and all the little beasts wore halos edged in gold. Mary saw a face, but it was not God. It was her own. Go away, she mouthed, go home. Little worms and crawly bugs, bright, metallic beetles, gathered around her, beneath her. A man came out of the house across the street. He did not see her. He went into the house, the door like a mouth swallowed him whole, and the windows, great, glaring eyes, stared back at her. Next a woman came out in a bonnet like the old woman in the shoe, her face as wrinkled as a ginger cookie.

"Missy, are you all right. Missy, wake up."

And shortly, or was it the following day or two days, several men in periwigs arrived in a chaise.

"Mistress Wollstonecraft, we are the Lunacy Committee from Bedlam Infirmary, I am Dr. Monro, and *you* are a dangerous and incurable lunatic."

CHAPTER 30

SHE WANTED TO TELL them she was not a dangerous lunatic, but somehow she had lost the ability to talk. All her words seemed to have settled at the base of her stomach, like a pile of stones that she could not dredge up, spit out.

I am not a lunatic who must be taken to Bedlam, is what she tried to say to the august members of the committee. On the contrary, I am the author of *A Vindication of the Rights of Woman* and many journalistic pieces, including *The Rights of Man*, and a novel, *Mary, a Fiction*. I am thirty-three and have lived my life in the service of others. I have been a schoolmistress and a governess, and a dear friend to one Fanny Blood of Hoxton, now deceased, and Joseph Johnson of St. Paul's Churchyard, a gentleman (in a manner of speaking) and a scholar. I am an important lady. My life and being are not without accomplishment. I am merely tired, is all. She felt so very tired out. Surely a famous lady can take a rest under the shade of a tree in the quiet earth of a yard.

Fuseli had once said that she talked with her eyes, and that what she said was: Save me, save me. But that was a hundred years ago on the other side of the truth. If lunacy is your search, she wanted to tell the men, I would suggest knocking on the Fuselis' door. But no. The Fuselis were gone. The men bundled her up in a blanket and took her away as fast as they could to Bedlam. She rode on the floor of the carriage, bumping along like a sack of potatoes, the words rustling in her stomach like dry leaves in autumn. Already, she thought, they are treating me like an animal.

" 'Tis a shame," one of the committee said.

"Ah, that it is."

"A shame and a pity."

"Ah, that it is."

"A crying shame and a pity."

"Ah, that it is."

"These days."

"It is the Revolution across the Channel that makes them so. It is like the tarantella, that mad Spanish dance induced by the bite of a tarantula. Madness is a frenzy and a habit. It comes in bread and oranges, sometimes the water."

"It is an Italian dance."

"I hear in France the women bare their breasts in battle like the ancient Amazons."

"Is that so? I should like to see them charge."

"Some wear pantaloons."

"Lord have mercy."

The carriage stopped and she was thrust over a shoulder, taken into a courtyard where there were chickens pecking in the dirt, pens of ducks, and children squatting around marbles. The gate was opened and she was delivered on a stone-cold floor.

"This one, she was lying down in mud two days. She cannot talk and does not walk. She has no decency and has stained herself. Some say it is lovesickness."

"Lovesickness." The matron guffawed. "We will rid her of that."

Mary was stripped of her soiled clothes, washed, and put in a shift so rough it chafed her skin until it bled. The matron led her up two flights of stairs to a room full of beds.

"So she can walk. Good," the woman said.

Mary was chained by one arm to the wall, so that she had to sit on her bed with her arm up all day and all night. She prayed to the God she had given up either to let them release her arm or to cut it off. She prayed to her mother who was dead to save her. She prayed to her sisters, who were in Wales now, and she prayed to Joseph. Nobody came, and in the morning she was still there, her arm fixed to the wall. Such agony was beyond belief.

There were twenty of them, women chained and suffering from melancholias, troubles, disappointments, grief, love, jealousy, pride, frights, manias, misfortunes. In the room adjoining theirs were men confined with the "English coffin," a device like a door, with a hole for the face and manacles on either side, and a wheel which pulled their limbs tighter every time they, the lunatics, moved. There was a machine for men and women which swung the person until quiet. Others who were permitted some mobility were in strait waistcoats. The truly docile got to lie in straw. They were the straw people. They were purged and bled, submitted to cold baths. Opium, extract of hyoscyamus, camphor, julep, and nitre were administered to the hopeful cases. Mary hoped to be a hopeful case and get enough opium to make her see the Lord Mayor himself and an angelic choir singing Hosannas.

One man sang all day, "Drink and drive care away, / Wine does wonders every day, / And sing tantararara, brave sport." Others, not chained or rendered exhausted by the purging and bloodletting, ran up and down the halls. And, Fridays, ladies and gentlemen would pay for tickets to witness and be entertained by the antics of the lunatics. The lunatics cooperatively stuck out their tongues, displayed their genitals, and urinated in their straw.

On the second day, Mary was unchained. Her eyes had become huge and wide and she could not lower her arm. She cried, though she could not utter a word. On the fifth day, she could lower her arm and stopped crying. Resting her head against the wall, she went to sleep. Her arm still felt as if it was going to fall off. The matron said that since she was gentle she would soon move to straw.

After a week, she was able to walk about and to sleep on her bed stretched out, not all crouched up against the wall like a bird mending its wing. It was then that she became more aware of her surroundings.

There was a woman who thought an animal lived inside her, not a tapeworm, but a round, furry beast with sharp little teeth which gnawed on her stomach and would soon come through. Another woman imagined an animal clinging to her arm, like a sloth. There was a man who must expose himself at dinner. Nobody cared, for there were naked people all about. Of the two hundred inmates, few were modest. One man invited Mary to Comus's Court where the Devil was to preside. A man who called himself a Preadamite went about only in his blanket because Adam was clothed in flesh. The others called him the Methodist.

In general, people were plagued with manias or melancholias, were either frantic and prone to violent gestures or were full of despair. Others huddled all day in a corner, legs drawn up, arms wrapped around legs, their faces a mask of sorrow. There were a few people who went from one extreme to another. The same man might be jolly and talking very fast one day, laughing and carrying on, and yet want to die the very next morning.

Mary slept for days at a time and then would stay awake every night all night. In her head ran a chant which went: I have to be dead, I have to be dead.

The dark halls, and locked cells, the shackles, the naked men, the great shouting and moaning, piteous cries in the night, the periodic parade of curious onlookers, seemed more than she could take at times. I am come to this, she thought. And yet it also seemed that it had always been, that Bedlam was her life. She lost track of what she had been before. Henry, his wife, Thursday-night dinners, her books, even her sisters appeared as only dim figures. A black silhouette table set on the edge of the world, at the tip of a desert, was peopled with paper cutouts: Blake in a top hat; a crouching, scabbed-crab of a man—that must be Paine; a radiant boy-god, Christie; and Godwin, a shadowy who-are-you; and Joseph, sweet Puck, prince of the fairies. Mary, light and airy, hung on the edges.

She no longer wanted to tell the Lunacy Committee that she was an author, that she could earn her own living, that she lived by her wits, that they must let her out immediately. She was not sure who she was, what she had done. She thought about Fanny, the dearest, sweetest friend a person could have, but the actual image was fuzzy and indistinct. Mary's main concern was bread and water, gravy on Sunday, being taken downstairs and outside to the jericho with a dozen women, Saturday-night washing, a dull, unaccountable succession of days, sleeps, get-ups. She was happy not to be chained, happy to get an extra crust, and would lapse into a fuzzy, hypnotic, almost euphoric state when somebody combed her hair with her fingers, scratching for lice, or when the sunlight in the afternoon hit her feet, traveled to her chin. That was like taking a warm bath.

One day Mary remembered what she had read of the actress Susannah Cibber's relative, the Chicken Man, who was put in Newgate for a few small debts and ended up frozen to death inside his mattress, all the feathers adhering to his excrement-covered body.

"The Chicken Man," Mary wanted to tell somebody, "crept inside his mattress, it was so cold. When they opened the door, he ran out, all the feathers sticking to his filthy body, but they caught him, put him back."

"Poor lad," she could imagine the woman who walked about with rags in her arm saying.

"We are lucky, are we not," a man would interject. "We and our straw."

"We most definitely are not lucky. Some people are sitting pretty in this world. My former mistress who locked me here. Is she any better than anybody else? Birth. Birth is all." This would be the servant incarcerated for an improper attitude. She mumbled all day that vengeance was hers.

"We are not the Chicken Man."

"But I have lost my mind," Mary protested.

"You will find it, dear. I am sure it is not far away. You know that nursery song. Leave it alone and it will come home, wagging its tail behind it."

There were days on which Mary felt happy. Comfortable. As if she had arrived where she belonged, finally. This was her home, her life. Nobody knew where she was anymore. She drew her blanket around her. Her blanket, her skin which she was thickening by a daily application of spit and pee, protected the pile of words at the base of her stomach.

Sometimes she was coherent and lucid, and she could not understand what had happened to her. Then she would stare longingly out the window at the branches of a lone tree. The leaves had turned from green to yellow and then in one windy night fallen to the ground.

This is not a coach on a trip and we all get off, she said to herself, or a ship at sea like the one to Portugal, but a stone building with bars on the windows. I am famous and nobody knows where I am or who I am or what I am or why I am.

She dreamed occasionally of Fuseli. She saw him in her tree, not like Blake's angels, but with all his stuffed animals, the beavers and foxes, a ferret, the squirrels and woodchuck, raccoon. Except they were alive and prowled the branches when the wind blew. The leaves then would shake like a chandelier. Mary could not quite remember what he looked like anymore. More vivid was his wife, plump and sweaty, unpleasant. Thursday-night dinners, her sisters, her other life—when had that taken place, and how? Maybe it was Atlantan time and they were underwater, moving very slowly. Maybe the straw was seaweed. Maybe they were merpeople and they ate, not watery meat stew from wooden bowls, but watery fish stew from cockleshells. Maybe she was back at the Kingsborough estate. Maybe she was dead and this was heaven, and God was matron. Mary might have been in Bedlam for years. The outside world was engulfed, contained, obliterated by the reality of the hospital. Yet, one visiting day, approaching her bed was a person who was familiar to her, a small, foxlike face, very pointy, very blue-blue eyes, a slow smile.

"Three weeks," Joseph shouted in her ear, "I have been looking for you. When you did not come back that night, I grew frantic. I have been out of my mind with worry." He put his hand over his eyes, started to cry. Across from him, a man was defecating in the straw. Nearby, a couple were copulating. Dinner had just been served. Mary's gown was torn, her face dirty.

"I knew you were not feeling well, Mary, but this?"

She had not recognized him at first. Of course, she knew who he was when he started talking. And he was so clean. This man was so clean.

"The Fuselis are in the country," he said. "Yes, I went to their house, but it was locked up. I wrote your sisters in Wales, but they could not come. This was a guess, just a guess. My God, Mary, what has happened to you?" He began to cry again, clasped her body to him. "I have been so worried." He moved back. She smelled terrible and there were lice and other vermin on her skin. "My God," he said. "They do not clean you here? Can you talk? Mary?"

"She cannot talk no more," the woman with the bundle of rags said. "Only sometimes she talks."

"I do not care. My darling girl, I am going to get you out of here immediately. I will teach you to talk again."

Mary blinked rapidly.

He opened her mouth, looked in. "It is there. The tongue is there. Say something. Say anything. Say Joseph, you dirty dog."

She shrugged.

"Mary, I want you to come out with me, I want to take you home."

She shrugged.

"Mary, you are not a lunatic. Do you understand? It was too much, too much—Fuseli, your book, everything, that is all. Your mind could not hold up with the weight. But now you are better and everything is fine. You feel too deeply, think too much. It is the strain. You are too melancholy. God, Mary, pull yourself together. This Fuseli thing—I did not realize how serious it was. How dare they call anybody else a lunatic. They put you here to get rid of you. I am sure of it. There is nothing wrong with you. A nice bath, a good meal, new clothes. And your voice will come back. How can you want to stay in this, this pit? You, you are a sensible girl."

She shrugged.

The man who sang the drinking song sauntered by without a stitch of clothing on.

"Drink and drive care away, tra-la," the man sang.

"Sir, who is that man in the blue blanket," Joseph asked. "The one over there?"

"Brown blanket, sir. He is the Methodist, a Preadamite."

"There is no such thing as a Preadamite."

"Well, not now, of course."

"Ever."

Mary was getting a headache. It was too confusing. Why did everybody always want something from her, for her to do something, to be something, talk, write. She felt enormously tired. Could not Joseph see how tired she was. Joseph himself looked tired. Why keep up? Her gown slipped down over her shoulders.

"My God, Mary. Cover up." He pushed her gown together. "You are going to Paris, are you not, to write something for me on the Revolution. After your *Rights of Woman*, surely all of England will be eager to read . . ."

Mary looked off into the distance.

"Mary. What is wrong with you?"
She thumped her breast.
"Ah, your heart."

> *With all thy quickening powers,*
> *Kindle a flame of sacred love*
> *In these cold hearts of ours.*

It was part of a hymn Mrs. Price used to sing. Mary wanted to explain: I am not like the Chicken Man who had to stay inside his mattress to keep warm with all the feathers glued to his stinking body. I am not a relative of Susannah Cibber . . . I have a blanket. I am more than Lady Kingsborough, who is a lady. I am not Eliza and Everina. Would that I were Fanny. But I am not.

The woman who had been a servant, who had been hovering, came forth.

"Usually she is very quiet, and then she cries."

"Thank you, miss. Mary, do you know that you are read all over the world, that people want to meet you, that your intelligence and your talent mean something . . . My God, if they knew you were here. How did you get here, get this way? Less than a month ago you were furiously writing day and night. I do not understand this."

Mary felt very sleepy. She let her body, already slanting, fall down on the bed.

"No," Joseph said. "Definitely not. You are going home. I am going to cure you myself. Just stay put. I will get you out."

Joseph went away for a while, returned.

And so the sun was very bright when Mary emerged, and the street seemed full of loud noises and dense commotion. Joseph had to hold her waist tightly. He escorted her home, took her up to her own bed. She could hear sparrows from outside her window, and Joseph had placed a vase of daylilies on her desk. Her new shift had been washed and pressed. Mrs. Mason came upstairs with a bowl of hot water and a rag and a plate of fruit, some cheese, a pot of tea.

"I am Mrs. Mason," Mrs. Mason said. "And we are going to begin again."

GILBERT

All the world is a stage, thought I; and few are there in it who do not play the part they have learnt by rote; and those who do not seem marks set up to be pelted at by fortune; or rather as signposts, which point out the road to others, whilst forced to stand still themselves amidst the mud and dust.

Mary wrote this in her *Letters from Sweden.* Yet practically all the literature on female conduct at the time advised a course of action the opposite of what she had taken.

Dr. James Fordyce's *Sermons to Young Women* (1765) called women who wished to study abstract philosophy "masculine," and told them to be meek and mild, soft little lambs.

Dr. John Gregory, in *A Father's Legacy to His Daughters* (1774), cautioned women to conceal their good sense and appear flighty.

On the other hand, Mary was influenced by Catharine Macaulay. She felt that Macaulay's keen understanding of abstract ideas was not particularly masculine, but rather that of a highly intelligent human being.

Lady Mary Wortley Montagu in 1739 argued in *Women Not Inferior to Man* that women were slaves, but could be teachers, physicians, lawyers, even soldiers.

Abigail Adams, on May 7, 1776, wrote to her husband, John Adams, who was attending the Continental Congress in Philadelphia: "I cannot say that I think you very generous to the ladies; for, whilst you are proclaiming peace and good will to men, emancipating all nations, you insist upon retaining an absolute power over wives."

Mary wrote in *A Vindication of the Rights of Woman* in 1792:

Women are told from their infancy, and taught by the example of their mothers, that a little knowledge of human weakness, justly termed cunning, softness of temper, outward *obedience, and a scrupulous attention to a puerile kind of propriety, will obtain for them the protection of man; and should they be beautiful, everything else is needless, for, at least, twenty years of their lives.*

Mary had long been skeptical of the notion of protection. Kindness and civility seemed the exception, not the rule, in men. To Mary, softness of temper in a woman was not necessarily desirable. Marriage, she had learned, was not always a refuge. In fact, much of what she had been led to believe about men and women was a deception, as Fuseli told her. At an address on Charlotte Street, according to one source, "London men chose to be birched, whipped, fustigated, scourged, needle-pricked, half hanged, holly-brushed, fuse-brushed, butcher-brushed, curry-combed, phlebotomized by women." And also at the Berkeley House, another such establishment, women could be raised or lowered on a kind of machine/chair for the pleasure of men.

One estimate at the time numbered fifty thousand prostitutes in London.

During the eighteenth century the prostitutes were often middle-class women, women who would not be haymakers or slopworkers, ones who came from families which could not provide an attractive dowry and women who were not permitted to remain in the homes of brothers or other relatives and could not become, as Mary did, a lady's companion, schoolmistress, or governess.

The salary of a governess at the time was between twelve and forty pounds a year. A male tutor received at least fifty pounds. Hairdressing, millinery, mantua-making, dentistry, originally female occupations, were being taken over by men, and midwives were being supplanted by physicians trained at the Royal College of Surgeons.

Women were butchers, and kept cook shops, and did silk winding, stitching of stays, and quilting. They were weavers, actresses. Women came on foot from Shropshire to work in the market gardens around London. They picked fruit, weeded, were involved in carrying loads of fruit to Covent Garden. They were all the worst things: cindersifters, slopworkers, ragpickers, bunters. They were ballad sellers and match sellers. They hawked fish and cat and dog food, the most noisome occupations.

An account of the fruit pickers' life: "The women carry on their heads baskets weighing from 40 to 50 pounds and make two turns a day, thirteen miles each day. Their diet is coarse and simple. They drink tea and small beer. They sleep on straw in hovels and barns and they often burst an artery or drop down dead from the effect of heat and over-exertion."

WHEN MARY WAS a young child living in Laugharne, she used to sit in the kitchen with Annie. While Annie scrubbed pots with fuller's earth and French chalk, Mary would read her alphabet book, bought from a cart: A was an acorn that grows on an oak; B was a boy who delights in his book. Was G a girl? Not at all. G was a griffin, of him pray take heed.

She read about Jack the Giant-Killer and the History of Tom Thumb and the Death and Burial of Cock Robin. When older, she read *The Life and Strange and Surprising Adventures of Robinson Crusoe*, and the *History of England in a Series of Letters from a Nobleman to his Son*, by Oliver Goldsmith.

She read *Goody Two-Shoes* and *The History of Little Fanny*, a story, need it be said, about a disobedient little girl who strays from home and becomes a dirty beggar. She is restored to her former station by a generous dame and, of course, learns the error of her ways. Another of young Mary's books was *The School of Manners, or Rules for Children's Behaviour*. Chapter I had short and mixed precepts:

1. *Fear God.*
2. *Honor the King.*
3. *Reverence thy Parents.*
4. *Submit to thy Superiors.*

Chapter IV features "Behavior at the Table."

1. *Come not to the Table unwashed or uncombed.*
2. *Hold not thy knife upright in thy hand,
   but lay it down at thy right hand . . .*

In her two books dealing with children, *Thoughts on the Education of Daughters* and *Original Stories*, Mary interested herself in morality and manners within a larger framework. She dealt with virtue and sincerity, and venerated goodness.

"Few are the modes of earning a subsistence," Mary wrote in her book on the education of daughters, "and those very humiliating." She went on to list them: "companion, schoolteacher, governess, and a few trades which are gradually falling into the hands of men."

Mary reviewed for the *Analytical Review* a book called *The Evils of Adultery and Prostitution; with an Inquiry into the Causes of their present alarming Increase, and some Means recommended for checking their Progress.*

Yet there was nothing that Mary read as a child or as an adult which prepared her for her life with her father, Mrs. Dawson, Eliza's escape, the trip to Portugal and Fanny's death, or her own incarceration in Bedlam. There seemed to be no relation between the written word and the events she had to confront. There were no guides, no handbooks, no examples, nothing to show her the way, comfort the heart.

She did not talk at Joseph's for four days. On the fifth day, in the morning, the sun streaming in her window, Mrs. Mason at her desk, Mary said: "I am not the Chicken Man."

"Of course not, dear."

Then Mrs. Mason realized what had happened.

"Joseph, Joseph," she called, running down the stairs, "Mary is talking."

Mary heard a clatter and much shuffling about and Joseph, in his nightshirt, appeared at the top of her stairs.

Mary said: "I am not the Chicken Man."

"Who are you, then?" Joseph asked.

"I am Mary Wollstonecraft of 72, St. Paul's Churchyard."

"And?"

"I am a writer."

"See," Mrs. Mason said, dancing about, clapping her hands. "She is better."

Mary blinked her eyes. A tear ran down her cheek.

"Let us take this slowly," Joseph said. "She is *getting* better. Let us not be too hasty."

"Miss Mary, would you like to take a walk?"

Mary shuddered.

"I think not quite yet," Joseph said. "Let us get her downstairs first."

"Yes."

"This is Monday. Why not try to have her fit as a fiddle by Thursday."

"Not Thursday dinner," Mary protested.

"You may be assured, Mary, that a certain person is incommunicado and incognito, a certain Thursday person is not welcome in our midst. Very persona non grata. Very."

"Forever?"

"Of course. Do you think for a second I could forgive him for what he has done to you? Ever in all eternity?"

"Joseph?" A heavily accented voice called from beneath the stairs. Then a head appeared, a torso, legs, feet. A stranger.

"Lars, this is Mary and Mrs. Mason. Mary, Mrs. Mason, Lars is from Norway and staying for a while."

Towheaded, boyish, with heavy brown eyes, short and shaggy as a pony, and in Joseph's dressing gown, of all things. Mary had a vision of Bedlam again—the straw, the shackles on the wall, the wandering people, swirling dust, nomads of the mind. Accept this, she said to herself. Accept Lars in Joseph's dressing gown. You have to or you will be finished. That is simply the way he is. Accept him, accept it.

"I do not ever want to be insane again," she said desperately.

"Of course you do not." Joseph reached out to hold her. Mrs. Mason came over to the other side.

"You English," Lars said. "So emotional."

Mary was shivering a little.

"Melancholia," Mrs. Mason explained to Lars. "All the poets get it. Whenever you hold a quill too long, visions come into the brain. Vapors and suchlike. It is in the ink."

"Oh, is that so?" Lars was surprised.

"Your mind needed a rest, that is what I think," Joseph said.

"She was insane? This girl?" Lars looked at her quizzically.

"She was not really insane," Mrs. Mason said. "So do not be frightened. She was insane only this much." Mrs. Mason held up her fingers to indicate an inch.

"I never want to be insane," Lars said. "Not any at all." He held his fingers up to a pinch.

"Paine has just gone to Paris," Joseph said. "Christie and his new wife are in Paris."

"Christie is married?"

"Everybody gets to go to France except us cooks," Mrs. Mason said, her hands on her hips.

"Oh, you do not want to be there. They shoot you up good, and chop-chop your head," Lars said.

"Thank you, Lars, for the vivid description of the Revolution."

"It is true, Joseph. I promise on my heart."

"I want to go," Mary said.

"Downstairs first," Joseph said.

"Downstairs today," Mary said, "and tomorrow France."

"She is a courageous little thing," Lars said.

Mary was as large as Lars and quite a bit older, and she wondered why he referred to her in the diminutive.

"I am as big as you," she said.

"Is that so," Lars said.

CHAPTER 33

IN PARIS, Mary stayed on the rue Meslée in a mansion belonging to French friends of Christie's, and that first week, December 1792, looking out of her window, she saw Louis XVI in his carriage being taken to his treason trial. He looked pale and drawn, quite ordinary, and Mary, though she was sympathetic to the Revolution, felt sorry for the king.

December 28, 1792

Dear Joseph,
The king is to be executed, I am afraid. I fear England is going to join the war against France. Do you remember how excited we still were at the table a year after the Bastille was stormed, and the march on Versailles demanded bread. And then the slight doubts which began when we heard of a certain invention of Joseph-Ignace Guillotin?
Yours in revolution, Mary

January 3, 1793

Dear Joseph,
I live in an immense mansion with sparkling white walls and many windows framed by ivy-green shutters. It is down the street from the Temple, where the royal family is incarcerated. It is hard not to feel a sense of fear and doom here. One's neighbor may inform on one for antirevolutionary activities to the Committee of Public Safety. Everybody is watching everybody.

April 16, 1793

Eliza, the French are still fops, even the bloodthirsty revolutionaries. I am heir, I am afraid, to the usual English prejudice against the French.

*I cannot speak their language well, and the daily anxiety of
life is great. I saw blood on the cobblestones and my heart stopped.
A woman told me not to look too long, to be careful of curiosity.
The guillotine, you know.*

May 17, 1793

*So, Everina, when it was time for me to leave the Christies' party,
there were marauding crowds of sansculottes roaming the streets
with torches. I am sure, though, that this will all die down and the
Revolution will return to its early, civilized ideals.*

*My house, I say my house, actually their house . . . what I
mean to say is that the people I was staying with have gone to the
country, escaped I believe, for though sympathetic with the Revolution, they are moneyed people, had perhaps aristocratic connections. So I am alone on rue Meslée. My room has a lady's desk
with lion-claw legs and inlaid brass. My bed board is mahogany
with rosewood parquetry, and the dresser has drawer handles
carved with cherubs.*

June 18, 1793

*Dear Eliza, I must say that I am in most sympathy with the Gi-
rondins. They believe that the family, as it is now, with the father
the head, is like a monarchy with the king as head, and they want
that changed. They believe that women should have the same
rights in the family as men and that we should also have equal
property rights. But now France is at war with the world, not just
with itself. Austria, Prussia, Belgium, England, all against
France. Foreigners are being arrested. Who knows what will happen. People say I should leave. My projected History of the Revolution, all the plans for female education, they say put aside.
Chaos reigns. They say use your head or you will not have one.
Some say the Revolution has been betrayed, gotten excessive, gone
too far. But at the same time, Eliza, women's clubs are springing
up all over Paris. Remember it was the women who brought the
royal family back from Versailles. And I cannot help, in my
lonely way, being excited. This is history, dear girl, history. People
here everywhere wish to have control of their own lives. I can un-*

derstand that. It is in the nature of people, if I may be so bold as to conjecture about our natures. The nature of men and women, those who will admit it, who will be strong enough to insist on it. Sadly, though I do not like her, they plan to execute the queen as well. The queen is to go before the knife. Is this a step in favor of the liberty of women? I am sounding rather confused myself. Coming? Going? Staying? Leaving? I would never count myself a counterrevolutionary, and yet I tremble to think this letter might reach other eyes.

October 3, 1793

Dear Joseph, I put myself at risk writing this letter to you at the English address. There is to be war between the two countries, n'est-ce pas? They have installed Madame Guillotine as a permanent fixture. Do you remember that hanging we went to? Every day is execution day here. The head falls into a small basket and they lift it high overhead. The crowd roars. Mothers knit stockings for their sons at the front right under the guillotine. I am reminded of Sir Gawain and the Green Knight. Remember? The Green Knight carried his own head away. One would wish that, would one not? All to be renewed and tried again. The world born green new-made. Or as in The Beggar's Opera, *the reprieve from the king coming at the last minute. Close, but in time. Of course, now there is no king, so who is to reprieve. We are running on death's clock here. Many heads, every day. The churches are to be done in. Not that I am religious. But it seems a pity. No excuse. No exception. Only execution.*

CHAPTER 34

ONLY A FEW BLOCKS away from where people were being led to their death, it was teatime at the Christies', eight in the evening, French style. There was a string quartet in one corner of the Christie drawing room, playing Boccherini. The musicians were in shabby powdered costume wigs and gold satin waistcoats. Tea and every other imaginable liquid were being served on silver trays. The room was furnished in sumptuous brocades, rosewoods, and carpets woven in mauve and salmon, cream and beige wool.

Christie had married a rich, giddy girl, mop-headed like himself, whom he called Jelly, short for Rebecca. They liked to entertain in a grand fashion and knew Paris, the old Paris of high culture and rich food, marvelous wines. Seeing no discrepancy between the way they lived and what was occurring on the streets, the Christies entertained with a revolutionary fervor. Christie, Mary noticed, kept himself upright, did not loll on the floor, and acted like an adult for a change. His wife was a consummate hostess, circulating among her guests with grace and charm.

"Mary," Jelly said. "I want you to meet Gilbert Imlay."

Mary looked at the man. That he was American was immediately obvious, for he was tall as a giant, brown as a Negro, his hair jet-black. Any blacker, Mary thought, and it would be night and he would need to put on a nightcap quickly. There was not a speck of powder on him. But, of course, powder was out of fashion in France and a real wig could not be found for love or money. Best not to wear a wig if one regarded one's head highly. He smelled of nun's soap and his clothing, this American's, was leather, as if the animal skin were his skin and he was naked.

"He is friends with Daniel Boone," Jelly whispered, buzzing by and pushing her forward. "Land. America. Money, dear."

"Really," Mary answered. She was not sure what was meant. The state of Kentucky seemed like Henry Fuseli's tree with dead stuffed animals. Wildlife, muskets, raccoon hats, and the forest did not stir her heart.

But this American person extended his hand to shake hers solidly, face to face. No finger kisses, bowing and scraping. "It is an honor to meet a fellow writer," he said in a deep voice.

Mary was always amused at all the people who called themselves writers. Many of them had hardly scribbled a line. She, on her fifth book, this one to be about the Revolution in France, did not really think of herself as "a writer."

"I do not presume to call myself a real writer, truth be told," he admitted. "The only thing I have to name my own is a technical and rather dull document: *A Topographical Description of the Western Territory of North America*."

"Well, Mr. Imlay, do not underestimate the amount of work any book takes, even a bad or a dull one. You are being modest, no doubt."

He smiled at her, tipped his teacup as in a toast. "Touché, Miss Wollstonecraft."

"It was nothing, Mr. Imlay."

"Yes, indeed, I understand you take us men to task in your book *A Vindication of the Rights of Woman*, something about women being able to do anything, to live as men . . . Sorry, the new etiquette is . . . What you mean is, live as rational human beings. That is what you mean, is it not. We are one in mind. That is it. I do hope this equality you speak of stops at the neck. Anatomy, however, is not my specialty. Are you rational, Miss Mary? In all circumstances? I am not. But that is neither here nor is it there or anywhere, is it? Beautiful eyes, you have."

"What color are they, Mr. Imlay?"

"They are hazel, changing in different lights, as mine are brown, Miss Wollstonecraft. You have nice eyes and your hair is brown."

"Your hair is black. It looks a good deal like a friend of mine's hair."

"I should like to meet your friend."

"My friend is dead."

"I am sorry. I, too, have lost friends. In battle. And magnificent teeth. You have the teeth of an American, Miss Wollstonecraft. They are your own? Yes, well, the English have such bad teeth."

"I am not a horse, Mr. Imlay, whose teeth must be examined before purchase."

"Indeed, not. But the horse is a noble creature. Did not Jonathan Swift make that point himself, more noble than human beings. In America, oh well . . . America."

He gave her a knowing look, and she cringed. She wanted to say she was only a few months out of Bedlam, and that she had only just learned to speak again, to think straight, to conduct herself properly in society, only just learned not to love Fuseli, could barely set pen to paper. Her body still felt frail and unsound, as if at the slightest tap all her bones would fall out of her skin. Her nose was sensitive and raw. Her eyes hurt. She no longer loved Fuseli, but where she had loved him, the tips of her fingers, under her lungs, in her mouth, felt empty and sore. She had come to France on a serious mission, to help draft educational reforms for the Revolution, to write her observations on the Revolution for Joseph.

In any event, she felt a refugee in France. She merely wanted to put herself together, to heal and become whole, and never, never to waste away her life again, as Bunyan would say, in the slough of despond. This meant, quite specifically, that she did not want to meet anybody, least of all an upstart American. She had seen others of his kind in Paris, and all of them, to a man, walked into rooms, salons, shops, as if they owned them. And they had the money to own them. God knows how they became so rich in that cow pasture of a country.

He put his hand thoughtfully on his chin, stepped nearer. "How did you come to be such a radical, Miss Wollstonecraft?"

She narrowed her eyes. "I suffered."

"As a woman?"

"As a human being, as a poor person, as a despised part of humanity, as a woman who was less than . . . and I read books about suffering, and I observed it all about me, and I have spoken to people and read books about our natures and what is possible to us as human beings. In America, you speak about the pursuit of happiness, do you not, and not merely for the rich. It seems . . ."

"I see."

"Do you really see?"

"I am trying to see."

"I doubt that you have suffered very much."

"Why do you say that?"

"You are an American. You are a man. You are tall. You are beautiful. In fact, what do you know?"

His leather clothes, soft suede breeches, the waistcoat of buckskin and shirt of cotton, his hose a beige cotton, his shoes carelessly buckled, were not inelegant, nor was he ingenuous. He had the civilized manner of a European born and bred in the city. However, he seemed intent on cultivating a rustic air of good-natured simplicity. His hair, his own, was very long and curly and carelessly tied behind with a simple thong. He had the face of a boy. He was, in fact, very handsome, the most handsome man she had ever seen.

"I am sorry I said that just now," she said, blinking very fast. "Really, I do not know anything about you. You probably have suffered as much as any of us." She felt embarrassed. He made her self-aware.

He saw her home to the rue Meslée because it was late and sans-culottes were about. He followed her into the house, as a matter of course. And then, ambling through the mansion, he walked before her, picking up things, feeling tables, petting chairs, fondling books.

"This is pretty," he said. "I like this, who plays the harpsichord, do you like Handel, how can one not? Do you play chess, not many women do, but then you are a famous authoress? Your book, I hear, states that brutal force has ruled the world. Am I right? And so what do you suggest? Are you not a little vixen yourself? Do not hide. I saw those sharp teeth. You feel women should be responsible for their own happiness. Are you happy? I hear you fell in love with Fuseli. Is he not a pornographer, that picture of his—*The Nightmare*. My goodness, have you ever had dreams like that, a demon lover straddling your knees and a wild white-eyed horse peering through the curtains, a rather crowded bedroom, would you not say? Ah yes, you English, pale boys. I hear Fuseli fancies pale boys. Is his publisher Joseph Johnson? He is your publisher, too, am I wrong? A small world. A very small world. Is that why you are here in France, getting over it all. Be a good girl, bring me a glass of wine. I would love to take you to the vineyards, spend a day in the sun, I miss the sun. We Americans love the sun. Talk to me, woman."

She ran downstairs to the pantry and wine cellar in great haste, my God, leaned against the cool walls, put her forehead against the cool walls, which had been painted in lime to trap flies. He was entirely out of hand. She could hear him pacing above. Quickly she pulled a bottle out from its groove in the wall. It was slippery. She looked at her hands. They were wet with sweat.

"Mary, Mary," he called. "Famous author, come out, come out wherever you are."

"Shortly, Gilbert." Or should it be Mr. Imlay? Gil? Mary wondered: Famous author? Am I famous? Is that why he is here now with me. She felt giddy, dizzy. Famous author? I am not that famous. And why the trembling? According to Hume, it must be allowed that when we know a power, that very circumstance is the cause by which it is enabled to produce the effect. We must therefore know both the cause and the effect.

"Mary."

"Yes." She looked quickly into the glass in the hallway to check. Yes, she was Mary. But not the Mary she used to know, the one who lived in the attic of Joseph Johnson's house.

"I feel so cramped here in Europe," he said, not crossing his legs the way the French and English did, his thighs too thick and muscular for that, but keeping his legs open. "In America," he said, "there is space. Here everything is so contained, so small. In America, not only can you walk about, but you can do things. You can do anything." And then he looked down. "Or you can fail miserably."

"I would like to go to America," Mary said, sipping her wine.

"Really?" He gave her a big, broad grin. "Maybe you will," he said. "Soon."

She looked up quickly. It was dark. She must light the candles, close the shutters. But in the gloom the paneled walls inlaid with gold leaf gleamed almost audibly, the rococo cabinets with hinged fronts and marquetry squeaked and crackled, the marble clock struck, and the writing desk of kingwood, tulipwood, and carved beechwood whistled.

I am in a forest of trees, a wood, Mary thought, and they are all chattering in their own language.

"Do not be afraid," Gilbert said, leaning forward a little, holding his glass under her chin. "Have you ever touched a buttercup flower to somebody's chin to see if he likes butter?"

"Do you like butter?" she asked.

"I love butter," he answered.

"Sometimes butter makes me ill."

He got up, started to walk around again. "I am naturally restless. Can you read music?" He picked up the sheet music on the harpsichord. It was Don Giovanni's seduction song to Elvira. He began to whistle the first bars. "Well, now." He finished his wine with one gulp. "Well, must be on my way." He extended his hand for another hearty handshake.

When he left, Mary fell into bed, quivering and spent. The man had taken up all the air in the house. She had to throw open the window, sit looking out at the street for a good hour, calm herself down. Then slowly and quietly she prepared for bed, hanging up her dress, putting paper in her shoes, taking down her hair and brushing it out. In the mirror, she saw a not so young woman with round cheeks, a flushed face. My hair is thinning a bit, she observed, although her breasts were still firm and hard. This American, she said to herself, jangles me, and renders me silly. He is too abrupt, too breezy, too presumptuous, too big, too handsome, too intelligent, too, too, too.

That night she dreamed she was in St. Paul's Cathedral, in the whispering gallery, where whispers carried across the church in loud echoes. All the pews, all the furniture was gone. The doors were wide open and a drafty wind whipped through like ice water. Where is everybody, where is everything, she thought, drawing her cloak about her chest. Can you read music, a voice said from behind the altar, but it sounded like: Can you read the writing on the wall. She looked up and there was nothing on the wall, nothing at all.

CHAPTER 35

THOMAS PAINE, who lived at White's Hotel in Paris and hosted dinners there for the expatriates, replicated Thursday nights more closely than the Christies' teatimes. Proceedings were loud and political. Port was not spared. Both Mary and Gilbert were to be seen there. The cuisine was hearty. It was at White's Hotel that Paine told an assembled group in December 1792 that the king was as good as dead.

"Trial is merely the event of formal accusation. To be accused is to be guilty."

Paine knew Danton, which was why he might have known about the king's fate. Outlawed in England for his republican sentiments and burned in effigy, Paine still pleaded for the king's life in Paris.

Mary felt at that time that the king should be spared, too. The king was born a king. Could he help it? Yes, Paine's guests replied. It seemed that they had in mind St. Francis, who gave up everything of his parents and walked naked into the world. Kings are not saints, she answered. "Why not?" they cried, banging the table. "We want justice."

In June of 1793, shortly after their first meeting, when Mary saw Imlay at one of Paine's dinners, he winked. Was that, she wondered, an American custom. What did he want?

Both Mary and Paine were sympathetic with the Girondin party, less radical than the Jacobins headed by Robespierre, who advocated Machiavellian tactics, the ends justifying the means. Mary had been invited to give a paper before the legal committee of the Girondins. This committee sought to break the power of the patriarchal family and give greater independence to women. She did not know where Imlay stood on these issues. She would have liked him to be an idealistic

American, an American revolutionary thinking in bold and fresh ways. However, she strongly suspected that he was there, at the Revolution, to make money.

"And do you know," Imlay said after the dinner with Paine that June night in 1793, and back at Mary's "immense *hôtel*," "that Diderot, the philosopher, has attacked traditional Christian attitudes on the family, family life, and so forth. He brings chastity and marriage into question. The act, you know . . ."

"Yes, Gilbert."

"Natural and pleasurable."

"Children, Gilbert, born of such unions, how are they to be cared for?"

"In common."

"I see."

"Why do you say 'I see' in such a way, Mary? In your work you call marriage licensed prostitution. How would you expect children to be taken care of?"

She said "I see" the way he said it. She even was beginning to smooth her hair down, the way he put his hand to his head. They were drinking wine and eating biscuits. Imlay had thrown himself onto the chaise. Mary had a headache. What she wondered was if there was anything in Rousseau or Voltaire or any of the *philosophes* which condoned violence. And if not, would the present events be perversions or even desecrations of their ideas of liberty, equality, and fraternity? And then having believed that the king's life should be spared, would she be a traitor to the cause, the original cause.

"Really, Mary, we are living in the most exciting city on earth during its most exciting time. Are you not delighted?"

Mary smiled. "A little."

"A little?" He bounded up, set his elbows on his knees.

He was such a boy, she thought, in his enthusiasms. He reminded her of Richard.

"A little?" he repeated, pacing about, throwing up his arms. "A little? Only a little?"

She had forgotten what "a little" referred to. "All right. Very much."

"Ah, yes, of course, I thought so. I know you like to play the demure young miss, moderate and contained, and so, so English, is that it? But, madam, I conjecture that your brain is a whole city aflame. Like the London fire during Pepys's time. What started it? A small fire in a bakery."

She laughed.

He was hard to resist. And she was not doing an adequate job of it, realizing as she dressed for still another of Paine's dinners that she was dressing with Imlay in mind. Her dress was a simple white muslin that night, high-waisted in the French fashion, with a ribbon under her bust and around her neck. Two red ribbons. A blue hem, and so she was quite the French patriot, or the American. When she saw him, her cheeks became rosy, as if she had been out walking at a fast and determined pace.

"You looked very nice tonight," he said, back at rue Meslée. Their after-dinner talks were becoming a habit. "But there is something else I wish you to wear."

As he reached in his pocket, Mary felt warmth grow on her neck and back. A present. She could not remember getting a present from anybody. She was thrilled that he had gotten her a small gift. She had known him only a short while. But he was impulsive and rapid in his affections and interests.

"And so," he said, pulling out a black silk stocking.

Flustered, she said: "A stocking, one stocking, how am I to wear that?"

"Over your eyes, my dear."

Quick as a wink he rushed over and tied it around her eyes so she could not see.

"Life is a mystery, Mary," he said, leading her, thus blindfolded, to the bedroom. Then he had her lie down and, without her seeing, unlaced her bodice and took off her stays, undoing the ribbons carefully, so he could see her full top, and then he loosened the string of her skirts.

"Gil, I have not bathed in weeks." She knew what zealots Americans were for bathwater.

"It is fine, Mary. Just relax." And he pulled off her shoes and rolled down her stockings. Presto, she was naked and worrying about her long thighs and full belly. Her blindfold was wet, but·he would not be able to tell she was crying. She lay for a while, assuming that he looked at her carefully, running one finger up and down her sides; then he flipped her over and rubbed her posterior for quite some time, as if she must be soothed after a long horseback ride. Then very gently he dressed her, lifting her arms up for the sleeves and her hips for the skirts. The stays were not pulled as tightly as she would have it, but she was hardly in the frame of mind to request hard pulls, for she had the sensation of floating or dozing off, a soothing and slightly tingling feeling. She dared not think: I am naked, I am sad. I am naked. I am disappointed. I am naked and I am humiliated. I am naked and here I am with a man again; these things are perilous, this is not the time for this, I am naked and I am not ready for this and how humiliated I am. I am tired, old, I hate him, I better stop him, explain. My body is a poor paltry thing better left unseen, I am naked and I have not bathed in two weeks except for my hands and face, is this the behavior of an intelligent woman, how can I get away, I am naked and I am ugly and he is the most handsome man I have ever seen.

"Mary," he said, undoing the stocking from her eyes.

"Yes." She sat up, blinked.

"Thank you." He was sitting beside her on the bed.

"For what?"

"Letting me see you."

"Oh, that." She acted as if it was nothing.

"People are going to lose their heads here. I do not want you to lose yours."

"Of course not, of course I will not."

"Good."

Saw Imlay again, Joseph, talked about losing my head. Yes, these are heady times, but he meant heart, not head. The real head chopper is situated not far from here. I passed by, saw the blood-stained cobblestones and shiny blade. It is a monument to horror. We live with terror here. An everyday thing. Lines for bread, and anybody can be stopped for papers. We have to show identification at every turn in the street. But do not ask me to leave. Now more than ever, I wish to stay. Love to you, my dear. Citizen Mary

July 30, 1793

Dear Mary, I detect a sad note in your last correspondence. Do not tell me that you have fallen in love again. Must you always be in love? And an American? Actually Paine wrote me as much. Christie has mentioned him. My dear, I have my sources. Remember, Americans are wild and irresponsible people. Mostly children from what I have heard, particularly the men who play soldier and Indian, just a game, but in truth they kill people. Their constitution gives them the right to bear arms. And slavery, do you not know that despite the rhetoric of their revolution, Africans are treated worse than the most miserable apprentice.

My suggestion to you is to observe, take notes, and leave as soon as possible. It will be a bloodbath and as an English citizen you will be most vulnerable. You can write your book in England, and for all our infringements on personal liberty, at least you do not have to worry about losing your head. You have a beautiful head. I love you. God keep you.   Joseph

"GILBERT IMLAY is nothing but a cheap adventurer from New Jersey, though he calls himself a frontiersman," Joseph Johnson told William Godwin, one of the few Thursday-night regulars left in London.

Johnson was not overly fond of the ponderous Godwin, but what could he do? Nobody was around. Christie, in Paris, had written that Mary seemed quite taken with a certain American of dubious reputation.

"He seems a fraud," Joseph went on, a little fretfully.

"Are not we all?" Mrs. Mason said, as she set before them her latest concoction, a frothy dish of trifle made of sponge-cake and custard and raspberry jam and sherry with a little touch of cinnamon.

"To a greater or lesser degree, perhaps." Godwin was reserved and judicious in his comments. He had recently published his *Political Justice*.

"We'll see, we'll see. Yet Imlay is known as 'Captain' in Europe, though he served in Washington's forces in the American Revolutionary War as only a lieutenant and very briefly."

"A summer soldier," Godwin said, quoting Paine.

"Basically," Joseph said, offering Godwin his excellent tobacco, "basically, Gilbert Imlay is a fugitive from justice and an impostor. The Kentucky courts have cases pending against him for trespass, default on debts, and fraud. He sold people land he did not own, making much of a supposed connection with Daniel Boone. He came to Paris to present to the Committee of Public Safety his plan of arming frontiersmen under French leadership to fight the Spanish presence in the Mississippi Valley, thus engaging the United States in war with the European powers. A commitment of 750,000 pounds he believes will guarantee success."

"My God, he is involved in that scheme? I thought it was Brissot's idea." Godwin had no real taste for danger. Johnson did. The table with just the two of them looked like a coffin to Godwin.

"In fact, both Imlay and Mary are connected to Brissot, she for her educational reform ideas. You know Brissot is a member of the Committees of Public Safety and Foreign Affairs. But what if favor goes against him? The political climate is so volatile. You see, not only would Brissot's Louisiana/Mississippi plan gain France a foothold on the American continent, and some very valuable land at that, but it would also distract some of the fighting away from France itself. You know, the Austrians, the Prussians, and the Belgians threaten France, and soon we, too, will, no doubt."

"And Mary?" Godwin did not know Mary well. They had sat across from each other now and then on Thursday nights, yet rarely talked.

CHAPTER 37

THE TIME Gilbert and Mary made love in the vineyard, the grass was slippery-smooth as silk, and the smell of ripening grapes was heavy and intoxicating. The sun caught in her eye, a yellow sliver of it, making tears; she felt she was in the clouds. One hundred miles north, the clouds were smoke from cannons.

He kissed for hours, it seemed—on her eyes, each lid, her nose, sticking his tongue up her nostrils and in her ears. He batted his long, feathery lashes against her ears, so that she felt he was painting her ears black with the brushstrokes of his lashes. He said he loved everything she could do with her mouth. He meant talking, he loved to hear her talk. She had a beautiful voice. And kissing. He meant kissing. He loved to kiss her. She kissed wonderfully.

They had seen a body in the tall grass, not a mark on it, but several days dead in the tall grass. Each pretended not to see it.

He did not shove his tongue in her mouth as Fuseli had done. Fuseli's tongue, in retrospect, now that she no longer liked him, seemed coated and like a big green pickle floating in a barrel in a stall on a London bridge. Fuseli kissed with a forward thrust which would do justice to His Majesty's fencing master. Sometimes Imlay pressed gently, dryly; he nipped and tucked, gave gentle little bites, taking the tongue and running all around along the top of her lip, the bottom; then, with a cautious lift with tongue and finger, he opened her mouth and, with a soft pressure, inserted his tongue into the cave of her mouth—exploring. If he were blind, she thought, he could see with his tongue.

The dead body was a peasant. He had blue trousers, loose and straight, wooden shoes. His open eyes stared at the sun like cooked eggs.

Gilbert felt under her tongue with his tongue and around the sides with his tongue, sliding up and down her handsome teeth. She really did not like her teeth fiddled with.

The dead man's hair was brown and oily. Ants clung to the strands as if straddling a bridge.

"I hear you are hatching a war on the American continent."

"Who told you that? Is that what you talk about in your women's clubs? Dangerous gossip, my dear, dangerous gossip."

"I feel . . ."

"Faint?"

"No, strange."

"These are strange times."

Later, when she was back in England, the notes for her book on the Revolution would include:

EXECUTED WOMEN

Olympe de Gouges, who had founded women's clubs, and composed appeals for the abolition of the slave trade, and was for instituting public workshops for the unemployed and a national theater for women, was sent to the guillotine on charges of treason. (She went to her death courageously.)

Madame Roland, a Girondin. (She helped a poor frightened man face the guillotine bravely, then climbed the steps herself.)

Charlotte Corday, a staunch Girondin and the assassin of Marat, who she felt was betraying the Revolution. (She believed that romantic love and other tender emotions cease to touch the heart of a woman who aspires to knowledge.)

Marie Antoinette, who was considered by Mirabeau the only man in the house, following her husband, Louis Capet. Her brown hair turned white, on the eve of her execution. (She accidentally trod on one of the executioner's toes and said: I beg your pardon. I hope I did not hurt you.)

Many of the women who had stormed Versailles for bread, who had brought the king and queen back to Paris, and had been members of the clubs to support the Revolution and liberalize the divorce laws and gain educational rights, were executed.

It could be at any moment, Mary felt, a knock at the door, a thump on the stairs, the steady beat of the drum. *L'état, c'est Robespierre.*

Charges: treason, conspiracy, supporting the enemies of the Revolution, counterrevolutionary thoughts and actions, the state must be cleansed of undesirable elements, crimes against the people, un-French activities, an ill-placed smile. For example:

On your doorstep the baker pauses. He has been selling bread to a woman who was married to a man who knew the cousin of a woman guillotined for hoarding fabric—cambric, chintz, Persian. Furthermore, this baker sheds tears at inappropriate moments as when a pet would be kicked to death by a soldier of the Revolutionary Army on his street, and once when he saw a picture of the dead queen, he put his hand to his heart, exclaimed softly: *Mon Dieu.* He is executed, clearly guilty, and you, who talked with him, go, too, a neighbor goes who was looking out of the window at the time, and his wife, who is married to him. You think on your way of your misspent life. You hope you will not soil yourself. They said the blade did not hurt, but felt very cool on the neck. *Mon Dieu.*

Danton, who had a very large head, a head like a lion's, was taken to the blade for arguing against the excesses of the Terror.

Brissot (Mary's friend and ally) was taken for his moderate sympathies.

The guillotine was moved to the Place de la Révolution, beside the Tuileries Gardens, which were leafy and lovely in spring and summer.

Condorcet himself, one of the engineers of the Revolution, who was arrested and officially condemned to death while he was in hiding, poisoned himself in jail. He was one of the few *conventionnels* who espoused full rights for women.

The blade was a siren who sang in the night, the blade was a vampire who needed fresh blood in order to live. The blade had a life of its own. When not in use, it was draped in a large black cloth, its skirts and dress, the people said. Madame goes dancing.

"What has happened to the Revolution? What do you do when all you have espoused goes awry?" Mary asked Gilbert in late fall 1793, when they were making love upstairs in her room. They always seemed to have political discussions at such times. She had been a Republican, worn the red hat with Blake, belonged to the Jacobin Club. She had argued for liberty, believed in equality, and who would not foster fraternity in his heart?

"Do not take politics so seriously," Gilbert said. "It is a game of winners and losers, that is all." He was pulling on his clothes. This was not a good moment, she knew, the putting on of clothes. You are awkward, you turn away from each other, you are ready to rejoin the world.

"What about equality and liberty?"

"Words to get people out of bed. I love the taste of you," he said.

"I am too frightened to be doing this anymore, Gilbert."

"It is the best time to be doing it. Now be a good girl, Mary."

"All my ideals have been crushed. Anyway, I am dressed."

"Ideals? Not illusions? You have beautiful legs."

She knew she could no longer write Eliza or Everina, and especially not Joseph, for mail between England and France was being seized. She no longer saw her friends in Paris, for *they* were being seized. At twilight, which was when people were being hauled away, she would hear the drum, for the summons came with a child beating the drum. Then came the men with the documents and manacles, the women with their tears and lamentations. In the name of the Republic. All the English were being rounded up.

"Why don't I get you papers that say you're my wife? Americans are safe. America is not at war with France. As my wife, you will be a citizen of America."

"Posing as your wife, Gilbert?"

"Yes, just a slight deception to remain alive, my dear. A real ceremony for two adult people is hardly necessary."

She did not say anything.

"I know how much you value your freedom, Mary. So this is simply a practical measure."

Now Gilbert and Mary are in the drawing room. It is an empty, windy house. When the residents left, they went quietly through the back door, taking only what they could carry in their hands. It is a fine, aristocratic house, not good to be seen in. Now Mary and Gilbert seem swallowed up by the many rooms. Their footsteps echo and their voices come out hollow, as if funneled through tin. The world is falling away on either side and nobody cares. You look wonderful on a bed, he tells her, tying her to the posts. Let us keep you there. But where was she to appear, anyway? All of Paris was in prison, under sentence, or dead. Torture was expected. It was in the air. Death seeped into the water.

They were in the kitchen. Terror was a palpable thing, like food. The air was thick and the smell of blood moved over central Paris in a heavy blanket. Mary was cooking kidney. The smell of urine mixed with the blood. Some people came out of their houses, stood at their doorways with hands on their hips, but most people stayed inside, drew their curtains. Sometimes Mary fell into deep sleeps in the middle of the day, ate whatever she could find, forgot to comb her hair. Gilbert ran out and bought bread, wine, flowers.

"You are my prisoner," he said each time he tied her up. "The most famous woman in Europe."

"Oh, save me, save me" were her lines. She felt awkward, unsure, not quite real. He hurt her, but it seemed important to be strong, not let on.

But once she said: "Stop."

"You know what stop means," he said.

At first the bruises were green and red, then blue and black, softening to smudges of brown. He liked to lick them like an eager little dog. Remembering Eliza's bruises, Mary thought, my God, perhaps she loved him.

They are on the top floor, in the maid's bed. The empty bottles are arranged around the bed like a green army at attention.

"What do you think the man in the vineyard died of, Gilbert?"

"Shot in the back, a coward's death."

"By now he will have vines growing in his hair and a leaf for a mouth, flowers for eyes . . . was he a soldier?"

"Mary, do not start in with the disgusting."

"What do you think our death will be like?" It seemed very close, actually. Sometimes, when he was whipping her, she felt the next step *was* death. It was all one, inside the house and outside on the streets. She felt caught in a swirl. Time was distorted. She felt both lost and found out, that is, she forgot herself, what she had been—the writer and scholar—and remembered certain childhood things—her father's angry voice, wetting herself during a beating, Annie's insistent requests. All over again, she was the humiliated little child. "I cannot help but be disgusting, Gil. I am in France. *We* are in France."

"There is a saying that, before the English are taught to worship God, they are taught to detest Frenchmen. When war between England and France was declared, some of the members of the Convention wanted to make it clear that war was being waged against King George and his government, not the English people. Marat, who was still alive at that time, laughed out loud. He knew how much the English hate the French."

"I do hate the French," Mary said. "They are making it impossible for anybody to ever have hope again. What are we to think of human nature, the possibilities of change in the society?"

There had been screams throughout the night before. In Mary's opinion, the English would never be capable of something like the Terror, or the Americans, either.

"They may not do it as fast," Gilbert said, "but they do it, you do it, the English kill as well as the next."

"Each other? Do we kill each other?"

"Of course. The poor go down daily, do they not? In poorhouses and orphanages, in Newgate and Bedlam, at the hanging tree, in shops and factories, on the street, in the colonies, everywhere."

Bedlam. She had not told him. Sometimes she felt she was back there again—those confusing days. She felt ill, wretched.

"I want to tell you something, Gilbert." She was standing now, in the drawing room, weaving a little, but trying to be straight and tall, strong.

"I need to tell you, Gilbert."

"The English are perhaps more subtle about it." He had lit the opium pipe, passed it to her. "Sit down, Mary, will you."

So she let it pass.

Some days later he was sitting on the bed in his shirt, one foot dangling.

"I love to wash my genitals in your bowl," he said, looking over at her tenderly, walking over to the armoire. "Maybe we should tidy the place, wash."

"I need to tell you something, Gilbert."

"Yes," he said. "Scratch my back, would you."

He came over, sat on the edge of the bed. "The left shoulder, right there, up a little higher, down, down, ah, right there."

"Do you love me," she asked.

"Sometimes."

"Right now?"

"Yes."

"There is something you should know, Gilbert."

"Gracious, woman, there are many things I should know."

"What I want to tell you is, I am with child." She felt his back tense up immediately. He did not turn around.

"What?"

"Baby. We are to have a baby."

"My God." He held his chest as if wounded. "Let us go downstairs."

"What is the difficulty, Gilbert?" She had no clothes on and felt in dire need of a dress, if not a suit of armor. She reached down to the floor for her skirts.

"This is about the worst time in the history of mankind, Mary, and the worst place on earth, for that sort of thing. I thought you were wearing a sponge like every advanced woman, like the woman you are. Are you so backward that you cannot take responsibility for yourself?"

"Did you ever see me put one on?"

"You can put them on before. You can walk in them, everything. I thought you were knowledgeable about these things."

"Yes, but I am not French and lascivious," she huffed.

"You English, such snobs."

"You Americans, so demeaning." He was making her sick.

"What is that supposed to mean?"

"And you are prudes, American prudes."

"If we are prudes, then you are licentious dogs."

"We are not licentious at all, Gilbert."

"Our country was founded by Puritans, Mary."

"That is not something I would advertise."

"Your country was founded by hypocrites," he said. "Shall I read to you the advertisements in the *Covent Garden Magazine*, better known as the *Amorous Repository*, and I quote: *5 shillings for a temporary favor, half a guinea for a night's lodging*."

She sang:

> To Banbury came I,
> Where I saw a Puritan
> Hanging of his cat on Monday
> For killing a mouse on Sunday.

"That is not what we are about in America at all."

"Oh, no? Hand me my skirts and bodice."

"Do you want me to leave? I could leave right now, rather than suffer fools kindly."

She looked at him. Panic clutched her heart. "Oh, Gilbert, do not leave me. I need you."

She thought of the room without him, how empty it would feel, and the house without him, how huge it would seem, and Paris, unendurable, and the world itself, a vacant, vast desert where she would wander with her baby, her orphan.

"I will not leave you, Mary," he said softly. "No, I will not leave." He patted her hand.

"Do you promise?"

"Yes, I promise."

"Everybody always leaves me," she said in a small voice.

"I will not."

"Do you promise to *never* leave me." The minute the words were out of her mouth, she realized she had gone too far. He stiffened.

"I have to vomit. Pardon me." She got off the bed, padded over to her washbowl, and delivered the contents of breakfast—two rolls, a piece of cheese, strong French coffee—onto the water Gilbert had used for washing himself a minute before.

"Could you get me a cup of water, please."

When he left the room, she hastily threw the contents of the bowl out the window, lest it make her ill again, drew on her skirts, and, without her stays, tied on her bodice.

"Take little sips, my dear, just little sips. We do not want the boy to be thirsty and hungry." He handed her the water.

"Boy?"

"Every man wants a son."

"I see. We go from 'This is just utter hell' to 'Be careful of my son.' Your mind can do that, make those jumps?"

"Shh, I want you to get some rest. You cannot let anything trouble you."

"I am not tired. It is only morning."

"You are tired. You need to rest. You must do exactly as I say from now on."

CHAPTER 38

IT WAS LATE FALL, then, 1793. The Vendée uprising was put down at the cost of 250,000 lives. But Mary liked to lie on her back and watch her stomach, as she had tried to see her legs grow when she was a child. She would stay up all night with a candle, but not see a thing. It happened when you were not looking, she supposed. Her nipples, though, which were always sensitive, became excruciatingly aware of touch and sound. A simple tune that Gilbert sang could make them strain and smart. Cloth, air, a light change in temperature, would make her jump in pain. They seemed long as dunce caps, had a little hum to them. Usually they were thimbles. Now they were fishhooks with fishes. And a long, dark line etched itself between them to her belly button. It looked like a dusky path through the Sahara. A windy trail to the woods. The long, wide road to perdition.

Certain smells made her retch. Sausage cooking and festering flowers were enough to make her gag. She hated eggs, butter, and milk. Food was becoming scarce in Paris, and even bread was dear. She could have stood bread. She lived on tea and hard sailor biscuits.

"One good thing," Gilbert said, "is they do not guillotine pregnant women."

"They wait until after the baby is born."

"The Terror will be over by then."

"We will see." They were saying these terrible things in jest, for Mary was registered as Gilbert's wife. They were careful.

In the early evening, Mary was most happy. Her stomach would be settled, and she would have slept in the afternoon. She liked to sit at the window facing the street and sew little clothes for the baby out of cloth cut from the left-behind dresses and curtains of the household. Blue satin shifts, and shirts made from blue-black taffeta, red velvet jackets, booties of Belgian lace, trousers with a braided seam. The house was cleaned up now, the kitchen in order. No more tie-up games and bruises (not good for the baby) and sleepy days blending into long nights (not good for the baby).

She found herself chatting with neighbor women about nursing and swaddling and when to start solid food and how to treat the navel and at what age they walked, talked, balked. She had to tie up her swollen ankles, lift her feet up.

"What happened to your *History of the French Revolution*?" Gilbert asked, rubbing her stomach with aloe. He liked her stomach and her breasts and the slow, heavy way she walked.

"Oh, all in good time."

She never felt less like reading and writing in her life. She just wanted to sit, sit in the mild winter sun, sit quietly. Landlocked by the Revolution, she could not write home, write to anybody, which she was happy for, the privacy, the chance to savor her pregnancy all on her own. She could have sat growing a baby forever. Particularly since, the larger she grew, the more amorous Gilbert became.

Here are the ways they made love:

1. She is sitting on his crotch, while he lies on his back, his legs up, her legs between his, his strong body holding her up, and his hands easing her up and down. That first afternoon was so quiet, the sun streaming down, and somewhere a drum rolling. Was it the guillotine they were signaling? A trial? A funeral?

2. She is on her side, one leg raised akimbo; he fitting inside and she pushing hard against him with her hips. Screaming on their street. Mary envisions women hanging on the coattails of the Committee of Public Safety as they carry away their husbands. Babies and children all set up a wail.

3. She is on her stomach, flat down; he on top; she having to be raised up a little on her knees, and their backs slippery with sweat. Mary imagined the people who owned the house she lived in, foraging in the forest like animals, eating roots and berries, sleeping in hollows or nests of pine.

4. Then both of them are belly to belly, she off at an angle, working hips. She sees blood on the street in front of the house in the shape of an oak leaf. It expands to an octopus.

5. Another position: he is on his side, both her legs thrown over him, his penis neatly fitted between her closed legs. She had heard that when the head came off, with the guillotine, it blinked, grimaced, had an expression.

6. He kneels above her, she twists to one side, and he is holding one of her legs up at his shoulder. Were tortures still used? Yes, of course, as always. The rack. Drawing and quartering. The Iron Maiden. Like in Bedlam.

7. She is rolling back, both her legs over his shoulders. Gil, Gil, they are coming to get us, the Committee of Public Safety. Shh, he'd say. No, no, no, they cannot. He had registered her as his wife, both Americans and not at war with France. She was safe.

8. She is standing, and this is hard because of his great height, and he coming behind her, with one of her feet raised and resting on the bed. Sometimes, even though she was safe, she thought she heard a knock at the door.

9. Gil liked her stretched on the marble top of the dresser, her breasts smashed flat as a cockleshell, and her behind hanging there, like a piece of meat ready to be cut down. The knocking is low and steadily increases in volume, speed.

10. He is holding her up, her legs wrapped around him. He is wearing her clothes, her bonnet, her skirts and bodice. There *is* a knock at the door.

"Put on your clothes," Gilbert spat.

"You are wearing my clothes," she whispered.

"God." He started tearing her clothes off.

"Gil."

"Shh."

"Gil, I am frightened."

"Get under the bed," he whispered.

She fell to the floor, still naked, crawled to the bed, sandwiched herself underneath, carefully moving the chamber pot to one side, trying not to make a sound.

Gilbert shed himself of her skirts and bodice, but still in her flat straw bonnet with ribbon ties, he tiptoed to the side of the window, moved over slowly to the curtain. Holding it in front of him, he looked down at the street.

"Have mercy," he uttered.

"What? Is it? Is it . . ."

He nodded. "I am not sure, strangers." He came over to her, crawled beside her.

"Is the wardrobe better, Mary, to hide in?"

"No. They will look there first."

The knocking was louder.

"Are there any secret hiding places? The linen closet, the pantry. Anything that can be locked from within?"

"The lady's bedroom, and within that, her powder room."

"We need to crawl very quietly."

"Will we be arrested?" Mary sobbed.

"Be quiet."

Mary inched her way, moving like a snake, Gilbert right behind her, holding her foot. The knocking was deafening, or maybe it was the drum, or was it her heart, or maybe she was dead already and that was what the center of the earth sounded like. She pushed the door open, slid into the room. There was powder all over the floor from when the lady and gentleman of the house had powdered their hair. It seemed like dust from a long time ago, dust of the ages. Gilbert stood up, locked the door. She remembered that the front door had a long bar across it, as if it were the gate to the city. That was good. To break the door open, they would need a battering ram. Mary and Gil were now in the powder room. She stood up and pulled Gilbert after her. The floor was covered with a fine powder. It seemed ironic to her that they were hiding and wading in a major symbol of the Old Regime.

"Dear heart," he said. "Let us pray for our delivery."

"Gilbert. I cannot."

"Why not?"

"You look so funny in my hat." She giggled. "Naked and in my hat."

He snatched it off.

"Now you must pray."

"Dear, I cannot."

"Have you become an atheist?"

"I am."

"Like that rascal Tom Paine?"

"He is not an atheist. He is a Deist."

"And you are not even that? Mary, is it not wise to observe, on the off-chance that . . ."

"If God were there, He would know I was being insincere. And if God were there, He would not have let my friend Fanny die miserably, nor would He permit the Terror. So it stands quite badly for Him if He is there. Thus, if He is there He is totally unacceptable to me as an active principle in the universe. Even as author of the universe, He is not beyond recall. I totally dismiss Him. And so, if you wish, I can pray to the sky."

He sighed.

"Sorry," she said.

"Shh, can you hear anything?"

"No."

They sat down. Gilbert sneezed.

"It is all that stupid aristocratic powder, Gil."

"I suppose you would rather have some democratic dirt. This closet is saving our life, I hope."

He had said "life," "our life" as if they were one. At that moment she thought she *could* go to her death, their death together. Of course, the guillotine would not be the means of her choice, but still . . .

"We are going to have to wait until it is safe."

"But, Gilbert, really, all I have to say is that I am the author of *A Vindication of the Rights of Woman*." She had not brought that to mind in a good while.

"Mary, are you insane? Do you think anybody cares?"

"They do not care?" She was crestfallen. "I am the most famous . . ." She used to be. She could recall a time when . . .

"Come, now. Nobody knows, nobody cares. Just be quiet."

"A is for acorn," she whispered. "F is for fear."

CHAPTER 39

THEY WAITED through the afternoon, staring at the walls. There were no windows, no light, and it was very close. It was like Bedlam, and Mary felt like screaming, but she did not. Mary thought she was too frightened to sleep, and she did not like to sleep naked, she begged him to get a blanket from the bed, but he felt that someone might be lurking below on the street, would see him snaking his way to the bed. She cried softly, rocked herself, thought of Fanny, of lame Richard, Dr. Price, Joseph. At some point, not knowing when, she fell asleep. She woke up in silence. Gil was curled beside her, his thumb in his mouth, and the other hand between his legs. He could have been an overgrown child, with his hair around his face. He had no hair on his chest. She did not know if it was day or night, except that light was coming through the crack between the door and the floor. She went back to sleep almost happily.

"Mary, Mary."

She was in a large house full of children and pets, brightly colored birds in cages, bowls of fish, shaggy house dogs, and exotic, slant-eyed cats who purred continuously. There were pretty pictures on the wall and baskets of fruit, beautiful curtains, and comfortable chairs, sumptuous carpets. The children kept saying: Mother, Mother, watch me. The women, all mothers, watched from a large stone-inlaid patio with arbors of climbing roses and woodbine hanging down. Somebody, the royal gardener, in a blue wig and powder-blue suit and blue stockings, was going about with a pair of huge shears, decapitating the roses. I love you best of all, more than any of them, somebody blew into her ear warmly. It was Joseph, dressed in her clothes. She looked up. A thunderstorm was coming from the east. Blue rocky clouds rolled in, somersaulting each other, crashing out sparks of lightning. A male voice said: Mary, Mary.

"I am going to look, see if they are still here."

Her mouth was sticky, full of sleep. Her body was creased by the pattern in the floor, and the creases were full of dirty powder. She felt like a wrinkled map of the world.

Gilbert undid the latch cautiously. Tiptoeing through the room, he got to the hall. She stayed in the bedroom, saw him go down the stairs. The sun splotched the hallway carpet with circles of yellow. Dust rose in a cone. Orange spirals swirled madly right and left. She also saw big black dots. All this seemed to come from behind her eyelids. Her insides gurgled and pressed. She wanted to use the chamber pot.

"They are gone," Gil said, running back up the stairs. "But I am sure they will be back."

"No."

"Oh, yes."

"What are we going to do, Gil?"

"We will not be here. In fact, we should leave this very moment."

Mary looked down. Her pregnant breasts were full and sore. Her stomach was growing. The smell, sight, sound of food made her ill. The thought, in itself, of travel fatigued her beyond hope.

"I cannot."

"You have to if you value your head."

"I feel sick, Gilbert."

"I am sorry."

"I can hardly move. It is probably just a scare. They will not be back. You said we were safe. They dare not touch Americans. Perhaps it is nothing at all and we are needlessly frightened."

"Get your bodice on, gather some clothes. We have to leave before the hour is out. When they come back, they will have the tools to open the front door and will be able open all the other doors in the house without any trouble. Do not be so helpless. Do not fall apart on me, Mary, not now."

"But where are we going? I have no place to go. I doubt that we could get out of France, cross the Channel. It will be worse. At least here we are in a house."

"We will hire a coach, one with curtains, keeping our portmanteaus inside. And we will head out of Paris to the country. We will find someplace. They will be back and a house is nothing, Mary, nothing. Not the least protection. Do you understand?"

"What if we are seized, Gil, brought back."

"What if, what if. What if we stay here?"

"The Terror is blowing over."

"You know the Terror is getting worse. They will take us. We will appear before the Revolutionary Tribunal, the Committee of Public Safety, be put in the Luxembourg prison, taken out, led to the blade. Do not fool yourself. Please make haste."

Mary put her hand around her neck. "But we will be found innocent, released. We have *citoyen américain* and *citoyenne américaine* on the door under our names."

"They will try us, if that is what you call it, and we will be found guilty."

"Of what?"

"Anything, Mary, everything. You know how it goes. You are English, that is enough. We were friends and worked with Brissot, who is now executed. They are looking for Condorcet, another friend."

"And our heads will be severed from our necks because we have friends who are guilty of nothing more than being of the wrong party?"

"My dear woman, they do not even need that excuse."

Mary had an image of herself kneeling before the guillotine, that awful second between the lift and fall of the blade.

"Will you get your things together, Mary, and stop yammering. We have no time for this. Are you not the courageous girl who said women should be like men?"

"Like human beings."

"Strong?"

"Strong." She did not feel strong. She tried to move fast, but her feet seemed half rooted to the ground. Midway up the stairs, she paused, turned. "But where will the baby be born?"

"In the country, Mary."

"What if . . ."

"Without a head, you will not give birth anywhere. You will die, the child will die, two in one. Dead, the end, no more, *tu comprends*?"

"I thought you said they do not behead a woman with child."

"From the birthing stool to the guillotine, my dear."

She had a vision of her former self, the self who had insisted that her sister leave her husband. She could now understand Eliza's hesitation and inertia, and she could see herself as her sister, desperately holding on to the familiar for its own sake, in the wish for all to be as it should, but she reminded herself that she was not her sister but herself. She, Mary, was resolute, firm, not afraid.

She rushed into her bedroom, grabbed up a few dresses, got her stays, which she treasured above all, and would someday, she hoped, wear again. She stuffed the clothing, all her books and her papers, the work she was doing on the Revolution, her Wedgwood vase, her Hume, her Voltaire, the portrait of Sarah Siddons, the baby clothes she had made, all into her big trunk. Then she stopped. Fetching the clothes, getting the coach, fleeing before somebody returned. Mother's locket, the baby. Was her life to be forever circling in on itself?

"Mary, Mary, the coach is coming shortly."

She was wearing the locket she had bought for herself, and carrying the baby within her. This baby would not be left behind; she had the locket.

She hurried downstairs, grabbed up a loaf of bread from the pantry, a chunk of cheese and sausage, a jar of jelly, the last of the coffee, a tin of tea, two bottles of wine for Gilbert, sailor biscuits for herself. She filled two green wine bottles with water, corked them. She remembered her brush and mirror, ran back upstairs, used the chamber pot twice, emptying it out the window, came back. Gil was standing by the front door completely dressed, only his hair in disarray.

"Do you have everything?"

"Yes," she said, looking at him, her hand on her stomach.

"I have the coach," he said. "Are you ready?"

"I am ready."

The curtains were drawn in the coach, but Mary could see through them. Once again, peeking through one side of the curtain, she witnessed the slow, impeded dance of the muffled, barely distinct townspeople. French people, not English people, but looking the same as when she and Eliza escaped. The air was sparkly, the people were sprinkled with mist, it was a dream and the city an enchanted forest.

I am forever traveling through a vague, unaccountable country, she thought. The coach must travel through soup, thick, dun-colored soup. People in this land move through their lives in silence and pain without any awareness of their own beauty.

"You have saved my life," Mary said to Imlay. "Why?"

"Why not?"

"No, really, why?" Because you love me, she hoped.

"The mother of my son," he answered. "My son."

"I see." She put her hands over her stomach. "It seems that I am always getting out of town, one way or another."

CHAPTER 40

CAN YOU READ MUSIC?

Gil had asked that the first day, standing by the harpsichord in the house on rue Meslée.

For some reason, it sounded like: Can you *eat* music.

It made her think of the crisp, fluted paper cups containing sweet-meats, and black raisins, like the flies in the kitchen. Marchpane with licorice lines. Then it would be Haydn very tasty, Handel melting in the mouth, Mozart enjoyed at twilight with a nice glass of claret, and minuets gobbled up and stuffed straightaway, down you go, one, two, three.

Now she and Gil read recipes in bed. Puddings and flan, celery soup, pigeon pie, and savories of every sort. Oh, yum, he would say.

Once, when he had made love to her backward, she kneeling against the bed, his hand on her, he said: "You are so swollen, so wet, you are dripping into my hand like pink meat on the spit dripping fat."

And the next day those parts were like sore soft folds of a pink rabbit nose. She remembered Annie, the maid, and the child who was herself, and the dank, fetid smell of a body washed only at Christmas and Easter. How she had hated that, yet was strangely drawn, as if the secret thing, sleeping calmly beneath the skirts, needed to be noted and made much of, served like a little hearthside saint.

She and Gilbert found a house in Neuilly, a small village at the edge of the Bois de Boulogne. It was a place full of trees and vine-covered walls just leafing out. Each day came with a soft pink light and left the same way, politely, kindly. It was a few weeks before the baby's birth. They liked to sit in the evening without candle or lantern. Mary loved it. In the day, she sat in the small parlor of their cottage

warming her feet on the footstool where a patch of sun would fall at
a certain time. Looking out the window at the blue trumpet flowers
spilling over the garden wall, she would dream off, content with her
growing baby. It was a new life. Paris, the blood, the huge crossbars
of the guillotine, the pronouncements and declarations of death, seemed
to Mary remote enough to be impossible.

Often in the morning she was sick, going behind the garden to
the hay field and vomiting copiously into the stiff green grass. Bits of
food and saliva stuck to the stalks like jewels. Coming back inside, she
would have to sit still for a while, calm her body. Mary liked to
concentrate by closing her eyes, making her mind go inward. I am
forming your limbs, she would say to herself inside herself. She visualized a little neck, firm and strong, not to be snapped, and a head
developing flowerlike on its stalk. I am making your toes. She saw
them, little pink buds, uncurl, press flat. I create your arms. They
stretched out, supple and strong. Be a boy, be a boy, she hummed as
she sat sewing little baby clothes. She imagined him stumbling after
a butterfly in the garden, or holding out his arms to be lifted up. Her
little man. She saw him on a wooden horse. Not like Ned: I am master
here. But in good sport.

Gil had to spend a lot of time away. Paris and Le Havre, very
surreptitiously, of course, leaving in the night, getting back in the early
hours of the morning a week later, that sort of thing. The danger had
not passed. He spoke of going to Sweden. Grain was in fact now his
business, feeding the troops; rope, too, and other supplies. But he had
to be careful. With the death of Brissot, the Mississippi/Louisiana plan
had fallen apart. Gilbert for a long time had no friends in the government. Catch as catch can, he explained.

Whom was he supplying, Mary wondered, that he had to be so
careful. Surely, if he was providing bread and weapons to the armies
of the Revolution, the Revolution would not want to hurt him. She
did not understand why she and Gil had been a target of the Revolution
in the first place. And yet the Revolution under Robespierre executed
many friends. Look at Danton. Desmoulins. Madame Roland. The
others.

"Do you understand," Gil said at dinner—veal stew, brought in by the neighbor lady—"that I am trying to make things better for all of us, and that only that keeps me away from you? That is why I am in Paris, only for you, my dear, the baby."

"Yes, I understand." Sometimes he made Mary feel like a stupid child. She stared down into her plate. "Why is missing you," she sniffed, "a sin?"

"It is not a sin. I am not saying that, now, am I?"

"I know I am fat and unattractive."

"And very sorry for yourself." He ran his finger along her front. "Do not be so childish. And how is my son?" He rested his head against her stomach. "Hello in there? Gilbert IV?"

"Gilbert IV?"

"Who else? This time I may be gone a week. Do you think you can manage? Hello, Gilbert." He knocked. "Anybody home?"

Who would want to stay with her now, anyway? She vomited in the morning and slept in the afternoon. Grand company. There were frequent trips to the jericho. Very romantic. Suppertime, she would try for a pleasant demeanor but find herself exhausted again. And were she not sick, she could have cooked simple dishes. Sometimes she did, with mixed results. The plum pudding she made was all wrong. Her concentration was sporadic. That was it. Her brain was turning into mush. It was hard to read, impossible to write. She had not only lost her figure, and her mind, but her complexion suffered, too. It was pale, not prettily so, but pasty pale, with red bumps on her chin, and her hair had gone lank and oily. Gil called her gypsy, teased her. She did not appreciate it.

"Go write your book, Mary. That should keep you occupied."

"Do not tell me to *go* write my book."

"Does motherhood render one imbecilic? Once you were one of the most intelligent women in Europe."

"Once?"

"Once."

"But now that I feel ill and tired, am fat and ugly, and am not an intelligent woman at all, I know you do not love me anymore. I get tired of having to be clever and witty. Nobody else is, and their husbands love them."

"I am not your husband."

"I know it," she snapped.

"Mary. I am losing patience here."

He looked across the room. The gardener had brought berries, which lay on a silver platter in the middle of the table. There was soup, potato-and-leek, on the stove, left by a neighbor lady. On the wall, not removed by the former inhabitants, was a picture of a mother reading a story to her children. All seemed to be taken care of. The furniture was, if too big and too much for a small country cottage, tasteful, bright, and cheerful. Mary had books to read. She was reading Shakespeare again. "Mary, I have tried to provide you with everything to gladden your heart and lift your spirits. What more do you want?"

"Gladden the heart and lift the spirits. You sound like a medicine. Gilbert, do you love me?" She looked at him questioningly.

"And do not ask me that. I hear it too often."

It was a recurrent question, one, she knew, he was tired of, and yet she could not help but keep asking, it was her nature. She had to know. She always *had* to know. "Do you love me?"

"Sometimes."

"Sometimes?"

"Right now?"

"No, and the more you ask me, the less I do."

"Oh, Gil." She felt a large weight had fallen on her chest. "Gil, you must."

"Mary, I am getting tired of having to reassure you. Have you no faith in me, in yourself? What is all this about. I save your life in Paris, take out papers for you as my wife. I have not deserted you. I am sitting right here. I have not run away. What more could you ask for?"

"My father . . ."

"I am not your father."

"Joseph Johnson and Fuseli."

"I am not Johnson and Fuseli, either. Will you give *me* a chance? Look at me. What do you see?"

She looked at him. She never stopped looking at him. "You are the world's most handsome man, and I adore you."

"Come now, why not say most handsome man in France and

America. I have heard that the Chinese have very handsome men."

She laughed.

"Tell me, honestly, what do you see, Mary?"

"Will you swear that you love me?"

"No, I will not. I will tell you what you see: I am just a man. I cannot make up for all that you have suffered. I am fallible, too. I make mistakes."

Somehow, those words made her heart squeeze shut.

"How fallible, Gil?"

"Fallible."

CHAPTER 41

WHEN THE MIDWIFE was summoned by the new gardener, they were living in Le Havre. Gil was away. Mary imagined the gardener walking through the village around the port, his straw hat entangled in vines and his hands thick with soil. He would have to part the vines veiling his hat, poke his head in the window. Beg pardon, is Mistress Beauchamps at home. She could swear he looked a very sight, the Green Man himself.

Mary imagined them scurrying around the midwife's messy house, getting the necessaries together in a big cloth bag, and then each holding his or her hat down, rushing up the hill to the cottage, other wives following, and curious young girls, dogs and cats taking up the rear, the little band of violin players. The whole town, alerted, would stream up.

For there was a good crowd about in the room and in the yard when Fanny was born, and a merry crowd at that. There was plenty of wine, cheese, and bread fried with butter and herbs. The midwife rubbed Mary's stomach with aloe as she sat on the birthing stool, a steaming pan beneath to send up soothing clouds of heat to dull the pain. Some of the women sang saucy songs, and one of the village men came in to dance, holding his shirt high above his stomach. You like me, you like me? he asked Mary in English. And a little girl sat in the corner weaving flowers into a crown for Mary to wear after the birth. There seemed so much going on, so much noise and wine and cooking, that Mary had been only vaguely aware of the pains contracting her stomach. And then suddenly the midwife and three other women were holding her arms and asking her to push.

Mary pushed down hard, and as she did so, it occurred to her that she was not ready for this moment, that she had not given a thought to actually having the child, and that its presence would change her life. What am I doing here, Mary wondered, and why, why am I doing this? As her body arched up in pain, she felt as if something, something had taken her over. She, Mary, had nothing to do with it. This baby was just coming through her, and without even her permission. When her body arched up again, Mary thought for a few seconds that she had escaped the confines of flesh and flown up to the sky, up beyond the roof. It was an exquisitely painful sensation, with a dull, buzzing sound like bees at honey. When her body arched up again, Mary cried out to herself: Now, now I know why I am alive. After all these years, I have joined the universe.

It was a girl.

For one flashing moment, it occurred to Mary to keep it a secret. She could wrap the baby up, dress it like a boy. But when Gilbert arrived two days later, back from his trip, he caught her changing the child's rag.

"I am sorry, Gilbert. I am so sorry. Please do not be angry."

He looked down, pursed his lips to spit, swallowed it. Mary felt a failure.

"Oh, stop crying. You had a girl. It cannot be helped."

"I am a girl," Mary said, "and, and . . . well." She sat down and uncovered her breast to feed the baby. She had not developed great ease with nursing yet. The child was always missing the nipple or would suck a while and grow angry, balling her little fists and doubling her legs in a frustrated cry.

"You are a fine girl, Mary, a wonderful girl, my own girl I now have two remarkable girls." And he kissed the top of her head and rested his finger upon the soft head of the baby. "It is merely my name, my line. A son . . ."

"The next one, Gilbert, I promise."

"Yes, yes. Fine."

Already she saw there would be no next one, no anymore. He did not look once at the child's face, and hardly at her, but went into the other room for a bottle of stout smuggled from England. He said he had to leave again, soon. That is what he said, maybe a week or two this time, and soon. Mary wondered where he stayed, did not ask.

Christie's, he said once, but she doubted it. At White's Hotel with Paine? Paine, she knew, had been in prison since January—it was rumored, slated for execution.

"How is old Tom Paine these days?" Mary asked.

"Fine indeed, fit as a fiddle. He sends you his love."

"Mine to him," Mary said.

"What are you going to call it?" Gilbert asked, getting out his pipe.

"Her. I want to name her Fanny, Gilbert, Frances Elizabeth, after my friend, my dear friend who died, and after Eliza, my sister. Fanny's baby was named Mary, and Eliza's baby was named Mary. Both of the Marys have died. Eliza's child died of dysentery when Mr. Bishop gave the baby to his sister. And Fanny's Mary died shortly before her mother. They were both buried in a small, shady Protestant cemetery on a hill outside Lisbon overlooking the port. This child . . ."

"Spare me the details."

"I have told you, Gil, about my friend, Fanny Blood, who was at school with me and died in Portugal?"

"Yes, you have told me about a hundred times."

"I see."

"Whatever you like, Mary. Call the child whatever you like."

"The midwife said it was always best that the first is a girl, so that she can help with the other children."

"Yes, yes."

"And I am very strong."

"Can I?" Gil put his hand on her lap. She winced.

"Not for a while, Gilbert. It tore and had to be stitched like a dress hem."

"This?" He put his mouth on her breasts. She drew back.

"It is a well-known fact that such carryings-on can poison the milk, Gilbert."

He shook his head, sighed. "You can do nothing. Is that right? Good for nothing."

"I can kiss you, Gilbert, and with my mouth I can . . . You always said you loved my mouth."

"It is not important."

"It is not?"

"No, nothing is important. I told you. Do you realize that my whole trip to Paris may be for naught. My whole life is a start and a stop, lots of maybes between. Maybe I will never be a rich man. Maybe I will always be on the borders of wealth, but never in the country."

"I do not mind."

"*I* mind."

"Rope, grain, is it not a good business?"

He looked at her with his eyebrows lifted.

"You are going just to Paris, right?"

"For now. Who knows tomorrow. Maybe Sweden."

He looked more angry than he had ever been. No longer in buckskins, he looked English in cloth breeches and waistcoat. They did not become him. He looked like a child who had outgrown his clothes.

"It is not easy to support a family, you know."

"I know."

"And I am doing my best."

"Tie me up, Gilbert. Do it. We can just do it."

"You do not mean that."

"I do." She winced a little, thinking of her stitches and the raw feeling as all would come apart. "Do not worry," she said. "It will be fine."

"The stitches?"

"Fine."

"Do you mean it?"

"Yes. Hurry, though, because the baby will be waking up soon. I want to be yours the way you like me. I want to make you happy."

She had to move carefully to get her shift off while he went for the riding crop. Just then the baby woke up, started to scream.

"Damn it," he said. "Damn it to hell."

Mary began to cry.

"Oh, all of you, all of you." And he threw down the riding crop, fastened himself together, and turned to her before throwing a clean shirt and waistcoat in his portmanteau.

"You know this cannot continue," he said.

"What? What do you mean."

"You know what I mean."

When he slammed the door, she wanted to follow, but she had the baby in her arms, could not walk very well, and it was dark. The night was huge and empty. She wanted to die.

"I hate you," she spat in the little baby's face, shaking her little baby body like a rag doll. "I hate you for ruining my life."

HOW MARY FIRST KNEW was the smell, a new smell, not *his* summer sweat or their sex or the odor of bay leaves or her own fragrance made of roses soaked in alcohol or the delicious pink smell of the baby. It was a cheap twopenny scent bought from a cart on the street, not a proper shop. It was a kind of tarnished, Frenchified odor. Distinctly sickening.

So he has been to a whore, she thought. The idea was hurtful, but not fatal. A whore was not a mistress, and she was nursing, what could the poor man do.

Then came moments when he would not meet her eyes or times when she turned to catch him glancing at her nostalgically, as if for the last time. If she confronted him, meeting his gaze, he would look away quickly, his eyes sliding off her face like two eggs slipping off a saucer plate.

"I am tired," he said.

"Of me?"

The taste in her mouth felt like dry dust. The tiny bedroom in the cottage, with the rose coverlet in honor of Mrs. Price, now seemed close and confining, the fabric of the bed cover wilted and ridiculously feminine. "Are you tired of me?" she repeated.

"Of quarreling."

"So soon?" She said this with the chilly cheer of the lost and forgotten. "I will stop nursing Fanny, Gilbert."

"Do not bother."

"Oh God, Gilbert, you are killing me."

"Why so melodramatic?"

"What is it?"

"You have a beautiful smile," he said, turning to her. "You really do."

"Smiles are beautiful by definition, Gilbert."

From her experience with Henry, Mary had learned that "beautiful" was a euphemism for "I love my wife" or "Your days are numbered" or "This has all been a grand mistake" or "There are so many things to do and see, goodbye" or "You belong in an asylum."

From experience, if she were to dissect jealousy, she would first find a pie. Then she would cut it in quarters and pieces of eight, getting down to sixteenths, like music, and eating it until each note had been absorbed by her body and entered the roots of her hair. His smell was not bay leaves or the warm leathery smell of himself or a baby smell, little Fanny after a bath, buttery and milky, soft skull, wrinkled monkey hand.

"I am not seeing anybody in the sense that you think, but of course, I *see* people. I see lots of people, men *and* women. What is the harm in that? Yes, I know you are here all day with the baby. Yes, I know you do not meet many adults. Why is it you are not writing. Surely that is what you came to Paris to do, and here you are, each day free. You do not have to worry about earning a living. I do that. You do not have to worry about being dragged off and killed. I have to worry about that."

His eyes would not meet hers, but gazed over and out the window right over her shoulder, and at night he lay on his back, stared up at the ceiling, and then would ball up like a snail. Sometimes he sat in the chair with a coverlet over his feet.

"A strumpet," she said. "A sorry slut and bona-fide whore."

Tom Christie, visiting for a day in the country, had mentioned that he had seen Gilbert with one of Mary's friends. Boyish and silly as ever, he rattled on. Indeed, he had not known that Mary had a friend who was an actress in a traveling street show. Dogs who could walk on their front legs, a man in fool's motley who juggled balls and told lewd stories. And then they had passed the hat.

> *Fair nasty nymph, be clear and kind*
> *And all my joys restore*
> *By using paper still behind*

And sponges for before.
And dancing girls with tambourines, singing tra-la-la.

"My friends are governesses and teachers, writers, artists," Mary said. "They are not out on the streets whirling their skirts. Pray tell me the appearance of this person." I have no friends, she said to herself, none at all of any occupation.

Christie shuffled and cleared his throat, looked down. "Tiny as a girl, no, nothing much fore or aft, but big eyes and a mass of hair, golden red, brown, thin little arms."

He begged off, had to hurry back, backed off and out. A hasty goodbye was said by all. Goodbye, goodbye. Goodbye, Christie.

Mary stayed up late that night, sitting with the baby in her lap, her posture very erect. She had scrubbed the floor and bathed herself and the child.

When Gil came home, he entered the house like a thief. "Oh, hello, Mary, still up?"

"Nice of you to come home, Gil."

"Of course I come home, Mary, where else would I go?" He put down his package, took off his jacket and shoes.

"To your whore's, your strumpet's, your slut's. Or does she live on the street where she performs."

"Agnes is an actress, Mary, like your own Sarah Siddons," he said wearily, not bothering to prevaricate.

"Hardly that."

"No matter." He sat down, stretched his legs out on the stool, peaked his hands, blew through his mouth.

"What does she look like?"

"Not anything wonderful."

"Answer me, Gil, is she beautiful?"

He stood up, wavered a little. The cottage was blanketed in a deep fog, with only outlines of trees showing, shadows of houses; a faint smudge of earth marked the road, indicated that it was not deep space they were floating in.

"Gil?"

He sighed.

"She is beautiful, Gil?"

"She is not beautiful, Mary." And with the most dreamy of voices, he began to describe her. A little cherry-red mouth, small tongue, a dainty ankle, an eager, childlike expression. She was slim and had long, delicate fingers. Her laughter was like little bells and she laughed often and over very little. Agnes was young, strong, and sweet. "Precious and dear, not beautiful."

Young, Mary thought, feeling about one hundred years old. Young. It was a girl he loved and she was not even beautiful. You do not have to be beautiful. Young is enough.

"She is always happy," Gilbert added. "She is satisfied with her lot. She does not complain."

"I suppose I am not and never happy."

"Hardly ever. You are one of the most unhappy people I know, Mary, and I cannot make you happy."

"Why do you say that?" She sat down. How heavy she felt. She got up, went into their bedroom, lay down. This is not happening, she said to herself.

"She was almost chosen Goddess of Reason," he shouted after her.

"Goddess of Reason? This is what they did for women, to women, made them mock royalty instead of giving them rights."

"Well, also to churches, for the lack of churches. It was a consolation of sorts."

"Yes, every village girl had the opportunity to wear a crown . . . This is disgusting. You know better than that, Gil. How could you associate yourself with something so silly, so deceptive. Anyway, Robespierre abolished the Cult of Reason and reinstated the Supreme Being."

"The thing is, I am in love, Mary." He said this wistfully. "God help me, I am in love."

He put his hands to his face, began to cry.

For a moment, Mary wanted to comfort him. Then she realized why he was crying. She needed to comfort herself.

"Do you remember the time we made love outside, Gil?"

"Vaguely."

"The bank of honeysuckle, the smell of new-mowed grass? You said: We are going to take this very slowly. You looked at my face as you undressed me."

"The dead man."

"The dead man."

"Yes," he said blankly.

"And that when we make love, you always say: Yes, yes, yes."

"I cannot stay here anymore, Mary. You understand."

"How long . . ." Mary squeaked out, "have you been . . . seeing . . ." Her voice was failing her.

"Since Fanny, since Fanny was born."

Mary put her elbow on the bed, her hands over her eyes. He still stood before her.

"Because I could not . . . Because Fanny is a girl, is that why?"

"No."

But she knew that was the reason.

"It is not that, not any large thing."

"What, then?"

"All the little things."

"Like what?"

"Like you talk too fast, too much. You are the master of all opinions, the one with the most knowledge. I can never say anything. I know you are more clever than I am, but . . ."

"I will never speak again, Gil. These are my last words."

"You are too ardent, too demanding, you wear me out, Mary."

"I will be quiet as a mouse, never say a word, and never bother you for lovemaking or even kiss you when you do not want it."

"See how much you are talking now?"

"Those are my last words, I promise."

"And you are always reading and writing. Your books are everywhere, under the bed and all over the floor by the bed, and on the table where we are supposed to eat, and on the chaise. You tuck them in chairs and cover the kitchen shelf, and where there should be plates there are books, and . . ."

"Books are my living and essential to my soul. They are body and soul to me, Gilbert. I have not worked on anything in months. You are the one who keeps telling me to write the book. But for you, for you, no more."

Mary got up and began collecting all the books. She opened the front door, threw them out.

"Mary, you do not . . ."

"I insist. If it offends thee, I will pluck out its eye. And that is final. And those are my last words."

"You do not manage a house well. You are not good with the servant. You let her do whatever she wants. You sit down with her, eat with her."

"You are completely right." Mary slammed the front door. The house looked barren without books, her books. There were still many on the shelf, and yes, under the bed, and in the kitchen, but she had made a start. "I promise to be more attentive to household matters. And now that I do not have my books and am not talking, it should be easy."

"Are they your last words?"

"Yes. My very last words."

"And you do not know how to make a man feel good about himself. You are not affectionate."

"I thought you said I was too affectionate."

"Not in the right way."

"Oh." She tried to think of how she should be.

"And you bite your fingernails."

"Surely, Gil . . ."

"You cannot carry a tune, and your stomach sticks out . . . and . . ."

"I will take singing lessons and my stomach is going back in."

"You have marks on it."

"I got those marks, Gil, from having your child."

She was doomed, she knew it.

"Let us go to America, Gil. I want to live there in the land of the free. I want to live with you always and forever. I want to become a Puritan and hunt in the forest. I will bake bread, weave stockings, smoke peace pipes."

"America is not such a good idea."

He was going to the wardrobe, pulling out his shirts and breeches, a waistcoat, stockings, and other pairs of shoes.

"Gil," she cried. "Do not leave."

"And you are very insistent on having me be what you want me to be, instead of accepting who I am."

She held her breath, tried not to say it, could not control herself: "That's a bold and brazen lie. You are stupid and weak, I grant you that, but I embrace it, accept you for everything you are not and are and will be. You grub after money, but cannot make an honest living. You are condescending to the poor, obsequious to the rich, and generally a fool. You are arrogant on the basis of very little. You are tall and strong, but lack a chin. You have the hands of a woman. Your bottom is too fleshy. You break wind at moments that are very inconvenient, and you get food on your cravat. You eat like a pig, drink like a fish, snore like a horse, make love like a bull, and go after women like a dog. You are a pen of animals. You are also a coward and a schemer. I hate you."

"Good." He reached up for his portmanteau. "And you contradict yourself. One moment you love me, accept me, the next hate."

"I love you, truly I do. Gil, I am sorry. Please, I take that all back. Oh God, what did I say?" She clutched her arms to herself. "I did not mean a word of it."

"And the fact that you hate me and I have all those terrible qualities straight out of the barnyard should make it easy for you to tolerate my absence."

"Do not leave me, Gil." She started to pull her hair.

"I shall and I will. You will not want for money, Miss Famous Authoress."

"Author."

"See, even now you cannot hold your tongue, but must correct me."

"I am never going to say another word, Gil. Never."

"Well, I will not be here to hear your silence."

He was going through the house, picking up his belongings. A paperweight. His quills and paper. A cameo of his mother and father. Tom Paine's early pamphlets.

"I will share you with her." Mary was flailing around, wringing her hands.

"No, Mary."

"If you can come home twice each week. Little Fanny . . ."

"No."

"Once each week, Gil. Once?"

"No, Mary, the answer is no, no, no."

He stood at the door. Night was lifting. She could see his face, which she loved, which she adored, which she could not live without.

"I am going now, Mary."

"You cannot go. You have a child."

"We are not married, Mary."

"We are good as married."

"You wrote that, and I quote, 'marriage is legalized prostitution,' and have told me personally . . ."

"I do not believe it anymore."

"It does not matter anymore."

"Please, Gil, please."

"Mary, you were a fever that I got over."

Mary felt her stomach contract. Her bowels loosen.

"Are those your last words, Gilbert? I am a fever you got over?"

"Yes. We are dead, Mary, we are all dead."

"No, no, we are not, Gilbert. We are alive forever."

"Spare me, Mary, the theatrics."

And then, in her mind, it started to snow in the vineyard, covering Gilbert Imlay and Mary Wollstonecraft in a soft white blanket, their limbs locked in an eternal embrace. Everything that had been holding its breath became frozen: the heavy scent of sun-browned grapes, sweet honey flowers, the grinding cry of crickets, snake grass, the dead body, a dog barking somewhere, and the sound of horses pulling a cart on the road below.

CHAPTER 43

DID IT END THERE, frozen in time? It did not end there. Neither of them had the courage. It dragged on untidily for a good while longer. There was a hasty return some months after the confession, a chagrined apology, and for one whole hour Mary thought her heart would burst in gratitude as they lay on the bed together and he kissed her eyebrows, the tip of her nose, the lobes of her ears, called her bunny, asked her if she was hungry, got up and fed her morsels of bread which he pinched off the loaf one by one. She could not remember feeling so happy. Then, when Fanny was nearly a year old, Gilbert made a proposal.

"I want you to do something for me," he said in the dark, tracing a pattern on her back. "A little business."

"Anything," she said.

It was thus that Mary found herself in a ship at the mercy of wind and a piercing cold rain in the choppy black waters of the North Sea—she, the baby Fanny, and her French maid, Marguerite, who prayed day and night that she would return safely to solid ground, Europe, if possible, and please God, best of all, Mother France. Mary wished Marguerite would be quiet. Their mission was to go to Gothenburg, Copenhagen, and Oslo. Gilbert had designated Mary, "wife and best friend," as his trusted emissary and deputy. She, who had left Paris in fright, was assigned the task of buying grain and iron, lumber and rope for the Revolutionary Army. The trip, though Gilbert had assured her that it would be tame, like punting across an English garden pond, proved treacherous.

In fact, Mary felt she was being sent into enemy territory to get a treaty signed. She felt he might have actually planned a storm at sea, hoped for a fatal resolution to their relationship. She did not know what to think. Like Marguerite, she longed for land, and sick to her stomach, she knew the trip was her last stratagem. And imbedded deeper than that was the secret knowledge that it would not make any difference. During his last visit to her, in a day's time, Gilbert already had grown inattentive. And two days later, when she closed up the house, Mary had found a piece of lace, not hers, folded in a copy of Shakespeare's sonnets Gilbert had somehow left behind.

Yet he had said, "It will be fine," patting her back. "I have made the trip several times myself. It will do you good to get away, get out of the house. You and the baby need some air." He had looked out the window to the meadow below as if he were looking out at a calm sea. "Another adventure," he added vaguely. "You will love it."

"It is not a brisk morning walk, this trip," Mary returned.

"Would I expose you to a bad experience, danger, anything like that?" He had a stupid smile on his face. It reminded her of the monkey she had seen in Portugal.

"No, of course not. I know you love me, Gilbert."

The morning the ship, a vessel carrying a cargo of furniture and kitchen utensils bound for Finland, approached the rocky coast of Sweden, the water was too rough for the ship to dock. Mary, the maid, and baby Fanny were set in a rowboat, pointed in the right direction.

"A few strokes," the captain said, "and you will be ashore."

Truly, it did not look far. Mary had rowed on the Avon, and as a child in Yorkshire had pottered in boats on the river Swale. But once set adrift, she noticed immediately that the sea was not a still English river on a hot summer day. The water was black and choppy. Little whitecaps lapped the sides of the rowboat, spilled over. She could imagine sinking down, not to the refuge of some civilized Atlantis, but to all the mythical horrors of nautical superstition—snakes and beasts, whirlpools and maelstroms.

"You row," Mary said to the maid. "I will hold the baby."

"I do not know how," Marguerite cried, "and I cannot swim and I have not made confession and I am still a virgin."

"Newton died a virgin, nuns and priests are virgins, what does virgin matter?"

"Who is Newton? A sailor? Have mercy on his soul."

"Newton is . . . For the love of God, row, Marguerite, row."

The clouds were bundled in ominous masses. Clusters of seabirds honked plaintively as they careened above. The lighthouse, set on a separate island with its black-and-white swirls, seemed to waver and wobble as the boat bobbed up and down. A lone figure on a promontory waving them in wore a long skirt which flapped like flags.

"Damn you, Gilbert," Mary hissed between her teeth. "Damn you to hell."

"Madame?"

"Here, take the baby. I will row. A is an acorn, B is a boy. Gilbert, you scoundrel, you will be the death of me yet."

"Madame."

"Hold on, Marguerite, hold on."

"God is good, madame."

"Is He, now?"

Mary felt like cursing God and dying. You who are not there, may you take note: I curse you. And Gilbert: Bane of my existence, may you be struck by a bolt of lightning in your privates on the way to supper. Her father: I hate you, hate you to death. And her brother Ned: Let life depart from your body and worms eat out your mouth. But as if her fury propelled her, they steadily gained on the land, and a small sandy inlet finally appeared.

"God *is* good," Marguerite intoned, falling to her knees in the watery bottom of their leaking boat.

"Maybe," Mary admitted grudgingly, feeling her aching arms.

On the beach, when the lighthouse keeper's wife took her right arm, Mary winced in pain. She felt as she had when her arms were chained up in Bedlam. Her skirts from wading in, pulling the boat ashore, were sopping and caked with salt. The lighthouse keeper's wife pulled the boat up onto the sand, and helped Mary and Marguerite with the baby scramble along the beach and struggle to the rocks. The three women hauled themselves to a little path, made their way through a clump of trees shaped by the wind into streaming heads of hair. Marguerite sobbed softly. The baby, who had been stunned into silence, let out a wail. The lighthouse keeper's wife muttered what sounded like strange imprecations in a guttural language. *This* is hell, Mary thought, not flames and brimstone. She imagined herself buried on that cold, barren land. They would have to hack the earth to dig a hole, and it would have to be a shallow one at that. Dead, she would hear the waves crash against the black rocks and the wind moan each night. High-stepping storks would prick at her bones and Druid-like priests would chant celebratory songs to pagan Gods over her dead eyes and bare skull.

But the lighthouse keeper spoke English and they had a roaring fire going in the hearth. He fetched Mary's trunk from the boat, and while his wife busied herself with tea and a kind of hot gruel which she served in wooden bowls, he spoke of a village nearby and a coach on the mainland which went all the way to Gothenburg. Mary's old treasure trunk, the same one she had taken to the Kingsborough estate, arrived with at Joseph's, and brought with her to Paris, stood in the corner. It had rested in the rowboat between them, and now Mary thought of it as her insurance, her security. She felt she had escaped death once again. She still had her Rousseau, her Locke, her portrait of Sarah Siddons, and a few dresses, her stays. She was still Mary. At this moment, she conjectured, Gilbert would be lighting a candle, dining, looking at the sky. He seemed worlds away, but all the more dear. She forgave him. It would be fine.

After a dinner of salt fish, and strawberries, and fresh milk, the lighthouse keeper took Mary up the long, winding stairs to see the eye of the lighthouse. The stairway seemed to have no end, and when Mary looked down the circular stairwell to the base, the lighthouse keeper's wife, holding little Fanny, looked like a doll figure, distressingly small. Finally they came out on a circular floor; in the middle was a huge oakwood fire. Ribbons of thick silvered metal, intricately interwoven, prismatic, and as ornate as any chandelier and elegant as a diamond, ringed the fire. Every hour of the night and on misty days, the lighthouse keeper had to crank the rope which wound around the metal reflectors and made them rotate when released. A little door led to a narrow walkway around the lighthouse, guarded by a frail railing. Looking down made Mary queasy. The sand on the beach was black, slate-gray, like shale or obsidian, and a forlorn little clothesline held a blue skirt, blue pants, and a tea towel. That line told a whole life, peopled a sorry little story.

Sweden, Mary found, was like a harsh, unforgiving fairy tale with

figures larger than life—the woodman, the witch, the beautiful princess, the dashing prince. The people were giants, fair, with thick red
lips, and wooden shoes, blotchy red cheeks and hands big as paws and
scads of white-blond hair. In the case of the women, their hair was
braided and wrapped about their heads, festooned in ribbons and dirty
twine, and in the case of the men, cropped short in a straight fringe
around their heads. Mary felt small, paltry, insignificant, pampered.

In the coach to Gothenburg, traveling through forests of fir and
pine, juniper and strange brambles, she expected to see reindeer and
lurking wolves, animals with thick coats and black eyes. The houses
were made of logs, and antlers over the doors signaled victory over
wild forces. She, the baby, and Marguerite stayed overnight in a building as vast as a Viking king's reception room or a huge hunting lodge.
That night, the wind through the trees swept the roof of the inn like
a vast broom sweeping clean the world. Mary, Marguerite, and the
baby huddled together on one bed. Mary had taken all the clothes out
of her trunk, put them over the coverlet. She had heard that in winter
the men of the village cut holes in the ice, bathed in the winter pond,
while below them fish, like hibernating bears, lay nuzzled in the mud.
Marguerite called on God once again. She wanted to be made warm.

"We must be brave and strong," Mary told her maid gently. But
she admitted to herself at that moment not only that she was frightened
by the dark and vast emptiness of the place but that she recognized
once again that all was lost for her, that she was, in fact, a solitary
walker, that her love with Gilbert had been lonely love, that he, in
fact, did not love, and that she was sent away because he was too
cowardly to leave her. The bleak landscape made everything clear.
There were no distractions.

In the day, the baby whined, had dysentery, so the coach smelled
like spoiled pastry and soured milk. Moistening the child's mouth with
water stored in a bottle, Mary was reminded of Eliza's baby who had
died. Water and salt. Water and salt. By the time they got to Gothenburg, though the child's bottom was raw and bleeding, her lips were
no longer parched and she was swallowing the water, reviving a bit.
Mary herself, fatigued, bone-cold, sad beyond memory, expected some
solace in the city. She was able, finally, to nurse her baby.

Gothenberg proved to be cold comfort, however. Their room in an inn was draped in baby rags. Nothing ever seemed to get dry. Mary imagined water rats beneath them. In damp skirts, she met the solicitor with whom she was to negotiate. Her nose was running. She had sores on her lips. His office was small and close, smelling of ink and rot. The seams of the wall and baseboards had a greenish tinge, and mushrooms sprouted from the mold in corners. The afternoon had a listless quality. The scratching of quill upon paper sounded like rodents skittering across glass. The sun coming in through the narrow panes offered meager consolation.

"Yes, yes," the man said, rolling up the paper, adjusting the ends of the scroll neatly. "We have oak trees hundreds of years old. Tell your husband winter is coming."

Mary wrote Gilbert faithfully as if she had not lost her faith in him. Writing was a habit. She kept notes of her letters. Who knows, she thought, maybe I can publish them someday. She remembered how, in Portugal, her faith in God had left her. The day her faith left, the world suddenly became very empty: color and taste, meaning and measure—all joy departed from her. In Portugal she was reminded of a childhood picture of the wind, Zephyr, the puffed cheeks, slitty eyes emerging from the clouds. Yet it was the opposite. Currents, ruffles, breezes, twittering birds escaped back into the clouds, were sucked up, gone forever. The world got very still. She knew at that moment that she would be dead, dead for good and all time. There was no paradise to come, no fire to fear. It was hard for her to move, impossible to eat. Terror clutched her heart. But she had to get on a boat, go back to her school, that was her life. By the time she got back to England, she was back to herself, and she merely took up as if nothing had changed.

She wondered how it would be with the loss of Gilbert, if it would be that bad. Her connection with him was tenuous at best, torture at worst, yet it was familiar and had given her life meaning. I am the author, she reasoned, but I have no authority here. So, faithfully, she wrote him about the countryside. They were chatty, wifely letters, whistles in the dark.

She had visited Versailles once in a coach with Gilbert, walked down the Galerie des Glaces, the Hall of Mirrors. That day she saw herself reflected what seemed a hundred times. I people a room, she said to herself, I am the world. Her life then had seemed so rich, so full, so foreign compared to the austerity she saw without and felt within now. Outside, in the gardens of Versailles, the statues appeared gilded by the sun. The sun in France, unlike the Scandinavian sun, was brilliant, full of gladness, spilling over roads and carts, children and peasants without restraint. It was butter. Her life had been butter. Have you ever, Gilbert had asked, touched a buttercup to your chin?

CHAPTER 44

"YOU KNOW," Joseph Johnson said in a pinched-lip way her first day back in London. "You know he cannot return to Kentucky, ever. He is a fugitive from justice. Trespass, and default on debts. And his wild scheme for getting the Spanish colonies in the Mississippi Valley back in French hands! Gracious, child, he has no world perspective, no altruistic inclinations at all. The man is a criminal. He is a recitation of degradation. Unfortunately, there are many such individuals in the colonies."

Joseph seemed to have aged, become smaller, tighter.

"The United States, no longer colonies."

"A fine point, my dear. And they burned women accused of being witches until only a short time ago."

"We burned witches here, too."

"They have slavery."

"We transport slaves, and all our colonies have slavery."

"That is the government."

"It is people. People have slaves, people are slaves."

"A fine point."

"Thousands upon thousands of people died in the year of the Reign of Terror in France, Joseph. The Americans do not have a monopoly on cruelty, as surprising as that may sound."

"Yes, but you—you had direct experience with American cruelty."

"We got along well. We were alike."

"Oh no, how can you say that. You are the city, my dear. He is some little village. That slut he is seeing, she is just a cow pasture. You are so complicated, so finely tuned. You have street lights and cobblestones and coach stands and baths and theaters and fine buildings and tea gardens. Mary, you are London. He is a couple of cottages, a public house, a church, market on Saturday, and a small lane running through. The actress is only soil and grass. Do not mix with riffraff."

"If I do not mix with 'riffraff,' I will always be lonely, for that is all there is."

"No, Mary, no."

The drawing room was cluttered with new chairs, and Joseph appeared a little confused. When Joseph opened the door, Mary started to weep, the tears spilling onto little Fanny, who began to cry, too. The child took up crying later on, also. Sometimes Mary could not quiet her. Fanny would be clean, fed, held, and everything Mary could think of, and still she would cry inconsolably. Mary, at her wit's end, would have to give her laudanum in a little baby spoon, the same one Henry used for porridge earlier.

"Is she hungry, in pain, what is the matter?" Joseph got very nervous when the baby cried. Mary had been at the old house at St. Paul's Churchyard for a week, in her old bedroom, and Fanny would not stop crying. Fanny slept in a crib and Mary had a new bed, but Mary knew they would have to move to their own apartment, but where? She had spent all her *Vindication* money, had barely started her new work on the Revolution. The first volume had come out in December 1794, the year Fanny was born. Now the child occupied all her time. And unfortunately the baby had a sour disposition, was not particularly pretty, with a puckered face, cloudy blue eyes, and hair the color of coal and texture of straw, and she often bit Mary raw when nursing. Had Gilbert been that way as a baby?

"The man was no good, my dear, do you at least know that?" Joseph could not get off the topic.

"Yes, yes, I know. I *do* know. He is no good." But she did not care. She still loved him.

"And to chose an actress, a shallow little bird, I hear, over you, the most intellectual woman in Europe. How common."

"It is common. You are right. Most men, even intelligent men, do not like intellectual, intelligent women. They like young beautiful women, not brilliant old ones. It is very common."

Mary considered the actress Gil had chosen a girl, not a woman, although she was certainly a grownup. He even referred to her as "the girl." Which made Mary wonder. Her name was Agnes. Gilbert, when he was through, had described her in detail. She was slight, that was true, and childish, and not even a real actress, but a street minstrel with long, ringleted hair the color of copper and eyes a startling blue and lips which were big and full and hung open a little. This girl liked to dress up. No doubt that was her idea of art. But her skin was smooth, not riddled with motherhood, and Mary could understand it all; *her* skin was slack and broken into parallel stripes of purple and pink hue over her whole stomach. Every night she rubbed thick cream over it, but it did no good. The midwife had called them tiger stripes or baby marks.

"I became ugly having Fanny," Mary said.

"Mary, you have to stop blaming yourself for his departure," Joseph said.

Joseph could be irritating. Mary found nothing substantially changed at Joseph's house at St. Paul's Churchyard. She had been through a revolution, had a child, been destroyed. Meanwhile, Mrs. Mason still appeared on most days with a cheery Hello, Mistress Mary. The first day she had added: And what a beautiful child. Yours? Why, I declare, she has gone and had a baby. And the large grandfather clock, Joseph's pride and joy, still ticked and gonged each and every hour in the hallway. Once a month, Joseph still oiled the parts. Joseph still edited the *Analytical Review* in fits and starts. And there were the interminable Thursday-night dinners. Christie no longer helped with the *Review*. And Paine was still alive in Paris, they believed. It was a sad bunch, an old, cranky set at Thursday night.

"I was jealous and clinging," Mary continued. "I became uninteresting. That is my fault."

"Mary, why is it you refuse to see him as he is. Imlay is a scamp and a roamer. When are you going to fall in love with somebody who is good for you, good to you? A good person."

"Like you, Joseph?"

"Well"—and he appeared very flustered—"not quite. No, a nice man, a kind man."

"He sounds boring, whoever he is, and not attractive."

"Fuseli was not attractive."

"Right, he was ugly, but so ugly, Joseph, as to be beautiful. He was a kind of wonder of the world. You know he was remarkable."

"Well, that is the problem right there, you see. Why do you find abasement exciting? Fuseli treated you badly, too. Remember from the beginning . . . I told you."

"It *is* my fault. I should have sent the baby out, not nursed her myself."

They were standing up in the drawing room for this little discussion. Neither would sit down, despite the large population of chairs.

"But you said he wanted you to nurse."

"He did, but I should have known better."

"Mary, you must promise not to get sick over this one, go to the asylum, or anything like that. They are not worth it."

"How can I be sick, Joseph? I am dead. He killed me."

CHAPTER 45

At the end of an affair, lovers gather up things, give back trinkets. Books and little mementos, ribbons and slips of paper, feathers and leaves . . . As if reclaiming each object is a way of coming to grips, an effort to once again place oneself in the world. This is the way I was before you, we seem to say, and I can go back to that and still be, still exist.

I write now with great sadness, Eliza. Oh, he was a bad, bad boy. And my passion for him was dark and terrifying. I was the dreamer and the dreamt. We are kissing and I open my eyes to see his mouth half open, his lower lip full and his teeth bared. He looks so much like a child and a wild animal—the white, evenly spaced, perfect teeth, the sharp nippers and the pink inside the lip, so tender and vulnerable—that I am moved beyond myself.

Eliza, I could not fall asleep before he did, for I must be awake if he was awake. We were always together; it was natural. He was, if anything, fascinated by my mind. I think our affair was woven of words. I had to sing for my supper. That is the price of being a clever woman. Had I been beautiful, looking at me would have been enough, and perhaps would have kept him with me longer, for what are words. One can always read a book.

Eliza, I was gathering up my clothes. I could not bear angry words when naked. You like, he said once, to cover yourself up with cloth and lies. Not so. Fights require armor, one's most dignified self.

But Gilbert walked about naked as we fought, picking up things, for he must touch things constantly, as if his hands not affixed to something would fall off. He read books, turning and smoothing pages as if they imparted their messages through the pads of his fingers. He ate food that way, too, putting down his fork like a foreign object not meant for use.

"Savage," I'd say. "Noble savage."

He liked to comb his fingers through my hair, and he patted and stroked, fondled every part of me, kneading my head as if to touch brains, and with his toes paddled my back, taking Hume's idea of knowledge conveyed through the senses to the extreme—the extremities, the sense of touch.

It was strange that he loved an actress and my first love was an actress, Sarah Siddons, who inspired me to go out into the world to make a mark.

I saw Mrs. Siddons as a child, when our family moved from Wales to Richmond. Can you remember? We sat in the gallery. Our grandfather was visiting and took us all to see Gay's Beggar's Opera. Mrs. Siddons played sweet Polly Peachum, the wife of the highwayman.

It was the most wonderful night of my childhood, Eliza, that night at the theater, seeing the row of candles ranged across the front of the stage, the names written on the boxes: Shakespeare, Sheridan, Jonson, Goldsmith in gold letters. The Lord Mayor of Richmond sat in Congreve's box. There was much trafficking of food in the pit and general hullabaloo, but when Mrs. Siddons spoke the famous lines, we all held our breath.

"O Macheath, was it for this we parted? Taken! Imprisoned! Tried! Hanged! Cruel reflection! I'll stay with thee 'till death. No force shall tear thy dear wife from thee now."

The people in the pit were shouting and crying out, telling her that her lover was betraying her.

When our illusions, Eliza—though this is a letter I will never send you, I am only writing this letter for myself, to myself through you—yes, Eliza, when our illusions about people fall away, we realize that what we have constructed is a whole story of love made up of bits and pieces of wishes and hope, how we would like it to be rather than seeing what it is. Gilbert was ordinary, weak, unfaithful. And if he was also a golden angel, beautiful and resplendent, then he was the one I constructed along the lines *of Milton's angel, the one who would not serve, the one who fell forever. We had our year, the first part in Paris, and then nearing the child's birth and Paris becoming too dangerous, we moved to Neuilly, Le Havre. In Paris, Committees prevailed: the Committee of Public Welfare, the Committee of Surveillance. Tribunals and sessions, courts and the guillotine. The women who trooped to Versailles to get the king (chief baker) to get the bread to feed the children to fuel the discontent to raise a revolution to kill the king to be at war within, French against French, and without: Britain, Prussia, Austria—these women lost. I lost.*

History was happening all about us, and within us, also, that is what I mean, Eliza, but Gil and I, except for his trips to the warehouse in Paris, to Le Havre, to Sweden, lived inside our few rooms, and tried to ignore it, acting out an ancient and venerable drama. We were lovers seemingly oblivious of the world as it came crashing down around us. Is there a lesson to be learned? We were crashing down as well, for Gil was as cruel as the Revolution, and I was as hapless as the slaughtered masses.

Melancholy sours mother's milk. My sister, I love you and miss you. Our lives are held up by a web of loyalties which defy authority and logic.

MRS. MASON took her to the butcher on a Tuesday. The insides of the pig they bought had to be boiled for three days. Then the offal had to be cleaned and the animal's tongue, heart, and liver were baked with sweet herbs and onions. A pudding was made late that Thursday with apples, eggs, cream, and bread crumbs soaked in brandy. Mary was feeling poorly, but she sat down to dinner. After dinner, the gentlemen of the Thursday-night eating club were going to a cock-fight.

"How can you," she said to Joseph when he told her.

"It is great fun, much gambling."

"It is cruel."

"They fight anyway."

"To the death?"

"Yes."

"I am very disappointed in you."

"Oh, gracious me. I am not a saint, you know that."

"I mean it. They wear silver spurs, I am told, and tear each other up."

"Oh, Mary, I wish I could be the person you want me to be, but I am not."

"But you publish books, Joseph, against cruelty to animals."

"Do you practice everything you advocate?"

"I am trying."

"So am I."

"Not very hard."

"How do you know?"

She stomped upstairs to work on the continuation of her work on France.

Page, she said to her paper, you never deceive me or disappoint me or betray me or leave me. You are always there waiting for me. The tabula rasa.

The problem was, however, Mary had not paid close attention. Her first volume dealt only with the first six months of the Revolution. Her note-taking had degenerated, after she met Gilbert, into mere sentences, an occasional observation. She had hoped to offer an eye-witness account of the events of 1793 and 1794. And now his face seemed blotted on every page she tried to write. *L'état, c'est* Gilbert Imlay. Stop that, she would tell herself, stop it right now.

Her book, of necessity, would have to be based on other documents. It could not be reported through direct observation.

Thus, it was to be a dry, dusty exercise. What she longed for was to be outside. It was autumn—frail, tenuous, pale—but not cold. She wanted to go out to tea. She wanted to go riding down the street. She wanted to go to the museum. She wanted to hear Mozart and Haydn, Handel's *Water Music*. She wanted to buy a great bunch of ice-green taffeta, spotted muslin, be fitted for new dresses, tiered skirts, pleated bodices. She wanted to gorge herself on novels and sweetmeats and buy new writing paper, a heavy cream-colored bond. She wanted a lover who would tickle her toes, call her Maria, bring coffee to her bed, make love slowly, leave her alone. She wanted a woman friend who would laugh and whisper secrets as the two of them strewed crumbs and pastry flakes across the big bed. You are beautiful, her friend would say. No, *you* are beautiful. No, *you* are. Mary wanted to write a novel, this time, which would bring to life the ideas she had expressed in *A Vindication*. She wanted to create a truly independent woman, place her in the world, watch her make her way. She wanted to suggest truths which were not obvious and therefore needed a story for demonstration.

No, she did not want any of this. She did not want to live. She could not savor anything and all seemed equally uninteresting. She had no will, no good reason for getting up in the morning.

She sat at her desk. Since the new bed, her desk had to be jammed against the wall. No more view of the sky through the window. She was at the point in her research that had to do with the Law of Suspects, which provided for the arrest and judgment of all persons who, although they had done nothing against liberty, had nevertheless done nothing for it. Any person in France had only to be accused by another to be brought before the Tribunal, with his life at stake. How would anyone know whether the other person had done nothing for liberty? Many felt disgusted with France. Surely it would collapse soon of the weight of its own wars.

Furthermore, it had created a crisis in European political thought, because those who had espoused the Revolution or the idea of revolution were now intellectually without a home. Where would they now turn for their hope and inspiration, what kind of government could they support, who were the heroes and heroines, what was the role of ideas in human political life, and did one then have to accept, with Hobbes, a pessimistic view of human nature? France was the mob, the riot, the common people, the peasant and the worker, as had been England during the anti-Papist Gordon Riots in 1780. What amazed Mary was that the common people turned out to be more vicious than the despots who oppressed them. Since that was the case, what had happened to the ideals of democracy?

In practice, people liked to make fun of the British penchant for debauchery and violence: drunk for a penny, dead drunk for two. Ben Franklin had remarked that within one year, 1769, there had been riots in England about corn, elections, workhouses, colliers, weavers, coal-heavers, smugglers; customhouse officers and excisemen had been murdered. Indeed, Lord North had once robbed, Horace Walpole shot at. Earlier, grandstands had been built around Tyburn Tree, the hanging tree, and at the drop of a hat, men shed their shirts, engaged in boxing matches. Yet all that seemed almost play, compared to the Revolution in France.

Fanny was crying.

Fanny had been crying an incessant, nagging drone all afternoon. Sometimes Mary wished she were deaf or Fanny completely mute. Impatiently, Mary picked the unhappy child from her crib and undid her bodice. The child sucked on her nipples rapaciously for a few seconds, then turned away, started crying again.

"For God's sake," Mary thought. "Just drink."

When Mary shoved the baby back to her breast, the baby bit her.

"You are impossible," Mary breathed. "What do you want?"

Mary ripped her away from her breast, shook her. The baby's head wobbled, the face got very red, and then the child started to cry more earnestly than ever. Mary put her back at her breast. The baby turned her head away, pummeled with her fists, kicked her feet. Mary felt like crying herself. She put the baby back down.

"For a pound," she said to herself. "For a shilling, I would . . ." Mary shook her head. "My God. Heaven help me."

She gathered her wits, went downstairs for a cup of tea to calm herself, staying down as long as she could. When she went back upstairs, the baby was still crying. Mary leaned down, put her face very close to Fanny's. The tiny eyes took her in, narrowed to slits, and the child began crying again. Mary picked her up, slapped her a little, thumped her face down in her crib.

"There," Mary said to herself. "That is all the attention you get."

The baby cried all the harder.

"Hush," Mary hissed. She paced back and forth. She picked her up again, undid her bodice, shoved a breast in her little face.

"You want this?" she seethed. "Is this what you want?"

The baby turned away, doubled up, messed in her clothing. Mary changed her, put her back down.

"You are filthy," Mary said. "And I hate you."

The child worked her legs, balled up her fists, and squalled. Mary picked her up, brought her close to her face.

"I will never get any writing done again in my life, thanks to you," Mary said. "What am I living for? Why do I not just die? Would you like to see me dead? Are you trying to kill me? Your father left me because of you. You, that is right. And you are not even pretty, not even good-natured, not even quiet. Have you no sense, either?"

Fanny doubled herself into a knot, extending her legs straight out, let out an awful smell, and commenced crying.

"You are an ugly thing, a plucked chicken, a rag and fiddle. Stop crying before I kill you."

Mary shook her up roughly, then becoming aware of what she was doing, began to rock her, and paced with her on her shoulder. Then she put the baby back in her crib.

"There, there, there." Mary was in tears. She thought of taking the quill, digging it into Fanny's eye. She thought of hanging her out the window by one foot. She thought of crushing the infant's bones with her bare hands.

"If you knew what I was thinking, you would stop crying," she said.

But it seemed as though Fanny intended to cry for all eternity, come what may.

"I have had enough."

At that moment, Mary felt she was in one of her dreams. Moving very slowly, she made her way over to the baby, picked her up, lifted her over her head, and threw her against the wall.

It made a little thud. The bundle of cloth trembled a second, became very quiet. Dear God, Mary thought, I have killed it. Shaking, she tiptoed over, turned it over with her foot. The baby's wide-open eyes stared at her. It was just like the dead man on the hill.

That quiet, that still.

"It *is* dead," Mary realized. "I have killed my own child."

Mary sat down on her bed, stared at the base of the wall where the bundle lay. I have killed my own child. Dear God, she thought, I have killed my own flesh and blood. Mary got up, walked over. The features at rest were pretty and very sad. And I had thought her ugly and killed her for it. Like the man in Bath who did not like my looks.

Mary put her head in her hands, started to weep. "My poor baby." She remembered the woman in Bedlam who carried the bundle of rags and asked you to look at her baby. Mary wondered if she would be doing the same in Newgate.

Then she noticed the baby blink, shiver a little, and it began to cry again, wailing pitifully for several minutes. And then, with little choking sobs, Fanny fell asleep.

Mary's teeth chattered and her legs could not support her. She did not want to touch the child.

"Joseph," she cried out. "Joseph."

Then she remembered that he was at the cockfight.

"Mrs. Mason, Mrs. Mason."

"What is it?" Mrs. Mason was drying her hands on her skirts when she came lumbering up the stairs.

"Over there." Mary pointed to the bundle thrown against the wall.

"Fanny," Mrs. Mason cried, rushing over to get her. "Fanny, what are you doing there?" She picked her up. "What are you doing on the floor, precious lamb?"

The baby let out a little gurgle.

"She looks like you, Mary."

"She does?"

"What a beautiful little girl."

"Do you really think so?"

"Oh yes, Mary. You have a child, something to live for, something in the world that is yours."

"I have my books."

"Oh yes, Mary, but books are books. This is a living person, somebody who will love you and remember you, who will care for you."

"Mrs. Mason, I want her to go to the wet nurse to live until she is older."

"You are going to send her away?"

"Yes."

"Why?"

"She will be happier."

"Without you? How can that be?"

Mrs. Mason tucked Fanny in her crib.

"I am not a good mother. Babies frighten me. She will be happier with a wet nurse, Mrs. Mason. I am not patient enough. And when she is weaned she can come back to me and be happy with me. When she can understand stories, words. I promise she will be much better without me." Mary was out of breath.

"You think she will be happy without you?"

"Surely so." Mary sat at her desk, her head low.

"But you are the mother, Mary."

"I know."

"And all you have written about parents and children, that parents should raise their children, not nurses and nannies. Your *Thoughts on the Education of Daughters*?"

"I know," Mary said, with her head down. "But for Fanny's own good. So that she can grow up."

"Mary, you just need to get out more."

"I do, but that is not the solution. I, I do not like . . . little children. So I am not a human being, a real woman, or a good mother. I am a beast, Mrs. Mason. Say it."

"No, you are not a beast."

"Well, maybe I am not suited to be a mother, a real mother. I do not like babies. I am not good with them, for them."

"Everybody is suited. Animals are suited."

"Well, maybe I am not well."

"You are well enough. You talk beautifully."

"One can talk a lot, like King George, and be mad."

"Are you saying you are mad?" Mrs. Mason put her hands on her hips.

"No, I am not saying that. I do not mean that. I mean, I am not good for her now. Fanny needs a good motherly mother." Mary knew that in Mrs. Mason's eyes to reject your child was worse than murder. But Mary did not want to commit murder.

"The wet nurses take on many children, Miss Mary, they do. People send their children to the country to die. That is what happens, Mary. Five babies, one wet nurse, a small country cottage. Nobody gets enough. It is dark and damp."

"Her chances are better. I will pay a lot of money for a good nurse. If Fanny stays, she will die here with me. She will be happier without me. I love her, I think, but really I keep saying it, it is a painful admission, but she will be happier, better, without me."

"You are a new mother. It takes a while. You will get used to it. You will learn."

"No, I will not." Mary flailed her arms about. "For God's sake, Mrs. Mason, I threw her across the room."

"It was an accident."

"No, it was not."

"We all do things we regret, Miss Mary."

"I do not want to regret killing her."

CHAPTER 47

DEATH IS SUPPOSED to come on a pale horse. But if an animal is to carry death, Mary thought, it should be a wild boar, its tusks dripping foam and its eyes wild with despair. It should snarl and paw the ground with its forked hoof, raising puffs of dust behind it. It should smell of defecation and taste of musty fornication. Its wormy, piggly tail should stand straight up. When it charged, the gown of its rider should flow behind, and the legs, up and open, would not reveal the opening Easter lily or the wrinkled snail of winter. It would be an empty hole.

Horses, white horses, she found altogether too benign to carry such a messenger, unless, of course, death was to come as a quiet sleep and immense relief after a long, hard life. In her dreams, up in Joseph's attic, Mary dreamed a death as soft and white as the first snow of winter. Outside her window, falling on the roofs of London, delicate flakes would winnow down right and left, over the shoulder, on the head, until the streets were covered and the houses wrapped with white fur, rabbit ears.

Other white things:

She remembered as a child in Wales seeing a pale horse with a freckled gray rump nibble the grass of the church graveyard. And the white-breasted sea gulls and the herons, wild geese in the winter and white primroses in the spring, all the white sheep on the hill like low-flung clouds, with legs brushing against the grass.

And she wanted it all back, rest and reclamation, hers. She wanted Fanny to be happy at the wet nurse's; Joseph to stop worrying; her sisters to stop writing for money; people to stop asking, Where is the child's father, how was the Revolution, see you have kept your head, hah-hah, is Robespierre as ugly as they say, when is your next book coming out.

That day Joseph Johnson's medicine chest was unlocked. All the little glass bottles were there, each labeled. She read: Mis: Odontal, croc metal tenebirth, R: Jalab, Lenet amygdal Tsacr. Greek. A little booklet wedged between the slates holding the vials in place was a little more comprehensible.

For apoplexy, swallow a glass of urine of a healthy person, mixed with salt to induce vomiting.

For gout, apply live earthworms to the affected part until they swell.

For cataract, blow dried, powdered human excrement onto the affected area.

There were remedies to treat ailments from constipation to nervous disorders—senna leaves, myrrh, asafetida, mortar and pestle, measuring scales, a long, pointed tube for enemas.

Yet what she wanted was not there.

Oh dear, she thought. But Mrs. Mason was out, and after almost a whole day of rummaging through the house, Mary found it. Not in the medicine chest, not in a bedroom, but downstairs in the pantry, wedged between the cowslip jam and the pickles, which made her wonder about Mrs. Mason. Mrs. Mason was at the draper's, or somewhere, on Joseph's instruction. Joseph was not home either, but at his coffeehouse.

Laudanum, she thought to herself, balm to my heart, laudanum laudanum. Mrs. Mason's laudanum was the color of a lover's sperm, the Milky Way, the big white bear of visions, bones clicking, and the very thing to bring respite for life's insomnia, a soft white feather bed, liquid oblivion. Laudanum had a sweet, smoky taste, and it went down smoothly and gently. Aphrodisiac, anesthesia.

Mary wandered outside, holding her arms overhead. It was a drizzly, late Thursday afternoon, 1795, and though it was only autumn, the air was already without promise and hope of anything better. Above her head, Mary held two pages of a letter written to Imlay. One page was titled "Meditation on Jealousy"; the other, "Meditation on Suicide." The ink from the pages ran down her hand, making new veins crisscross the old. There goes misery, she thought, and the word "misery" ran down and off the page onto her wrists, pooling in the curve of her elbow.

She had settled on her course of action the day before as she was having tea and tea cakes, a good strong cup of black Bohea with Joseph.

"You are looking much better," Joseph had said.

Actually, she had been happy. She felt free of everything. Indeed, Joseph had been glad to see her smile. Mary had talked with Mrs. Mason at length. Mary almost felt alive. She had gone to bed not dreading dreams. She had awakened with fresh energy. The Battersea Bridge that rainy Thursday was her first choice, but there were too many people about. She feared discovery. It was almost as if she were carrying on an illicit affair and eluding a suspicious wife. Standing near the edge of the bridge, she felt outside any law, and yet, as a standard-bearer for despair, she considered herself her own law *and* country. This was a higher calling. She supposed saints felt that way. The damp bricks of the bridge were both hard and slippery, and the thin soles of her shoes were soggy, offering no protection. She welcomed discomfort.

The rest of her clothing was similarly chosen for the occasion— not the flowing gowns of a stage tragedian, but skirts of a suitably heavy fabric to effect a thorough drowning. She did not wish to float downstream like a lily pad, head aloft and legs wavery tendrils. She did not want a buoyant bodice. She wished to sink hard and fast. And so it was wool skirts, for cotton and linen would have been far too light, and her overskirt, at least ten yards of cloth, was caught up at the sides and back in heavy gathers. Large bows held these in place. It is because I am famous, she said to herself, that I can afford to adorn myself in a manner appropriate for a quick death. The petticoat, although of cotton, was quilted, with rucked detail and a fringed hem and pleated decorations. The belt over her bodice was wide, ribboned and embroidered.

It was raining hard by the time she got to Putney Bridge, and she walked back and forth until her skirts were drenched with rainwater. She knew she would sink straightaway. Yet she was shivering and worried that she would catch an ague. Silly, she said to herself, soon you will be beyond the ague and all illnesses. She touched her face. It was smooth, unwrinkled. And if not left in the water too long, she would be a pretty corpse.

Gil, summoned from France for the funeral, would lean down,

see her beautiful, pale face, unmarred like that of Hamlet's Ophelia, and her body thin as a girl's, no stomach sticking out anymore, her hands crossed on her chest like lilies. They would comb her hair in two long waves. Fulham Church would have plenty of tapers illuminating her wistful smile, and oh, how he would cry that it came to this, that it came to this. I did not mean it, want it, he would protest, and if only . . . He would remember her large nipples and the smooth skin, fine wit, how she looked when she laughed, her lower lip, her nose all twisted up, and the night she had sat astride him, reciting: I am a fat horse riding to Banbury Cross.

What she feared most, however, was what she had seen once in Bath when a drowned woman was brought up dead after several days. The woman's face was full of algae, and slops were caught in the hair, awful lumps, and little fishes woven into the slops and hair lay dead, like decayed jewelry, with lines of excrement hanging from them. The face was that of a witch, pinched like a closed door and riddled with bumps and large carbuncles. The belly had been bloated and the fingers waterlogged to webby paddles. This was not a noble Atlantean from the deep, green-hued and clean. This woman was blue, covered in sludge, grotesquely deformed.

The other frightening prospect for Mary was the actual sensation of dying. She just wanted to be dead. To be on the other side of it. She wanted it to happen without delay, without pain. When she thought of jumping off the bridge, her stomach buckled and her breath caught. It would be the horrible sensation of falling from a tall place. Yet other methods, such as cutting herself, would be unthinkable. Too painful, too messy. She clutched the droopy pages of her meditations on jealousy and suicide like flowers, a nun's bouquet.

Mary's dress was now completely soaked. She walked back and forth, not only delaying but also insuring a fast trip downward, no flotation of skirts. She wanted them to hang down limply. Seeping milk from her breasts stained her bodice. Perfect, she thought. More weight. Another few minutes.

She imagined the cool water massaging her burning eyes and flowing into the hole in her chest where her heart had once resided, soothing away all pain, all torment, all Gil gone. She would no longer have to be clever or funny or entertaining or perform or be alluring. She did not have to fear abandonment or hurt or humiliation. She could rest. The choppy black waves beckoned to her. White-topped fingers called:

Jump, jump.

Clutching her meditations to her for dear life, Mary looked about, saw nobody on the bridge or nearby. Quickly she hoisted herself up on the low wall, and squeezing her eyes shut, she tried to gather in the memory of his body—his narrow chest, long legs, and soft black hair—and of the quality of his fine mind. But, of course, he did not have such a fine mind, and certainly not one she could regret missing. Or she should be thinking of her writing, her literary standing. But how little that meant in situations like this. Or her dear child.

"Fanny," she called out over the Thames. "Fanny."

She was thinking of her friend.

The wind scooped up Mary's hair and hollowed her stomach and rushes of frigid air hit her mouth and throat. She remembered standing on the edge of the boat going to Portugal. Then she jumped.

It seemed forever going down.

Then all of a sudden, she hit.

She hit the water with a cold shock.

Then she felt herself begin to lose consciousness.

Then it was black night.

Then come home, Everina said, come home, our mother will not last long. She asks you to tend to her.

How can she ask for me, she hates me.

Wicked girl.

Why not Ned.

A man.

Her son.

Or you.

You know how the sickroom smell offends me. Eliza has her husband to tend to, her child.

I suppose you think my employment is of no consequence.

Mrs. Dawson would understand. Mother cannot last more than a few weeks, at the most.

Mrs. Dawson did not understand. And Mary traveled from Bath to Richmond, wondering about her next shilling.

The sickroom smell Everina had objected to was of rotting flesh, very similar to the offal thrown from the butcher's in the street for the dogs to eat. It was close and dark, the curtains drawn. Even the outside shutters had been banged shut, latched. The form on the bed was still and the hair on the head on the pillow was like matted straw.

Nobody has combed her hair, Mary said.

Comb her hair? She is dying, Everina answered.

She is not dead yet.

There was a chamber pot filled with vomit beside the bed, and a cat was lapping it.

Take that out, Mary said. Immediately.

So fussy, what matter if the cat eats it here or in the yard?

Mamma? Mary said gently.

Who is it? The voice rasped together like insect wings.

It is I, Mary.

Mary who?

Mary had to catch her breath. Mary, Mary your daughter, Mary, that's who.

Oh, you.

I have come all the way from Bath, Mother, I have come from far. I have been traveling for days.

I am dying, you know.

She is very sick, Mary told Everina, who was waiting outside the door, the chamber pot in her hand filled with mucus and blood.

"Are you surprised?"

Their father was sitting in the kitchen, his feet up on the table. One year and his hair had gone white and sparse, and his chin was no longer separate from his neck.

Annie was in Scotland. No doubt parting the tartan, Mary mused.

Father will marry again, Everina said. They always do.

Mr. Bishop, Eliza's husband, looked and walked like their father. Maybe it was simply the way men walked, and if Mr. Bishop did not like the dinner, he swept it off the table with one blow of the hand.

Eliza's little baby whined constantly.

It was Mary's job to change her mother's dressings. Each morning she would peel the cloth from the breasts. The muslin clung, and Mary would take the tip with her fingernail, lift very gently, very slowly while her mother screamed in pain.

It would take a good ten minutes, and then a fresh one was put on. The cancer puffed out in great knots of a summer squash left out in the field to ooze and pop.

Her mother resisted having her bandages removed, but it was not hard to hold her down, she was so weak. The arms were like sticks, the flesh hung loose and wobbly. Her legs Mary could no longer look at, and her femaleness had collapsed into a mockery of itself.

Worms and bloodletting had been tried, purges and salves. The local barber had been called in with his razors and knives, but he would have none of it. Hot and cold compresses, clean linen, and lots of gin, that was the strategy the physician recommended. Her mother could not swallow more than a sip at a time.

It was Mary's job to boil the rags on a fire in the yard, hang them up to dry. It was cold, the earth packed shut, and the steam from the great kettle rising high into the air was seen for miles around. Water thrown out from the kettle furrowed the earth and chickens pecked at it, walking daintily tiptoe on their claws. It was early spring by now and the landscape bleak and dreary, but Mary could remember how it turned pink and lavender, soft yellow, in a month or so. As a child, she had looked out over the castle tower to the river Swale, dreamed of getting away and becoming a great actress like Mrs. Siddons.

One day, going into her mother's room, she found her dead.

Mary went back into the room with a bowl of water and a sponge, and she carefully undressed her mother, slipping the sleeves from the shoulders gently as if the breast could still feel. It lay like its sister breast now, cold and quiet, no fever, no throbbing. The lump was just a lump, the breast a breast, the woman a woman, once her mother, now no longer.

And her mother's skin had become chicken skin. This is what we come to, Mary thought, combing out the limp hair and putting rouge on the cheeks. Her mother had said the day before, almost sighed: Just a little patience, Mary, and it will all be over.

Why is it, Mary thought, looking down at the body, that while we may hate our fathers, we forgive them, but we can never forgive our mothers?

"Mother, Mother."

"She is waking, she is alive, quick, quick, lift her head."

"Mary, Mary."

Cold, damp, black night, torches streaming orange trails. Fulham church, dead, or dead.

She could hear the fog bell. Fog in hell?

"The beach, missy, you are on the shore."

"Keep her warm."

"Shh, shh."

"You were drowning."

A man with a large red nose leaned in, drew back. Mary felt dizzy. She began to shiver.

"Somebody get a cloak, a blanket, brandy, hot tea."

Beneath her body, she felt something soft and squishy.

"We saved you," a man said. "From the river."

"We thought you were dead."

Another man, holding a piece of mirror, said: "We were looking for your breath. You are on the beach. These watermen saved you from your fall when you were leaning forward to catch your papers."

"My meditations." She could hear the swell of the tide. "My meditations."

"You were floating, and you had fainted, but your head did not go down."

The bridge, the cold rush of wind, the icy grab of water, she remembered.

"Where do you live?"

"Who are you?"

"She is a famous writer."

Mary sat up, reached for the mirror, held it up. At first she did not see her face, but gradually it wobbled up, came onto the surface. She looked into her own eyes.

Mary gazed longingly into the mirror. What is it, she thought. What is happening to me? Why do I feel so happy? At that moment Mary fell in love with herself.

Why? How?

Because she was alive and that was all there was.

WILLIAM

CHAPTER 48

BY THE END OF the eighteenth century, London had twenty hospitals or asylums for the sick and lame, 107 almshouses for the old, eighteen for the indigent, seventeen dispensaries, forty-one free schools, seventeen other schools for deserted and poor children, and 165 parish schools.

Besides the baths attached to many of the great hotels and coffeehouses, there were eleven public baths, including the seawater bath. Mail and stagecoaches pulled up at the principal inns. A good place to have a luncheon was the Cheshire Cheese off Fleet Street. Nearby was the Barley Mow, where roasted and boiled potatoes were served every day and roasted potatoes every evening during the winter season. The Queen's Arms Eating House in Bird-in-Hand Court, Cheapside, had an excellent ordinary meal every day at three or four o'clock. There were eighteen tea places and innumerable coffeehouses and pubs.

A good meal could be had in a cookshop for one shilling. The rent of houses on trading streets was from thirty to forty pounds per annum, and in the great squares, two hundred to three hundred. A furnished room went for one to five guineas, and on the second floor it was two-thirds the price. The coaches, parked in various places such as Islington Green, Shoreditch Church, and Fleet Street, opposite Mitre Court, cost one shilling per mile.

Kew Gardens, a favorite recreation spot, was four miles south of Kensington, across the Thames. It was laid out with great taste. The greenhouse, built in 1761, extended 145 feet in front, was thirty feet wide and twenty-five feet high. In the gardens, there was an aviary, a flower garden, a menagerie with Chinese pheasants, and in the basin, stocked with waterfowl, there was a pavilion in the Chinese manner. In addition, scattered throughout the grounds there were Temples of

Bellona, Pan, Solitude, and Augustus. Mary, of course, sat in the Temple of Solitude. This was when she began to get better from her near-drowning and could move about unaided. William Godwin sometimes accompanied her. She found him an antidote to Gilbert Imlay, for Godwin believed that "our only true felicity consists in the expansion of our intellectual powers, the knowledge of truth, and the practice of virtue."

On Princess Street, Hanover Square, Merlin's Mechanical Museum had a clock, a hydraulic vase, a model of a cruising frigate, a mechanical juggler playing with cups and balls, a barrel harpsichord, and a magic lantern. Godwin liked the hydraulic vase best. Mary liked the magic lantern. The black shadows of puppet silhouette figures, mounted on a disk and lighted by candles, were projected on a screen; cranked by a kind of organ-grinder's handle, the disk went round and round, and on the screen were ladies at a dance, or a ship sailing the sea, or children bouncing balls.

CHAPTER 49

MARY REMEMBERED the first time she was hurt. She was in a small circle at the end of the road. The strange half cast of the evening light made it seem like an arena. The dust was rising up in a cone of light and the rose petals were falling down. Her nose was clogged and she could not breathe. Stop, stop, she wanted to shout, but it would not stop. The bad boys continued to throw dirt balls at her.

Waking from her dream of death on the shore of the Thames, Mary had been seized with a sharp sense of joy. All her senses awoke and her awareness of herself was poignant and painful. The smell of decay emanating from her wet clothes reminded her of being on the punt in the river at Bath, of the estuary at Laugharne. The sound of the people mumbling in the background, the heavy, swinging dirge of concern was reminiscent of Paris during the Revolution. Mary saw lights from across the Thames that night as if they were the bobbing fishing boats lighting up in the Bay of Lisbon. Lisboa, they called it. She sank back onto the sand.

The London rain had stopped, and the moon rising bright and full promised Mary that she would do great things someday. She *had* done great things. Yet it did not seem to matter, the great things. It was the someday. That was what mattered. She had a someday.

Why had she done it, they whispered on the riverbank. Why did she try to kill herself?

For love, somebody said.

Ah, love.

The lack of it.

Where is her mother?

Where is her father?

Where is her husband?

They say she used to dress in black all the time.

A pity and a shame.

They say she is a famous writer.

Then she is rich.

If I were rich, I would not kill myself. I would spend my money. And a woman rich on her own work? She must be lonely. She must be a man in disguise.

Midwives babble.

Slop-carriers smell.

Seamstresses have a way of looking in their laps.

Coachmen whistle.

I, for one, would never do something like that.

You would miss your beer too much, that is why.

There is no missing, no tears in the grave.

The boatmen who saved Mary rowed her downstream to Black-friar Stairs, with two boatloads of men and women following behind. They carried her up Ludgate Hill to Joseph's place, swinging her in a blanket done up like a hammock. It was a procession, torches aloft with swirls of flame bleeding into the night. Occasionally a face was illuminated—skewed mouths, a narrow sweep of cheek, red eyes, a crumpled row of teeth.

"We are here, this is it," Mary declared.

Joseph opened the door.

"My God, Mary. What is this?"

"The lady fell in the river," one of the men said.

The troops were welcomed in, given brandy. Mrs. Mason brought up loaves of bread, pickles, cold meats. They ate, they toasted, they left. Meanwhile, Mary had been placed in front of the big parlor fire, Mrs. Mason washed and changed her, and then she was swaddled in clean warm covers and set in the chair.

"Mary, you scared us to death," Joseph exclaimed. "My dear, how could you do something like that? Your dear baby girl, your work, me. How could you do this to me? You are ready to throw away your life because some idiot tumbles after a sorry slut, a strumpet actress, a little wench. Another thing is that all of this, and not just this but the little excursion into Bedlam and so forth, and you know of what

I speak, is not at all, not in the least good for your literary reputation . . . Am I making sense? Do you understand of what I speak?"

"I beg to differ," Mrs. Mason put in. "The public loves to see the human drama . . . When I learned that, and I forget her name, is it Miss Burney or Miss More, perhaps Miss Foster, who was disinherited by her grandfather and was abandoned by her husband and died in great distress, well, needless to say, I wanted to read her *The Old Maid* all the more."

"Mrs. Mason . . ."

"Sorry, sir, did not mean to . . ."

"Mason . . ."

"Chop-chop, down into the shop, and more brandy. Never known a problem a brandy could not cure, and I said to him, I did, Mind your manners and tuck in your shirt. Men are so loose these days, Miss Mary . . ."

"Mrs. Mason, we must be gentle with Miss Mary."

"I am a lamb," Mrs. Mason agreed.

"Mary, say something to me."

"The cat has got her tongue, Mr. Johnson, I do declare, just like when she was in the lunatic asylum."

"Mrs. Mason, the brandy. Off with you."

"I have seen it before. They cannot clear their throat. Struck dumb, dumbfounded, dummy . . ."

"Mary, shake your head if you mean yes. Can you hear us?"

Mary shook her head.

"See. She heard you say dummy, Mrs. Mason. Apologize this instant."

"May God forgive me and may He nail me to the cross and pluck out my eyes and pour hot oil on my toes . . . But she did tell them how to get here. She *can* talk."

"Mason."

"Sorry."

Mary was once again in Joseph's silky, slithery robe. Perhaps she had never taken it off. The room was mostly the same. He had added new things to his house while she was in Paris—a polished steel grate for the fireplace, a settee, a marble table with a gilded eagle set on a plinth base, and a Chinese-style chair, other chairs. He had a walnut cabinet and bookcases, a satinwood Pembroke table with drop leaves, a chair in the Sheraton style, and a candle stand. She had seen these things before, but not seen them. Mrs. Mason was wearing a new dress, this one green and grainy. Mary's vision seemed clearer now, more focused. Connections were easier. She suspected that her book *The Rights of Woman*, which had sold so well, was what had made the current additions to Joseph's eclectic décor and Mrs. Mason's massive wardrobe possible.

"And, Mason, this talking business. Do not overwhelm her."

Everything overwhelmed Mary. The world was loud and falling in on her in large waves. See me, see me, everything seemed to be saying. Objects and people were everywhere she turned. Her own body posed a challenge. The wet tips of her hair were like writhing worms set to skate down her back. The fire blazing in the grate contained her sisters' faces in the flames. The needlepoint lion on the back of the chair hissed and roared. Mary could talk, but she did not want to say a word yet. It would only have added to the confusion of things.

"Just a little bite," Mrs. Mason said, pressing a morsel of cake to Mary's mouth.

"Mary," Joseph said.

"Just a little bite, my love."

Mary remembered something that impressed her in Paris, during the executions. Few brought before the Tribunal escaped the guillotine. The red carts were full as they lurched over the Pont-Neuf and into the rue Saint-Honoré, passing the palace of the Louvre, where the French kings had lived before Versailles, moving slowly, the streets clogged with onlookers, passing the Tuileries and its gardens, the Manège, the Jacobins Club, and on to the rue Nationale and the Place de la Révolution, where the crowd, in their red hats, resembled a field on fire, on and on, a long slow descent into hell. Meantime, the vendors hawked their wares: Little cakes, little cakes. Mary felt then like crying: Little cakes, little lives. Now she felt like saying: Little cakes, just a bite.

"She has received a shock, Mrs. Mason. We must get her upstairs."

"I know that, sir. But one must eat to live."

"I am more worried that she does not talk," Joseph said. "Do not force her to eat."

"Now, Miss Mary, I know you have seen trouble, my dear, with that bad Mr. Inlaws, is that his name? I mean the American, my dear, what do you expect. Savages pure and simple. Some be convicts. And they go for anything that moves among the trees. Yes, indeed, that's how they are. Anything that moves, they shoot at, or the other, that is how they are. It just has to move. I do not wish to make you sad. Now I want you to taste this savory porridge. And if you do not take it down nicely, I will get somebody up here to hold open your mouth until you do. That is a good girl."

Mary opened her mouth. "Where is Fanny?" she asked. "I do not want porridge."

"She can talk," Mrs. Mason declared. "Miss Mary can talk again."

Joseph sighed. "Thank God."

"She is at the wet nurse, Miss Mary, as you asked. She is fine. And you have your readers to regard. You are a responsibility to the public, missy. You do not merely belong to yourself, so that you can dispose of yourself at your will. You will worry your poor sisters to death. They love you dearly and that is the end of that. Family is family. And think of the men who saved your life, fishing you out of the dirty water. My goodness, you cannot *not* eat. Think of me. If you should die, Mr. Johnson will show me the door and that is without doubt. So be a good girl now, eat your porridge, and I will bring you some bread."

Whatever happened, Mary wondered, to the bread that was lost at the bakery, the family bread which had made their father angry and their mother miserable. Was it still moldering away in some corner— W for Wollstonecraft grown fuzzy and peppered with green, in time a fossil.

"Mrs. Mason, let her sleep now."

"The raveled sleave of care?" Mary asked.

"What should I tell the Thursday-nighters, Mary, that all is well, that you are recuperating nicely, that you have forgotten that scoundrel of an American, that you are ready to go on with your book on the Revolution in France?"

"Is it true what I heard about the queen, that going up the stairs to the guillotine," Mrs. Mason interjected, "she accidentally stepped on the executioner's foot, and that she begged his pardon? So she was a real lady, after all. Me, I would have to be drunk as a lord to get within sight of the guillotine. They say it is fearsome. Do you think they would have executed Lord North—just because he was our prime minister, he would be cut?"

"And Pitt, our prime minister, what if we sacked and chopped him. One day top of the heap, the next day bottom of the barrel. My God, just to think of it makes my neck tingle. You are lucky you got out of the country safely. We were so worried over here. And Mr. Paine, Mr. Paine of all people, put in jail. They say the queen's hair went white overnight. What you need, Mary, to set you to rights is some good English roast beef."

Mrs. Mason and Joseph helped her upstairs. Mercifully, they went downstairs, leaving her alone. Mary could hear Mrs. Mason muttering for a while, and then it was very quiet, as if the house closed in on itself and she lived in the middle of silence.

In her dream, Gilbert was wearing her skirts and her hat and he put his fingers up her. She was very wet. They were on the hill of the vineyard, and when they turned the body over, it was Marat with his short legs and sores all over his body. His hair was in a pigtail, with the plait encased in a black silk sheath. English wildflowers surrounded him: rosebay willow herbs, ragged robins, dog roses, foxgloves, lords-and-ladies, common mallows.

He is dead, Mary said.

From too much wine, Gilbert explained.

No, Mr. Justice's Thumb.

What is that, Gilbert asked.

"It is the Act of Flagellation, Gilbert, giving a man the right to beat his wife as long as he uses a stick no thicker than his thumb. It is the rule of thumb. You see, he is a woman in pantaloons."

Gilbert put his thumb in her, declared what a good boy am I, and whipped her all soundly and put her to bed.

"I do not want to wake her." Joseph spoke softly, standing at the foot of her bed. Somebody with a large head, spectacles, stood with him. Mary squinted her eyes, pretended to be asleep.

"She has received a considerable shock," the stranger said.

"But she will drift back. They do," Joseph added.

"He, this Imlay fellow, a regular Squire Western out of Fielding's *Tom Jones*, am I right, Joseph?"

"More the dissolute Viscount Squanderfield of Hogarth's *Marriage à la Mode*, I had heard. We've discussed him before. He is not worth comment."

"In any event, here she is, undone, Joseph, not even one of those Fleet marriages that they once did so quickly around Fleet prison."

"I thought you did not believe in marriage, William?"

"No, but I do not believe in ruining a person, either."

"What is between?" Joseph cleared his throat.

"Celibacy, my friend. One grows quite used to it."

The bed Joseph had bought Mary when she returned from France was massive. It took up much of the little attic room, had carved bedposts, hangings. She hid among the pillows now. Who was this? But she peeked around, caught a glimpse of sharp-toed, red morocco slippers, a green coat, and crimson underwaistcoat. Who was this fool? He looked vaguely familiar.

"Opie wants to paint her again. There are all sorts of requests."

"Reynolds? Dead. Thank God Hogarth is dead, too. No telling how he would render her."

The window was open. Mary could hear birds. It was morning?

"Her *Vindication of the Rights of Woman* alone will insure her a place in history. But what is so amazing is that she is still that bedraggled, bereft woman standing on my porch begging for lodging. The first time I saw her, I said to myself: Let me keep at least one woman off the street. Last night, looking at her in my bathrobe, brought it all home to me, full circle, full circle without a doubt, as if she had done nothing in the last eight years. Off the streets, only to be delivered to the asylum, and then into the river she goes. The contrast between her accomplishments and her feelings about herself . . . quite amazing. She works very fast and is not careful. Brilliant, but messy. *Rights of Woman* was done in a few feverish months. Then, when it is all over with, she looks around for the man who will be the least kind to her. Kindness is a foreign idea to Mary. She would have to ask me to translate it, and still would not grasp its meaning. She has very little experience, for all her writing of what-should-be, of what is possible among civilized beings."

"But *she* is kind, Joseph, is she not?"

"To a fault. But it does not do her any good. And she has known Dr. Price, other good men."

"Maybe she needs . . ."

"But what more can happen, William? What else can she do to herself?"

"Maybe it is all spent and she will come back."

Come back to what, Mary wondered.

Joseph tapped his foot, his hands behind his back. "How can she produce anything under such circumstances. It is stop and go, high and low."

"Quite common, Joseph, among poets."

"It plagues my own heart, and so it is at some risk I attend to her." He shook his head. "The trouble is, I look at Mary, see myself. I try not to see it in her. For, if such a vital, intelligent, courageous being can become so downcast, who is safe?"

"Yes, and look at Collins, Christopher Smart, William Cowper, the unfortunate Chatterton, dead at eighteen, a genius, supposedly, or a great fraud, however you look at it, they are all melancholics."

"But she is not a poet."

"She is, Joseph. She has that cast of mind, that sensibility. Fancy, enthusiasm, passion, a certain kind of outlook which is uncharacteristic in the general run of things."

"What kind?"

"Sad."

"But sometimes she is so merry and will talk for hours in the most happy manner."

Mary did not think that was true. Around Joseph it was hard to get even one word in, let alone hours of words.

"Like King George, who talked for nineteen hours straight until he collapsed. It is not pure melancholy, my good man, but a pendulum swinging back and forth. Very interesting people. They seem like the rest of us, and then quite out of the blue they will be stung by crippling sadness, and for days sometimes, weeks, even months be completely inaccessible. Or they can be extremely happy. They can stay up all night working on something and chatter, chatter, chatter, or they can sleep around the clock."

William scratched his bald head. "The road of excess, Blake says, leads to the palace of wisdom."

Joseph leaned against the wall, his hands in his pockets.

"Sometimes it leads to self-destruction. Is she religious? A Methodist, Joseph, in spirit."

"Good God, no. Those ranters and ravers? Not at all. She has been influenced by Dissenting thought through Dr. Price but was Church of England, basically. Price was the first person to see how very intelligent she was and to begin to direct her reading. She has had a rather difficult time of it. Since childhood, I must say. Her father . . . and her mother . . . Mary always feels she is going to show them. Show them what, I wonder. Her mother is dead and her father remarried and is a drunkard. Then each man . . . She has ended up without much faith at all in God or man. Is it any wonder? I truly believe we must love our fathers to love God, do you not concur, William?"

"Many men, Joseph?"

"No, not many. But two I know of, William. There may be more. There was some rumbling about the oldest son at the Kingsborough estate. But I think not. He was sixteen and an invalid. Fuseli, a good thirty-five. This Imlay, I do not know. Perhaps a little younger than she. But he was a mature man, in body."

Mary felt like laughing out loud, but covered her mouth with the sheet.

Joseph went to the window. "You know, it is strange to hear you say that she may have a poet's nature, because her work, well, it is prose and advocates reason. She urges women again and again to be reasonable."

"Maybe she is urging herself, Joseph. Writing is a kind of becoming, a discovery and a beginning, and not necessarily an arrival. We write because we must, because we hope to be."

This intrigued Mary. The man was sounding like Dr. Price.

"She writes to show them, all who have harmed her."

"Maybe she writes to show herself." William Godwin looked over at Mary.

"To show herself what?"

"That she can. It is a way of saying: I live."

"For her it is 'I live.' Hah!" Joseph said. "She feels others do not want her to live."

"Well, tell me, it is really suicide, is it not, which should be called the English malady? Rather than the spleen? Foreign visitors are always amazed at how easily we decide our own deaths. Have you ever read Cheyne's *The Natural Method of Curing the Diseases of the Body and the Disorders of the Mind Depending on the Body*? Fresh air, fresh milk, that's what he recommends. Get out of London."

"Surely you know what Samuel Johnson said: If a man is tired of London, he is tired of life. And we are a nation of beefeaters. That is what we use cattle for, not milk."

"Yes, my good fellow, she is tired of life. That is it exactly, and there are three hundred asylums in our fair land, London with its share—and beefeaters? How many people do you know with gout?" Joseph said.

"There are all kinds of suicide, my friend. Hanging oneself is suicide, diving from bridges is suicide, but there are other ways in which we can destroy ourselves and yet still walk about."

Mary listened carefully. Who was this?

"And she is one of the most famous women in the world. Sad, is it not, this struggle?" Joseph said.

Mary wondered if they thought the most famous woman in the world had lost her hearing. Why did they talk about her as if she were not there?

"Last night, I was sitting quietly going over a manuscript by Blake."

"Blake is remarkable, Joseph."

"I think so, William."

"He is remarkable and something very strange."

"Yes, something very interesting. A mystic."

"Do you think so?"

"Anyway, it was night when I heard knocking. Is it Old Bailey summoning me to account for my politics? Are the French landed at Dover Beach? The long and short of it was that they had Mary. She appeared neither dead nor alive."

"Did it not seem odd to you that she was not home?"

"It did and it did not. I was not thinking too much. Maybe she had met somebody, I thought she might, I do not know. I cannot think of everything all the time, you know. Now, however, I must think of how to get her well, happy."

"Thursday-night dinner. Prompt her to participate. Inspire her to get up each day, get dressed, go out, encourage her to attend to her duties."

"It may be hard, William. She can be obstinate."

"Indeed. But consider this: somebody like Burke would have her in Bedlam again. Over the gates of Bedlam are two statues: one of extreme madness, and the other of dark melancholy. It is frightening."

"No, no, never that. But you have been very helpful. Just talking to you. I am grateful for your advice and consolation, William."

"Think nothing of it, dear fellow."

Think nothing of it? Now she recognized that this great authority on melancholy disorders was none other than William Godwin, writer, philosopher, and with opinions, she hated to admit, very like her own. This Godwin, like everybody else she knew who came from a Dissenting family and who had been a Dissenting minister, was a Johnny-come-lately to life and letters. That he could hold a quill had indicated to him that he was a writer.

Unfortunately, he *was* a writer. For, if she was the most famous woman, he surely was the most famous man. *Political Justice* and the novel *Caleb Williams* alone had made his reputation. The novel began with the sentence: "My life has for several years been a theater of calamity." But he was pompous and ugly. She could not believe that, though the price of the first edition of *Caleb Williams* was set at over a pound, three thousand copies had been sold. Furthermore, she had to grant, reluctantly, that his ideas were not only similar to hers, but even more radical. He proposed that private property be eliminated, that vice is a natural product of circumstances, that government is a source of evil, and that the necessary revolution must be bloodless.

Yet, soon as he left, she called to Joseph.

"Mary, what is it," Joseph asked, running up the stairs.

"I hate him," she said. "I hate his shoes, his coats, his advice, his big face. I hate *him*."

CHAPTER 50

THERE WAS the heavy smell of honeysuckle, and the taste of the grass in her mouth.

In the distance she saw a man lying in the grass with spots of blood on his waistcoat, but she pretended she did not see because she and Gilbert were going to make love. Looking over Gilbert's shoulder, she saw the sky, the clouds galloping heavy-hipped across the mountain, the sun a ring of flattened fire, and the black cool shadows of leaves. The wind brought the sound of cannons, snaps of gunfire. Set out on a cloth beside Gilbert was a picnic dinner of pancakes and pigeon, Madeira wine, Wiltshire cheese. Baby Fanny was at that picnic, nested within her.

Mary woke up, called for Mrs. Mason. She did not feel well. Chills started at her feet and set her shivering all the way to the top of her head. They wrapped her in warm blankets until she felt she was going to smother and burn up. When the fever began to cool, they ducked her in the washtub filled with cold water.

"It would be a pity," Mrs. Mason said, "to have her die after being rescued."

For days Mary was alternately hot and cold. She had a vision of Armageddon, the battle staged in Ireland, and she and her charges sitting upstairs in the window seat watching it below on the green heath. In the dream, she walked about on the Kingsborough estate in her long blue cloak. On the train of her cloak, cross-legged, sat the three little girls. Richard, her first love, hobbled on the outskirts like Dr. Santos in Portugal. And Fanny, not baby Fanny, but her dear friend Fanny, soared in the sky like a kite. Richard held the string and asked Mary if she wanted to hold it, but she did not catch hold well enough and the kite spiraled away, higher and higher, until she could not see it anymore.

"You can sit up for a little nourishment, can you not?"

Mary opened her eyes. Mrs. Mason loomed above her, blocking the window. Mary wondered if it was sunny. There was a fire going in the grate.

"Gruel?" Mary said.

"Aye, so we are better if we can complain about the food."

Mary sat up.

"I suppose you would prefer roast beef and Yorkshire pudding with all the trimmings, and jelly and soft bread?"

"Yes, I would."

"Aye, so she is much better."

Mary *did* feel better.

The room was warm, the window was the color of slate.

"Have my sisters written?"

"Not a word."

Mary shook her head, slid back down in bed.

"Not a word, Miss Mary, and Joseph sent off to them over two weeks it is."

"I have been sick that long?"

"Aye, it was the river water, that rainy day. The water made you ill."

"And Fanny?"

"At the wet nurse still."

"How do I look?"

"We are getting better and better if we care for our looks. You look thin. You look thin, my dear. Your face has drawn in and your eyes gotten bigger and your ears stick out and your neck looks like a chicken's neck and your nose is a grand beak . . ."

"Wonderful, Mrs. Mason. You make me feel wonderful."

"I do not make mention of legs, and, Miss Mary, you have lost your front, and your back is . . ."

"Where is Joseph?"

"Joseph is out."

"Ah, I see."

"Heavens, just until this evening."

"Oh."

"You should eat this. I will leave it on your bedstand, and then you should rest some more. I will come back to check you, but do not try to get up without help. You will find that your legs will not be used to your body and will not do as you tell them."

But as soon as Mrs. Mason left, Mary got up and went to her writing table, holding on to the wall for support. In her night shift, with her thin face and bunchy hair, she knew she must look like a mad poet or an exiled prince.

November 3, 1795

I hope that Joseph has not alarmed you unduly. I am doing well again. I suppose I was close to death. The world looks different from the vantage of death. You see less in general and more in detail. Without your life, there is less interference between you and the world. The world is more itself, and in a sense a veil is lifted. For example, there is the expanse of the street with the vendors and the peddlers and the buildings and the coaches and the people walking about with parasols and walking sticks. And then you notice that the little child is weeping silently in the corner and the vendor has lost his teeth and the dog has three legs, like the Hogarth painting "Gin Lane" with the intoxicated mother reaching for snuff, the baby falling off the steps, the dog eating the bone with the man, a corpse being put in a coffin, the pawnbroker examining a saw, the suicide hanging from a rafter, bricks falling off the building.

It seemed a rather silly letter, and not really what she had intended to say. She wanted simply to say that she was different, that she had changed, and the world, if not completely happy, was somehow more meaningful in particular and mundane ways. The dailiness of life, which had at one time almost defeated her, now was a triumph. She did not need a grand passion or a dramatic crisis to animate her bones or stir her imagination. It was enough that she could see the sun outside her window or smell coffee or hear Joseph whistling downstairs. She would be happy never to partake of romantic love again. And, anyway, she planned to get a book out of her experience with Imlay, reconstruct her notes taken at the end into letters from Sweden, Denmark, and Norway.

CHAPTER 51

MARY COMPLETED the *Letters* and Johnson published them in January 1796. She worked on the *Analytical Review* as an editor, went on short outings with William Godwin, who had taken an interest in her health, and attended Thursday-night dinners, retiring early. It was a quiet time for her. She was on the mend.

And then it was summer and there were flowers all over. Peonies, York and Lancaster roses, and carnations, nasturtiums, blue gentians, pink sweet peas, geraniums and love-in-a-mist. Trees, full-leafed, grew along all the streets. There were beeches, oaks, elms, willows, birches, cedars, and ash. Green, green canopies, green bowers, walls of greenery, green.

Mary's body seemed to flower, too—first her toes, nursing baby bunnies, and then her sharp, arrow ankles. Her buttermilk calves, warmed by the sunlight, swam smooth as silk, and her knees knocked together like fresh-cut wood. Her eyes were milky-raw. Sunlight hurt. But she could walk. And she could talk. Mrs. Mason dressed her hair in the French style and Mary put on her pretty shoes.

"I am to be up and about, tra-la."

"You know, Mary, no need to rush into anything."

They were in the kitchen. Mrs. Mason was making a fish stew. Mary could hear horses clumping along the cobblestones, criers hawking wares. It seemed she had been asleep a hundred years.

"The world is alive, Mrs. Mason. I am alive."

"Indeed you are. But you know what I mean, all the same."

"You mean . . ." Mary smiled knowingly.

"Yes, exactly that. Let them look, is all I say. They can look . . ."

"But no talking?"

"No talking. For, you know, first comes the mouth and then the hands. And where there are hands, hips are sure to be. Thighs follow hips. And not far behind are knees."

"And then those nasty feet."

"Well may you laugh."

"I am not laughing. But Blake is married." He had invited her to his printshop.

"Famous last words, madam."

"And he is quite ugly."

"We have heard that as well, have we not? Ugly is as ugly does."

"Mrs. Mason, I have finished. Look at me, I am old."

"You look very fetching, Miss Mary, and you know that you are a fine figure of a woman, no matter your age, and there be some whose humors are attuned to the melodies of love more than others. There are some whose blood runs high and hot. Age cannot quench, nor . . ."

"Weather subdue? A friend, dear Mrs. Mason, am I not permitted a friend? He is an old friend."

Mr. Blake had written: You must come and see me.

"What do you think Blake really wants, Miss Mary?"

"God only knows."

"God does know. Blake talks to Him firsthand, and daily, is what I hear." Mrs. Mason licked her thumb and raised her finger heavenward. " 'William,' God says, 'mind your manners and be a good boy.' "

"Blake *is* a good boy, Mrs. Mason."

"Ah, and a nasty one."

The kitchen smelled of the ocean at low tide. Mrs. Mason was shelling clams and cockles and mussels for the stew. Mary did not like fish heads and fish eyes staring up at you, and the shiny bits of scale that floated to the top of the brew with the froth bubbling like dirty soap. She was glad she was not going to be home for dinner.

"Surely I should see him, Mrs. Mason. He is the one who did pictures for my book *Original Stories*."

"Am I stopping you? I am merely warning you. I know how it starts. Old times, old thoughts, he can remember, you can remember, so jolly that is, and meanwhile you fool yourself into believing you are newborn, baptized in the river, and you cannot go back, oh no, cannot be touched by claims made years ago. It is just talk, you think, light and easy. No harm. No danger. But the past can hang heavy on your mind, Mary. Like an iron pot fixed on the hook. Will not let go. Blake is part of that past, is he not? Fuseli was his good friend, Thursday-night dinners, the revolutionary spirit and what-have-you. Soon you are the person you were, having the trouble you used to have, and Joseph and I, we are rushing to the hospital or dragging the river or combing the countryside. More babies, more silence, more sadness."

"More books, Mrs. Mason." Mary got up from her chair.

"You need that misery for books?"

"No, I am not saying that. I am not saying I need misery for books. From now on, just books. No misery. I am not the silly girl you think. You do not have to worry. Furthermore, Blake is harmless."

"As a snake, Miss Mary, as a snake in the grass."

Mr. Blake's printshop in Lambeth was a low wooden building with a lopsided door facing the street. The windows were askew, and the roof ready to collapse. Mary carefully pushed open the door, stepped in gingerly. Copper plates lay all about like broken dishes after a domestic fight. Chisels and scrapers and burnishers were scattered across the low tables like dirty silverware. The air in the room was hot and damp. Mary could barely breathe. There was the scent of ink and fresh-cut paper and something else she could not name. Oranges, perhaps. That smell always reminded her of Portugal. A tall ladder rested against one wall. The walls were painted in wide, pale stripes —a sandy yellow, pale pink, lavender, and misty green. It was like being enclosed in a tropical rainbow. The floor was sticky with grime. Mary had trouble making her way across the room. Her feet would stick, unstick. Blake was way off in one corner of this steamy caldron by the press, singing merrily to himself and loosening the huge wooden screw attached to the platen which pressed the paper; he looked like something spawned from a cow-pat. His face was dirty. His neck sweaty. And his arms were steeped in stain. His sparse hair was matted into peaks and owl ears. Mrs. Mason need not have worried that Mary would be lured into amorous adventure. Blake was unsavory at best, repulsive at worst.

"Mary, how nice to see you," he shouted across the room.

She moved toward him, nearly slipped on something on the floor, righted herself, laughed.

"Mary, my love, you look wonderful." He clasped her in his arms, released her. "My goodness, I have dirtied your fine dress. No matter. Let me take another look at you. My goodness, to the Revolution and back. Madame Guillotine. Let me look at your neck. Are the French not tired of war? I must tell you that I thought of you. We all thought of you. Fondly. And I realized that I had always neglected you and not been the friend I should, the friend I wanted to be, the friend, my dear, you needed. Need I say more?"

Like Fuseli, Blake had a large and impressive head placed on a small body. Blake's body, however, seemed inconsequential, merely a vehicle for moving the head about. Head and the hands, that was what was important to Blake, was it not?

"I heard about your *Songs of Innocence and Experience*, William," Mary said, loosening the ribbons of her hat, trying to breathe.

"Ah, did you, now?"

"And I wish to understand *The Book of Urizen*."

"It is about separations, my dear, separations."

Mary felt hot, a little queasy. She looked about, but there were no chairs in the shop. If she did not sit down soon, she would collapse.

"I wanted to ask you something in particular, William."

"One print and then I am yours, Mary, love."

He lowered the platen by tightening the screw. It came down on a sheet of paper. Blake let it rest some minutes and then slowly tightened the screw, brought the apparatus up again.

"It is the poison tree again," Blake explained. "Illuminated printing. The whole page, printing and illustration, in one."

"I had heard about your invention. And I am familiar with the poison tree poem. I myself have written about managing the temper."

"Yes, I am a genius, should anybody ask." Blake laughed, wiped his hands on a dirty rag.

Mary blew air down her bodice, lifted her skirts a little.

"Ah yes, and the tree, the tree of mystery, the tree I have just printed. My dear, it is not only man's tree here, but God's also. Do you see, Mary? It is a tree of life, knowledge, regeneration, forgiveness, and it is full of poison. Yes, poison. But do not be frightened. It is the tree which the demiurge, God's helper, watered with his tears and Adam's tree and also the tree on which Christ was nailed King of the Tree—'A Poison Tree,' just a child's poem, as you see."

Blake stood stiff and straight.

"*I was angry with my friend,*" he began.

"*I told my wrath, my wrath did end.*" He bent low, swept the ground with his rag.

"*I was angry with my foe.*" He saluted to the ceiling.

"*I told it not, my wrath did grow.*" He mopped his forehead, sighed deeply.

"*And I water'd it in fears,*

"*Night & morning with my tears.*" He pretended to cry, wiped a tear.

"*And I sunned it with smiles,*

"*And with soft deceitful wiles.*" He did a little twirl, one finger pointed to the top of his head, one knee up.

"*And it grew both day and night.*" His voice gathered volume.

"*Till it bore an apple bright.*" He showed the shape of an apple with his hands, boomed out:

"*And my foe beheld it shine,*

"*And he knew that it was mine.*" He lifted his finger as in "Hark, hark, the lark."

"*And into my garden stole.*" He tiptoed around the shop like a stealthy thief.

"*When the night had veil'd the pole:*

"*In the morning glad I see*

"*My foe outstretch'd beneath the tree.*" Blake fell on the ground as if dead.

"Blake, get up." Mary was rather astounded by his performance. "Blake!"

He lay inert on the filthy floor.

"William Blake!"

One eye opened. "I am dead," he said.

"You are not dead. Gracious. Please do get up."

He scrambled up. "Did you think I was dead?"

"Not for an instant."

"You think I am a fool."

"I think you are foolish."

"If I am to be a fool, it is a holy fool."

She had had this discussion before. It was quite the fashion. Why was everybody so intent on being a fool, holy or otherwise?

"William, I want to ask you . . ."

"It is always the simpleton who marries the princess. Would you marry me, Mary?"

"I believe you are already married, William, and I am not a princess."

"Right you are. But, as you know, three is the mystical number. Both of us have fancied three, have we not?" He smiled knowingly.

Mary thought: Maybe Mrs. Mason was right. These are dangerous waters. "Let me be clear, William. I do not have long to visit."

"Let us see what we have for our luncheon, shall we? You cannot leave without eating, and eating without leaving would mean that you are trapped here forever and ever. Snow would fall, Mary. This whole place would be blanketed. And rain, rain the like of which has never been reported in the history of Albion. Day and night. A Flood. Finally, in the dead of night, after everybody in every house, castle, and inn was on their knees . . ."

"You are quite mad, mad as Joseph, but I will stay for a light repast and I am off."

"A light repast, indeed. Follow me and I will lead you straight to the way and the light."

"The light of flames is more like it."

"Oh, you modern women."

Blake pranced ahead. Mary followed him out of a back door into a walled garden.

"Behold the Garden." Blake bowed low.

"The Garden" was forest, not cultivation. Bushes overgrew each other in mad competition for sun. Untrimmed, they had the wild and desperate look of unkempt bearded men who wander the street in a muddle and beg for money. Vine tendrils throttled each other in a lacy profusion. Roots dug into the earth like fierce claws. Flower stems tangled and strangled each other. Daisies pushed up against roses. Lilies of the valley and pansies were trampled by nasturiums and geraniums. Hollyhocks, pink and crimson and yellow, stood against the fissured wall. Ivy choked the trunks of sickly-looking trees, and statuary and birdbaths tumbled over in clumps of weeds like petulant children who would not come in for dinner. It was a splash of obscene color. It was a riot of flowers disgorging their insides, exposing their sexual parts. Sticky yellow pollen bombarded the nose, and big fat bumblebees hung sullenly in the air, contemplating eminent human targets.

"My goodness." Mary had a headache. "Is this Rousseau's nature or God's horticulture, William? Tell me, what have we here?"

It looked like the devil's handiwork.

"My dear Mary, we live in a failed Utopia. Vestiges and remnants of a great civilization lie all about us." Blake waved his hands in grandiose fashion. "I want you to consider another approach to the Gates of Heaven. Do not dwell on things of this earth."

"Another approach? I am not dying yet."

"Oh, but you will."

"Not for a while, Blake. I want to know how to live, not how to die. If this is the entrance to the next world, goodbye. I am not ready."

"They are one and the same, dying, living, living dying."

"I think they feel different, Blake. I think it is something like all and nothing."

"Oh, metaphysics." Blake shrugged.

"Not my strong point, I am afraid."

"You *should* be afraid. Metaphysics will get you in the end and make mincemeat of your body. Catherine, oh Catherine," Blake called out. "A guest is here. Come out, come out, wherever you are."

Blake's wife came out of a little door in a house set alongside the garden. At first, Mary thought she was wearing a slim brown dress, but as she moved forward, it was apparent that she wore no clothes at all. So the stories were true. For a second, Mary felt delighted. She could hardly wait to tell Mrs. Mason.

"Dear Catherine," Blake said, taking his wife's breasts in his hands, giving them each a swift kiss.

"Excuse me," Mary said. "I have interrupted."

"Not at all, Mary," Blake reassured her.

Mrs. Blake giggled, held her legs together daintily. She had long, brown nipples like sticks of chocolate and not much hair on her mound. It looked like a plump, bumpy silk purse filled with rose petals and cloves, the kind to scent clothes in a drawer.

"I think perhaps I should be getting on." Mary had a sudden urge to laugh, cry, urinate, run.

"No, stay," Mrs. Blake said. "I am going to serve our luncheon shortly. You must not be put off by my God-given body. I hardly ever wear clothes in summer if I can help it. Do not be alarmed. Will and I like to be as close to nature as we can manage."

"That is quite right, my dear." Blake looked at his little wife approvingly. "It is quite warm outside, is it not, Mary?"

Mary stole a glance at Mrs. Blake. It was hard not to be disconcerted. And she felt disoriented. But, of course, Captain Cook on his travels had met naked people who thought clothing ignoble. The American Indians and African slaves did not wear much clothing. And there was Friday in Defoe's *Robinson Crusoe.* Wherever it was hot, nudity was practical. Furthermore, the great artists painted nudes. She, herself, had been naked in the act of love. She should not be bothered by such an innocuous sight. English people could be so narrow and pinched. She had traveled, knew better.

"The body is a beautiful thing," Blake said.

"When you are sixteen," Mary said.

"What was that? I heard a strange sound. Is it the trumpets of Armageddon?"

"Nothing, William, dear. Nothing at all. A little gas."

The heat of the day made it seem like Portugal. Mary remembered the last quixotic gestures—the donkeys on the hill silhouetted like black paper cutouts on a magic lantern forever moving around and around, Fanny's racking cough, and then the torture on the beach. Mary had only rarely seen Fanny's body, and mostly when she was sick. By then, it was so wasted as to be hardly a woman's. It was a child's. Mary's mother's body when sick had been repulsive, almost animal, like the beached fish she had found once on the sand of the

estuary, bloated and smeary with oozing pus. Mrs. Blake was brown
and round, a pert little doll, not at all displeasing.

"Sit, Mary." Blake indicated a seat under a tree.

"You will eat with us?" Blake's wife asked, not waiting for an
answer, and turning to enter the house, which was not unlike the
printshop in design. The sun, high overhead, glittered through the
tree branches. Mary felt a little dizzy. Mrs. Blake's backside had dim-
ples like the cheeks of a face. How curious. Mary felt as if she were
dreaming herself in a dream.

"I hear, Miss Mary," Blake began, "that you have had a dark
night of the soul."

"I visited Atlantis," Mary answered, slipping her gloves into her
purse, swallowing hard.

"Did you see the green king under the water?"

"I saw their president. They do not have kings."

"And what did he say, Mary?"

"She said to go back to my own kind, that I was not finished with
my life yet, that life was life, good and bad, and that there was nothing
else."

"Ah yes, the atheist's dream, the best materialism can do."

Mary was sweating and her stays were poking into her breasts.
She had not been so completely dressed in several weeks. Her skin
was still tender. Her waistband was too tight. The sleeves cut into her
armpits. How comfortable Mrs. Blake must feel.

"It is my belief, Mary, that our life is a descent from the eternal
world to the material existence. When my brother Robert died, I saw
him ascend to the ceiling clapping his hands for joy."

"I was wondering, given your inquiry into the human mind,
Blake, what you think about innocence after knowledge."

"I must wash, Mary, before we dine. Please excuse me."

Mary was glad of the opportunity to be alone a minute, for she
must plan how to leave gracefully.

It has been very nice, but I promised Joseph I would come back
straightaway.

Thank you for the lovely afternoon, but I am not completely well.

Well, well, how late it has become.

Yes, I am working on my next book. That reminds me, I must be going.

"You will not mind if I, too, disrobe, Mary?" Blake called out from the bushes.

"Not at all," Mary replied, a little too shrilly. God help me, she muttered. How much will I be asked to stand?

Blake had been dressed in blue breeches and a white cotton shirt with the sleeves rolled up, and a large apron, when he ambled to the back of the garden to the pump and cleaned his hands for lunch. He emerged from behind a spray of leaves as the natural man. His body was compact and rather brown, like his wife's. The pouch of his testicles looked like a marble sack, and the little purple worm of his penis trembled and filled, waved back and forth.

"Blake, tell it to behave."

"Surely you have seen a naked man before, Mary."

"Not recently."

"All the more reason." He took her hand, rested it on his lap. "My best friend," he said of his organ.

Mary sighed. She was more than a little tired of men and their best friend.

"I am through with all that, William."

"My dear."

"I categorically reject . . ."

"My dear."

As his wife appeared with a tray of food, Blake immediately dropped Mary's hand.

"You should really take off your clothes, Mary," Mrs. Blake said. "You look terribly tight, if you understand the meaning of constriction. As in boa constrictor. It is such a hot day. You would be surprised how wonderful it feels to have the breeze play about your bare skin. I am always closer to God this way, the way of innocence. William says this is an act of fidelity, and that we are faithful in this way to the spirit as well as the law."

"I am not that uncomfortable, thank you, Mrs. Blake. May I have a glass of wine?"

"Before the fall, when we were innocent, we had no awareness of our naked state," Mrs. Blake continued, putting her hand on Mary's shoulder.

"So I have heard," Mary said. "But it is now."

"Now is the time, Catherine," Blake interrupted, "for you to bring the White Lisbon for Mary."

"Of course." Mrs. Blake sidled off into the little house, humming "Oh dear, what can the matter be? Johnny's so long at the fair."

"She is a dear, dear precious love," Blake said, shaking his head sadly. "I . . ."

"Yes, you love her."

"How did you know?"

"Because you, Blake, are a fool."

"For loving my wife?"

"For telling me of it while . . ."

"But she is very sweet."

And Mary was happy to observe also that there was somebody in the world with a bigger bottom than hers.

At the table Blake said grace, thanking a number of beings Mary had never heard of before. They sounded like Assyrian griffins and Zoroastrian deities. Then he thanked the food itself for giving up its life so he, William Blake, could be whole and sound, and his wife for being such a splendid cook, and the day for being beautiful, and the tree for shading them, and all of God's creatures for being themselves. Mrs. Blake said it was enough now, she was hungry as a bear.

"Very well. And thank you, Mary Wollstonecraft, for gracing our humble table."

They sat at a little table built into a tree. Their benches were rough wood. Mary wondered about splinters, for by then she had had several glasses of wine and had taken off her clothes, too, which lay in a heap like an exotic mushroom, ledged and highly polished, and sprouted especially to complement the scene. Mary felt fine. Clothes *were* quite the bother. Mrs. Blake had been right about the air. Mary felt her nipples were so long and hard that birds could perch on them. Her hips spread comfortably beneath her, and she let her stomach go slack. Why not?

Mrs. Blake had put a homespun cloth on the table, set out large pottery bowls. It was a simple meal of cold lentils and hot mustard, dandelion greens, toasted bread, and small, tart apples. Mary had camomile tea drizzled with honey, some more wine.

"Simple pleasures are the best," Blake said, farting loudly.

"Is that Armageddon I hear?" Mrs. Blake giggled.

"I visited Dr. Price's church at Newington Green when I came back from France," Mary said quickly, trying to be sensible and uplift the conversation. She crossed her legs in a ladylike manner. "They put up a plaque. I copied it." Mary extracted a piece of paper from her knit handbag. "Look." She handed it to Blake.

> *To the Memory of Richard Price*
> *26 years minister of this chapter*
> *Died at Hackney, Middlesex, April 19, 1791.*
> *Theologian, Philosopher, Mathematician*
> *Friend to Freedom as to Virtue*
> *Brother of Man*
> *Lover of Truth as of God;*
> *His eminent talents were matched*
> *by his integrity, simplicity and*
> *goodness of heart;*
> *His moral dignity by his profound humility.*

"Very nice, Mary. Such an example to emulate."

"My meager talent is not matched by humility, I am afraid," she confessed.

"Humility is something I do not own, either," Blake admitted.

"I, too," Mrs. Blake chimed in. "I am very unhumble in all that I do and see and be and am."

"I have not been a good sister of man," Mary continued.

"I have not been a good sister, either," Mrs. Blake concurred. "Decidedly bad, that's the kind of sister I am. Bad, bad, bad." She hit herself on the bottom, smack, smack, smack. Blake watched with interest. "I punish myself regularly, Mary."

"You do?"

"Well, now, you have certainly been a good sister to women, Mary," Blake said.

"I feel just like your sister," Mrs. Blake comforted. "Your twin sister. I think maybe we grew up together sometime. Your mother was my mother and my mother was your mother and . . ."

"Catherine, I think maybe . . ."

"Blake, you do not understand. I want to be a better person."

"I think you are a perfectly wonderful person, if you ask me." Mrs. Blake stroked Mary's hair. Mary could have purred like a cat. Her legs felt wonderful. She noticed when Catherine Blake got up that her legs were sturdy and scarred with scratches and bites, little bruises and cuts. She had a child's legs, as if she constantly slipped and fell while running about. Mary's own legs used to look like that. So did Fanny's.

"I do not want to be a better person," Blake said.

"You do not?"

"I do not, either. I want to be a perfectly awful person in everything I do."

"Catherine."

"Surely she can say what she wishes, William."

"She has had too much to drink. Catherine, do you want to go to your room?"

"No." Catherine hung her head, pouted.

"The idea of perfection is arbitrary, something thought up," Blake said.

"No, dear husband. God is perfect. That is where that idea comes from. We cannot, according to God, be 'as the gods,' as Lucifer tempted, we cannot know good and evil, but we must be God-like, as near perfect as possible, whatever that means. That is what is left us in this weary world. Oh, my." Mrs. Blake yawned.

"That is exactly what I came to ask—the possibility of innocence after knowledge." Mary sighed. She could see the end of the afternoon. Nothing too bad had happened. Nothing more was *going* to happen. What was a little nakedness among friends, anyway?

"You mean," Mrs. Blake took up, "how can we have an open heart, an open mind, after all we suffer and all the suffering we cause."

"Yes," Mary said, looking at Mrs. Blake with some interest. The woman was not stupid. People had merely assumed so.

"I do not think we can aspire to goodness, Mary. Do you? Did you read my poem 'The Human Abstract,' or 'Divine Image'? They were handed about."

Blake stood up.

"*Cruelty has a Human Heart*," he began.

"William," Mrs. Blake pleaded.

"*And Jealousy a Human Face.*" Blake made a scowling, angry face.

"I think Mary is tired, William."

"*Terror the Human Form Divine.*" Blake jumped up, making his penis wobble in a circle.

Mrs. Blake rolled her eyes. "William, I think you have had a drop too many."

"*And Secrecy the Human Dress.*" Blake curtsied, holding a flap of his thigh out like a skirt.

"*The Human Dress is forged Iron.*" He marched about.

"*The Human Form a fiery Forge.*" He hammered the air.

Mrs. Blake shrugged. "No point. No point."

"*The Human Face a Furnace seal'd,*

"*The Human Heart its hungry Gorge.*"

"Thank you, William, and now will you finish your meal?"

"All of our so-called human virtues are in response to poverty and fear, man-made things, Mary." He shoveled in the lentils. "But do not mind me. Follow your own stories. You like the one about Sir Gawain and the Green Knight. The Green Knight sends Sir Gawain on a quest to find himself. Sir Gawain is tested and tempted and spared. You like the continent under the water which rises again. We all have the capacity for regeneration and growth. Yet, while the thought of our century—Rousseau, Locke, David Hume, Voltaire—may tell you what is, what should be, and how we think, none of those thinkers, Mary, can truly tell you how to live your life. You must read yourself and discover yourself."

Mrs. Blake held her finger up. "Discover yourself."

"Catherine," Blake said.

"You would have us live as Christ, is that it?" Mary smirked.

"No, I would say live as Job."

"You would say be as Mary, Christ's mother." Mary knew the New Testament was in there somewhere. It was everybody's frame of reference.

"No, I would say be, Mary, as *you* are, and I have said to the worm: Thou art my mother, and my sister. Be as the worm, my dear. Have some more wine."

"Yes, have some more worms, Mary."

"Catherine."

The air hitting her bare flesh was exquisite. Mrs. Blake had been so right. They were now, Mrs. Blake and Blake himself, kissing her back. Mrs. Blake had tiny, wet little kisses. Blake kissed dry and hard. Mary's back felt wonderful. She was drunk, too. Her senses were both sensitive and blunted. A minute before, she was ready to leave. Now she wanted to move in.

"I plan to devote myself to learning," Mary announced to the sky at large, feeling she must make some amends. "As soon as I get home."

"Good idea, Mary." Mrs. Blake was working up to her neck with the kisses.

"Catherine and I are your handmaidens," Blake said, gently rubbing Mary's shoulders.

"We want to lay hands on you, Miss Mary."

Mary had always wondered what handmaidens were.

"I think we should anoint her," Mrs. Blake said.

"Anoint?" Mary remembered they did that in the Bible.

Blake went off into the bushes. The wide arc of his glistening urine hit a broad leaf like welcome rain.

"She is so pale, William," Mrs. Blake observed when he came back.

"I feel a little tipsy, to tell the truth, Mrs. Blake."

"The planet is tipping these days," Mrs. Blake affirmed. "Soon it will be the vernal equinox."

"That is in the spring, dear. Next is the autumn."

The sun was making a pattern between the leaves of the trees like bits of tinker's tin. Mary wondered if she was losing her mind, going to faint.

"We live in ruins," Blake said.

"It is the wine, Mary." Mrs. Blake had taken Mary's hair down and was combing it through with her fingers, and placing rosebuds around her face. "If I were you, I would wear my hair down about my shoulders like Ophelia, the poor dear."

"I do not know what to do, Blake. I have survived much. I feel duty-bound to make good use of the rest of my time."

"Follow your heart," Mrs. Blake suggested.

"Who knows what to do?" Blake asked.

"I do, dear. I do just what I please."

"Catherine, please."

"So how do you act?" Mary wanted to know, but not urgently. Everything in good time. The sun was still high in the sky.

"You close your eyes, jump."

"I always peek," Mrs. Blake confessed.

"It sounds like suicide, the bridge."

"No, not that."

"But what if it is wrong, what you do, what you jump into?"

"Only God is perfect, did we not mention that here this afternoon? Mary, I do think you are very pretty. Do you think my backside is a wee too big?"

"Not at all, Mrs. Blake. It is exactly right. No backside can be too big as far as I am concerned, and men, too. It is quite their thing. Only God is perfect, remember?"

"I think it is time for a laying on of hands," Mrs. Blake said. "It is healing to the person. It is never wrong. It is right. You cannot go wrong with a laying on of hands. It is an old practice of the Romans, I hear. I wish my breasts were like yours, Mary, ladylike, delicate."

"Wrong is not the right word, I think, for what we do, Mary," Blake said, "so long as what we do springs from passion. So long as the choice we make is a passionate one."

"What do you mean by passion?"

"I mean," Blake explained, his face big as a moon over her, "the mind holds on to things, will not let go, and our bodies follow suit."

"He means the heart, not the will," Mrs. Blake elucidated.

Mrs. Blake's breasts jiggled back and forth. She was by far the more interesting-looking of the two. Blake, though, had a nice mind.

Hearts and minds were not supposed to be pretty. Mary thought of her heart as a slippery black octopus she saw hanging up in the fish market in Portugal, the tentacles curling and uncurling. It could crush you in its embrace, she had heard, even when half dead.

"How do you feel, Mary?"

"Quite well, Blake." At least she was not supping on fish stew. Indeed, it seemed natural and good at that moment to be there on the ground without her clothes, being petted and pawed by two small brownish people, a man and a woman, not so different after all. Hands, arms, legs, hearts, minds.

"Let go," Blake said.

Mary turned sideways, looked out at the garden.

"Let go," his wife repeated.

"Go forth," Blake intoned.

"Go forth," his little wife repeated.

Were they trying to exorcise the evil spirits within her? Let go of what? The trappings of civilization? The material world? Were they trying to convert her to some strange Eastern rite? Witches, she had read, cavorted naked in the woods. Were little devils escaping her body, little licks of flame speeding away into the undergrowth like shooting stars trailing fire?

"It feels very nice," Mary said. She felt both dreamy and alert. Where her mind started and her body ended was not clear, did not seem to matter. Wrong and right blended into one. God looked at the world and it was good.

Then, without meaning to, she noticed in the tangle of vines and from behind the bushes the tiger and the lamb. The tiger was fierce and frightening, the lamb gentle. From within a nearby rose, at its swollen base, a worm crawled out. The Daughters of Albion sighed and swayed. Great muscular men heaved and hummed. Little sooty chimney sweeps danced around trees, sang hosannas. Newton sat on the ocean's floor, compass in hand; a man reached for the moon. And a puckish fellow in waistcoat and top hat and with a walking stick rushed away.

There was the play of light, the heat, the buzzing of bees. She was tired. She was dizzy. She felt vaguely sick to her stomach.

"Blake," Mary whispered. "Blake, I am afraid."

"Do not be," he said.

"It has been a very unusual afternoon."

"It is all a vision, Mary. Take comfort."

"Take comfort," Mrs. Blake whispered, kissing the edge of Mary's lips. "It is all very real."

CHAPTER 52

ST. PANCRAS CHURCH was within walking distance of Godwin's house. Mary had taken rooms opposite his. They had decided that keeping their own separate quarters would be best, since they were both independent thinkers and needed their own domains. The church was on a little hill. Farmlands all about it gave it the look of a monument, but it was less pretentious than most churches and was almost a chapel in mood. The idea of marriage, of course, was unsavory to both of them. It would not be easy to face their freethinking friends. However, the circumstances merited such a gesture.

It was a small, intimate church with whitewashed walls and broad beams, and an awning over the altar with the sun embroidered on it gave it a Mediterranean look. In fact, marriage would be a great embarrassment, given all that they had written against it. Behind the altar was a triptych of Christ on the cross. There were other paintings, medieval in appearance. The one Mary liked was of Mary, her foot on the moon, and eyes dazed slits gazing heavenward for help. Other celestial suggestions, Mary thought, such as Leda and the Swan or Eve tempting Lucifer, could be made at little cost to orthodoxy. It could almost have been a pagan church combining several pantheistic elements. This marriage was one of practical considerations, she told herself.

Mary was wearing a new dress, pink silk with lace cuffs, tight sleeves, and the skirts bunched over her swollen stomach, and the lacy collar wide over her shoulders. She had a bouquet of pink primroses, to match her costume, and her hair was dressed in a full upsweep, with little tendrils loose underneath a small square of lace. She had never been so elegant and she wished Gilbert could see her as she walked down the aisle to William Godwin. If William were Gilbert, he would be hopping and skipping down the aisle, doing somersaults, some prank, and at the very moment of union, he would be laughing, his head thrown back, the world in harmony, his joy cosmic and catching. He would not care who was looking at his long, unruly body, elbows out, wrists showing beneath his shirt. Am I the love of your life, he would ask, huh, huh? running backward in front of her. Tell me truthfully, tell me, tell me true. Am I the love of your life? You are the love of my life, she would answer. In the bedroom in Paris, he could not wait for the bed, but would begin to kiss her at the door, and then, sinking to the floor, would take her right there. So it was in a daze of disbelief that she heard: Do you, Mary Wollstonecraft, take William Godwin as your lawfully wedded.

Godwin was wearing a blue coat, yellow cassimere breeches, and very white silk stockings. His hair was plaited behind, and Mary thought he looked ridiculous.

In her heart of hearts, she wanted to run out, hoped that the roof would collapse, or a lightning bolt break open the floor between them, making visible in jagged relief the abyss, the roar of the ocean.

Dearly beloved, this wedding cannot go on.

The church would get very quiet. All faint rustling would cease. Slowly, everybody would turn to the figure in the back, the tall man in buckskin, his raven hair straggly and his bright eyes flashing.

Yes, that is correct: she cannot marry another. I love her. I have always loved her. I will always love her. I want to take her to America. My horse is waiting.

She would find herself walking to him, going slowly up the aisle in airy, slow jumps, for she had always been moving toward him, and his smile was as familiar as her own. Getting up in back of him on a pale horse, a patient animal, she would pat its sides, kiss his neck, throw a kiss to the breeze and the brethren. Thus they would cross the sea in a day and a half of steady galloping, emerging from the waves in Boston. My wife is tired, do you have a bed? We have traveled far.

Godwin signed the license: bachelor. Mary signed it: spinster.

How had they gotten to this point?

She remembered that at Johnson's table Godwin had called her

a "philosophic sloven"—or was it Fuseli? Was he addressing her clothing or her mind? Actually, *he* was very slovenly. Was his turnabout
interest in her merely due to her near death and illness? She remembered his discourse on melancholy at her bedside.

Now, somehow, they were married. It had happened very fast.

She found on her first visit that Godwin's quarters were cramped
and filled with odd objects. He seemed to be, as many were during
his time, a collector of sorts—with his turtle eggs and stuffed owl,
sheets of paper, musical scores. At least, with the exception of the owl,
there were none of the stuffed wildlife there had been at Fuseli's house.

After the marriage ceremony, attended only by Joseph Johnson,
Little Fanny, and her nurse, they planned to go to the Adam and Eve
tea garden. That night, after tea, Mary was to return to her rooms
across the street from his house. They had both agreed that if they
were to be married, they would at least maintain their freedom of
movement. They planned that each day they would meet for tea or
send a note across. It was quite the best arrangement, Godwin acknowledged, for did they not have books to write and others to read
and much to be done. Mary said: Yes, it is best.

In her first book, *Mary, a Fiction*, where she called marriage
legalized prostitution, Mary had her heroine wish for a world where
there is neither marrying nor giving in marriage. Yet surely this arrangement with Godwin was quite the best solution, given that she
was pregnant. And she wished to keep it in perspective. However, she
felt her breath catch and lodge in a small spot under her heart when
William made the suggestion that they keep separate residences. Not
just separate beds or separate bedrooms, but separate houses, as if they
were a rich couple, one in the country, the other in town, except that
they were both in town, across from each other.

"We will visit each other at night?" she asked shyly, not looking
up from her lap.

"Oh, yes, of course," he answered, coming behind her, patting
her back like a good fellow.

During her first visit to his quarters, after her sickness, when she
began to go about, seek answers, he asked her, writer to writer: "Yes,
well, and what are you working on?" He cleared a place on a chair

and sat down, left her standing. "That is why you came, is it not, to discuss your work? Oh, you need a chair, do you not?"

"I have just published *Letters Written During a Short Residence in Sweden, Norway, Denmark*, and I am working on a novel exemplifying some of my ideas in *A Vindication*, much in the way your *Caleb Williams* related to your *Political Justice*," she called to him as he went into the other room.

"How interesting," he shouted back.

Mary was brought a chair that had two good legs, a third serviceable, and the fourth about to go.

"In this book, *The Wrongs of Woman, or Maria*, Maria is put in a private asylum by her husband so he may gain her dowry. There is an attendant in the madhouse, Jemima, who was once a thief. She had also been a prostitute at one time, this attendant. The two women, one rich, the other poor, become fast friends."

"You treat the prostitute sympathetically?"

"Of course." She looked over her chipped teacup, caught his eye, looked down, cleared her throat. "Can I have a better chair, please? I am afraid this may fall down."

Mary waited. Godwin reappeared with a large upholstered relic. Mary had to help him drag it into his study. She sat down, comfortable at last.

"It is all economics, William, why women choose to be prostitutes instead of spinsters. There is that account in *The Times* of the two unfortunate sisters who starved to death in the privacy of their own parlor. If women were permitted other means to a livelihood, well, then, we should be doctors and solicitors, apothecaries, master tradeswomen, instead of starving spinsters or pathetic prostitutes."

When they emerged from the church on their wedding day, it was raining. There was no pale freckled horse in this churchyard. William held the umbrella up above her. It was a black umbrella and did not help the gloom. "I feel strange," Mary told Godwin.

"I thought you liked graveyards and ruins."

"I see my future."

"My dear, it is all our futures."

"No, this is particular."

"Do not be so tragic," Godwin said. "What you need is a good tickle, that is what you need, and a good cup of tea."

"What I need, what I need is . . ."

"Do not say it, dear. You are now a respectable married woman."

"I have a premonition, William."

"So do I. Our wedding dinner: ham, three boiled fowls, roasted duck, plum tart, apple tart, pears, nuts, wine, cider and beer. What do you think?"

During her second visit to his rooms, Mary sat opposite Godwin. He placed himself in a large cherrywood rocking chair. The walls of his study were plaster, with medallions, trophies, and urns in flat relief, and set with panels. The whole place, like his clothing, seemed overdone, as if it could not make up its mind about anything.

"I understand you *were* in Bedlam," William Godwin said, "like your character."

"Yes. Lovesickness."

"And jumping in the river?"

"Lovesickness."

"Ah, yes. I have heard of that, but I have never been in love."

"You have never been in love?" In truth, she had heard that he lived among his books like a bachelor, a monk.

"No." He shrugged in a very charming way, smiled sadly, pushed back his hair. "There *are* other things."

"Of course."

"Where is your child?"

"In . . ." and she faltered. "In the country. Fresh air, you know. The city is not a good place to raise a child."

"Yes, yes, quite right. But you are not afraid of anything, are you? You keep coming back."

"Coming back?"

"To the world, facing the world, trying."

"Trying what?"

"The full life. I wish I could be more like you."

They had to walk home from the wedding very slowly. The nurse followed with Fanny. Mary's stomach felt huge, and her legs hurt. She felt damp and irritable. Then the rain stopped. The sun came out. Snails and slugs lined the road. Godwin was wearing buckled shoes, Mary dainty pink silk slippers to match her dress. Mary's armpits felt like baked clams.

"Do not be sad on your wedding day, Mary."

"I am not sad."

"Your new book, the one you are working on, is not going well. That is it."

"That is not *it*."

"Is it because Fanny is an unhappy child?"

"Fanny is only two and a half. How can she be an unhappy child. She is a fussy child, that is all."

Fanny had been brought home to Joseph's and would now live with Mary across from Godwin.

"You miss Joseph, his house."

"I do not."

She did miss Joseph, his house. She missed the very walls, his hodgepodge of new chairs, the bellows for the fireplace, the smell of anise and flour, the air, her room in the attic. They belonged to her, and she used the objects in the house as a means of accommodating herself to the world. Two paces to the right after the front door was the rusty mirror. The china cabinet was something she looked upon at every dinner. There were crumbs on her floor swept to the corner years ago, and a Reynolds in the drawing room which Blake hated, but was what she always looked at before going outside. On seeing Joseph studying a manuscript or Mrs. Mason rolling out a pie crust in the kitchen, Mary would feel content and at peace with herself. There were always visitors, Joseph was always suggesting something, something was always occurring, what was occurring was always exciting.

"Let us pack up today and go out for a nice cup of tea," Joseph might say.

"Look smart, Mary, I want you to meet somebody."

"What-ho? A ride in the country?"

"Going to Fleet Street to the printer, anybody want to come along? I will buy you a meat pie."

"I was on my way, Mary, to my coffeehouse on Cheapside, and a huge man stands in my way. I try to go around him, but I move, he moves. Kind sir, I say, what is it you would like? A shilling? A box in the ear? Touch me, just touch me, he says. Nobody has touched me in years. He leaned down, Mary, and I put my hand on his face, tenderly."

Mary began blinking very fast.

"A lady gave me a box on Ludgate Hill as I was bound for the Barley Mow, Salisbury Court, Mary. I wanted a nice piece of roast. Sir, says the lady, I entrust this box to your care. You must guard it with your life. Should you lose it, I will be done for. On the third Friday of next month, be at London Bridge with the box. I will be wearing a straw bonnet with wood cherries and a plaid taffeta dress. Do not be frightened."

Mrs. Mason, Joseph, and Mary held their breath as the mystery box was opened. Mary expected snakes, Mrs. Mason money, Joseph some important documents. When it was opened and they peered in, there was absolutely nothing inside. Nothing.

"This is a various, nefarious, carious life," Joseph concluded.

"You mean curious."

"I mean carious."

"I have never seen that word in the Dictionary, Joseph."

"You will. Give it time."

"Yes, I do miss Joseph, Mrs. Mason, the household, William. I cannot help it."

The third visit with Godwin after her sickness, when she began to go about, tea was brought in, poured. Mary pointed her toes demurely, drew them back under her dress, pointed her toes and drew them back, wondered if the privy was in the yard. Godwin looked different, better really, than at Thursday-night dinners and better than when he was whispering with Joseph in her room, and much better than during their excursions to Kew Gardens and Mechanical Museum, and much, much better than he had looked during her other two visits to his room. She was beginning to like him.

"Perhaps I should leave now," Mary said abruptly. She did not want to feel this way.

"Do not go," William Godwin said, taking her hand.

In the morning, back at Joseph's house, she wrote a note to him:

Consider what has passed as a fever of your imagination; one of the slight mortal shakes to which you are liable—and I—will become again a Solitary Walker. *Adieu.*

Godwin wrote back:

Ours was a sober and dignified happiness; and its very sobriety served to give it additional voluptuousness.

"This is our wedding day and you do not love me," Godwin said, shaking his head sadly back and forth.

"You are my husband. This *is* our wedding day." She longed for the soft snow, weeks of gray skies, bad weather. She wished he would be quiet.

"Well, then."

"But I have a good bit to be sad about," she said petulantly. "My father was a brute, my mother stupid, my sisters helpless, my brother indifferent, my lovers faithless . . ."

"I am not faithless, Mary. And those lovers were there for a reason."

"What reason?"

"They are like Stations of the Cross."

"Come now. Stations of the Cross? It is not the face of God I am to see at the end."

"No, your own face."

"And anyway, William, I know you do not love me."

"I do love you."

"You are marrying me because I am pregnant."

"That *is* why I am marrying you, but not why I love you. You are pregnant because I love you, loved you."

Godwin's lovemaking had been gentle and thoughtful. He was

rather awkward, yet touchingly romantic. He started by stroking her face. Nobody had ever paid that much attention to her face before, not even Gil.

Godwin's house was a handsome structure with a stucco exterior, with bow-windowed bays, and two classical columns flanking the front door. Nothing foretold the mess within. He shook out the umbrella.

"Put Fanny in for her nap," Mary instructed. Then she turned to Godwin. "I do not understand your logic, William, about marriage and love."

"Because it is logical, Mary."

"I write about being logical."

"I know you do."

"I thought we were going to the Adam and Eve tea garden," Mary said.

"Are we quarreling on our wedding day?"

"Yes," she said. "We are."

They went into the drawing room.

"No, you are not faithless, William. But it has nothing to do with me." Mary pulled off her gloves, finger by finger, threw her gloves across the room, hitting the stuffed owl in the face.

"You do not have to take out your frustrations on poor Peckie."

"I wish Peck would just wither up and die."

"He is dead."

"Disappear, then."

"Peckie has been in my family three generations."

"So you have told me one hundred times."

"With whom, then, does my fidelity to you have to do if not with you?"

"With yourself. Your ideals, your habits. I need a chair, William, for God's sake, I am with child. You always sit down and leave me standing or perched on some rickety excuse for a seat."

"Of course. We cannot blame the world, Mary, for our lives. It is up to each one of us to pick up the reins, make something of our time on earth."

"Chair, not reins. Could you pick up a chair?"

"Immediately, my love." He ran into the next room, lugged back a heavy upholstered chair.

Mary sat down. "At last."

"Of course, my dear."

"Please spare the platitudes, William. I am not a Methodist hearing a sermon in a tent, nor am I somebody passed out in Gin Lane needing a spiritual lift."

"It is *your* pregnancy," Godwin said. "After all."

"Your chance-medley system of avoiding conception, that is what this is." She pointed to her stomach.

"It is scientific."

"It is bad science."

"There is no such thing."

"Whatever you say, William. Nevertheless, I am pregnant, but it is hardly anything that you need to attend to. Women are born to suffer."

"Balderdash." He went to the window. "I think we can go now. You are angry with me because I am not Gilbert."

"That is ridiculous."

"Is it, really?" He looked stricken.

"It is ridiculous."

"Believe me, that man would have been the death of you, Mary."

"I believe you." But as long as they had died together, it would have been fine, beautiful even.

"We should have asked Joseph to come along with us," he said.

She noticed that Godwin was nervous when the two of them were alone.

"You did not have to marry me, William, just because of the child."

"But I wanted to," he said. "Can you accept that I love you, that somebody loves you with all his heart?"

"Sometimes. Sometimes I can."

"What is so hard about it. This is our wedding day, Mary, for Christ's sake."

"Right."

"What do you think weddings are about?"

"Property."

"Exactly. We are both so rich."

She sniffed a little.

"I think I may take a little rest, Mary. Care to join me? The wedding walk has tired me out."

"No, I think I may take a ride over to Joseph's, give Mrs. Mason the news . . ."

"Right."

She got her gloves off Peckie's face and went down the stairs, out onto the street. I am married, she said to herself. Mrs. Godwin, if you please. It did please her, and on her ride over to Joseph's she kept her glove off, letting the sun sparkle on the plain gold band William had given her. I will not eat you off, she said to the ring. No, I will love you and cherish you.

In fact, the first thing Mrs. Mason said was: "What a beautiful ring."

The second thing she said was: "It is your wedding day, Miss Mary, what are you doing here?"

"I do not know if I like being a married lady, Mrs. Mason."

"Come on, Mary, give it a chance. Three hours is hardly time enough to judge."

"Two hours." Mary was breathing hard, as if marriage were a kind of sack, sewed at the top, with her trapped inside. "Already I am . . ."

"No, no."

"Is Joseph home?"

"Mary, Mary." He came forth, took both her hands, kissed her on the cheek, drew her in the house. "So happy to see you again. You look just beautiful," he said. "What should we do, where should we go? Tea, anyone?"

CHAPTER 53

WHEN MARY FELT her stomach squeeze in and out like an accordion and her sides ripple like twisted candy, she had a note delivered across the street to William and asked her maid, Rose, to fetch the midwife. Fanny was sent to stay at Joseph's.

Mary had started to sweat profusely early in the day. Now she could not walk. So she sat in a chair while Rose stripped the room of covers and blankets, tablecloths, rugs, all that might catch and hold dust. Curtains were pulled back and knotted. And kettles of hot, boiling water were brought up from the kitchen and used to scour the floor. Mary wished she had seen to all this earlier. Instead, she was trying to finish her book *Maria, or the Wrongs of Woman*. But there were freshly washed sheets, not just as was usual, but sheets sponged with a mixture of spirits of wine, turpentine, and camphor to keep the bugs out. And she had a clean nightdress.

"I think it will go well," Mary said, remembering Fanny's birth.

There was a knock at the door.

"Who is it, the midwife?" Rose asked angrily.

"It is I, the father."

"No men," Rose said.

"I am coming in, like it or not."

He ambled in, looked sadly at Mary, who was sitting up in a chair, a good sturdy one.

"The baby," he said, taking her hand. "Does he hurt you? Is he hurting you?"

"Yes, a little." She winced.

"You are an angel," he said.

"Do not say that. It means I am dead."

"I mean on earth, as in darling angel."

The room seemed too bright to her. The walls seemed to glare and demand attention. She would have much preferred having the baby in her old room at Joseph's, with its woody smell and great height from the street. This was only one story above the ground, with low ceilings, and the street busy and noisy. The room at Joseph's was like a tree house. She could hear birds there, crows and pigeons, and in the spring and summer, robins and blue jays, sparrows.

"Fanny is fine," Godwin said, patting Mary's knee.

"Mm."

"Joseph is amusing her. She is not distressed and is eager for her baby brother."

"Yes, well . . . Is Joseph coming?"

"We do not need Joseph."

"*I* need him."

"So who is it you love, Gilbert or Joseph? I am tired of Joseph this, Joseph that."

"William, I am in labor. Kindly do not accuse me of any wrongdoing. I love you. You are my husband. It is just that Joseph has been my friend for so long."

"You are tired. You wish to rest in the bed. The midwife is to be here shortly. I still think you should use a doctor, a surgeon. Can I do anything? Are you comfortable? Would you rather be across the street in my establishment? I am sorry, please forgive me."

"We have talked about it, William. I am fine."

A sudden pain clutched at her sides. She squeezed his hand.

"Oh, Mary, I cannot stand to see you suffer. I am sorry I am so jealous."

"I would like some coffee."

"I will bring it immediately."

"William."

"Yes, dear." He turned around.

"Nothing."

"I will bring the coffee." He smiled at her.

"William."

"Yes, darling. Tell me."

"You have been a good husband to me."

"And I will keep right on being a good husband."

"William, what if it is not a boy?"

"If it is not a boy?" William stared off into space, as if he had never considered that possibility.

"If it is not a boy, William, if it is"—and here she hesitated using the word—"a girl, if it is a girl."

"You are a girl, Mary. I would hope that she is just like you. Intelligent and witty, full of ideas and pranks."

"Look like me?"

"Oh, yes. And everything like you. Maybe not your melancholy, but that is largely due to your life. We would give her a good life, a happy life, just like little Fanny. She would be a happy Mary. I would love her dearly."

"I am a happy Mary."

"Yes, yes, you are a dear girl."

Mary put her head back.

"What is it, Mary, what did I say?"

When Mary turned to William, tears were streaming down her face.

"What did you say, William? What did you say? The nicest thing anybody has ever said to me."

"Really?" He looked puzzled. "I will see what is keeping the midwife. You get in bed."

"I am too tired to get in bed."

"Oh, Mary, do not be that way."

"What way? I am too tired." A great weariness washed over her.

"No, no. You must get up on the bed. Rose, help me get her up."

"Why does everything have to be such a struggle?"

"Now you are getting contrary again. You cannot have the baby in the chair, Mary."

"I am too tired to get in bed, and that is that. In France I had the baby in a chair, a birthing chair."

"We do not have a birthing chair. Now listen, I will be back shortly, and I want you to stop fretting. Do not fret."

For days she had lain about fretting, but not about the delivery. Her book read like a cheap romance. Yet how was she to inject high-mindedness in something as emotional as the forceful incarceration in an asylum of a hapless young woman by a greedy husband. William had been patient through all this. She had been cranky. Her life had been well ordered. Fanny would be brought to the parlor after dinner, cleaned up, in a pretty dress, and on her best behavior. She would solemnly reach out her little hand for a shake and then curtsy demurely. At three, Fanny was not a bad child, merely somber, weepy, prone to fits of frustration and pique. It was obvious she was not to be a beauty, or even passably pretty. She did not seem particularly clever, either. Mary took that as a great injustice. The child, slow and gloomy, the cause of Gilbert's departure, and a continuous problem, the child could at least be something distinguished.

Sometimes Mary would suffer a guilty pang for these thoughts and for her daily inattention, because in all she had written dealing with children and parents she advocated direct parental concern and involvement. Here she was, exactly the negligent parent she cautioned against. It was not that she did not love Fanny, or at least the idea of Fanny, it was simply that . . . she did not love her. You are supposed to love your child. If you did not, you were a . . . All people, however humble, love their children. Even animals. The thing was, if Fanny was to be Gilbert, and she did resemble him terribly, then why . . . could she not truly *be* Gilbert?

Now, this next child was not planned or hoped for. William had assured her of the efficacy of his scientific method, that it was quite safe to indulge if indulgence was frequent, reasoning that grass seldom grows on a path well-trodden. Then her age, thirty-seven. She thought pregnancy unlikely. This pregnancy, perhaps because of her age, was harder. She could not bound around as she had in France, playing in the meadow behind the cottage and digging flower beds in the kitchen garden.

This time she felt as if she were dragging around a huge tail, like one of the exotic animals Captain Cook had brought from his trip in the South Seas, or one of the grotesques painted by Hogarth. She felt like something stuffed and housed in the British Museum.

When she read pages in her book over again, she could not believe how bad they were. William said: Do not read things over too many times. That is the problem. Still, the new pages seemed forced and unnatural. Characters showed themselves limp and lifeless; the story appeared boring and stupid.

"What are you doing out of the bed?" A little old lady rushed in with a basket in one hand and sheets in another.

"Up, up, up in that bed. I am Mrs. McCamb, the midwife, and do not forget that. I say, you do."

"Where is my regular midwife? Where is Mrs. Colin?"

"She is attending to another woman, her daughter. Now, Missy Mary, I want you to spread your legs."

"How is my girl doing?" Godwin popped his head around the door.

"Who is that?" Mrs. McCamb asked.

"My husband." Mary felt for the first time happy with that idea. "He is my husband."

"Oh, so we have a husband, do we. Tell him the rules around here: no men until baby." Mrs. McCamb went to the door, closed it firmly in Godwin's face.

"It is his baby as much as mine," Mary protested.

"No, it is not. You know it is your baby. You see it sticking up there inside of you. The man must take it on faith that it is his baby."

Mary could hear Godwin's footsteps descending the stairs. He was not one to go to the tavern. Instead, he would sit in her study, nurse a glass of port.

"He wants a son, am I not right?" the midwife huffed, busying herself in the corner. "Where would we all be if all the sons they wanted were born? Nobody to give birth."

Rose was standing in the corner, folding sheets. There were enough sheets to drape a path from London to Bath and back. And while there was the air of bustling and busy preparation in the room, nothing really seemed to be getting done. The baby, which had been so eager before, had curled up, gone to sleep.

"Now lie back and do not kick and do not scream. I am going to put my finger in you, missy, check to see if this baby is truly ready to meet the world."

"The baby is resting," Mary said.

"Yes, fine. Hold still."

Mary clenched her teeth. The woman's finger felt like a knife. Mary's body contorted into a bright fist of pain.

"Oh, dear," Mary cried out. For it did not feel the way Fanny had. This baby felt knotted and obstinate, and the sides of her womb felt scraped, sore.

"This is nothing, just the beginning. The child has some time yet."

"Rose, bring me my manuscript."

"No, no, none of that. Sleep. If you can, sleep. You need strength."

Mary closed her eyes, could not sleep, could not think of anything. She saw bright colors, circles of them. She remembered chickens pecking in the mud behind her mother's house, the coach ride delivering Eliza from perdition into travail, the vision she had at Blake's.

"Here you are, lassie." The midwife took off her night shift and, tying a bracelet of rags around Mary's right wrist, hitched it to the bedpost.

"No," Mary said. "No. I will hold still. I will not kick or anything."

"Rose," the midwife said. "Come and help me."

The two of them were too strong for Mary. Furthermore, Mary did not want to hurt them. They tied up both her hands and then her feet, so that Mary was spread open, exposed naked on the bed and unable to move.

"Before, I could move about freely," Mary said. "With Fanny I squatted in a chair and the women rubbed aloe on my stomach and heated water with herbs underneath me so that the pain would not be as much. We drank wine. In France, they . . . This is like torture."

"Filthy Frenchy, papist habits," the midwife said. "You are in a God-fearing, civilized country, Mrs. Wollstonecraft, and this is how we birth our babies, in a most sanitary and proper way."

The pain came again.

"Oh my, oh, have mercy, oh dear." And she let out a shriek.

William on the stairs. "Mary, are you all right?" William's head poking in.

"Out, out, shoo."

"Is she all right?"

"She is having your baby, sir."

"Does she need help, more help? I could call a doctor."

"Sir, would you please go downstairs."

The midwife slammed the door shut. "Men," she said.

"I *want* Mrs. Mason," Mary said. "I want a woman, a midwife."

"I am a woman, I am a midwife, so hush your mouth."

Another pain swooped down, pierced her straight across the abdomen, and twisted her to one side.

"I am going to die," Mary said. "I know I am going to die."

"No, my dear, you will not die, it will just feel that way."

Something caught her again, wrung her body out like a wet cloth.

"You must save your strength, missy, you will need it. Do not give in to girlish fancy."

The midwife was pacing back and forth with great serious intent. She whispered something to Rose, who left the room quickly.

"I am going to die, is that what you told her."

"No, I did not tell her that. I told her it would be soon."

"That I die?"

"Madam, you are having a baby. Soon for the baby to come."

There were steaming kettles and soaking rags, rags drying from a little line, and dry rags folded up. There were extra sheets on the chairs, and Mary's dressing gown. Little blankets for the baby were piled in a basket by the bed. Mary felt as if she were going to suffocate in a mountain of cloth.

"Think of your little family," the midwife said.

Mary closed her eyes a minute. No, she was not going to die, how silly.

"You will soon have a wonderful baby."

Wonderful, Mary mused. Full of wonders. The idea seemed a Christmas package tied up in bows and pretty paper that must pass through her, land on the base of the bed.

"Ten is what I have. Ten, all alive and now married."

The midwife had a long, soft white beard on her chin like a nanny goat and a huge mole on her cheek from which grew several coarse black strands. Mary recognized her from a dream.

"Oh dear, it is coming again." The pain twisted her sides like the red-blood streams of a barber pole.

"Breathe," the woman said. "Breathe."

Mary breathed.

"Take short quick breaths, like a dog. Ever see a dog give birth?"

"Mary, Mary, Mrs. Mason is here."

"What is *this*?" The midwife looked at Mrs. Mason's huge bulk with considerable disdain.

"Mrs. Mason."

Mrs. Mason arched her eyebrows. "Is this a rag shop?" she asked.

"Ump," replied the midwife.

"And why is Miss Mary so hot-looking? Rose? Where is that lazy girl? And why is she tied up like a prisoner going to the gallows? Rose?"

Rose put her head in around the door.

"Listen, get some chipped ice for your mistress. And some ice cream. They are downstairs. I brought some from Mr. Johnson's. And cool water. There are some jars setting in the basement. And some stiff paper to make a proper fan. Take these witch caldrons out of here. And a good sharp knife, needle and thread. Boil those first. How long has she been going? Do not answer. And wash your hands and arms very well. Tie your hair up in a tight cloth. Do not be slopping about. Undo those curtains knotted up at the window. Make it cool and dark in here so she can sleep between pains. I want no noise, no commotion, perfect peace and quiet."

Mrs. Mason undid Mary's hands and feet, put her night shift back on her.

"What are you waiting for," Mrs. Mason said, turning to the midwife, with her hands on her hips. "You can go. You are dismissed."

"My pay."

"Mr. Godwin will pay you."

"Mr. Godwin?"

"Her husband."

"But she is Mrs. Wollstonecraft."

Mrs. Mason sighed. "Yes, and he is Mr. Godwin."

"Well, mark my words. This is going to be something you wished you never set foot in. That baby is turned around, or has the cord around its neck. It is not a normal birth."

"Oh no," Mary wailed. "It is coming again, the pain is coming again."

"Breathe fast like a little puppy. That's right. In, out, in out."

"I want William with me."

"Rose, fetch Mr. Godwin."

"But it is not suitable that the husband . . ."

"It will make her feel better. Get him. Hurry."

Finally, at about six in the afternoon, after almost ten hours of labor, Mary said: "I love you, William, but I am going to die. I am going to die in a characteristically female way. Is that not funny? I have suffered all the indignities and partaken in all the travail of my sex."

She had almost said Gilbert. I love you, Gilbert. But that was merely force of habit. She did love William.

"You are not going to die," William insisted. "I will not let you die in a female or male way or any way."

"Mr. Godwin, I believe the baby is coming quite soon now, so you best go downstairs. We will call you, sir."

Rose had been putting the ice wrapped in rags on Mary's head, and moistening her lips. Mrs. Mason attended to Mary's legs. She had Mary bring them up high.

"Mary, I may be putting my hand inside of you to turn the baby around. I think it may be backward, or breech. The cord may be around its neck. It will not take long, but it will be painful. Remember that you are getting a baby from this. This pain is to bring you something. Ask God to help you."

"God has never helped me before. Surely He will not now. I want to jump out of the window," Mary sobbed. "I want the end of this."

"There, there, Miss Mary."

It was a very hot night. It stretched out like old string. The windows were closed, a new supply of ice was brought up, Mary felt so raw, so on the edge of her life, that she could easily die.

"I have asked Mr. Godwin to call his friend Dr. Fordyce."

"The surgeon?" Mary whimpered. "The surgeon," she repeated softly. "Not the surgeon."

"We need forceps, Miss Mary. He will have them."

"I do not want the surgeon."

"Shh, shh."

"No, no forceps." She felt her body arch up high on the flat face of the clock and be pinned there, floundering and flapping, tail to head like a fish in a bucket.

"Push, darling, push. It is coming now. Push hard. Rose, rags please, the sheets, bring me the scissors."

"Oh no," Mary shrieked. "Oh, Mother, Mother, help me."

It was searing fire between her legs. She could stretch no further.

"Push, Mary, one more push. The head is out."

"We do not need forceps. It is coming."

"The baby is coming," Mary said jubilantly. "The baby is coming," she screamed. "I do not need forceps."

She did not think she could push any harder, but her body took over her will, and in an enormous effort, the baby was expelled.

"Oh, my God," Mary cried. "It is over, thank God it is over."

"A beautiful little girl, Miss Mary."

Then it cried and Mary fell back into the depths of the pillows and went fast asleep.

CHAPTER 54

AT FIRST IT SOUNDED like the restless lisping of cricket wings. Then she saw them in the corner, whispering.

"Mary." A man moved toward her, his shirt sleeves rolled up and his cravat and waistcoat off. His long form gave off a shadow like a praying mantis on the wall behind.

"The baby," she said. "Where is the baby?"

"A healthy girl."

It was Dr. Fordyce. She had met him at Joseph's Thursday nights. What was he doing there in her bedroom?

Was she dreaming this shadowy nightmare, the woman, the white-orbed horse, the imp? And the blood was still pouring out of her. Mrs. Mason had not tied her up with rags. Why the delay, and these people?

"William," she called.

"Yes, Mary." Her husband moved forward. He looked gaunt and drawn.

"William, what?" Mrs. Mason was avoiding her eyes.

"Mary," Dr. Fordyce said, gently resting his hand on her leg. "I have some opium and gin I wish you to take. It will lessen the pain."

She propped herself up. "What pain? The baby is born."

"The afterbirth, Miss Mary," Mrs. Mason said.

"The afterbirth is still inside, Mrs. Godwin," Dr. Fordyce said.

Wollstonecraft. That is my name, though all she felt was blood and sore stomach, wretched legs, bruised arms, a woman, a wench, a wretch. She could feel all her insides as if they sat on her chest, exposed to the air—blue lungs and orange heart, collapsed sick womb, and snaky intestines, and the tunnel to the womb red-rimmed, ragged. But she was still Mary Wollstonecraft.

"Yes, it is inside and I must go in with my hand and pull it out bit by bit. It is going to be very painful, but if we were to leave it inside, you would die of infection."

Mary fell back on the pillow. "I am not strong enough for more pain. To put your hand way up inside, to pull the pieces from . . . it would kill me. Please have some mercy."

"The opium . . ."

"I cannot take opium, or gin, it will spoil my milk. I cannot go through with this. I cannot."

"Very well, Mrs. Godwin. I will not be responsible for the consequences."

"Oh, Mary," William said. "If I could serve in your place, I would."

"I am not strong enough. I know this, William. People die. People die in droves in the lying-in hospitals. We are cheap. We are expendable. They do not care."

"Dr. Fordyce cares. He knows your books, Mary."

"My books? What are my books? It is my body. Can you not see what is happening?" She was delirious with fear. "We die, we die, side by side. What do books have to do with it? We are our bodies. We die."

"You are the most famous woman in Europe and England."

"No, I am not. That was for five minutes, years ago. Now, now I am just a woman, just a body. Do not let him kill me."

"For me," William said. "Do it for me. I will stay with you through it all. And this is your very own room, *your* bedroom. Underneath is your study, your kitchen and drawing room. You are not in the lying-in hospital. You will not die."

"I am in Bedlam and they are torturing me."

"No, my dear, your own room."

"My book is bad, William. I will be remembered for a bad book. That book, *Maria*, is bad."

"Mary, you are not going to die. I will not let you."

"I said the same thing to my friend Fanny, and she died. Fanny died."

"She had consumption, dear. You are a perfectly healthy woman with a long life ahead of you."

"My milk."

"The child can stay at the wet nurse."

"Fanny did, not this one. This one I want to do right."

"Our Father," began Rose, kneeling by the side of the bed.

"Stop that." Mrs. Mason hoisted her up. "No churchy talk around here. The woman is fine."

"I want you two ladies to hold her legs," the doctor said.

"Hold my legs?"

"So you do not kick, Mrs. Godwin. The pain is quite, quite . . ."

At times the pain was so intense that Mary prayed to the God she no longer believed in to make her die. Anything would be better. The doctor's hand inserted way up her womb was a barber's razor of sharpness, and the doctor's fingers picking up and ripping the bits of tissue off, butcher hooks. He had a tool, scissors it seemed, which tore flesh, ate flesh off the sides of her womb, jawed off the flesh. She felt like the sea turtle she had seen on the docks of Lisbon with his flippers pulled, his eyes poked out, and still its mouth was working. A woman had a pole pushed up her on Store Street. Mary had read about it. They found her still alive but bleeding copiously. She died when they pulled it out. That is how it felt, what she experienced.

"William, if I die, I want the girls raised . . ."

"You are not to die. You *will* not die. I will not *let* you die."

The first light of morning shone through the curtains.

"You are bearing up extraordinarily well," the doctor said.

This last time he went in, Mary thought she had finally paid the price in full for her existence on earth.

CHAPTER 55

I DID LOVE my dolls as a child. My first one had a wooden head and silk arms attached with wire to wooden forearms and hands. She had glass eyes, a gown of green silk with a closely fitted bodice, quilted silk petticoat, and braid-trimmed shoes.

I would strap her to my back as I made my way over hill and dale, through fields and up to the Laugharne Castle, the ruins where we would play, Everina, Eliza, and I, king and queen, lady-in-waiting.

I lost my wax doll in a field, and my last doll, the one with a papier-mâché painted face and leather body, Eliza cried for, begged for, until I gave it to her. Here, take it if you love her so much.

And then the ninny promptly lost her.

Gilbert bought a little riding crop to use on me. He liked to switch it up and down my back. I would wince and the next day he would take my bodice off and, kneeling behind my seated form, would gently kiss each bruise.

For Fuseli I was dreamy and demonic. Languorously, I was to plead for love. Kind sir, if you please.

Children's games.

In a dream, Gilbert slit me open from stem to stern with a fine pair of dressmaking scissors. He opened me up, crushed my ribs, and, pulling my skin about him like a cape, hovered there, a great bat in a cavity filled with blood.

You have the eyes of a doe, I told him once. He laughed as he undressed me, saying in turn:

You have beautiful feet.

Lovely shoulders.

Such pretty breasts.

Gil, are you listening to me?

Of course. Are you not a famous lady? And I adore your legs, admire your tiny waist and wrists.

Until I found myself flattered head to toe, and lo and behold, quite naked as well.

Now I am here, again naked. But alone. Yet I find myself still talking to him, making him listener by my thoughts, present through love. Yet I also love William, my husband. Gilbert is the love of my life, and William the love of my death.

I am talking to myself and can even be heard whispering into the pillow. It is at night that I open *The Book of Shadows*. They all come, my lovers, my characters, my many words. They tiptoe in, kiss my feet. Fanny and the Mary of *Mary, a Fiction*, and Crazy Robin and Mrs. Mason from *Original Stories*.

Dear Eliza, I think I am dying.

They do not say so, but their faces tell it.

"Mary," Joseph said. "Please save your strength."

"Have you seen the baby?"

"Yes."

"What color are her eyes?"

"Blue."

Ah, blue eyes at last, Mary thought.

"Joseph, I am never going to be well again, am I?"

"Gracious, Mary. Why say something so dire?"

"And my baby, and Fanny, I will never see them. I know it. I know it."

The new baby had been sent to a wet nurse right off. Mary's breasts ached with milk. Nightly, William squeezed them for some relief, but in the morning she woke to fever and leaked sour milk down her chest and across her stomach.

Mary's bed gown was an expensive Indian print, bought on White-chapel Street. It sat waiting for her among the cambric and chintz, Persian and black bombazine, crepe, muslin, cotton, linen, and wool.

I will take six yards of that, Mary said, pointing without asking the price, for she was heady with success. Finally, the continued sales of the second edition of her *A Vindication of the Rights of Woman*, published late in 1792, had made her financially independent. She could send money to Eliza and Everina. She could buy pies from the pie man on the street. She could go to the tea gardens. She and Joseph had taken a sedan chair to the dressmaker that day, for once a sedan chair, although she was afraid God or somebody would redress the balance by striking her down dead for extreme presumption.

Dr. Fordyce did not know why she was not getting better.

I never had a bed gown before that time, Gil, just my linen shift to sleep in and for a long time my one woolen black dress worn daily in and out. Now fallen to pieces, both have become a border of diamond-shaped patches on my quilt. I have several black dresses now, and a blue and a green, my wedding pink, other colors.

It was too hot for the quilt. It was too hot for anything. Mary was burning with fever. All the windows were flung open to the street, and though it was cobbled, clouds of dust and dirt were thrown up to the bed, sticking to her skin, making her hotter. When she pulled the rope, Rose would appear.

"Oh, Miss Mary, oh, Miss Mary."

Gil, my stomach is wet with sweat like that time in the vineyard, but now rags are placed between my legs to stanch the flow of blood.

"You have childbed fever," Mrs. Mason said.

Mary knew of it. It was rampant in lying-in hospitals.

> *Heart Cakes.*
> *Cherries, O, ripe cherries*
> *Wall Fleet Oysters,*
> *Hog's Puddings, Barcelona filberts.*

Street cries cut through Mary's mind, and she knew that after she died, the same tunes would be played in the same places, nothing changed, just as, when Fanny died, people went about washing their clothes and children skipped rope as if nothing had happened in the world.

Coaches came in from the country in her mind, and on the stairs she heard William's real footsteps. He dragged his right leg a little. There was an unevenness in his step, a hesitancy. The doorknob turned.

"Mary."

His large head was bowed, his nose red. He had been crying in her study. She could hear him from upstairs and should she, were she able to go downstairs, she would see the leather of her desk smeared with his tears.

"The children," he says, taking her hand.

He tries not to look at my body. Look, I want to say, it is my body, the same. This is Mary, all in one piece.

The damage is on the inside, Gil. Only the blood stanched with rags gives a hint. Enough blood to flood the street, lap the little hill of St. Pancras, where William and I were married. We came in on a wave of blood, I want to say, straight from the altar to the altar.

"The children," William says again.

"I do not want to think of them."

"Mary."

She rises up on her elbows, gives him a good look. "William, will you stop Mary, Marying me."

He laughs, takes her hand.

"A fine kettle of fish is this," she says.

We are an enlightened couple who called in the doctor, the educated medical man of the future, and what should happen?

I might as well have birthed in a mud hut, Mary thought. She and William laugh at the absurdity. Here, at the edge of the eighteenth century, in an age of science and reason—can you imagine? We have the calculus. We have vaccination. We have the Social Contract. Iron bridges. The flying shuttle. Enclosure. Ships laden with cargoes ring the globe. *The Spirit of the Laws*. We have all that, and I am dying of simple childbed fever. Women have been dying of this forever. What kind of progress has been made, and for whom? They laugh over the irony of it all. She laughs, even though it pains her.

How can I be dying, Gil, if I can still laugh, is what I would like to know.

The canopy had been taken down from the bed and the windows thrown open.

> *Three rows a penny pins*
> *Short, whites, and mid-dl-ings.*
> *Buy my dish of great eels?*

Songs, penny a sheet.
Dumplings-ho.

Mary Wollstonecraft thought she heard the street criers hawking their wares, and all day carriages and horses clip-clopped on the new cobblestones. This was progress in London, 1797. The streets were paved and light shone (whale oil) on major corners all night.

She was burning up with fever, and so ice was brought out from the sawdust and damp earth underground, unwrapped and chipped, placed on her cracked lips. She remembered when they had brought it in last winter from a man who came in a cart, his horse shaking with cold.

"I could be skating," she said to the maid now, trying to banish that image—the man with rags around his red hands, the horse's bony rump. "Maybe we could make some ice cream, Rose."

"Oh, yes, ma'am. Ice cream would be a treat."

"I should like some ice cream before I die."

"Oh, ma'am, do not say it so."

On Mary's Windsor chair was her bed gown. The blue and red flowers ran together, pooled at the corner of her eyes. Indian print. In England, women had lost their eyesight embroidering such things. Such sacrifice would no longer be necessary, for pressed print had become all the rage in London.

When Mary bought the print, she had chided herself: Here I am, subject to fickle fashion.

She remembered when she worked with her friend Fanny Blood and sat sewing by the cold dark fireplace all night so some lady could go to a ball suitably attired, and yet had the lady not wanted her dress, she and Fanny would not have had their dinner.

And when Mary ate her dinners, the overworked farmer and poor laborer hovered over her shoulder, and the woman in the market, bent and abject, reappeared. Each object had its shadow, and all contained a hidden cost. Dresses were spotted with the blood of pricked fingers. Furniture resembled coffins, and every coach was measured to the rhythm of the whip.

The second time she and Gilbert Imlay made love, she had to

bring up the poor weavers who had spun the muslin of their sheets, remarking on their wretched lives, wondering at their slavery to their craft.

Gilbert said: Who is this rabble you have invited to our bedding, are they in fact woven flat with the threads so that we in our lust lie on their faces, cavort in their misery. Stop it, Mary, you must stop suffering on behalf of the whole wretched world. I forbid it.

I hate tears, he warned her that second time. I hate demonstrations of the sorrowful sort.

No crying, she repeated obediently.

You must be happy, he commanded.

I am, she said, wiping her cheeks dry like a good girl, but sniffing a little. Why were Americans always happy? It was in their national rhetoric. Life, liberty, and the pursuit of happiness.

Joseph, though, could be properly dour. Yet the first time she met him, he had been merry, full of pranks. He had egged her on, kept her at bay, not revealed himself.

She had left behind at the inn her one trunk with her favorite books: Rousseau's *Solitary Walker*, Young's *Night Thoughts*, Locke's *Essay Concerning Human Understanding*, Milton's *Paradise Lost*, and a linen shift, a bodice, a Wedgwood vase, which was a gift, a manuscript of sorts, and a portrait of the actress Sarah Siddons. She wore the blue cloak she had made when she had started out as a governess, and the black dress, which was to be how people noted her in London. The lady in the black dress, the one who walks about as if she were a man on important business. That's what they would say of her after a while.

Ah, I am your publisher? Joseph Johnson gave her a good look up and down, taking in her skirts sodden with rain, her serious mouth, unpowdered hair, which, wet, had fallen in a tumble about her shoulders.

Mary Wollstonecraft, well, well, well. Maybe I am indeed your publisher. Come in, my dear. He had pursed his lips together and led her to his drawing room, where a hot, big fire begged her attendance.

Joseph Johnson had made her take off her wet skirts and bodice and stays, and given her his dressing gown to wear. He had dried her feet and hair, given her claret. He unlocked the tea caddy, served her tea from a kettle kept on the fireplace. Strong black tea with a spoonful of whisky that went down smooth but burned her throat, warmed her chest.

Joseph Johnson was a neat, spare man with a tight mouth and pretty eyes. His home was his office and his office was a mess and he dared to publish books on the evils of the slave trade, advocated that Jews should be tolerated, that children should not be put to work but sent to schools provided by the state, and that women should have access to all the goods and services of society. Mary's books—one was about the education of daughters, and the other, a novel, about a woman forced to marry a man she did not love—were just his sort of thing.

I like your writing, he told her, I like the way you think.

Let us leave it at that, she answered.

Her room looked out on the green dome of St. Paul's on one side. Thursdays, Johnson had dinners to which all sorts of thinkers were invited—Dissenters, English Jacobins, poor artists, the engraver William Blake, the revolutionary Tom Paine, the artist John Opie, who felt Mary's fine cheekbones with his thumbs, wanted to paint her.

It had been so lovely that fateful evening, with the scent of sweet peas and the sounds of boat bells on the Thames. The St. Paul church bells were rung on the hour. The faithful flocked to the services. Mary could hear dinners from the other houses being cleaned up. The last coach had come into the stand. The day was tucking up.

As she came in from the privy and made her way up the back stairs, she heard voices, soft night voices. The door of Johnson's bedroom was ajar, and it was then she saw the young man, smooth-cheeked as a girl, long hair curling down his neck, and bare buttocks smooth as polished stone.

"Oh, Joseph," she had cried when he visited her sickbed, sitting demurely on the side, the tears dropping off his face like jewelry. "I am done for, in truth. This is no mere playacting. Do you remember our best moments? I had thought, during those times, and am now proved right, that nobody is permitted to be so happy, that I would be punished for presumption . . ."

"Do not be ridiculous, Mary. Such excess does not suit you."

"Do you promise I am not dying, Joseph?"

He looked at her, smiled sadly. "I promise, Mary."

"Why are you crying, then?"

"I am like a sentimental fop in a silly shilling novel," he said, his voice cracking and his trembling hand digging out his handkerchief. "You cannot die, Mary, for what would I do without you. I love you, I have always loved you."

"But . . ."

"It does not matter. I love you."

Maybe it is Joseph, she wondered, maybe it has always been Joseph.

"I am not dying," Mary said. "Because I still have to think of you. I cannot give up the thought of you, Joseph."

"Mary, you are too kind."

"I cannot live without the knowledge of your beauty, Joseph. I mean, the knowledge of your beauty must, it has to go on. It cannot be dropped. I must keep thinking it, and so I must keep living it."

"I am not beautiful, Mary."

"Oh, yes, you are."

When William came upstairs and looked at her body stretched out on the bed, he said, "Dear one," putting his head at her feet. She pedaled his hair. That she had learned from Gil. He loved her feet, or so Gilbert said. She had always been vain about them, wearing dainty shoes stitched in needlepoint and tied with a satin bow even when she had few clothes.

The time she had too much wine, Gil made her sleep with her feet sticking out from under the quilts.

So you do not get sick, Gil said, that is why the feet out. He knew the tricks. She had been sick, so sick with drink that time that she had roared about the room. She had moaned and cried. That was after she knew about the actress. And he, the cause, had been the cure, taking care of her when she was besotted and stupid, undressing her, putting her in bed, patting her back, making her sleep with her feet sticking out.

"*Now* I am dying. Now, William, when I am doing what everybody expects. I am married, have children, I am like everybody else. I am respectable. I am quiet. I am doing what they want. I am not a brazen strumpet. I am not in Bedlam. I am not jumping off any bridge. I want to live. How can I be punished like this?"

"Do not leave me, dear girl." He would hold on to her hair, her arm, her foot, as if keeping her from the jaws of hell.

"I am trying not to, William."

Sometimes she felt that she would not disappoint them, that she would get up, go the window, walk about like a good girl, a well girl. She wanted to see sedan chairs moving up and down, coaches coming in from the country, stopping at an inn. She longed to be in a coach herself, go to Kew Gardens to see the menagerie, the pheasants and waterfowl, the aviary, the Temple of the Sun, Temple of Bellona, Temple of Pan. Stages left from Piccadilly every quarter of an hour. She could go if she could just get downstairs, out the door, onto the street.

> *Rue, sage, and mint, farthing a bunch.*
> *Fresh cabbage.*
> *Nice Yorkshire cakes.*

She would walk downstairs, at least that, see what the cook was preparing for dinner. She would walk out into the back garden, let the air go through her hair, smell the peonies. She dreamed of it.

Except that she had no hair. Her hair had been cut off. And she could no longer walk. And blood was seeping out of her body.

She could not imagine not knowing the world. And only a short time before, there had been no thought of dying. She had been buoyant and gay. She had dressed her hair, hummed, and for two hours worked on her new book. The character, Jemima, had taken hold of her imagination, was beginning to live on her own. The book did not seem so bad now. She wanted to finish it. Jemima paced the confines of her mind, made herself comfortable in Mary's brain. Jemima moved furniture about, opened the windows, aired the rugs.

"I am beginning to see the world through Jemima's eyes," Mary told William at tea several days before the baby came. Thinking about it, Mary made Jemima's eyes a green-blue, like the water in the estuary

at Laugharne, like Annie's. Mary's hair was brown, Jemima's a honey-
yellow. Mary's life had been hard, Jemima's was harder.

My book, Mary liked to say, as if it, like the child she had and
the child she was going to have, both belonged to and was separate
from her.

She and William had planned a dinner to celebrate the child
expected any day. They were going to invite friends, Blake and Joseph
Johnson, and William's friends Thomas Holcroft and John Opie, who
had promised to paint the baby's portrait, as he had done both Mary's
and William's.

The early pains were not severe. She remembered them from
having Fanny. She sent a note over to William's house from her rooms.
All had seemed well, at first. But the labor was slow, and instead of
keeping the midwife, or Mrs. Mason, they had called in a physician
trained at Oxford, certified by the Royal College. William had insisted.
Secretly, Mary had wanted just a midwife, like the old woman she
had in Le Havre birthing Fanny, her first, named for the dear dead
friend Fanny Blood.

That was France; this was London.

London, alone under the white sheet, the man at the end, hidden
like a ghost, working between her legs, the room silent and her things
stripped away, all very sanitary, cold, and frightening.

In France, one of the women of the host of helpers proposed a
toast, a toast to the mother and child.

Giggling and gurgling, Mary had been a little tipsy at her baby's
birthday party. That first birth had not been solemn or quiet, dark or
distant, but like the baby's conception, sunny and tasting of wine, and
her belly, glistening like a great grape ripe for the picking, expelled
in a gush of fluid her daughter, Fanny Imlay.

Hello in there, Gil used to knock, putting his head on Mary's
belly.

"Where is the baby, where is Fanny," Mary cried to William on
the fourth day of her childbed fever. "Where is my baby, my girls."

"They have been sent away, Mary."

Much of the time Mary was with Gilbert, she could not dream.
It seemed that his dreams took all the space. The room would get

crowded with a full night's dreaming, all the dream people bumping into each other, dream to dream, hello, very nice to meet you. Yes, I am the one in the gypsy circus. Here, let me take off my horse head. Mary, more sherry? Yes, as I was saying, the price of cake in Paris has skyrocketed since the war. All the supplies are going to the front, to fight the Austrians and the Prussians. And in the distance could be heard hooves and musket fire, the heavy thud of cannons, the screams of children, the wailing of mothers.

Mary is standing in the downstairs hallway, calling up from the floor of little cream octagon tiles through the circular staircase to her upstairs bedroom.

"Get your things together. We must leave immediately."

And so they had packed their belongings in a great rush and traveled with the greatest haste through the back streets of Paris, the hissing and smack of the whip providing the rhythm of their departure. Mary was afraid that if she looked behind she would see the devil, not a handsome one, not Milton's Lucifer, but the one on the wild boar's back, in fast pursuit, its robes flying behind it.

Gilbert, are we there yet?

Soon, Mary, soon.

The gardener put berries on a silver platter in the middle of the table, and the arbor was a tangled mass of twigs, and Mary would sit by the window sunning herself and rubbing the juice of the aloe plant on her widening stomach.

"Mary?"

Like most women, Mary did not wear drawers, pantaloons, or pantalettes. They were worn only when skating on the ice or by little girls at play or by servants who must climb ladders or by prostitutes who wished to tease or by dancers who must whirl about. Some argued that they were useful when riding horseback, and a famous doctor had recommended that, "by stopping the passage of air, pantaloons prevented rheumatism and other discomforts." But Mary considered pantaloons uncomfortable and mannish. It was enough that she wore her stays, which cupped her breasts high. Besides, Gilbert sometimes was in such a need, tumbling her breasts out of her bodice and pushing her skirt up on the floor, at the door, before they got to the bed.

She is on the edge of the bridge. Beneath its curved base, there are echoes of gulls, little splashes as they swoop down to catch a fish. All the boatmen are far away. Empty boats are pulled up on the sand. In the distance she can see a few solitary men hurrying home, their wide-brimmed hats flopping up and down.

She is more frightened of falling off the edge than of being dead forever. In her hand are two pages of a letter written to Imlay: a meditation on jealousy; a meditation on suicide. They are white bouquets clutched in her fist, the blue ink running down her hand like new veins. Jealousy crisscrosses her palm, rings her wrist. Suicide, the word, dribbles off the page between her fingers, coming out a runny blue on the backs of her hands. Wind whips up suddenly and her skirts billow out. She almost loses her balance on the bridge. She has second and third and fourth thoughts. The wind rushes in at her ears. The water comes up at her, hard and fast. Unimaginable coldness assails her body, numbs her nerves. Her legs are like loose tendrils underneath her skirt, which is holding her up like a lily pad. She presses it down with her hands, tries to push herself beneath the water.

"Why have they taken my hair away, William, my hair. That is what they do before they guillotine you."

Her arms, almost too weak to lift, went up to her head.

"Because of the fever, Mary."

"But I need my hair. I do not wear wigs. How am I to go outside?"

Mary had always dressed her hair simply, powdering it only twice when she could afford to, abandoning the style when George III put a tax on powder and the English Jacobins dressed like peasants, like common people. She was a common person, after all, did not have to pretend. She had never worn a wig.

Heart cakes.

Cherries, O, ripe cherries.

"How can life go on without me, William, without my permission?"

She would not perceive the world, she understood, but it would be there. She would be dead, and all of philosophy would be of no use. Those learned men, their brave words, Hume and Rousseau, where were they now? Their words sat on the pages of books. How did their philosophies serve them in death? It was of no use to her. She was not any closer to the meaning of her life now. All that was left was her sufferings, recorded in her few words, and her girls. To live would be a nice piece of mutton with mint jelly, the sound of a fiddle tuning to Handel, a lace handkerchief her mother used to blot her forehead on a hot day, her grandfather's walking stick, a ride in the country, her desk.

Mary's desk was large and covered in black leather. It was a man's desk, for she disdained the frail legs, marquetry top of a lady's desk meant only for dainty letters and household lists. She was a scribbler, had always written, and then made a living at it. Her desk was her workplace, her desk was her life. She could live for her desk alone.

Or at tea at Vauxhall, hearing the flutes, or eating a treacle tart or a Cornish pasty, or plum pudding, a vase by Wedgwood, an elegant dress made of Indian cotton, or going into a home designed by Robert Adam—cool, swift lines, airy, open, Rome.

Cockles, mussels, alive-o.

Fine potatoes,

Buy my clove water.

I am to die here in this room, shut away, the world muffled in wool, William in my study sobbing, his face nose down on the torn and worn leather of my desk, my two girls, Fanny and the baby, taken away, my hair cut, my body naked, my room stripped bare, everything pared down, my life contracting to the size of this room, fit to the measurement of a bed, I who have been to France, Portugal, Sweden, and Ireland, and lived in Yorkshire, Wales, Bath, am relegated finally to this small place where I must wait patiently for my inevitable end. They all go on tiptoe shh, shh, don't disturb me, she's dying. How I want to be disturbed, awakened, kept alive.

Scissors and razors to grind.

Strawberries, scarlet strawberries.

For the birth and afterward, she took nothing. No medicines, only a tiny sip of wine. The pain was beyond imagination, but when they offered laudanum on her third day of fever, she refused.

"Pain is my brother and sister. No laudanum, thank you, and no holy men, either, draped in black," she instructed.

For she thought: Pain is feeling at least, at least that. She wanted to feel, feel everything, she wanted to keep feeling. She kept her eyes open, tried not to sleep, wanted noise, pinched her arms to stay awake.

"At least I can still feel something," she said to herself, panicking when her toes went numb, calling out:

"William, I am dying. Get my sisters."

"They are coming, Mary. Hold on."

"The famous Mary Wollstonecraft, author of *A Vindication of the Rights of Woman*, cannot even get her sisters to attend her deathbed," she said to William.

"Do not say that. They must come from Wales. They will be here."

On the fifth day of fever, Mary could no longer sit up.

That was when her sisters swept into her room.

"Did you know," Everina said, "that Ann Radcliffe got six hundred pounds for her novel *The Italian*, topping her *Mysteries of Udolpho* by some hundred pounds. Can you fancy that?"

"Thank you for bringing me the news, Everina."

"I think you can walk it off, Mary," Eliza said. "Just get up and walk." She hiccupped. "You have always been so strong. This is so unlike you."

On the sixth day, they brought two puppies into the room.

"Puppies? You bring puppies?" Mary thought of her father's hanged hunting dogs, Mrs. Kingsborough's pets. "You bring puppies to amuse me?"

"No, ma'am." Rose hung her head.

"Mary," William began, "Mary, the puppies are to relieve your breasts, help you stop the blood from flowing out, tighten your poor, sore womb. The puppies, Mary, are to make the milk come out, draw your insides in. The puppies are to suckle at your breasts."

"Oh, no," Mary moaned. "No, please, no. No puppies."

CHAPTER 56

IN THE DREAM, it was a soft spring day, the light spreading in thin fingers across London. In the dream she was on a horse, a pale horse, going across Putney Bridge. She did not know where she was going or where she had been. But she rode faster and faster.

Then she heard somebody hawking *The Times*, calling something out. She turned around. Was it the reprieve from the king? The horseman was all in green and he had on a coat made of feathers.

Read it in *The Times*, he called out: She is dead. She is dead.

"A is for acorn," Mary intoned in her dream. "F is forever. And L? L is for love."

CHAPTER 57

A FEW MONTHS after Mary's death, Godwin published his *Memoirs of the Author of A Vindication of the Rights of Woman*, which was to some extent an account of her life. Joseph Johnson published it. Thanks to Godwin's honest discussion of her emotional entanglements, her suicide attempt, and her religious disaffection, her work was largely ignored for some years. The Tory press at the time of the *Memoirs* designated Godwin a pimp and Wollstonecraft a whore.

In America, Mary Wollstonecraft was accused of encouraging women to take up sport, for she initiated young virgins into the exercise of ice skating, a "most slippery diversion."

Only a woman's magazine, the *Monthly Visitor*, defended her by stating that she had strong passions, strong understanding: "She was a woman of high genius; and, as she felt the whole strength of her powers, she thought herself lifted, in a degree, above the ordinary trammels of civil communities."

Yet, despite the criticism, *A Vindication of the Rights of Woman* had gone through four American editions and six British editions one hundred years after its initial publication.

In 1812 Fanny Imlay, the first child, at age twenty-two, after her aunts Eliza and Everina rejected her plea for living quarters, quietly checked into an inn. Holing up in her room, she dreamed of suicide. The walls seemed to ooze, and the floor buckle. She sat at a small wooden table, thought of all the unhappy people who had inhabited the room. Having been a miserable, fussy child, Fanny Imlay grew into a melancholy young woman, accomplishing what her mother had attempted on Putney Bridge. Fanny's body was identified by her mother's stays. M.W. was inscribed on one whalebone.

Tom Christie died of fever in Surinam the same year Mary died.

His best years were with Johnson and the magazine, lolling on the floor. In Paris, at the height of the Revolution, he had entertained lavishly.

Joseph Johnson died in 1809.

Gilbert Imlay died in 1828.

William Godwin remarried and lived until 1836.

Everina and Eliza ran a school together in Dublin until the 1830s, when Eliza died.

Tom Paine, buried in America, was dug up and made off with by a couple of admirers. His early biographers attacked him for being an atheist.

William Blake was buried, according to the extant burial record, at Bunhill Fields Burying Ground on Friday, August 17, 1827, at 1:00 p.m., by an undertaker located in Piccadilly. Obituaries appeared in the principal London papers and reviews. But of course his spirit had joyously ascended long before.

In 1814 Mary Wollstonecraft Godwin, Mary's second child (who was born in 1797), was courted by her husband-to-be, Percy Shelley, in the St. Pancras churchyard, over Mary's grave. Delicate, clever, and lovely, Mary leaned up against her mother's stone, struck a pose appropriate to a romantic heroine. Her grandmother would have approved of the way she carried herself. This Mary, unlike her mother, was languid and aristocratic. Her dress that day was a beige taffeta (she had a more subtle taste than her mother), low cut, that fell fairly close to the body. This Mary had magnificent hands, gently sloping shoulders, and a very sweet face.

"My mother's stone," she said prettily to Shelley, who was married at the time. "My mother was very handsome, was known to be witty and brilliant, and had a weakness for beautiful men."

Shelley, of course, was very beautiful himself. He had long, flowing hair, a slight body, the face of a girl with piercing brown eyes. He sported an open collar, flowing scarves. He had style, verve. He was graceful, splendidly intelligent. He thought Mary leaning up against her mother's gravestone in her nice dress was a woman who "could feel poetry and understand philosophy." Mary thought Shelley was the most interesting man she had ever met. Shelley admired Mary's father's stance on social reform, and he was getting tired of his wife, Harriet. Mary was not happy with her stepmother. Percy thought anything was possible. Prometheus was his hero. He idolized Icarus. Mary had an Oriental sense of fatality. She was dreamy, unformed. She wondered why he liked her. He knew she loved him.

"Until my father, that is. My mother fell in love with beautiful men until my father, William Godwin. My father is not beautiful." This Mary was more beautiful than her mother, though perhaps she lacked her energy and strong sensuality, and she did not have her father's depth. But Shelley had these qualities in abundance.

"And then she learned her lesson about beautiful men?"

"Yes, she learned her lesson, married a sensible man, settled down, and died," Mary said. Mary, herself, was quite sensible. At sixteen, she wanted to live long, make her mark. She had her mother's appetites, some of her abilities, but was determined not to be a spendthrift with her emotions.

"That is the way it goes, is it not? Learn lesson, die. I hate the way of the world," he said.

The way of the world ground people down, made martyrs of the unsuspecting, and destroyed whatever pleasure was to be had. That was his view of things. Percy sympathized with those gathered beneath him. The tombstones leaning up against each other looked like a sorrowful army on the march home from a lost battle.

"She was married in that church, Percy. They walked home, had a quarrel. I rolled in her stomach, banging my fists for them to stop. I wanted peace. My birth was horrendous."

The church, St. Pancras, where Mary Wollstonecraft had been married to William Godwin, was closed. The small spire poked up into the night air valiant and free. The Fleet River flowed below silently. Mary thought of Leander swimming to Hero each night. She held her breath a moment. All was still.

"What is that, that sound, Percy?"

"A skylark."

"I do not think so."

"Only a lark, Mary, would be so happy."

"You have the neck of an Easter lily," she said. "Is that what you would have me say. Skylarks and lilies. Primroses and sweets. Cold and hot. Here and there, now and then."

"That sounds like your mother, a yes and a no in one sentence. A compliment and a rough cuff."

"I am her daughter, Percy."

"What about Fanny Imlay, who is always so angry, so downcast?"

"Also her child. We are all her children." It sounded as if her mother had been an ancient goddess giving birth to the world, a Ceres.

"Indeed. Your mother had a passion for beautiful men and pretty clothes, good food, and was melancholy much of the time. Is that you *and* Fanny Imlay? Is that the world, how we all are?"

"To be human is to be full of contradictions, Percy, that much I know." She had learned that at her Uncle Joseph's knee.

"I hear she did not like children, led a kind of ragamuffin existence, only owned a few sticks of furniture her whole life, supported her sisters much of the time. She was quite the conversationalist at that salon Joseph Johnson ran, dashed off strongly worded, clumsily organized books after dinner, spilled wine, translated freely, took off her skirts readily, yet held no man, including God, in high esteem. Was she a man in woman's clothing?"

"She was an Intellectual Beauty, as you would say." Percy had ideas. Her father had ideas, too, but he was stern and distant. Percy spoke in capital letters, made points with his walking stick, yet was accessible, and when he touched your hand, you felt you wanted to faint.

"I wish I could have known her, Mary."

"Are you courting me or my mother, Percy?"

"I am full of love and longing for *you*." He put his hand on her cheek. "You are her worthy heir. I wish she were still alive. I love the world with everybody alive. I love the world as it might be."

She flinched at the word. She wondered what place love had in his philosophical constructions. Would he consider it part of his so-called Necessity? Yet he was as much a lover as he was a philosopher and poet. Indeed, he was notorious. Women swooned. She thought of herself falling in love. Her father had described her mother falling in love. It sounded like falling into a big vat of molasses—like one of the kettledrums in the colonies in which sugarcane was boiled for the making of rum. Falling in. Falling through the sky. Falling head over heels. In love.

"Your mother was full of feeling," Percy said, taking one of her curls between his fingers. "Are you?"

"She was full of ideas. Like you."

"I want to kiss you in all your secret places, Mary."

She shivered. Was this what the discussion was all about?

"My mother lies under here," she whispered. "The fever is burnt out of her, her bones are blanched clean. She is a skull, a hank of hair. I cannot kiss you here."

"She is alive and well. She lives, my dear, in your heart, in your mind."

"Please, Percy. I never even knew her. We met at my birth, said goodbye."

"Enough." He made a sweeping movement with his hand. "Let's lie here, please."

"On my mother's grave?"

"What better place? Stretch out. Savor what lies beneath."

Mary looked around. Stones and cold night. The shape of trees barely visible, the small church, sharp-edged in sun, but indistinct now.

"You are beautiful," he said.

"*You* are beautiful," she replied.

"You are in my power."

"No, I am not in your power, Percy. I am in my own power."

"My, my." His dark eyes glowed. His body smelled of wine and rosewater, a woman's scent. Mary felt a little dizzy. She looked up. The sky was dense and unyielding. She look down at the soft earth. Some of the stones were covered over with ivy as if the underworld not only had taken the body in death but wished to pull down the markers. She noticed that there were, in truth, a lot of birds. They went for the worms. Food for birds. Food for worms. Mary took a breath, knelt, and stretched herself across the grave as if to embrace what lay below. Pressing her mouth against the soft earth, she asked:

"Mother, may I?"